• • • • • •

Time didn't take away her memory, however, so Tish peered under the garage door and made a decision that went against her heart and her mind and her overall sense of right and wrong. Rather than get into her car and drive away to the job that paid her utility bills, rent and car note, Tish went back to her front door and opened it.

She stepped inside her quiet home and took a look back over her shoulder. She wished she hadn't. What she saw crawling out of the garage across the street was nothing like the Dino she knew and loved and shared a bed with while her brother and sister slept and her mother worked a night shift at American Airlines. What Tish saw was nothing like anything she had ever seen outside of a movie screen or even one of the horrific nightmares that plagued her sleep when her big brother got killed.

Dino slithered out of the darkness like a goblin and sprinted across the street with a speed that belied his obvious physical trauma. Tish wanted to slam the door closed before he got there. But by then she was completely terrified – not just of what sort of demon she had invited into her home, but she was also fearful of what his reaction would be if she rejected him this late in the game.

Dino mounted her front steps in one leap and slammed the door closed behind himself once he rushed inside.

"Lock it!" he ordered.

Tish fumbled with the deadbolt while Dino peeked through the curtains at the front of the house. He looked like he had a baseball tucked under his cheekbone. Dried blood was caked all the way down his neck and under his tee shirt. His skin was ashen, his clothes matted and dusty from his stay in the garage. He brought with him a stench that was immediately recognizable as death. Dino's eyes were wild. His hands trembled like he was running from Satan himself.

"*What you do?*" Tish squealed.

"I got shot," Dino told her plainly. "My homeboy is dead, and some girl got shot, too. They killed a little boy."

• • • • • •

1

# BLOOD FOR ISAIAH

I0589584

# BLOOD
# FOR
# ISAIAH

## KEITH THOMAS WALKER

KEITHWALKERBOOKS, INC
This is a UMS production

BLOOD FOR ISAIAH

**KEITHWALKERBOOKS**

Publishing Company
KeithWalkerBooks, Inc.
P.O. Box 331585
Fort Worth, TX 76163

For information write
KeithWalkerBooks, Inc.
P.O. Box 331585
Fort Worth, TX 76163

All characters in this book have no existence outside the
imagination of the author and have no relation whatsoever to
anyone bearing the same name or names.  They are not even
distantly inspired by any individual known or unknown to the
author and all incidents are pure invention.

ISBN-13 DIGIT: 978-0-9850500-6-1
ISBN-10 DIGIT: 0985050063
Library of Congress Control Number: 2014909471
Manufactured in the United States of America

First Edition

Visit us at www.keithwalkerbooks.com

*This book is for Jody Wayne Thomas*

# MORE BOOKS BY KEITH THOMAS WALKER

Fixin' Tyrone
How to Kill Your Husband
A Good Dude
Riding the Corporate Ladder
The Finley Sisters' Oath of Romance
Blow by Blow
Jewell and the Dapper Dan
Harlot
Plan C (And More KWB Shorts)
Dripping Chocolate
The Realest Ever
Jackson Memorial
Sleeping With the Strangler
Life After

## NOVELLAS

Might be Bi (Part One)
Harder

## POETRY COLLECTION

Poor Righteous Poet

Visit keithwalkerbooks.com for information about these and upcoming titles from KeithWalkerBooks

# ACKNOWLEGMENTS

Of course I would like to thank God, first and foremost, for giving me the creativity and drive to pursue my dreams and the understanding that I am nothing without Him. I would like to thank my wife for being my first and most important critic, and I would like to thank my mother for always pushing me to be the best I can be. I would like to thank Janae Hampton for being the best advisor, supporter and little sister a brother could ever have. I would also like to thank (in no particular order) Denise Bolds, Sabrina Scott, Beulah Neveu, Jason Owens, Sharon Blount, BRAB Book Club, and Uncle Steven Thomas, one love. I'd like to thank everyone who purchased and enjoyed one of my books. Everything I do has always been to please you. I know there are folks who mean the world to me that I'm failing to mention. I apologize ahead of time. Rest assured I'm grateful for everything you've done for me!

# BLOOD FOR ISAIAH

# CHAPTER ONE
## *JACOB AND DINO*

A poor guy can get by if he's good-looking.

And an ugly guy can get by if he has some money.

But a poor *and* ugly guy, shit, there's just no help for that.

Jacob didn't think his little brother was ugly, but beauty is in the eye of the beholder, and he grew up with Isaiah. He was three when Mama brought him home from the hospital. Isaiah was premature and small and weak back then, and the last ten years hadn't changed much of that. Isaiah was the smallest baby in daycare, and when he went to school, he was always the smallest boy in his class – smaller than some of the girls even. He was in the fifth grade now, but with his short stature, bony arms and pencil neck, Isaiah could easily pass for a fourth or even a third grader.

But it wasn't his size that made him ugly. Isaiah had a big nose that his face hadn't quite grown into yet. His eyes were beady, and his bifocals made them look even smaller – which by comparison, made his nose look much bigger than it actually was.

Not to mention Isaiah didn't care much about personal hygiene. You could often catch him with eye boogers or real-live nose boogers. Back in the second grade, some of his classmates caught him plucking boogers and smearing them directly onto his pants, rather than search for Klccncx or bathroom tissue.

When Jacob heard about it, he warned his little brother to show a little class. And Isaiah responded, "I don't like to get up in class, 'cause then they'll make fun of my flooding." By "flooding," Isaiah was referring to the high-water pants he had to wear back in those days. And incidentally, that was one of many things Jacob admired about his little brother: Isaiah looked like a nerd, and thankfully he backed it up with a head full of smarts. He was always one step ahead of everyone. He was a *If I do this, then this will happen,* and *If they do that, then that will happen* type of guy.

Unfortunately only the teachers cared about Isaiah's smarts, so the girls labeled him poor and ugly. Jacob and Isaiah's mom could hardly ever afford to get their hair cut in a timely matter, so the guys tacked *nappy* onto Isaiah's growing list of put-downs. Jacob was just as poor and nappy as his brother, but he was better-looking and bigger, so he didn't have to endure half the heckling Isaiah did.

Today's round of bullying left Isaiah with yet another pair of broken glasses. They were damaged at the hinge this time. Always prepared to make due with less, Isaiah had tried to fix his glasses at school by replacing the missing screw with a bent staple, but Jacob could see that more extensive repairs were needed. The tiny hinge was bent almost as badly as the staple, so even if Mama had a tiny screw lying around, it wouldn't fit unless they could straighten out the hinge first.

"He knocked them off your head, or what?" Jacob asked.

"Yeah, and then somebody stepped on them," Isaiah said, his face set in concentration as he tried to perfect his staple remedy.

Jacob didn't see how he could work on something so intricate; the way the bus was bouncing along the deteriorating streets in their neighborhood. He and Isaiah lived in what was commonly referred to as the "bad" part of town. There was a lot of crime but hardly ever any police chases, because you could blow a tire if you hit one of those potholes going over 40 miles per hour.

"What you do when he knocked 'em off?" Jacob asked his brother.

"I tried to pick them up, before somebody stepped on them," Isaiah said. "It was passing period."

"What'd you do when you picked 'em up?" Jacob asked.

"I saw they were broke. I tried to find the screw."

"I'm talking about the dude that hit you. What about him?"

"He walked off."

Jacob shook his head; more in despair than disappointment. "Why didn't you go after him?"

"I didn't want to start a fight," Isaiah said, still not looking up. His tongue protruded from the corner of his mouth, like a turtle's tail, which meant he was using the majority of his brain cells on the task at hand. Jacob sat back and waited for him to finish.

The bus was nearing the end of its route, and it was nearly empty. Other than the brothers, there were only three more kids eager to get home. They all sat in seats by themselves, but Jacob didn't feel self-conscious about sitting next to his brother. It was no secret Isaiah needed protecting, and the best way to do that was to let Isaiah have the window seat while Jacob blocked off any threats coming down the aisle.

Jacob was only thirteen, but he'd seen a lot of bad things in his short lifetime, and he had an underlying meanness about him. Everyone on the bus knew they'd have to go through him if they wanted to mess with Isaiah, and in two years no one had been bold enough to try that – not on the bus at least.

But things would be different when Jacob went to high school next year. Isaiah would move up to middle school, and he would have to ride the bus home by himself for the next three years. Jacob was pretty sure he couldn't prepare Isaiah in time, but he was a long way from giving up.

Isaiah finished whatever he was doing and put his glasses back on. He looked up and smiled at his brother, and Jacob almost wanted to slap him. He laughed instead and shook his head again.

"Boy, you know them glasses still crooked."

"I prolly need some tape," Isaiah agreed.

The thought of masking tape holding the arm on his glasses made Jacob laugh harder. That was the problem with these little heart-to-hearts. It was hard to stay focused with someone as unwittingly goofy as Isaiah.

"If you tape that arm on, you gon' have even more dudes picking on you. Plus you won't have no girlfriend, either."

"I don't have a girlfriend now," Isaiah said. "I never had a girlfriend."

"I know," Jacob said and his smile ebbed. "But for real, man, you can't let nobody knock your glasses off like that. You shoulda hit him back."

"But I had to get my glasses. You know I can't get new ones."

Once again, this was true. Their mother had two jobs. The one at the hospital had pretty good insurance, but Mama's vision plan only provided one pair of glasses per year. Their mother wisely waited until August before getting his glasses, but she didn't understand that the beginning of a new school year was prime season for bullies. Currently it was mid-October, so Isaiah would have to wait approximately ten months before he could get new glasses.

"How you let them break your glasses in the first six weeks?" Jacob chastised. "That's when you need to be the *most* careful."

"I tried," Isaiah said. "I told you; the first thing I did was look for my glasses."

"And when you saw they were broke, that didn't piss you off?" Jacob wanted to know. "It didn't make you wanna jump on that dude?"

Isaiah thought about that and shook his head.

"I'll get him for you tomorrow," Jacob said. "But I can't keep going to your school to beat up people. I'm in middle school. I ain't supposed to be fighting nobody in grade school. And when I get to high school, I'm not supposed to fight people in middle school no more."

"I don't want you to fight him," Isaiah said. "That just makes it worse."

"How come?"

"'Cause then they be saying, '*Look at the baby. He can't fight for himself. Leave him alone, or the baby will go tell his big brother.*'"

"They can say whatever they want," Jacob informed him, "so long as they not hitting you. Right now they talking about you *and* hitting you."

Isaiah continued to shake his head. "Teacher says it's my cross to bear."

"I can't stand your teacher," Jacob said, and he meant it. He was in Mrs. Turner's class himself three years back. There was supposed to be a law against teaching religion in schools, but she threw it in your face every chance she got. She didn't make the students pray, or anything that flagrant, but she prayed aloud herself every day: *"Thank you, Jesus, for this blessed morning. Open these chirren's hearts and minds, Lord, and guide my lesson plan."* Even the bullies were afraid to make fun of the way she said *children*, because God might strike them down.

"You know why Mama named you Jacob?" Isaiah asked.

"Yeah, but Mama's not as bad as Mrs. Turner."

"I like Mrs. Turner," Isaiah said. "She makes me feel better."

Jacob let it go because Isaiah needed to feel good at school by any means necessary. He wouldn't come against anything that helped his brother get through the day.

The bus slowed to a squeaky stop at the intersection of Crenshaw and Campbell, and the brothers made it to the front before the doors swung open. Some drivers want you to remain seated until the bus comes to a complete stop, but Mr. Barnett was fifty years old and more neglectful than a drunken babysitter. If you were stupid enough to stand in the aisle while the bus was moving, it wasn't his fault if you got violently jostled if he hit a pothole.

Isaiah jumped off first and then turned to wait for his brother.

"Bye, Mr. Barnett!" he called over Jacob's shoulder.

The bus driver grunted and closed the door as soon as Jacob was off the steps. He took off, leaving stinky exhaust fumes in his wake.

"Why you say bye to that man every day?" Jacob wondered. "He don't never say nothing back."

"I don't know," Isaiah said and turned; heading south on Campbell. His backpack was stuffed to the brim. His pants weren't high-water today, but they were too big and faded, and it was obvious they once belonged to his big brother.

Jacob followed for a few steps before pulling alongside.

"Do you have a girlfriend now?" Isaiah asked.

Jacob thought that was an odd question. "What you mean?"

The boys moved from the street to the sidewalk, where most of the shade was. Pecan shells cracked under their sneakers, but they didn't stoop to pick any of them up. The pecans on the ground were hollowed out by birds or insects. Most of the good pecans were scavenged already by the many junkies in their neighborhood. Jacob didn't know it, but you could get up to a dollar a pound for fresh pecans at the Marshall Grain feed store on Lancaster.

"Do you have a girlfriend yet," Isaiah asked, "or do you wait 'til you've been at school for a while?"

"I have a girlfriend," Jacob lied. There were a few girls he liked at school, but so far he didn't have the courage to talk to them. Jacob got a few new shirts and pairs of pants for school that year, but *new* didn't mean much when your wardrobe came from Walmart and Payless. Some girls could see past that. Some girls couldn't. It was hard to tell which ones.

"It's some girls at my school who already have boyfriends," Isaiah said. "I see them holding hands and kissing sometimes."

Jacob snorted. "You're ten years old, Isaiah. You don't need to be kissing or holding hands with *nobody*. You know what kind of girl be kissing when they're in the fifth grade?"

Isaiah shrugged.

"A ho," Jacob said. "They'll have a baby when they're in high school, or maybe even middle school. They can't have one now, because they haven't had their period. But once they do–"

"What's a period?"

Jacob frowned; not pleased he had to be the one to have these talks all the time. They had a dad, and he lived somewhere in this very city. Why couldn't he come home and share some knowledge with his son? Their father left for Stop N' Go when Isaiah was one years old and never came back. How long does it take to get a pack of Salem 100s?

"Girls have a period when they're twelve or thirteen," Jacob explained. "That's when they're ready to have a baby. They chest will get big, and their hips will, too. It's called *puberty*. Boys start growing hair on their face, and their voices get deeper."

"You don't have any hair on your face," Isaiah noticed.

"It doesn't happen at the same time for everybody," Jacob said.

"Your voice isn't deep, either."

"Shut up," Jacob said, his face growing warm. "Sometimes it don't happen until you're fourteen."

"But you still didn't say what a *period* is," Isaiah pressed. "I saw on South Park that it has something to do with blood."

"What you doing watching South Park?" Jacob questioned. "We don't even have cable. Where'd you see it?"

"At Shaun's house."

Shaun was a knucklehead who lived a few blocks down from them. Jacob didn't like him, because he was in a lot of "slow" classes at school. But Shaun never picked on Isaiah, and that made him tolerable.

"I'ma tell Mama you over there watching South Park," Jacob threatened.

"Don't," Isaiah said, his eyes growing wide.

Jacob kept a straight face, but inside he smiled. Isaiah was so smart, yet so naïve. After all these years, he didn't realize that Jacob *never* ratted him out, even when he deserved it.

"Then stop asking me about periods," Jacob said. "When it's time for you to find out, you'll find out – probably more than you want to know."

"Alright," Isaiah said and dropped it just like that. If it didn't involve standing up to a bully, Isaiah was obedient to his big brother without fail. He kicked a pecan shell into the Gregory's lawn as the boys neared the intersection of Campbell and Forbes Street.

Isaiah moved his backpack to the opposite shoulder and shaded his eyes from the sunlight. He was totally unaware that he would never need a new pair of glasses, find out what a period is or hear Mrs. Turner's illegal prayer at the beginning of class tomorrow morning.

● ● ● ● ● ●

Dino brought the lighter to his cigar and took a few short puffs. He removed the flame and took a long, satisfying drag. In the corner of his eye, he saw Tricky already reaching for his Zippo. Dino handed it to him and paid close attention to what he did with it afterwards. Tricky simply closed the lighter and slipped it into his front pocket. That was it.

Dino had been wondering how the hell Tricky kept up with the same lighter for two months in a lifestyle where the average lighter was misplaced in a couple of days. Dino thought some type of magic might be involved, but it turned out Tricky was only being attentive and diligent this whole time. Dino looked away lethargically, blowing a thick plume of blue and gray smoke from his mouth and nostrils.

It was warm outside but nowhere near the scorching temperatures that made Overbrook Meadows so miserable during the summertime. Most of the pecan trees on Forbes Street were already losing their leaves as well as their fruit, but things wouldn't cool down until early November.

Dino could hardly wait for winter. Not only did he have two leather coats he'd never worn, but he liked the idea of putting on more clothes to ward off the environment; sweatshirts, gloves, thick jeans and hoodies. The more clothes you put on, the more weapons and dope you could conceal on your person. That made everything more dangerous, which was more exciting in Dino's opinion.

He sat on the front steps of the Sicc Crips dope house with Tricky chilling next to him and three more comrades on the porch behind them. The Crips sold crack out of the house on Forbes Street, but it wasn't really a dope house per se. At this spot, they only sold bulk amounts of dope to drug peddlers, rather than users, which cut down on the traffic and consequently cut down on the amount of attention their spot garnished.

Dino took another drag of the marijuana-packed cigar and passed it to Tricky. He took it hesitantly, looking up and then down the long street with skittish eyes that reminded Dino of a squirrel. Dino looked back over his shoulder at T Lowe, who was leaning against the front door. Next to T Lowe, Stephon shifted his weight from one leg to the other, nibbling at his thumbnail. A skinny hoodlum named Peanut sat a few feet away on the only piece of furniture on the porch; a rusting folding chair that was already there when they rented the place.

There were a few more misfits inside the house. The rest of their gang was scattered across the city in similar dope spots T Lowe had set up for them. T Lowe was technically the leader of the Sicc Crips, but his power only went so far. Everyone knew the almighty dollar was the real glue that held them together.

Their dope houses were so profitable, all of the Sicc Crips were entitled to kickbacks every other month or so. Plus T Lowe allowed them free enterprise, which meant any member of the gang could keep the money from whatever ventures they had going on the side, as long as it didn't interfere with the operations of any of the dope houses.

It was this "free enterprise" clause that had everyone down in the dumps at that moment. Dino had been *blessed* with a three thousand dollar windfall less than an hour ago, but T Lowe had nothing but negativity for his successor.

"You shouldn't have done that, cuz."

Dino shook his head and rolled his eyes at him. "I don't see why not. He was out of bounds, and he got *got*. He should've known that was gon' happen."

The "He" in this scenario was a fourteen year old dealer named Pooky. Pooky rented an apartment a few streets down and had the gall to sell dime rocks all by himself. Dino simply walked in the front door, slapped him around a little bit and left after relieving Pooky of his drugs and money. Dino only got a few hundred in cash from the robbery, but the dope was the real prize; three of the prettiest thousand-dollar bricks he'd ever seen.

"He was selling to crackheads," T Lowe said, stating the obvious. "That don't put him in competition with us."

"How come it don't?" Dino asked without looking back at him. "Nigga was like, right around the corner."

"Minding his business," Stephon said. He stepped forward and took the blunt from Tricky.

Dino snorted. He didn't care too much for Stephon. There had always been underlying tension between the two. Two weeks ago, he finally figured out why Stephon got under his skin: T Lowe had rounded up the troops to do a driveby on a neighboring set that was disrespecting them, and Dino found himself in the backseat of a stolen Maxima with Stephon.

When it came time to do the do, the enemy surprised them with a well-orchestrated counter attack. When a few bullets slammed into the Maxima, Stephon yelped like a little girl and actually dropped his piece. He picked it up only after everything was over; as they made a speedy getaway. Stephon had looked around sheepishly, and Dino locked eyes with him. He didn't call him out right then, but his eyes told the whole story: *I saw what you did. You're a coward, and you will be exposed.*

"How much you get off him?" Tricky asked.

Dino grinned, showing off his bigger than normal teeth that gained him his nickname. Back in grade school, Dino hung out with a class clown named Michael Wilkinson. Marveling at Dino's elongated chops one day, Michael said he had teeth like a dinosaur, a T Rex to be exact. *"I'ma start calling you Baby Dino!"*

Dino didn't object to the moniker, because dinosaurs were vicious and deadly predators, so pretty soon everyone at school called him *Baby Dino*. As he matured, he dropped the *Baby* from his nickname. He was twenty years old now. Few of his homies knew where the name *Dino* came from, which was just fine with him.

"I only got a couple hundred," Dino said. "A couple slabs, too."

T Lowe stepped down off the porch. He took a few steps into the yard and turned to face his disciple. T Lowe was a good-looking guy. His skin was a smooth, dark bronze. He wore a thin goatee and a short crew cut. His eyebrows had the best natural arches; perfect for the look of disappointment he fixed on Dino.

"You took his dope, too?"

"No doubt," Dino said with a nod.

"*And* you whooped him?"

"I hit him a few times," Dino admitted.

T Lowe rotated and chewed on a toothpick that was poking from the corner of his mouth.

"And *why* you say you did that?"

Dino shrugged. He looked over at Tricky, who didn't have a comment.

"I told you he was right around the corner from us," Dino said to T Lowe. "That shit's bad for business."

"I already knew about him," T Lowe countered. "Pooky wasn't hurting us. He be selling nicks and dimes."

"Well, maybe I just wanted to rob him," Dino said, which was a lot closer to the truth.

The two men stared each other down, and Dino began to feel self-conscious, as he always did when T Lowe rebuked him. Aside from his monstrous teeth, Dino had a pudgy nose and kinky hair that didn't lay flat like T Lowe's did. Dino's complexion was dark, like the bottom of a grave. He considered that another flaw that pushed him towards the *ugly* side of life.

Because of his reputation and the money in his pocket, Dino could still have pretty much any girl he wanted, but T Lowe could pull a fine broad with his looks alone. Plus he had more money and a bigger rep than Dino.

"Which is it?" T Lowe asked. "You wanted to rob him, or you did it for the Sicc?"

"I did it for the Sicc," Dino said right away. "Everything I do is for the Sicc."

"Well, I think you should give it back," T Lowe said. "Where the dope at?"

"It's in there," Dino said, throwing a thumb over his shoulder. "But I ain't giving it back."

"What you mean?" T Lowe asked, almost daring Dino to defy his authority.

"I mean it's stupid to give it back now," Dino said. He tried to sound casual, but his blood was starting to boil. It was always someone with a lot of money who felt that less fortunate people should settle for less. T Lowe wouldn't feel this way if he didn't have his own nest egg stashed away.

Stephon stepped off the porch and stood next to their leader, which infuriated Dino even more.

"It's gon' be more trouble than it's worth," Stephon said.

"Shut yo bitch ass up," Dino replied.

"Don't talk to the little homey like that," T Lowe said.

Dino cut his eyes at both of them.

"Where it's at?" T Lowe asked.

"It's in the house," Dino said. "But I already told you; I'm keeping it. That's my lick."

"I thought you did it for the set."

"I did," Dino said. "But if y'all don't appreciate it, then fuck it. It's all mine now. Free enterprise."

T Lowe took a deep breath and let it out slowly. Dino watched his eyes and could almost see his inner conflict. On one hand, Dino's behavior amounted to insubordination. T Lowe could gather the crew and have a meeting to discuss the repercussions of such insolence.

On the other hand, Dino was the best soldier in the gang. His overall rank was second in command, but when it came to doing dirt, he was the number one man. No one in the gang was more willing to fight, steal or kill to protect the Sicc Crips' interests. Dino was the enforcer. He was the punisher. He was a rising ghetto superstar, and if T Lowe came down on him too many times, others might view it as jealousy.

"What about HB?" T Lowe asked, referring to Pooky's formidable big brother.

"What about him?" Dino said.

T Lowe frowned. HB, whose full nickname was *Head Buster*, was a very big deal in the city of Overbrook Meadows. He'd done ten years flat for armed robbery and another ten years for manslaughter that ran concurrently. HB fell right back into the bad life once paroled, but he moved most of his dope on the south side. He and the Sicc Crips never had dealings with one another, but everyone in the city knew HB was not to be fucked with. They called him "Head Buster" because of his one punch knock-out abilities, and HB had a notable arsenal as well.

"What you gon' do when HB comes looking for you?" T Lowe asked more directly.

"What you mean what *I'm* gon' do?" Dino asked. "What, we ain't in this shit together no more?"

T Lowe narrowed his eyes. This was a good example of the problem with free enterprise. If you allow your soldiers to generate their own capital on the side, then you would eventually find yourself responsible for situations you never sanctioned or condoned.

"You better think about this," T Lowe said. He walked past Dino on his way up the steps and back inside the house. Dino guessed he was going to get another blowjob from a sixteen year old they had in the back room. The bopper had been on a steady diet of semen and raw cocaine for the last three days. She was now a shell of a woman, totally used up and disgusting in Dino's opinion. But T Lowe would keep her around as long as she wanted to stay. In addition to being an ineffective leader, he was an insatiable pervert.

"So you gon' keep that nigga's shit?" Tricky asked when T Lowe was gone.

"Yeah, I'm keeping it," Dino replied.

Tricky tossed the butt of the cigar onto the front lawn, and Dino followed it with his eyes.

Down the street, Dino saw two young boys rounding the corner. They weren't a threat, so he gave them only half his attention. The older boy was always protective of the little one, and Dino had never spoken to either of them. He wanted to throw rocks at the runt with glasses every time he saw him, but the boys' mother paid the Sicc Crips a visit when T Lowe first opened up shop on Forbes Street six months ago.

"Don't y'all be messing with my boys," she had said. The way she stood there with a hand on her hip and her face set in a scowl would have been amusing in most cases, but there was something strange and strong in her eyes that had earned her respect, if not admiration from the guys who were on the porch that day.

"What you talking about?" Dino had asked her.

"When they be coming home from school, or whenever y'all see them, you better leave them alone," the young mother had said.

"Ma'am, we not gon' mess with your kids," T Lowe promised her.

"They don't want to be in your *gang*," the woman went on. "And they don't want none of your *drugs* either. If I find out y'all messing with them, best believe I'll come over here *myself*. You won't have to worry about the police."

"Ma'am, I assure you," T Lowe had said, "we don't want nothing to do with your kids, and we ain't gon' say nothing to them. I promise."

The woman stared them down for a few moments more before turning and marching back to her house across the street. Dino had watched her as she stepped, and it occurred to him that his life might have turned out differently if he had a mother like her in his life.

"You sure about that?" Tricky asked, snapping Dino from his daydream.

Dino looked up and saw that Tricky was now staring in the opposite direction. He followed his gaze and saw a two-toned Chrysler 300 slowly creeping up the block. All of the ballers in Overbrook Meadows had flashy rides specific to their personalities, and right away Dino knew that was HB's Chrysler coming to pay them a visit. And though a spray of frigid air washed over him, Dino stood and took a step forward, knowing his gang would stand behind him.

"Yeah I'm sure," he said. "That's my dope, and I'm keeping it."

# CHAPTER TWO
## *POOKY AND HEAD BUSTER*

At 3:42 pm, the sun was high in the sky; blazing down on them with nary a cumulus or thunder cloud to stifle its radiance. The sunlight gleamed off the hood of HB's two-toned Chrysler. Dino put a hand up to shade his eyes from the glare. He kept his sights on HB, who was in the driver's seat, pushing his ride in their direction from the right.

Next to HB, Pooky sat complacently in the passenger seat. When they got closer, Dino saw that Pooky had a bulky Dallas Cowboys jacket lying across his lap. Both of his hands disappeared beneath the jacket, and there was no doubt he concealed a weapon there.

Dino expected a driveby, but if Pooky was the shooter, HB would have come at them from the other direction; allowing for an unimpeded shot from the passenger window. But a driveby wasn't on HB's mind. He made this clear by pulling to a stop directly in front of T Lowe's dope spot, illegally parking on the left side of the street.

HB usually rocked the Isley Brothers from the sixteen speakers that were custom-built into his Chrysler as well as the two subwoofers he installed in the trunk, but his car was eerily quiet today. From the look on Pooky's face, Dino knew it had been a long, slow drive over to T Lowe's crack house. No music or blunts being passed, just talk about money, dope and murder.

Bloody murder.

"Oh, shit," Tricky called from the steps, and Stephon backed up a few paces; leaving Dino at the forefront of the mess he'd caused.

*Coward ass faggot,* Dino thought, but he didn't look over at Stephon with disgust twisting his lips. No, Dino's eyes remained fixed on HB, who returned the mean glare two-fold.

"That's him?" HB asked his brother.

"Yeah," Pooky said quietly. "That's him right there."

Pooky had a swollen lip, and his right eye was starting to close up. There was still blood on the chest of his white tee shirt from the altercation with Dino. Sweat poured from Pooky's head and pooled across his brow and atop his collar bones. His chest rose and fell like he'd sprinted all the way from the south side.

Dino's blood ran quick in his veins, too. Neurons fired up and down his spine with the speed of a locomotive, but Dino felt his core temperature cooling rather than heating up. He felt like he could see everything – all at once. His vision had never been so clear.

HB opened the door slowly and stepped out into the afternoon warmth. From the spot he vacated, Pooky now had a clear line of fire – except for the fact that his brother was standing right in the middle of it. Dino knew right away that he would use this to his advantage. No matter what went down, Dino would keep his body safely on the other side of HB's. Pooky wanted vengeance, but not badly enough to shoot through his brother.

Surely not.

HB closed the car door and stood next to his ride for a second. At six-foot six, he was taller than Dino and all of his cohorts. HB had a body built for football, with huge muscles stacked on his neck and chest, arms and shoulders. He wore an all-black tee shirt with black Dickey workpants and black Chuck Taylors. His skin was whiskey colored. His fists were like bowling balls. His eyes were too close together, and even his face was muscular.

His head was completely bald, and other than his eyebrows, there was no hair on his face. His skull looked so hard, Dino wondered if he would hurt his hand if he tried to punch him. That was a ridiculous thought, because the idea of going head-to-head with a guy like HB was sheer folly. Not only did Dino give up a hundred pounds to the head buster, but HB had a long list of fools he'd knocked out cold, most of them dating back to his days in the penitentiary.

Behind him, Dino heard Peanut knocking on the front window of their dope house.

"HB out here," Peanut called, almost in a whisper.

HB relaxed his hands and stepped closer to Dino. He stopped within ten feet – generally regarded as a respectable amount of space.

"You took my brother's shit?" he asked. His voice grumbled like an old motor.

Dino looked first to Pooky before responding. Pooky still had the coat draped over his lap. The muscles in his skinny forearms were flexing now. Dino looked back at the head buster.

"That's yo brother?"

"Yeah that's my brother," HB said. "Everybody know Pooky my brother."

"I don't know him," Dino said. Behind him he heard the screen door open and close – twice. HB followed these sounds, and then his eyes settled on Dino again.

"What you run up in his house for?" HB asked. "He wasn't fucking with y'all."

Dino liked to hear the word *y'all*. He liked it so much, a smile cracked the corner of his mouth. *That's right, cuz. It ain't me you got a problem with. It's **y'all**.*

"He was too close to us," Dino said. "I thought you worked on the south side."

HB was still calm, but his eyes darted here and there. Dino knew his mind was racing. HB was also a punisher and an enforcer, and Dino respected that. HB took in as much of the scene as he could before making a life-altering or possibly a life-ending decision. His eyes settled on Dino again.

"Y'all sell weight over here. My little brother selling dimes. Ain't no conflict."

"I didn't know what he was selling," Dino lied. "I just heard some nigga opened-up shop, and I went to see him."

"You went by yourself?"

"Yeah," Dino said. "I didn't think it was gonna be no trouble."

"You took his money *and* his dope?"

Dino checked his alignment before he replied. He couldn't see Pooky's face at all. HB didn't have a bulge under his shirt, but

Dino did. The .380 tucked next to his bladder was hot and heavy, begging to be set free.

"You know how that shit goes," Dino replied.

HB looked Dino up and down with his head cocking by degrees. "Nigga, who is you?" he asked, though his posture said, *Who the hell do you think you are?*

"Nigga, who is *you*?" Dino snapped back. "Don't come over here asking what my name is. You police or something?"

There was an audible gasp from somewhere behind him.

HB took a step forward with his hands rolled into bowling balls again. Dino reached towards his stomach, and that halted the big man's progress. HB's eyes swam from the now visible bulge in Dino's pants to the dark faces congregating behind him. He saw someone he recognized, and the tension melted off his face. His hands loosened up as well.

"Say, T Lowe," he called. "What's up with yo boy?"

T Lowe grudgingly stepped down from the porch. He stopped next to Dino, and they stood as a united front.

"He say he caught your brother slipping," T Lowe explained. "That ain't nothing I sent him to do."

"But is this yo boy or what?" HB asked. "He with y'all?"

"Yeah, he down with the Sicc," T Lowe said and Dino's chest swelled with pride.

Being in a gang meant a lot of different things to different people, and it was moments like this that meant the most to Dino. No matter how ugly he was, no matter how stupid, and no matter what fucked up things he did, the Sicc Crips would always have his back. Even the marines didn't have this kind of loyalty; they would court-martial your ass in a minute, if you went against the grain.

"So, what's really going on?" HB asked T Lowe. "You saying you cool with this shit he pulled?"

T Lowe gave Dino a stern look before responding. "The homies can make money however they want," he said. "So long as it don't interfere with the shit we got going on."

"So you got your boys out here renegading?" HB asked. "Whatever they feel like doing is cool?"

"I didn't say it was cool," T Lowe said. "I told him that shit wasn't right."

25

Dino's nostrils flared.  He couldn't believe T Lowe was distancing himself.

"Hell naw it wasn't right," HB agreed.  "If he wanted Pooky to move around, he should've gave him a warning or something. Better yet, if he didn't like what Pooky was doing over there, he should've come to *me*.  Pooky told him that was my shit."

T Lowe gave his soldier another hard look and then sighed. "I see where you coming from," he told HB.  "But we don't have everything figured out yet ourselves.  Give me a little time to talk to my nigga, and maybe we can–"

"Charge it to the game," Dino said abruptly.

HB's face registered surprise for the first time.  "Nigga, what?"

"Charge it to the game," Dino said more defiantly.

The phrase didn't really bear repeating because every gangster lived by that code:  If you loaned your partner a pistol, and he ended up getting busted with it, you don't demand that he replace it when he gets out.  You take the loss and let it go.

"You got me fucked up," HB said and took an unexpected step to the side.

Pooky came into view again.  Dino saw that he still had the coat lying over whatever weapon he had.  He stepped in the same direction as HB, until Pooky was out of his line of sight.

"I ain't charging shit to the game," HB said, his face stony and rigid.  "Who the fuck you think you is, little nigga?" he asked Dino.  "You got my brother for three bricks, and you think that shit's gon' fly?  Hell naw!  I ain't taking that loss."

When a man goes from talking about what he *may* or *may* not do to what he *will* and *won't*, trouble is soon to follow.  Dino was too deep in his own bravado to pump the brakes.

"Well, I don't know what to tell you," he said.  "I walked in a dope house today and got what I got.   That's how I get down. You can't come over here after the fact asking for that shit back.  If you and T Lowe cool or whatever, my bad.  I didn't know.  I'll leave yo brother alone from now on.  But this one today is a done deal. It's over.  Too late to take it back now."

HB let those words sink in, and then he surprised everyone with a smile.  He nodded at Dino and then at T Lowe.

"Say, I like this nigga," he said.  "You got some balls, boy. You remind me of myself, when I was young, coming up in the hood. Robbing niggas – if that's your hustle, I can dig it. You did your thing, and you came up. Pooky shouldn't have been in there by hisself in the first place. I give you your props, little homey. But we gon' have to have some diplomacy about this shit. Tell you what; I'll let you keep the money you took off him. I just want my slabs."

"How about I give *you* the money, and *I* keep the slabs?" Dino countered.

HB chuckled. "Don't be stupid, boy."

"I didn't go through all this shit for nothing," Dino said.

HB's smile went away again. "Alright. I'll let you keep *one*. Gimme the other two, and we straight."

All things considered, that was a good deal. But Dino shook his head.

"How about I give you one, and I keep two?"

T Lowe lowered his head and sighed. The veins in HB's neck swelled.

"I'm through playing with you," he announced.

"This ain't no game," Dino assured him.

"I come to you like a man," HB said. "I try to talk to you–"

"You ain't come to talk to me!" Dino blurted. "You got your brother over there hiding something under that coat. You run up on our set, trying to tell me what to do. You gon' *let me* keep the cash? Cuz, I already got the dope *and* the money. How you gon' *let me* do anything?"

HB pointed a hard, rigid finger at Dino's nose. "T Lowe, you'd better shut this ugly motherfucker up!"

Dino raised his shirt and put his hand on the butt of his pistol. "We got guns, just like y'all do!" he shouted.

"Alright, I got you," HB said, but he headed for his car, rather than mount an offensive.

Dino watched him closely, knowing full well it wasn't over that easily.

Instead of the driver's side, HB went to the trunk of the Chrysler. That was a total shock, because there was no way he'd have time to open it and use whatever he had tucked next to his spare tire. But it was just a ruse. As soon as HB approached the back of the car, he reached for the small of his back, where his heat had been all along.

Dino drew his own weapon. He had the drop on HB, but in the confusion, Dino momentarily forgot about the variable. When he looked back inside the car, Pooky had already tossed the Cowboys jacket to the side. His toy was now in full view. It was a Kalashnikov assault rifle, better known as an AK-47.

Pooky's eyes were wide and demented. He raised the barrel of his weapon just as Dino raised his. Dino totally disregarded HB at that moment, because the AK was the most prominent threat, and certainly someone else had a bead on HB by then. Hate it or love it, Dino was down with the Sicc, and the Sicc had to stay down with him, too – all the way down to the grave, if necessary.

● ● ● ● ● ●

"We should go the other way."

Isaiah noticed them first, because he always noticed everything. But even if he hadn't, it's not like Jacob wouldn't have seen them, too. It was hard to miss a guy parked virtually in the middle of the street, especially a guy as big as the bald-headed thug visiting the Sicc Crips that day.

Jacob looked around irritably, weighing their options. He and his little brother stood at the corner of Campbell and Forbes Street. The intersection was a T-bone, so they couldn't go to the right (nor would they want to, because that would be in the exact opposite direction of their faded yellow house with white trimming). They could continue forward, towards Berry Street, but that would also take them past their destination. Even if they made the block at the next street, they would still have to come down Forbes again from the other side.

And what Isaiah was referring to as "the other way" wasn't a very good option at all.

"What other way?" Jacob asked, just to be sure.

"The alley," Isaiah said, looking back the way they came.

Less than half a block behind them was an alleyway that ran behind the Josephson's house. The alley continued for a full block, allowing the brothers access to the backyard of their own home. But the city gave up on that stretch of land many years ago. In a better neighborhood, the neighbors might have banded together to keep the alley clean. But this wasn't a better

28

neighborhood. On this block, no one cared about any area outside of their property line.

When the boys were little, Jacob and Isaiah liked to play in that alley. The overgrown grass and shrubbery was nearly chest high – perfect for games of hide-and-seek, cops and robbers or wild African expeditions. But over the years things got more and more ugly back there. People used the alley as a junkyard; filling it with tree branches, bags of leaves, paint cans and other rubbish that couldn't be traced back to them.

Jacob was positive there were snakes and mice in that alley, but he was more worried about the filth and cockleburs and paint cans and how his new school pants would look once they jumped the fence and made it safely inside their backyard.

"I don't want to go that way," he said. "It's nasty. And they're not fighting or nothing."

"Mama said don't be out there when they're arguing," Isaiah said.

There was no need for the reminder. Jacob knew exactly what their mother said, because she said the same things almost every day:

*Don't be out there when those **thugs** are outside.*
*Don't even look out the window.*
*Don't open the door.*
*Don't be out there when they're arguing and fighting.*
*Don't talk to them, if they try to talk to you.*
*Don't go over there if they call you.*
*You come tell me.*
*I already went over there and talked to them, and I'll know about it, if you try to hang out with them.*
*Those boys ain't nothing but trouble, and we don't have nothing to do with them.*
*And for God's sake, if they **do** start shooting at somebody, hit the floor and lay there as long as you have to. Jesus Christ! I gotta get us the hell away from here!*

"They not arguing, and they not fighting," Jacob said. Their home was only two houses down. Jacob could see it and almost feel the air conditioner already. "Come on. We'll be in the house in thirty seconds."

He started walking, and Isaiah followed reluctantly.

"Come on," Jacob urged.  He reached back and pulled Isaiah's backpack, until his brother caught up.

"They're going to fight," Isaiah predicted.  He kept his eyes glued to the drama unfolding across the street.

Jacob watched too, but he did so more furtively.  In his short life, Jacob had come to understand that people don't like to be stared at when they're upset.  Such gawking was likely to bring about a response like, *Whatchoo looking at, fool?* at which point you'd be stuck in one of those all-too-familiar *nigga moments*.

By then there was no doubt that the hoodlums across the street were angry about something.  Even without looking them in the eyes, Jacob heard the intonations in their voices.  The big man was trying to sound calm, but he was becoming more and more frustrated.  The guy he was talking to – a kid really – was escalating things with a cocky attitude and total lack of respect.

"They're arguing now," Isaiah noted.

"We're almost there," Jacob said, and that was true.  They were already past the Josephson's yard; in front of Mrs. Hobart's place now.  Just twenty more paces, and they would be home, thirty tops.

Jacob held on to the loop at the top of his brother's backpack and pulled him along, because Isaiah was much shorter, and his legs didn't move as quickly.  To save even more time, Jacob began to cut through the Hobart's lawn.  This was another cardinal sin, and Isaiah resisted immediately.

"Hey!"

"Come on," Jacob muttered.

"We're not supposed to–"

"It don't matter.  We're cutting through.  Now do what I say!"

Jacob punctuated his last sentence with a forceful tug.  Not surprisingly, Isaiah tumbled forward, the huge bulk of his backpack driving his chest into the soft grass.

"Ow!"

"Get up," Jacob said.  He grabbed hold of his brother's arm and lifted Isaiah with hardly any effort.  Isaiah quickly dropped back to his knees to retrieve his glasses.

This had to be the most embarrassing thing ever.  It was bad enough Jacob had to care for his little brother so much, but now Isaiah was showing weakness in front of the toughest guys in the neighborhood. If the Crips saw him fall, they would laugh and call Isaiah names. They might throw rocks. Jacob was used to sticking up for his brother, but how could he stand up to all of them?

Fortunately the Crips across the street were too busy to notice Isaiah's clumsiness.

"*We got guns, just like y'all do*," one of them shouted.

"And, there's a gun," Isaiah said matter-of-factly.

Jacob's heart froze, and he gave the thugs his full attention then. The two men who were arguing had separated. The bigger man rushed to the back of the Chrysler 300. The younger guy pulled a pistol from underneath his shirt; just as plain as day, as if they were shooting a movie or something.

"*Come on!*" Jacob almost yelled it this time. He jabbed a shaky hand in his pocket as they stepped and wrapped his fingers around the shoestring he had in there. The shoestring was laced through one key; the one needed to unlock their front door. His mother preferred that Jacob wear the shoestring around his neck, but it was just as safe in his pocket. He couldn't afford even a fake gold necklace, and he sure as hell wasn't going to school with shoestring bling.

"*Come on!*" Jacob shouted, dragging his brother by the backpack again.

Isaiah followed a lot better this time, though his body was turned almost completely around, his eyes fixed on the excitement less than fifteen yards away.

*You too damned nosey for your own good!* Jacob thought, wondering if it was the jitters or the cold fingers of the Grim Reaper tip-tapping down his spine.

• • • • • •

HB didn't have a goddamned thing.

Running to the back of the Chrysler was a diversion.

This was Pooky's hit all along.

Dino didn't know any of this at the time, but he knew to keep his gun on the biggest threat. You can never go wrong with a plan like that.

Pooky had enough firepower and enough bullets to kill everyone outside and inside T Lowe's dope house. But HB mishandled one crucial detail when he came up with this plot for revenge: Pooky got beat up by Dino less than an hour ago. If he didn't stick up for himself when Dino walked out with his money and drugs, where would Pooky get his well of courage from now?

The opportunity for revenge makes a lot of gangsters trigger happy. It would have for Dino, and it no doubt would have for HB, too. But Pooky didn't have the heart of a warrior like them. Dino saw it in his eyes in the split second before all kinds of shit hit the fan. In a heartbeat that seemed to last forever, Dino pulled his weapon while Pooky was supposed to be cocking his. Dino aimed his pistol while Pooky was supposed to be firing his.

Dino got off the first shot, and time and space instantly converged as one. The sound of gunfire made the slow motion stop and become fast-forward instead. And Dino grinned, knowing he was well on his way to ghetto immortality.

*BAP!*

The first bullet flew through the Chrysler's open window and impacted with the passenger-side door panel, just a few inches from Pooky's right arm.

Dino squeezed again.

*BAP!*

The second shot was way off; slamming into the Chrysler's front fender.

By then something snapped in Pooky's head, and he realized things were not going as well as they'd mapped it out on the south side. They hadn't caught the Sicc Crips off guard. This wasn't the one-way shooting spree HB had envisioned. Instead, Pooky was caught up in the most dreaded nigga moment of all; a kill or be killed scenario. And when faced with those options, even a coward can find the nerve to pull the trigger.

Pooky raised the AK and let go with what had to be the biggest and loudest bullets in the world. The racket was immediately deafening; instilling chaos and fear in the hearts of everyone on the wrong end of the street sweeper.

As expected, the Sicc Crips began to scatter like flies – all except for one. Dino stood tall in the midst of adversity, because that's the stuff legends are made of. He wasn't too concerned with his own death, just as he wasn't concerned with the death of any of his comrades. What Dino wanted was to live forever. He wanted his story to be told:

*Did you hear about that nigga Dino?*

*HB came over there and tried to punk him, but Dino stood up to him.*

*Word?*

*Dino busted at HB and his brother.*

*He went hard.*

*Pour out some liquor.*

*That nigga was the shit.*

By then HB had completed his sneaky trip around his car, and he opened the passenger door behind his brother. He meant for Pooky to jump into the driver's seat. HB would climb in the vacated passenger side, and they would make a smooth getaway. But this plan was already spoiled because Pooky didn't start shooting in a timely matter, and they still had a Sicc Crip shooting back at them.

Undaunted, HB was determined to get back into his car. He shoved Pooky forward, totally oblivious to the fact that Pooky's finger was jammed on the Kalashnikov's trigger. The violent jolt sent AK bullets flying at T Lowe's dope house in all directions.

***TAT-TAT!***

***RAT-TAT-TAT-TAT!***

Dino heard screams behind him. He didn't know if they were from fright or from pain, but he did know that none of Pooky's bullets had hit him yet. This was proof that he was meant for glory. Rather than retreat, Dino pressed the attack, taking one, and then another bold step towards the Chrysler, though the driver's side window spat lead and fire like a dragon's breath.

With his third shot, Dino saw blood splatter, but Pooky and HB were so jumbled together, he didn't know which one he hit.

Dino's fourth bullet found a home as well. He didn't express any fear until Pooky made it to the driver's side of the vehicle. Rather than turn towards the steering wheel, Pooky stuck the AK out of the window and actually leaned out of the car. Maybe it was getting shot that woke him up. Maybe his brother's shoves knocked some of the bitch out of him. Dino didn't know what it was, but he saw that the look on Pooky's face was altogether different now. Pooky looked furious. Deranged, and downright *gangster*.

It's only natural to get away from something like that, and Dino's legs began to backpedal on their own accord. Murder was still on his mind, so Dino kept pulling the trigger as he retreated.

Something like a fiery baseball slammed into his cheek, and a flash of bloody red obscured Dino's vision completely for a few seconds. Before he could open his eyes, the heavy weight of someone's body crashed into the back of his legs, effectively bowling him over.

With his arms outstretched, Dino kept squeezing the trigger; determined to empty his clip before HB's Chrysler sped away. Dino only had four bullets left. One of them was named Chuck.

Chuck was mad as hell, and he wasn't bullshitting.

*Now I'm peeping you*
*Through this barrel of this gun*
*I'm looking you dead in the eyes*
*I'm bouncing with anticipation*
*C'mon*
*C'mon!*
*Pull the trigger, dog*
*Let me at em*

# CHAPTER THREE
## *MY BROTHER'S KEEPER*

Chuck was born two years ago in Raleigh, North Carolina. He wouldn't say he was *born* hating people, but he would be the first to admit that his birth was saturated with destructive tendencies. Just days old, Chuck had a good deal of cordite stuffed right under his butt. Beneath the cordite was a primer. His innards were held together with something his manufacturers called a *casing*.

Chuck didn't like his casing. Casings were the bitches of the bullet world. They were the snitches, the detective's dreams. They were the weakest link. And from the moment the casing was squeezed around him, Chuck wanted nothing more than to be free of it.

His full name was Semi-Jacket Hollow Point, but who wants to go by all of that? Even the shortened version, SJHP, was a bit much for his tastes. *Chuck* suited him just fine, so he took that name for himself. When you're a bullet, you can pretty much take whatever you want for yourself. Chuck was actually the name of the first inspector to caress him, hold him, and verify him a success.

He was placed in a box with twenty of his brothers, and this box was placed inside a larger box containing fifty more boxes of twenty. The time spent in that box measured only months, but

35

it felt like an eternity to Chuck. Some of his companions warned him to embrace the peaceful tranquility of the box, to hope he *never* got out of the box in fact, because when the box opened, he would die.

But what was that shit about? Chuck, as well as every other bullet, was born to die. The projectiles were starting to sound like casings in that box, so Chuck was elated when it was finally opened.

Unfortunately, Chuck found that he was not in Afghanistan, but in something called a *sporting goods store* instead. He got this news from WSSM, a Winchester Super Short Magnum who said he had been there for at least six months. Six months sounded like a life sentence, but Chuck bid his time. While waiting, he got next to a Walther P99 who claimed to have bloodied at least three people. He also met a Colt Python who had never been fired.

When his time to shine finally came, Chuck was ready. A young socialite bought the box he was in one broody winter morning and promptly stuffed him into the clip of her brand new handgun. He was six of eight and feeling great. The socialite's purse was stolen five months later, and Chuck found himself the property of a dopefiend named Marty.

Marty was a fool. He never considered using Chuck to go on a robbery spree, so he could have all the drugs he wanted. Instead, Marty immediately traded the whole .380, Chuck included, to a slanky dealer named Lennox for three ten-dollar crack rocks. Lennox was small time. He bought his working dope from the Sicc Crips on Forbes Street. Four months after landing the piece, Lennox sold the .380 to a thug named Dino for seventy-five dollars. Chuck had to wait only six days before Dino had use for him.

As Chuck zipped through the afternoon sunlight – his ride lasting only a fraction of a second – his heart filled with an elation only lottery winners could understand – he allowed himself a moment to contemplate life, loss and the meaning of it all. He decided he didn't give a flying shit about any of that, especially if he hit flesh and muscles.

He hit bone instead.

Chuck slammed into Isaiah's head, just above the right eye, and skated through the boy's skull like a mini rocket, taking a good deal of whatever he touched through a peach pit size hole he created on the way out. Isaiah was already lying prone on the ground – had been ever since he heard the first clap of gunfire – and the majority of his blood splattered onto the soft, green grass beneath his left ear.

With momentum ebbing, Chuck continued his route out of Isaiah's head and into a layer of topsoil dense with roots. His wild ride came to an end eight inches later when Chuck collided with a remarkably unyielding sandstone.

Beat, battered, and horribly misshapen, Chuck was forced to consider the brevity of his task compared to the painstakingly dull wait he endured. As his body temperature cooled, he decided it had all been worth it.

*Oh yeah, totally fucking worth it.*

● ● ● ● ● ●

The sound of screeching tires announced the deed was done.

Dino opened his eyes. His left eye squinted at the bright sunshine. He couldn't see anything but blood in his right eye. He thought he was dead, or close to it. He knew he got shot in the face, but he also felt pain in his left leg. He thought the pain in his face should be worse, but it wasn't that bad. It felt like his cheek was numb yet on fire at the same time. The throbbing in his leg was a totally different kind of pain. He pushed up with his arms, so he could see if his limb had been blown off somehow.

Behind him someone screamed. It was a female voice, and it wasn't very much of a scream at all; more like a low-pitched wail, what some might call a death rattle.

Staring down at his legs with his one good eye, Dino still couldn't assess the damage. There was a corpse draped across his knees. He knew this was the body that had knocked him over a few seconds ago. He wiped the blood from his eye, blinking furiously. The person on top of him didn't appear to be bleeding, so Dino pushed his shoulder.

"Say, man..."

Stephon's head popped up, and he looked around warily. "They gone?"

Seeing who it was, Dino's temper quickly got the best of him. *Coward ass faggot.* "Nigga, you hit?" he asked.

Stephon shook his head, marveling at Dino's new head wound.

"Get off me!" Dino snapped. He bucked when Stephon didn't immediately comply. "Nigga, get off me!"

Stephon checked the streets before getting up.

Dino looked back to the dope house and saw Tricky cowering in the bushes next to the steps. Peanut was no longer sitting in the metal folding chair on the porch. No one else was in sight, but the wails continued from inside the house.

Dino made it to his knees and scanned the street in both directions. Everything was eerily quiet, except for a ringing in his ears that would probably never go away completely.

*rat-tat*

*rat-tat-tat-tat*

Dino was sure HB wouldn't be back, but following up one driveby with another attack was not totally unheard of. Dino checked his pistol and saw that the clip was depleted. He turned back to the house and saw T Lowe peering out of the front door. T Lowe had a weapon in hand now, an SKS, but Dino knew he hadn't fired the gun. Dino also noticed that T Lowe was hesitant about coming outside.

"You alright?" Dino asked Tricky.

"Yeah, man." Tricky made it to his feet, and then he approached and gave Dino a hand. Tricky stared at Dino's face in amazement. "Damn, cuz. Yo shit's fucked off."

Dino put a hand to his wound and winced. Without a mirror, he didn't know what he was feeling. But he knew that his cheekbone was tender and wet and was starting to swell.

"The bullet still in there?" Dino asked.

Tricky leaned in close. "I don't know. Too much blood. It's on the side though, so probably not. Just skinned you. If it went the other way, you'd be dead."

"They gone?" That was T Lowe, still standing in the front door. Another dark face peered over his shoulder.

*Too scared to check on your homies?* Dino wondered. He didn't call T Lowe on it, though.

Not yet, anyway.

"Yeah, they gone," Dino said. "Somebody got shot in there?"

"That bitch got hit in the leg," T Lowe said. He stepped out onto the porch holding his SKS with both hands. He looked like a proper soldier now, but Dino already saw the truth.

"You bleeding bad," T Lowe said.

Dino felt the slickness on his neck and chest then. He thought it was sweat, but when he rubbed his collarbone, his hand came back red.

"Peanut dead?" T Lowe asked, staring down at the porch.

Dino didn't think so, but he mounted the steps and saw his partner crumpled next to the folding chair. Peanut was curled in a fetal position. His eyes were wide and unblinking. His mouth hung open. His shirt was wet, and a pool of blood grew steadily, originating from his midsection. Blood pooled under his nose and mouth as well.

Dino's mouth fell open. He dropped to one knee and reached slowly for Peanut's arm. By then Tricky had hopped onto the porch as well. He leaned over Dino's shoulder, and Dino could smell the Doritos Tricky had for lunch that day.

"Say, Peanut, man," Dino said. "Peanut?"

"He dead, man," T Lowe said. "Look at that nigga's eyes."

"He ain't breathing," Tricky agreed.

Dino withdrew his hand before making contact with Peanut's arm, as if he could catch his own death by touching a corpse.

"That nigga killed Peanut," Dino said, still watching his friend's face. He expected a blink or a shudder or at the least a spit bubble that would make him out to be a liar, but Peanut did not blink, and no air passed between his lips. Dino stared at the death mask for so long, it would forever be a part of his psyche. He would never be able to think about his homey without seeing his bloodied face.

"They killed my nigga," Dino said again, already trying to diminish any role he might have played in Peanut's untimely demise.

"*Help meeeee!*" The girl's screams were getting louder now, but her voice was faint.

Dino looked up at T Lowe and then stood. "Did you shoot back?" he asked.

39

T Lowe shook his head. "I ran in there to get my shit. They was already gone when I got back."

"Who shot back?" Dino asked. "I emptied my clip in that nigga's car. I know I hit somebody." It was good to establish these things early on.

T Lowe shook his head. "Didn't nobody else–"

Another bloodied Crip rushed through the front door, his eyes wide, his breaths quickened. "Say, this bitch finna *die*," he announced. Detroit was short and stocky with coppery red skin. His pants and hands were coated with blood, but none of it was his.

"I thought she got shot in the leg," Tricky said.

"She hit in the thigh," Detroit confirmed. "But it must've hit an artery or something. Bitch squirting blood like a faucet. She bleeding out. Shit's everywhere. We gotta get outta here!"

T Lowe handed Detroit the SKS. "Go put this in my car. Y'all got the shit bagged up?"

"Shorty's doing it now," Detroit said, and then looked down and asked, "Peanut dead?"

"He gone," Tricky confirmed.

Detroit looked up at Dino, and his big eyes grew even wider. "Damn, cuz. Yo shit's *jacked*. You gotta go to a doctor, cuz."

"Did you shoot back?" Dino asked.

Detroit shook his head, his jaw slack.

"I did," Dino said. "I emptied my–"

"What's up with that?" T Lowe was looking across the street now. Every eye followed his gaze. A few of the neighbors had come outside, and they were having a hard time deciding what they wanted to gawk at more; the Crips standing outside with guns and blood-smeared clothing or the small body lying in the yard of the yellow and white house across the street.

Dino took an awkward step forward, and his legs nearly gave out. The air left his body like he'd been punched in the stomach. His head spun. He stumbled to the banister and held onto it for support.

There was no doubt about whose body that was because his big brother was kneeling over him; still trying to protect the runt from a cruel, cruel world that was getting uglier by the second.

Dino staggered down the steps and stood next to Stephon. T Lowe and Tricky came and stood behind him. From that distance, none of them could see if the child was hurt or not. But they could read it in the tears that streamed down the face of the protective brother. They could see it in the eyes of the neighbors who looked from one crime scene to the other, their mouths hanging open behind their trembling fingers.

"They, they shot that little boy?" Detroit asked.

"Yeah," Dino said. An arctic wind rolled down his body. His mouth was drier than it had ever been. He swallowed roughly, his heart pounding. "They musta, they did–"

"Dino, you the one shot that boy," Stephon said, and something in Dino's mind cracked.

He swung as hard as he could; hoping to take Stephon's whole head off with just one punch. The blow landed awkwardly on the side of Stephon's neck, but it was hard enough to knock him down. Dino was immediately on top of him, throwing punches with all the ferocity he could muster. Stephon blocked as many of them as he could, but he couldn't block them all. Dino connected on the side of Stephon's head and then his mouth and then his temple again.

"*You made me!*" he blurted. Tears streamed down Dino's face. Even with all of the bravado in the world, he couldn't stop them. "*You fell on me!*" he cried. "*You made me fall!*"

"Hey! What – *Get off me, man!* Get–"

"Chill out, Dino!"

"*Man, get this nigga!*"

"Dino, man! Get off him!"

Strong hands yanked Dino from his prey. T Lowe swung him around so hard, Dino nearly lost his footing.

"Cuz, you need to get outta here!" T Lowe shouted. "Just *run*, man! We'll catch up with you later."

"But it was *him!*" Dino tried to lunge at Stephon again, but two people restrained him. "He didn't shoot back when we did that shit on Vaughn!" Dino cried. "I knew he was a ho then, but I didn't say nothing! He was too busy trying to save his own self! I was the only one shooting back, and he ran into me! *I was the only one trying to help!*"

Another fist flew into the fracas. This one was such a surprise, no one did anything for a few seconds. Jacob swung

41

again, landing a glancing blow on Dino's chin. The eighth-grader was crying and punching. The scene was so pitiful, Dino didn't even ward off the blows.

"Get on, little nigga." T Lowe pushed him away, but Jacob came right back.

"*I hate you,*" he bawled at Dino. Jacob's face was drenched with sweat and tears and snot that ran from his nose unabated. "*I hate you! I hate you!*"

"Man, let me go!" Dino ripped free from Detroit's grip. His remorse was a harness of tears and blood. He could barely lift his head from a pool of despair that was thick like quicksand.

Jacob tried to go after him again, but T Lowe grabbed the boy from behind. Jacob fought against him like a wild animal.

"*I hate you!*" the boy cried. His hands were red. His chest too was coated with Isaiah's blood. "*I hate y'all!*"

"*Y'all leave that boy alone!*"

Dino looked back and saw a few of the neighbors headed in their direction. The do-gooders never stood up to the Crips before, but Jacob's grief was much more than they could turn a blind eye to. It was the most appalling thing they had ever seen.

"Get out of here!" T Lowe yelled again. "Go, man! Just go!"

Dino looked around fretfully before taking heed. Sweat poured from his head, and it mingled with the blood in his eyes. The wound on his cheek pulsated, delivering the first tendrils of real pain.

"*Run, cuz!*"

Dino still wasn't going to do it, but the neighbors were getting closer, and at that moment T Lowe could hold Jacob back no longer. The boy broke free and charged like a pit bull dog, and Dino turned tail – not because he was afraid of Jacob, but because he finally understood that enough was enough. Even with blood rushing in his ears and his dreams of ghetto glory going up in flames, Dino knew that there was a line, and he had crossed it, and sometimes the only thing you can do is run.

Run away from it all.

Dino hit the streets like Jesse Owens in his prime, and Jacob took off right behind him. Around the first corner, as his sneakers clapped the pavement like a quarter horse, Dino found religion the way most gangsters do: Not in the church house, but in the ghetto, in the midst of sin; when all other options have failed and it's okay to believe in Jesus Christ or the Holy Spirit or whoever else might love you enough to offer unconditional compassion in your time of need.

*Oh Lord, what I'm gon' do now?* Dino pondered.
*Jesus, what I'm gon' do now?*

• • • • • •

Jacob and Isaiah were already on the ground when the automatic gunfire started.

The brothers both dove face-first into the grass at the sound of the two smaller gunshots, just as their mother told them to do. They'd made it all the way to their front porch by then, but Jacob never had a chance to unlock the door and get Isaiah into the relative safety of their home.

The first two shots were like something from a hellish nightmare. Jacob had lived in various ghettos throughout his life, and he'd grown accustomed to the sound of gunfire. But to hear it in such close proximity rattled his nerves like nothing ever had.

He reached back anxiously, his hand pawing the stiff blades of grass, until he came in contact with Isaiah's head. Jacob grabbed his shoulder and dared to look back at his brother. Isaiah looked up at him with terror widening his eyes as well.

"Stay down!" Jacob ordered, and Isaiah nodded, his whole body shivering like a wet kitten.

"I am!"

"Stay down!"

Jacob's chest thundered. He looked across the street just as the boy in the Chrysler opened up with the AK. The first gunshots they heard were loud, but the automatic gunfire was completely deafening. Jacob saw fire spitting from the Chrysler's front seat, and he was both amazed and terrified, confused and astounded. The Crips started to run in all directions, and Jacob waited to see one of them fall.

He wanted it.

For the past six months, the Crips had been the source of countless worries and precautions in Jacob's household. It was hard enough growing up poor, but even poor kids had some sense of normalcy in their day to day lives. Jacob didn't want to have to worry about whether the Crips were outside before he went to visit his friends down the street. He didn't want to have to lower his gaze every time he saw them. Even something as trivial as taking the trash out or bringing the bins back from the curb was an ordeal because of the Crips.

*Get em.*

Jacob couldn't stop the thought from creeping into his mind as the grass scratched his face and neck, nor did he want to stop it.

*Get em.*

*Get em all.*

There was a momentary lull in the gunfire when the bald man ran to the passenger side of the Chrysler, but it didn't last long. The AK ripped off another long burst, and Jacob felt Isaiah shuddering behind him. Jacob's heart shot up in his throat, and he looked back at his brother, expecting the worst. But Isaiah was still okay. He looked up at Jacob with his glasses off, his eyes wet with tears.

*"Why won't they stop?"* he cried.

"You're okay," Jacob told him and returned his attention to the gunfight. The bald man was inside his car now, and the boy with the AK was still shooting. Only one Crip remained standing in the front yard. Jacob's pulse quickened. He knew he was about to witness a murder, because there was no way the kid with the machine gun could miss him now.

Sure enough the Crip's face exploded in a spray of bright red, and he stumbled backwards. He kept firing his pistol at the car as he fell, and though Jacob hated everything about the thugs across the street, he couldn't help but feel like he was witnessing something powerful. Majestic even. Before crying out in pain or even reaching for the wound on his face, the Crip's mind was still on murder.

The Chrysler sped away then, and Jacob saw a real-live cloud of gun smoke lingering over the spot it vacated. The Crips were slow to access the damage on their end, and Jacob was too. He remained on the ground for a full thirty seconds before he was confident the shooting was really over.

"Isaiah."

He called out to his brother, but Isaiah didn't respond. Jacob reached back and nudged his brother's shoulder.

"Isaiah."

Once again there was no response.

More confused than worried, Jacob felt around until he found his brother's head.  He felt something wet spilling from Isaiah's mouth.  He jerked his hand away in revulsion, and in the half a second it took him to look down at his fingers, Jacob knew that wasn't Isaiah's mouth because there was no nose or eyes anywhere near the wetness he felt.

Jacob scrambled to a sitting position, staring first at his bloodied hand and then at his little brother, who lay quietly on his stomach.

"Isaiah?"

Jacob knew he wouldn't respond, because he saw the gore coating the grass.  But the sight was too much to bear or comprehend.  He could not accept what he was looking at.

"*Isaiah!*"

Jacob's energy was sucked from his body along with all the air in his lungs, and he barely had the strength to pull Isaiah's head into his lap.

"Come on, man.  Get up, Isaiah.  It's over now..."

Isaiah's eyes were closed.  That was a blessing.  Jacob knew he would have gone stark-raving mad if he had to stare into those lifeless orbs.  As he cradled his brother in his lap, Jacob's face twisted until it resembled the exaggerated makeup of a sad clown.  Tears streamed down his face, but Jacob was more concerned with the tears that were starting to dry on Isaiah's cheeks.  He wiped them with his thumb, leaving a thick smear of blood that was much worse by comparison.

"Come on, man. You gotta get up..." Jacob coughed and sniffled and sucked in a long string of mucus.  "Mama gon' be mad when she get home.  She gon' be mad at me."

Isaiah's head rolled loosely on his pencil neck.  Jacob felt blood soaking into his pants, all the way to his underwear.

By then the Crips across the street were moving around, and a few neighbors came outside to see what was going on.  Jacob looked up and saw Ms. Hobart standing on her sidewalk.  Ms. Hobart's mouth dropped open.  The look she fixed on Jacob said it all:

*What happened to your brother?*
*You were supposed to look after him.*

45

*How'd you let this happen?*
*What have you done?*

"No." Jacob shook his head and turned away from her.

Across the street the Crips were watching him, too, and Jacob knew they were thinking the same thing: He only had one thing to do; just one important goal in life, and he failed to accomplish it. Why didn't he throw his body over Isaiah's? Why didn't he take the alley like Isaiah suggested? All he had to do was get Isaiah from the bus stop to the house. Their mother trusted him, and he'd failed her miserably.

Jacob threw his head back, and a loud moan erupted from his chest and rattled past his trachea. He staggered to his feet like a drunkard and was already moving before he understood his destination. Across the street, the Crips were fighting – amongst themselves. Jacob balled his fists as he stepped through the dense gun smoke still lingering in the air. He didn't know who his target would be until the Crips separated the fighters and one of them yelled, "*You made me! You fell on me! You made me fall!*"

And then Jacob knew.

The murderer had already been shot in the face. He was crying, and he sounded remorseful about what happened to Isaiah, but Jacob didn't care. When he was close enough, Jacob threw his hardest punch at the Crip's head, trying his best to end the thug's life. The shooter backed away. No one intervened, so Jacob swung again and again.

Strong hands grabbed hold of him then. Jacob fought like hell to free himself.

"*I hate you!*" he screamed. "You killed my brother! I hate you! *I hate you!*"

The hands relaxed for a second, and Jacob charged the shooter again. But at the last moment, someone grabbed the back of his shirt and halted his momentum.

"*Y'all leave that boy alone!*" The voice came from Ms. Hobart across the street.

The hands on Jacob went slack again, and he immediately went after his brother's killer. The Crip was ready for him this time, though. He easily sidestepped Jacob like a bullfighter.

"Run, cuz!" somebody advised, and the shooter did just that. He took off down the street. Jacob gave chase before better sense could stop him.

The footrace lasted no more than eight blocks before Jacob's heart felt like it was on fire, and he knew he'd have to stop. It was illogical: The Crips drank beer and smoked pot every day. Jacob had virgin lungs and youth on his side, but Isaiah's killer gained more and more ground by the second. The murderer made wild turns at ever other block. He cut through lawns and jumped a back fence, and Jacob found himself in an unfamiliar alley when he followed.

His chest heaving, Jacob stopped in the middle of the trail, his body slumped over, his hands resting on his knees. He looked right and then left. He didn't see the shooter anywhere, but he heard thrashing in the bushes to his right, so he went that way.

Jacob emerged from the alley, scraped and bruised, at a T bone intersection on Burton Avenue. There was no sign of the killer, and there were no barking dogs or agitated bushes to give a clue as to which direction he went this time.

Crushed, Jacob put his hands to his face and screamed as loudly as he could. He heard sirens in the distance. The only thing he knew for sure was the killer hadn't gone in *that* direction. Those sirens were for Isaiah.

Defeated, Jacob turned and headed home. He dropped his head and cried and took slow, deliberate steps. His only hope, at that point, was that they'd have his brother scooped up off the lawn before he got there.

Before his mother got home from work.

# CHAPTER FOUR
## *DANCING WITH DEMONS*

Tammy Spencer stood in the doorway of room 475 shaking her head slowly. She took a deep breath and let it out an audible sigh.

*Great.*

Just two hours into her shift, she'd already mopped up after a vomiting grandmother in 467, a spilled catheter bag in 489 and now this.

The patient in room 475 had been there for nearly a month. It was always a chore to clean up after someone who stayed that long. Tammy was glad the kid survived his gunshot wound to the chest, but she wasn't at all pleased with the way his family and friends treated the room over the past twenty days.

There was no sense complaining though, so she put on a fresh pair of latex gloves and pushed her cart into the room. The floor was the best place to get started with jobs like this, so she reached for her broom and dustpan. Most of the debris was too big, however, so she returned the broom and grabbed one of the large trash bags instead.

Tammy's own reflection caught her eye on the other side of the room. She ambled over to the mirror to see if she looked as tired as she felt today. Purple had never been very flattering on her, but that was the color all of the housekeepers at Jackson Memorial wore. Tammy thought she looked *alright* in her scrub suit. She would prefer if the outfit showed off her waistline a little, but there was no one at the hospital that she felt the need to impress.

There were some cute nurses scattered about. A good number of them were black and single. But those guys never gave housekeepers a second look. Tammy's purple scrubs made her even more invisible to doctors – but it's not like she had a chance of scoring a physician in any outfit.

Tammy considered herself fairly attractive. She had smooth, mocha-colored skin, large brown eyes and full pink lips. Today she had her shoulder-length hair pulled back in a ponytail. But no doctor she ever met was interested in dating a middle school dropout.

Actually, Tammy did go back to get her GED, but that didn't change her lifestyle very much. Someone once told her GED stood for *Good Enough Diploma*, and Tammy was in agreement with that. She was good enough for her entry-level job at the hospital, and she was good enough for her part-time job as a waitress at Juan's Taquería. But good enough to date a doctor or a nurse? Yeah right.

Back in the doorway, another cart bumped into hers. Tammy turned to tell them she already had this assignment, but she saw that it was her friend Marissa.

"Boy, stop," Marissa said, laughing at someone in the hallway.

"I'm coming in there with you," a male voice responded.

"I don't need your help," Marissa told him, giggling. "I know how to make a bed."

The teenager followed her anyway with his hands firmly on Marissa's waist. Tammy put a hand on her hip and frowned at both of them. The boy looked up at her in surprise.

"Oh, it's somebody already in here." The youngster wore black Dickey pants with a gray collar shirt; the required uniform for employees in the patient transport department. His shirt wasn't tucked in, and his pants sagged midway down his ass. He sported a baby-afro and one gold tooth.

Patient transport was another entry-level position for good-enough people who didn't have any specific training.

"I told you I didn't need your help," Marissa told him.

"Alright. I'ma holler at you later," her friend replied. He stared deeply into Marissa's eyes and smiled dreamily before taking off. Tammy was pretty sure he would've given her a kiss if she wasn't there watching.

49

"You ought to be ashamed of yourself," she said when he was gone.

"What are you talking about?" Marissa asked. Still grinning, she slipped on a pair of gloves and looked around the cluttered room. "Damn, what happened in here?" she asked. "It look like they had three or *four* patients in this room."

Marissa was tall and thin, beautiful in Tammy's opinion. She was fair-skinned with small eyes, arched eyebrows and full, ruby lips.

"This is where that No-Info was," Tammy replied. "Don't you remember? He was here almost four weeks."

"That boy who got shot in the chest?" Marissa asked.

Tammy nodded. "I'm glad he made it out, but his people went to town in here. I think his mama and grandmama spent the night every day. People was coming in here with McDonald's every time I looked up."

"I still smell French fries," Marissa said with a smile.

"What you doing in here anyway?" Tammy asked. "I already picked up this job."

"I picked it up, too," Marissa said. "Cheryl put in for a second."

That was surprising. Tammy's supervisor rarely allowed two women to clean one room.

"Is it slow?"

"There was only one more job in the system," Marissa said. "What, you don't want my help?"

"Yeah I do," Tammy said. "The more the merrier." She picked up her trash bag, and the ladies got started on the task at hand. "What's up with that transporter?" Tammy asked after a while.

"What about him?" Marissa said. She held the bag open while Tammy scooped up most of the big stuff by hand.

"You kinda robbing the cradle a little bit, don't you think?"

Marissa grinned. "Girl, Demetrius is *nineteen*. He been out of school for a whole year already."

"Yeah, and you been out for twelve," Tammy said.

"You don't think he look good?"

"He's handsome," Tammy admitted. "But he seems a little childish to me. That gold tooth is ridiculous. Where he from, Houston or something?"

"Louisiana."

"One of those Katrina victims?"

"He lost everything," Marissa confirmed.

"He been working here for two years already," Tammy said. "He coulda bought a new belt by now."

"So you have noticed him," Marissa said with a sly smile.

"He used to make those same eyes at me," Tammy informed her. "But after I rolled my eyes at him enough times, he left me alone. I heard he was messing with somebody else in transport, too. You know everybody up here is a ho."

"I'm just having fun," Marissa said. "It's not like I'm falling in love or nothing."

"You slept with him?"

"A couple of times," Marissa admitted. "In the Meredith tower once."

Tammy's eyes widened. "You did it *here*?"

"Those transporters know some secret spots," Marissa told her. "Some spots don't nobody else know about."

"I don't know whether to laugh or cry," Tammy said.

"You never wanted a younger man?" her friend asked.

"Not that young," Tammy replied. "My oldest boy is going on fourteen. What would I look like with a nineteen year old boyfriend?"

"Which one's your oldest?"

"Jacob. And even *he* pulls up his pants and acts like he got some damned sense."

"*Tammy Spencer, please call extension 3793,*" the hospital operator announced over the PA system. "*Tammy Spencer, please call extension 3793,*" she repeated in the same monotone.

"I wonder what Cheryl wants now," Tammy said on her way to the nightstand where the patient's phone sat. "You sure she told you to help me in here?"

"Yeah," Marissa said. "I was sitting right there when she put it in the system."

Tammy dialed the extension, and her supervisor gave her a different number to call.

"What is it?" Marissa asked when Tammy hung up.

"She wants me to call one of my neighbors."

"Your house got broke into?" Marissa guessed.

"No, I doubt it," Tammy said, but she could think of no good reason why Ms. Hobart might be calling her at work. She never even gave Ms. Hobart her number at the hospital.

The middle-aged woman answered after four long rings. "Hello?"

"Ms. Hobart? This is Tammy. You, um, you called up to my job?"

"Oh, uh, yeah I did." The woman breathed heavily into the phone. "Baby, you need to come home. Something bad happened over here."

Tammy's heart was suddenly ice cold, and she couldn't draw in another breath. This call wasn't necessarily a surprise, because Tammy knew where she lived, and she worried about her circumstances all the time. The only surprise would be finding out exactly which bad thing happened. Burglary? Fire? Fight? Looting? Shooting? The possibilities were dreadfully infinite.

"Are you there, honey?"

"What happened?" Tammy asked in a hushed voice. Marissa came and stood next to her. Tammy didn't look up at her.

"Baby, this, I don't, I think there's some other people you should probably talk to." Ms. Hobart was uncharacteristically flustered. "There's some police here. I told them where you work, and–"

"My boys alright?" Tammy couldn't blink. She stared at the phone so hard her vision blurred. She couldn't look away. She couldn't move at all.

Ms. Hobart didn't answer for a long time. "There, um..." She sighed. Her voice quavered when she spoke again. "There's, um..."

Tammy dropped the phone and rushed out of the room. As soon as she stepped into the hallway, she saw two police officers at the nursing station. One of them worked for the hospital. His name was Warren, and Tammy liked him a lot. The other policeman wore plain clothes, but Tammy knew he was a cop right away. She could tell by the way he was dressed and by the way he looked at her. She could see in his eyes that this wasn't about a burglary, fire, fight or looting.

Tammy fell to her knees in the middle of the hallway and clasped her hands together in prayer. She prayed the men would turn around and walk off the unit and take whatever bad news they had with them.

But that didn't happen. The men walked directly to her. Warren moved more quickly when he saw that she had dropped to the floor. When he helped her up, Tammy wailed at the tears that glistened in his eyes.

• • • • • •

The two black and whites converged on him like lions going in for the kill. They stomped the brakes, and their tires came to a screeching halt no more than ten feet away. Both the passenger and driver's side doors flew open on both vehicles, and four cops sprang into action; drawing their pistols while remaining crouched behind the door panels.

"**STOP, OR WE'LL SHOOT!**"

"**HOLD IT RIGHT THERE!**"

"**HANDS UP! GET YOUR GODDAMNED HANDS UP!**"

Jacob looked up at them slowly, barely concerned about their threats or their guns. A part of him wanted to charge them. If they put a couple of bullets in his head, he wouldn't have to feel this hurt anymore. Plus Isaiah wouldn't be alone in the afterlife.

If it wasn't for his mom, Jacob might have been crazy enough to do it. But she would be all alone if he died, too. As much as he hated himself, he couldn't bring himself to do anything so selfish.

"**GET ON THE GROUND RIGHT NOW!**"

Jacob raised his bloody hands, but he did not drop to his knees. "It wasn't me," he said.

"**GET ON THE GODDAMNED GROUND!**"

"*It wasn't me!*" Jacob screamed back at them. Fresh tears filled his eyes and rolled down his cheeks. His voice cracked, and he wondered if he wasn't going through puberty after all.

"Hold on!" One of the cops put a hand in the air and implored his partners to show some restraint. "What's your name?" he called out.

"Jacob!"

"Hold on guys." The officer holstered his weapon and scanned the tense faces of his cohorts. "It's the brother," he said. "That's Jacob."

The enlightened cop stepped around his vehicle and approached the boy cautiously. Two of the other policemen lowered their weapons. The fourth kept his gun pointed at Jacob's chest, just in case.

"Hey, you alright?" the first officer asked. He put a strong hand on Jacob's shoulder. "You can put your hands down."

Jacob did as he was told.

"What's your last name?" the cop asked.

"Spencer." Jacob looked the man in his eyes and then lowered his gaze.

The cop nodded. "You chased the shooter over here?"

"Back there." Jacob shot a thumb over his shoulder. "On Burton. I lost him."

"Burton and what?"

"Miller."

"Do you know which direction he was headed?"

Jacob shook his head.

"Can you describe his clothing?"

Jacob shook his head.

"Is he still on foot?"

Jacob nodded.

"Anything el–"

"Shot in the face," Jacob said. "He got shot in the face."

The policeman turned to his partners. "Shooter last seen at Burton and Miller. Radio it in! No description on clothes, but the GSW to the face is confirmed. Perp is still on foot!"

One set of cops jumped in their vehicle and took off in the direction Jacob gave them. The third lawman took a seat in his cruiser and snatched up the radio.

"I'm officer Gunderson," the policeman told Jacob. "I'm really sorry about what happened to your brother. This guy that shot Isaiah, did you make any contact with him?" He looked down at Jacob's bloody hands. "Do you think you might have any evidence, any blood, or maybe you grabbed hold of his clothing?..."

Jacob shook his head and studied the dried DNA on his paws. The tears stung his eyes, and his vision blurred. "This is Isaiah's blood."

The cop nodded. He looked genuinely concerned and disheartened. "We need you to come with us," he said.

"To where?" Jacob asked.

"Down to the police station. The detectives would like to talk to you about the man who shot your brother. We need to get a statement, of everything you saw."

"I don't wanna go."

"Why not, son?"

"Where's Isaiah? What'd they do with him?"

"They're, taking care of Isaiah right now."

"Is he dead?" Jacob knew the answer. He already saw it for himself. But sometimes people pull through, even when they didn't have a pulse for thirty minutes or more.

Jacob met the policeman's smoky gray eyes, and the cop looked back towards the patrol car. After a moment, he summoned the strength to look the eighth-grader in the eyes like a man.

"Your brother has passed away," he confirmed.

Jacob's sinuses filled with moisture, and he brought a bloody fist to his mouth. "I gotta go home," he moaned. "Mama's going to, she wants me to stay with Isaiah."

"Your mother's going to meet us at the police station," the cop informed him.

"Y'all already told her?"

Officer Gunderson nodded. He put a hand on Jacob's shoulder and squeezed softly. "Come on," he said. "We got every cop in the city looking for the shooter. We'll get him. I need you to be strong, for your mom."

Another patrol car zipped past them with its sirens blaring, and Jacob noticed that the whole neighborhood was abuzz with similar noises. Somewhere above them, he heard the familiar *bhudda-bhudda-bhudda-bhudda* sound of a helicopter flying low.

Officer Gunderson took his bloody hand with no revulsion at all, and Jacob walked to the patrol car with him, vaguely aware that this was the first time an adult male had ever held his hand. His friends at school would think it was gay, but Jacob liked the feeling of strength and compassion in the policeman's touch. Isaiah would have liked it, too.

For the second time that day, Jacob cursed his father for not being there for them.

● ● ● ● ● ●

Dino lay on his belly, like a snake, listening to dogs, sirens, helicopters and what might have been the whole National Guard and Marine Corps searching for him. His face pulsated with each one of his heartbeats. He knew he shouldn't have his wound anywhere near the ground, but he couldn't stand up. He heard anxious voices nearby. He worried that if he stood, they would see him. And if they saw him, they would shoot him.

They wouldn't ask him to put his hands up, and they wouldn't care if he had a weapon or not. They would simply open fire, like they did with Bonnie and Clyde, because Dino was a bonafide gangster now. He was a killer of children, a menace to society, an American nightmare. The worst of the worst.

Dino lay on the filthy ground inside a decrepit garage that should have been demolished many moons ago. The garage was stuffed nearly to the brim with garbage and long-forgotten storage items. The smell of old trash and mildew mixed with his own sweat and blood was nearly overpowering.

To his left were old bicycle frames and spare bicycle parts that were rusty and covered with cobwebs. Behind the bike parts were cardboard boxes piled high against the wall. Dino didn't know what was in those boxes. There were dark stains on all of them. He imagined there might be body parts; left long ago by some unknown killer.

To his right was a 1974 El Camino that had four flats, no passenger door and piles of paint cans dumped haphazardly in the bed. The paint in those cans was completely dry, but Dino could still smell the primer, as if it was spilled just yesterday.

The rest of the garage was flooded with trash bags of varying shapes, sizes and colors. They were filled with clothes, papers and God only knew what else. Dino lay amongst these bags listening to his thundering heartbeats and watching the shadows and darkness play tricks with his mind. Pointy hangers stabbed at his legs and midsection, and Dino heard the constant scratching of what he assumed was a mama rat building a nest inside one of the trash bags six feet from his head.

Dino's face continued to bleed, and he noticed that a handful of ants were attracted to the bright red puddle under his face. He did not move his arm to shoo them away. He dared not. Any sudden moves might give him away, and they would send a police dog in there for sure.

The garage door was mostly closed, but there was a two foot gap at the bottom. This was where Dino made his entrance. This was where he got his fresh air, and it was also his only hope for survival. Through the gap, Dino could see directly across the street. And if he could somehow make it into the gray and black house over there, he knew Tish would help him.

The only problem was every cop in the city was waiting to see a bloodied gangster like him streak across the street. They had birdies in the sky, dogs on the prowl and fingers on hairpin triggers. Their eyes were everywhere, but Dino could only see the world through the two foot gap. He could see Tish's house well, but who's to say she was even home? Dino had been watching her house for thirty minutes, and he never even saw a curtain move.

Good sense implored him to wait and watch for a little while longer, but Dino knew that time was not on his side. Tish lived only thirty blocks away from the crime scene on Forbes Street, and the police were apt to expand their search pretty soon.

The only thing Dino knew for sure was the longer he stayed in the garage, the more likely they were to catch him. They knew he was on foot, so all of the vacant houses and abandoned garages would become a top priority. They might be working their way down Tish's street right now, for all he knew.

His options were few, and they were all fraught with danger: Either he could wait longer or he could go now. Spending another ten minutes in the garage would surely spell his doom, but darting across the street without knowing whether Tish was home or not could be just as risky. Maybe if...

Dino's thoughts trailed off, and he sucked in a sharp breath as his prayer was answered. He thought it was a mirage, but the vision did not go away when he rubbed his eyes. The front door of the black and gray house swung open, and Tish stepped out into the diminishing sunlight. Dino was so mystified by the blessing, he watched Tish close and lock the door before he remembered there was a very important reason he was waiting on her.

Keeping low, Dino scrambled to the front of the garage and lay flat on the pavement in front of the small gap. Tish was at her car by then.

"Tish!" Dino called out to her, wary of raising his voice over a whisper.

Tish didn't hear him at all. She opened her car door and removed her purse from her shoulder.

Dino knew he'd have no chance of getting her attention once she got in the car, so he threw caution to the wind and yelled this time.

***"Tish!"***

She paused and looked around. Tish was a pretty girl; a yellow-bone with red hair and light brown eyes. Dino would have made her his main squeeze in middle school, but Tish was also a big girl. Dino already had enough problems back in those days, with his ugly mug and dinosaur teeth. He didn't want to compound things by being a chubby chaser, too.

"*Over here!*" Dino shouted.

Tish looked towards the spooky garage, and her eyes narrowed. "Who's that?"

"*It's me, Dino!*" His heart raced. He heard sirens nearby; multiple sirens from multiple emergency vehicles. Someone was going to hear him. He was sure of it.

"Dino?" Tish frowned in confusion. She hadn't seen him since Dino dropped out of the ninth grade. "What you... Boy, what you doing over there?" She bent and peered in the gap. "Are you, are you in that garage? Come out of there."

"Can I come in?" Dino pleaded. She still couldn't see his face past the shadows, and Dino needed confirmation before he exposed himself. She might reject him, once she saw his condition. But if he could get her to open the door first, Dino was getting in that house. No matter how it went down, he was getting in there.

"I'm on my way to work!" Tish shouted, confusion still marring her soft features. "What's going on? What you doing here?"

"*I need your help!*" Dino cried. The pain and exasperation in his voice was real, and Tish couldn't help but respond to it. Her frown melted away, as if she found a box of sick kittens on her doorstep.

"What you want?" she asked. "I'm going to work, boy. Come out of there. This is crazy." She looked up and down her street. "What are all these sirens about? Are they looking for you?"

"Let me come inside for a second," Dino begged her. "I need to talk to you face-to-face. I got shot, Tish. I look bad. If I come out, I'll scare you."

Tish brought a hand to her chest, and the apprehension came back.

"*Please!*" Dino wailed. "Tish, I ain't never asked you for nothing. This is an emergency! This is as real as it gets. Don't turn your back on me. You're the only one who can help me right now."

Tish considered it for nearly a minute before closing her car door. "Alright, come on."

"Go ahead and open your front door," Dino instructed. "The police might be around here. I need to run over there real fast. Is there anybody standing outside? Any of your neighbors watching?"

His words made Tish hesitant again. But Dino had a prized fish on his hook, and he wasn't letting her get away.

"Come on," he pleaded. "I wouldn't never do nothing to hurt you. You know that. I ain't never did *nothing* to hurt you."

That was true, just as it was true that Tish always had a crush on Dino. Back in middle school, he exploited her love for personal gain. Dino said he liked her, but he kept their relationship low-key to avoid the harassment that was sure to follow if he walked down the hall with a big girl on his arm. Dino used to share his most intimate thoughts with Tish. Their phone conversations would continue late into the night sometimes. It was the closest thing she ever knew to real love – even though he would all but ignore her the next day at school.

When they got older, Dino made the transition from her secret boyfriend to her secret lover, but sex is always the complicating factor in such relationships. Tish could tolerate having a boyfriend none of her friends knew about, and she could even tolerate the way Dino let his friends make fun of her at school. But losing her virginity to a ghost was too much of a burden.

She eventually gave him an ultimatum: *Either accept me as your girlfriend, or go away.* Dino's pride took him in the opposite direction. Tish cried for him many a night, but time heals all wounds.

Time didn't take away her memory, however, so Tish peered under the garage door and made a decision that went against her heart and her mind and her overall sense of right and wrong. Rather than get into her car and drive away to the job that paid her utility bills, rent and car note, Tish went back to her front door and opened it.

She stepped inside her quiet home and took a look back over her shoulder. She wished she hadn't. What she saw crawling out of the garage across the street was nothing like the Dino she knew and loved and shared a bed with while her brother and sister slept and her mother worked a night shift at American Airlines. What Tish saw was nothing like anything she had ever seen outside of a movie screen or even one of the horrific nightmares that plagued her sleep when her big brother got killed.

Dino slithered out of the darkness like a goblin and sprinted across the street with a speed that belied his obvious physical trauma. Tish wanted to slam the door closed before he got there. But by then she was completely terrified – not just of what sort of demon she had invited into her home, but she was also fearful of what his reaction would be if she rejected him this late in the game.

Dino mounted her front steps in one leap and slammed the door closed behind himself once he rushed inside.

"Lock it!" he ordered.

Tish fumbled with the deadbolt while Dino peeked through the curtains at the front of the house. He looked like he had a baseball tucked under his cheekbone. Dried blood was caked all the way down his neck and under his tee shirt. His skin was ashen, his clothes matted and dusty from his stay in the garage. He brought with him a stench that was immediately recognizable as death. Dino's eyes were wild. His hands trembled like he was running from Satan himself.

"*What you do?*" Tish squealed.

"I got shot," Dino told her plainly. "My homeboy is dead, and some girl got shot, too. They killed a little boy."

"*Who?*" Tish implored, her eyes wet with tears. "Who killed a little boy?"

"The same people who trying to kill me," Dino told her. He looked her dead in the eyes. "They killed that little boy, and now they wanna kill me, 'cause I saw it."

Tish's bottom lip quivered. "You, you saw it?"

"I was standing *right there*," Dino said. "I done did some fucked up shit in my life, Tish. But I ain't never done nothing like that. Not even close."

# CHAPTER FIVE
## *ACCESSORY AFTER THE FACT*

Tammy Spencer had never been known to be faint of heart or prone to dizzy spells, but she needed help getting out of the car when the homicide detective arrived at the police station. Her legs felt like they were asleep, or maybe her brain diverted the blood meant for her limbs back to her chest where it was needed most. That would be only a temporary fix, because her heart was not merely broken. It was shredded and crushed and stomped under the foot of God Himself.

It was a wonder she went on living at all. Honestly, Tammy wouldn't mind if Jesus called her home right then. She would run towards the light and find her baby in the celestial glow. She would hold Isaiah's hand, and they would walk through the pearly gates together. If not for her surviving son, Tammy might have choked on her own sorrow to hasten her demise. But that was a selfish thought.

Jacob was with Isaiah when he died, and Tammy could only imagine the anguish he felt right now. He needed his mother to be strong for him, just as Tammy needed Jacob to be strong for her. And maybe in the midst of them supporting each other, they could find the courage to get through what was sure to be the hardest episode of their lives.

They still had to care for Isaiah. They had to find a funeral home and make arrangements for him. They had to put Isaiah in a box and watch him disappear into the ground. They had to live the rest of their lives without ever seeing him again – but first they had to get through today.

Inside the police station, Tammy felt like she'd walked into a carnival funhouse. The hallways tilted to and fro. She had to place a hand on the wall for support. Through her tears, everyone looked like they were crying, too, and that was proper and fitting. Isaiah was the twinkle in his mother's eye, and he was destined to be a bright light in the world one day. The bastards who killed him would never know the kindness and gentleness and beauty they extinguished. The whole planet became uglier without Isaiah. Every man, woman and child should mourn his passing.

The homicide detective held her hand tightly, and soon they reached an interrogation room where Jacob was waiting. Tammy cried out and rushed to embrace her only son. Jacob remained seated on a swivel chair. He buried his face in his mother's bosom and clamped his arms around her waist.

"You okay, baby? It's okay. Mama's here." She rubbed his neck and woefully kissed the top of his head.

Jacob became overwhelmed with wailing hiccoughs. His shoulders hitched, and he moaned into her chest. "*I'm sorry, Mama! I'm sorry.*"

"Shhh. It's not your fault, baby. Don't–"

"*It is!*" Jacob howled. "Isaiah wanted to go the other way, but I wouldn't let him! He, he knew it was trouble. I didn't listen to him."

The detective backed discreetly out of the room, and Tammy held her son's face with both hands. Jacob's eyes were nearly bloodshot. His lips were chapped, and his hair was kinked. Thick tears leaked from his eyes.

"Don't say that," Tammy told him, her voice quavering. "It's not your fault. Don't say it's your fault."

"*But it is,*" Jacob whined. His lips were curled in an impossible frown that made him look ten years younger.

"Stop it," Tammy implored him. "Look at me."

"It is my fault."

"*Look at me.*"

Jacob met his mother's eyes. "You don't, you don't know what happened."

Tammy reached for the only other chair in the room. She rolled it next to Jacob and continued to hold his trembling hands when she took a seat. "Okay," she whimpered, "then tell me."

"We, we, we was..."

"Calm down." She rubbed his fingers gently, yet fiercely.

"We, we got off the bus, and Isaiah saw them. He, he said we shouldn't go that way, 'cause they, they was getting ready to fight."

"That's not your–"

"He said we should take the back, back alley. He, he knew there was gonna be trouble. I didn't, I didn't listen to him."

"Baby, it's–"

"*I didn't want to get my pants dirty!*" Jacob blurted the awful truth that had been eating away at his soul like cancer. "*Isaiah wanted to do right, but I didn't want to get my pants dirty. And now he's dead!*"

His words hit Tammy like a kick to the chest. It was better not to know. It was better to think of this as some uncontrollable act of God. To hear that Isaiah's death was possibly avoidable added insult to injury. But Tammy knew Jacob's suffering was a hundred times worse. He watched her eyes, waiting to see if she would condemn him. Tammy concealed her disappointment as best she could.

"Jacob, you can, can't blame yourself for this." She wiped her nose with the back of her hand. "You hear me? Maybe you could've gone around the back, but that don't mean it would've turned out different. If God wanted to take Isaiah home, there's no stopping that."

"But Mama..."

"I'm not going to sit here and let you blame yourself, Jacob." Tammy summoned strength from an ancient reservoir heretofore untapped; reserves passed down from her grandmother and her great-grandmother who lost two boys to the Klan many years back.

"Those assholes across the street killed my baby, and they're the *only* ones responsible for this." Tammy spoke through gritted teeth. The anger made her voice stronger. Jacob listened intently.

"There's no reason you should have to take that alley," Tammy said. "This is a free country, and I pay my bills just like everybody else. That's *my* house. I don't deserve to have bullets flying at it. You don't deserve it either, Jacob. If those dumb niggas hadn't been out there shooting their guns, Isaiah would still be here. That's the end of the blame *right there*. You didn't do nothing but come home from school, and I'm not gonna let you feel guilty about that. You hear me?"

It took a while, but Jacob finally nodded. Tammy closed her eyes and held him closer, hoping she could absorb his pain and spare him some of the agony.

But in the back of her mind, Tammy could see her baby begging to take the back alley. She forced the thought away. Thinking about that might lead to resentment, and that was the last thing her small family unit needed at that point.

● ● ● ● ● ●

The detectives came back after a while so they could conduct a formal interview with Tammy present. They already told her most of the story on the way to the station, but it was still hard to hear it from Jacob's point of view. Tammy went through half a box of Kleenex before they concluded the questioning twenty minutes later.

Afterwards, the detective told them the shooter was most likely a member of a gang called the Sicc Crips. That wasn't surprising. Tammy had seen some of their graffiti spray-painted throughout the neighborhood. The detective brought in a big folder full of pictures of known gang members and asked Tammy and Jacob if they could point out anyone who might have hung out across the street.

This was a daunting task, because by rule Jacob didn't pay the Crips any direct attention. His mother taught him to avoid eye contact that might be perceived as a challenge or as interest in their gang. But Jacob did pick out one face he was sure about. It wasn't the shooter, but Jacob was positive this person was there when Isaiah got killed. He showed the picture to his mom, and Tammy was certain she'd seen him at the drug house over the past few months.

"I talked to him," she told the detective. "I went over there when they first moved in. I told him to leave my boys alone."

The policeman was surprised by this. "What'd he say?"

"He told me they wouldn't say anything to them. He promised to leave them alone."

The detective took the folder and turned it around, so he could see the thug in question.

"You got a good eye," he said after a few seconds. "This man is the purported leader of the Sicc Crips. We believe he's responsible for drug operations all over the city. Other witnesses have confirmed he was at the location today when Isaiah was shot."

"What, what's his name?" Jacob asked.

Tammy thought that was an odd question, and the detective did, too. He gave Jacob a wary look.

"Um, I'm sorry, but I can't give out the name of any of these suspects, until we make an arrest."

"Can I see the picture again?"

The detective reluctantly gave the folder back to him. Jacob studied T Lowe's mug shot for a long time. He memorized every line and contour on the Crip's face. If he ever met T Lowe again, he would recognize him. He would know right away this was one of the men who killed his brother.

Jacob and Tammy identified a few more hoodlums from the detective's big book of human waste, but the shooter's picture wasn't there.

"Maybe he's never been arrested," the detective offered. "Or maybe he wasn't identified as a gang member at the time of his arrest."

Jacob found that hard to believe. Isaiah's killer was a dark and ugly individual who looked like he'd been up to no good his whole life.

"In any event, it's not going to be hard to find someone who's been shot in the face," the detective assured them. "You can't just walk down the street with a big hole in your head. People will notice. Don't worry. We'll get him."

● ● ● ● ● ●

After the interview, Tammy was grateful to find her mother and sister waiting at the police station. Florence, the matriarch of the family, looked like she hadn't slept in days. Tammy's big sister, Pam, was even worse for wear. The three women came together for a group hug with Jacob sandwiched in the middle. Normally Jacob would've shied away from such affections, but he returned the embrace. He savored the familial togetherness.

"How'd you know we were here?" Tammy asked her mother.

"The police called," Florence said. "They got my number from Jacob." She put a hand on her grandson's head and tried to force a smile that didn't quite work.

"I wish they'd lock 'em all up," Pam said with a sneer. Her eyes were red and puffy. Her nose was, too. She wore no make-up at all, which was a huge rarity for her. "They should line 'em up and shoot 'em all," she said.

"Hush child," Florence told her. Tammy's mother had long, straight hair that was still all black. She was thin with hard lines on her face that gave away her age. "You don't need to be filling your heart with all that hate," Florence warned. "Vengeance is mine, says the Lord."

Jacob lowered his gaze so no one would see him roll his eyes at his grandmother. Everyone in his family was overly religious. Jacob loved Jesus as much as the next guy, but sometimes you have to look at things on a worldly, rather than a spiritual level. He had absolutely no problem with lining up all of the Crips in the world for a mass execution.

"Did y'all ride together?" Tammy asked her sister.

"Mama was already here when I got here," Pam said.

"I drove myself," Florence confirmed.

"Can you take Jacob home with you?" Tammy asked her mom. "I have to go pick up my car from the hospital. I'll come get Jacob when I'm done."

"You need a ride?" Pam asked.

"Yeah, I do," Tammy said. "The police said they'd take me, but if you want to—"

"Anything you need," Pam said. "You know I'm here for you."

Tammy knelt so she could look Jacob in his eyes. She rubbed his hair and then his cheeks. She kissed him on the forehead and wiped the tears from his face.

"I'll be back to pick you up in just a little while," she said. "You gonna be okay?"

"I wanna go with you," Jacob said.

"I wanna take you," Tammy said, "but I have one more stop to make before I get my car."

"Where?"

"I have to see my baby," Tammy said. She looked upward, hoping to keep the tears in, but it didn't work. "I have to go see Isaiah."

This was news to Pam. She stiffened visibly. Jacob nodded, expecting nothing less from his mother.

"Okay," he said.

"I'll pick you up as soon as I get my car," Tammy promised. She embraced him again and kissed him softly on the cheek. She stood and Jacob backed towards his grandmother. The older woman gripped his small hand in hers.

"Come on," Florence said. "Let's get you something to eat. Have you ate since you got out of school?"

Jacob shook his head. "I'm not hungry."

"Try to eat something," Tammy urged. "Even if you're not hungry, eat a little bit anyway. And drink some water."

Jacob nodded. He never looked so young and so fragile. When he and Florence were out of sight, Tammy put her hands over her face and allowed herself a good, strong cry. Pam held her firmly, and she almost broke down, too.

"Alright." Tammy pulled away first. She sniffled loudly and wiped her face with a well-worn paper towel. "Let's go, or we'll be standing here all night."

"Okay," Pam said. She regained most of her composure. "Why do, are you really going to see Isaiah? Mama said they already made a positive ID."

Tammy nodded. "I know, but I still have to see him."

"Where, where is he?" Pam asked. "I'm sorry. I don't know nothing about this, this kind of stuff."

"I think we only have one coroner's office," Tammy said. "On Main and Hemphill. I'll check with the detective before we leave."

"The police told you to go over there?"

"No. They tried to talk me out of it," Tammy said.

"I don't, I don't think I can go with you," Pam confided. "I mean, I can take you to it, but I'll have to wait in the lobby or something. I can't go in, in that room with you..."

"That's fine," Tammy said. "As long as you're there when I come out, that's all I need."

● ● ● ● ● ●

"That's not gon' work," Tish said.

She sat on the toilet lid while Dino leaned over the bathroom sink. He was clean now, freshly showered, and he still had a surprisingly nice physique, standing there in only his boxer shorts. As dire as their situation was, in the back of her mind Tish couldn't help but notice how nice it was to have a nearly naked man in her home – even one as badly hurt as Dino.

He had his injury mostly cleaned up, and it was clear that the bullet did not enter his head. He did have one hell of a graze wound, though. No amount of rubbing alcohol or Neosporin was going to make it better.

After icing it down for two hours, the swelling had gone down from baseball to tennis ball size. But Dino still needed medical attention. He definitely needed stitches. Tish thought someone should clean out the wound, too. Who knew if there were bullet fragments still in there? Antibiotics were a must. Dino took enough Tylenol to dull the pain for a while, but it would be back soon, with a vengeance.

"You got shot, boy," Tish reasoned. "You can't slap a Band-Aid on it and go on about your business."

"Do you see me putting a Band-Aid on it?" Dino snapped.

"You gon' have to put *something* on it," Tish countered. "You can't just walk around with the air and dust getting in it."

"You got some gauze?" Dino asked without looking away from the mirror. He squeezed the swollen area around his wound and winced in pain. A good amount of blood dribbled out. Tish looked away in disgust.

"No, Dino. I don't have no gauze. Do this look like a hospital to you?"

"It ain't gotta be a hospital for you to have some fucking gauze," he said with a sneer. "I know this ain't no goddamned hospital. Do I look like I'm retarded or something?" He wiped his cheek with a face towel that was already soiled with gore.

"You ain't gotta get no attitude."

"Well, don't be asking me no dumb ass questions."

"Hey, don't forget, I took off work for *you*," Tish reminded him. "And I lied to those police for you. I ain't never lied to no police, but I did it for you."

Dino couldn't forget that, because he'd surely be in jail by now if not for the cover-up. The police started their house-to-house inquiries fifteen minutes after he made it inside Tish's home. Dino assured her all she had to do was say she didn't know anything, and they would leave. But Tish was so nervous, he was sure she'd mess it up.

*What if they want to search the house?*

*What if they find out I'm lying?*

*I don't want to go to jail for you.*

Dino promised her she wouldn't go to jail if she stuck with the script. The police didn't have a warrant to search every house in the neighborhood, so they would have to go by her word alone. Dino hid in the bathroom when the cops pounded on the door. Tish went to answer it with her eyes so big, she looked like a hoot owl. But she returned a minute later looking relieved.

"They believed me," she said.

"I told you they would," Dino told her and gave her a slap on the rump.

That was nearly three hours ago, and the police hadn't been back since.

With no other bandage available, Dino found a couple of Band-Aids and stretched them across his wound in an X shape. He backed away from the sink and went to stand before his new accomplice. Tish remained seated. She looked up at him expectantly.

"I know what you did for me," Dino said. "And I ain't never gon' forget it."

Tish turned her body towards him, and Dino stepped conveniently between her chunky legs.

"The hard part is gon' be keeping quiet when the news comes out," Dino said. "They gon' be saying some bad shit about me. They might even say *I'm* the one who shot that kid."

"Why would they say that?"

"I told you; they trying to blame me," Dino reminded her. "If the police caught some of them, that's the first thing they gon' do, try to pin that little boy on me."

"Why don't you go to the police and tell them it wasn't you?"

"Why would they believe me?" Dino asked. "Plus I *did* get in a shootout with them niggas. If I go to the police, they can put me in jail just for that."

"How you know you *didn't* shoot that little boy then?" Tish asked.

Dino shook his head. "Tish, my bullet would have had to jump out of my gun, do a 360 in mid-air and fly back towards me, because that boy was *behind me* when he got shot. There's no way on God's green Earth I shot that boy."

"So, what you gon' do?"

"I need to meet up with the set tonight," Dino said. "Can you drop me off in Como?"

"You leaving?" Tish frowned.

Dino fought hard to conceal a snicker. Even after everything he'd told her, she still wanted him around. It was sad and funny at the same time.

"I gotta meet with my niggas."

"Are you coming back?" she asked.

Tish pouted with her lips poked out. Dino remembered how she used to wrap those lips around his dick back in high school. The thought caused a slight erection to grow. Tish grinned when she saw the lump in his boxers.

"What you got that thing in my face for?"

Dino shrugged, growing harder by the second. "I don't know. It's just there."

Tish pulled his drawers down. Dino's manhood popped up and brushed her chin.

"Ain't you supposed to be all shot up and hurt?" she asked.

"My dick ain't shot up," Dino said. He reached for the back of her head and guided her mouth until she took him all in. The initial sensation made Dino shudder. He could've ejaculated within seconds, but Tish would be a lot more pliable if he hooked her up first. After a minute he said, "Let's go to the bedroom."

Tish got up without a word and headed in that direction. Dino followed her, staring at her big, round ass as they walked.

● ● ● ● ● ●

Tish and Dino piled into her Honda at eight forty-five. By then it was completely dark outside, but the police presence hadn't diminished. Tish thought it was silly that Dino wanted to lie in the backseat rather than ride up front with her, but Dino followed his heart, and it turned out to be a good move. The cops didn't have roadblocks set up anymore, but they were still out in force. They peered into every vehicle they saw on the streets.

Tish was a nervous wreck, but things settled down when they got out of the neighborhood. And it was business as usual when they reached the west side of town. T Lowe had crack houses in almost every neighborhood in the city, but the Como dope spot was the official clubhouse for the gang. No one had to call a meeting. Dino knew his brothers would be there, because this is where the Sicc Crips always met when there was a crisis.

Tish made the last turn onto Shiloh Drive. Dino saw that there were no cars parked out front and only one vehicle in the driveway of the blue and white rent house. This was to be expected. T Lowe didn't like a lot of traffic at this sanctuary. The Sicc Crips either had to pull their car all the way into the backyard when they came here, get dropped off, or they could leave their ride at the park down the street and walk the two blocks to the house. Dino let Tish pass the house completely before he stopped her at the next corner.

"Let me out right here."

Tish looked around. "Where?"

"Right here is fine," Dino said, sitting up in the back seat. "I appreciate your help, girl. You did me a solid for real."

"Are you coming back?"

"I might," Dino said. "You gon' be there all night, right?"

"I already called-in."

"Alright, we'll see," Dino said, then, "Remember; don't tell nobody I came to your place today. Don't tell nobody where you dropped me off, neither. You already told the police I wasn't there. You could go to jail if you change your story now. You haven't seen me since high school, right?"

Tish nodded. "I won't forget."

Dino leaned forward and kissed behind her ear. He hated mushy, romantic shit like that, but sometimes you gotta do what you gotta do. His cousin Dee once told him, "*I'll kiss a Billy goat in the asshole to save my own ass.*" Dino felt the exact same way. And luckily Tish didn't smell like a Billy goat's rump. She smelled like Suave lotion and Baby Phat perfume with an underlying aroma of naïveté.

"Thanks, baby," Dino said and slipped out of the car and into the darkness.

Tish pulled away, and Dino ducked his cheek behind his shoulder as best he could as he made his way down Shiloh.

Not until Tish's car was out of sight did Dino consider the full burden he had placed on his gang. He wasn't expecting a standing ovation when he walked through the doors of T Lowe's dope house tonight, but now a persistent tingling in the back of his mind warned him that maybe he shouldn't meet up with his crew at all.

# CHAPTER SIX
## *ETERNAL REST*

"So, whose side you on?" Pam asked.

Tammy watched the sunset through the passenger side window, mostly in a daze. She had stomach cramps and heart cramps, and her head was throbbing.

"What?" she asked without looking away from the descending fire in the sky.

"What do you think about what Mama said?" Pam asked. "Is it wrong for me to hate those people? I really wish they was dead. If I had a gun, I could shoot some of them."

"Violence begets violence," Tammy said. "Mama's right. Vengeance belongs to the Lord."

"But it ain't fair," Pam said. "You know, some of these assholes out here killing and stealing from people, they go to prison and try to get converted. They become Christians, so when they die, they get to go to heaven? All they have to do is say they love Jesus, and they sorry, and they get to be in heaven right next to all the innocent people they hurt?"

Tammy didn't have the heart for a theological debate, but she expected this from her sister. When it came to religion, Pamela was the black sheep of the family; always questioning the rationality of the Bible and God's teachings.

"You know what's really bad," Tammy said, looking over at her.

Pam shook her head, watching both the road and her sister's doleful eyes.

"Jacob said Isaiah tried to warn him," Tammy confided. "Isaiah saw them about to fight or whatever, and he told Jacob

74

they should go around back, through the alley. Jacob didn't want to, 'cause he'd get his pants dirty."

Pam pursed her lips. "You not mad at him, are you?"

"Course not," Tammy said. "But when he told me, I did feel, something, like disappointment. I didn't show it. I mean, he don't know how I felt, but I did feel it. It just, it's messed up, you know?" Fresh tears rolled down her cheeks. "All these little decisions we make in life."

"We're raised to think God has a plan for us," Pam said, "and all our futures are wrote down already."

"I know," Tammy said. "That, that's what gets me. It's like, did Jacob really have a choice about which way to go? God *wanted* him to make that decision?"

"Don't even get me started," Pam said.

"And what about Ernest?" Tammy said. "I wouldn't even be living in Poly, if Ernest didn't run out on us. So God wanted me to live across the street from them fools? Is He *making* this happen, or allowing it to happen?"

"You starting to sound like me," Pam noticed.

"No, I do have faith," Tammy countered. "It's just, my baby's dead, and, and, and it's okay to wonder why." She brushed the tears from her cheeks with cold, shaky fingers. "I know God has a plan for me. I'm just, I just don't see what taking my baby has to do with it."

Pam reached for her sister's hand and squeezed it tightly.

Tammy closed her eyes and prayed for forgiveness before she said anything else. It was not her place to understand God's motives, and this was not the first innocent blood God shed – or allowed to be shed. The Bible was full of tales of despair much worse than hers.

● ● ● ● ● ●

The medical examiner's office was a hulking building with five stories and a huge clock tower that poked the clouds. The offices were mostly deserted at this time of day. Pam had no trouble finding a parking spot near the main entrance. Tammy's heart began to knock in her chest as soon as her sister turned off the ignition. Pam studied her eyes.

"Are, are you scared?"

Tammy shook her head but said, "A little."

"Why do you wanna do this?" Pam asked. "The police said they don't need you to identify him."

"I have to," Tammy replied. "How can I know my baby's gone, if I don't see it for myself?"

"Why don't you wait 'til he gets to the funeral home," Pam suggested. She was crying again. The bags under her eyes looked like inner tubes.

"I can't go home tonight until I see him," Tammy said. "I have to see him."

Pam still didn't understand, but she wasn't a mother, and she knew there were complexities her sister couldn't explain.

"Okay, well, I'm ready if you are."

Tammy opened the car door. "I'm ready."

The hallways were completely empty in the large building, but there was a security guard manning the first information desk they approached. The guard looked the ladies over curiously. Tammy guessed it was her work scrubs that threw him off.

"Can I help you?"

"I came to see my son," Tammy said with a boldness she didn't feel anywhere in her body.

The guard's eyes narrowed. "Your son? He's, um..."

"He died today," Tammy said. "The police said he's here now."

"What's his name?"

"Isaiah Spencer."

The guard entered the name in his computer. After a few moments he said, "I don't believe they're expecting you."

"I told the police I was coming."

"Do you have some type of identification?"

Tammy dug her wallet from her purse, her anxiety slowly giving way to frustration.

"One moment," the guard said as he picked up his phone.

"I don't like it here," Pam whispered while he spoke with his superiors.

Tammy nodded but was too apprehensive to respond.

"I get bad vibes," Pam said with a shudder.

Tammy nodded, her eyes still on the guard.

He hung up the phone. "Here you go," he said, returning her driver's license. "It'll be just one minute. The Deputy Medical

Examiner is on his way out to see you. You can have a seat, if you like." He gestured towards a row of chairs to the right of his desk. "I'm very sorry for your loss."

Tammy and Pam sat down and didn't speak at all for three minutes. A gentleman of Arab descent finally appeared in the hallway. He wore a white lab coat over a white button down and khaki slacks. He was young and handsome. He didn't look like the kind of person who removed and weighed dead people's organs on a daily basis.

"Hi," he said. "I'm Dr. Malik."

Tammy stood. "I'm Tammy Spencer."

He offered a hand to shake. Tammy took it, noticing her palm was completely moist.

"Right this way," he said.

Tammy took a deep breath before going with him.

"I'll be right here," Pam said, looking like she saw a ghost.

The doctor led Tammy down a narrow hallway that had closed office doors on either side.

"I apologize for your loss," Dr. Malik said as they walked. "This is always a hard thing, especially when it's a child."

Tammy nodded. "Thank you."

"Did the police explain the nature of his injury?" the doctor asked.

"They said he, he got shot in the head."

"That's correct," Dr. Malik said.

Tammy thought he would go into detail about what brain layers and lobes the bullet passed through, but thankfully he left it at that.

"There were multiple shooters involved in this murder," the doctor said. "So what I have to do is determine the trajectory of the bullet that killed your son, so we can help the police determine which shooter fired the fatal shot."

Jacob already told the police who killed Isaiah, but Tammy kept quiet, mainly because her throat was squeezing closed.

The doctor turned down another corridor and stopped at a stainless steel door that was different from the rest. He turned his back on it and looked Tammy in the eyes.

"Ms. Spencer, you do understand that we've already identified your son? There is no need for you, at this point, to view him. This can be a very traumatizing experience. We do not recommend anyone go through this unnecessarily. If you would like to see your son, it would be much better if you do so once he's moved to the funeral home."

"I want to see him now."

The Deputy Medical Examiner half nodded. He turned and opened the metal door. A cool breath of air rushed out to greet them. Goosebumps sprouted on Tammy's arms, and her legs grew stiff. She tasted acid in the back of her throat. Her eyes were focused and unblinking. She had to force herself to get moving when the doctor entered the cool room.

Tammy expected to see her son right away, but this was merely an antechamber. The smell of medicine was strong. There was a metal table in the center of the room, but it was empty. There were glass shelves covering all of the walls. Tammy saw syringes and instruments she didn't care to know the uses of. Everything was clean and sterilized, but the scent of death lingered in the air. That smell would always be there, no matter how often they scrubbed the surfaces and mopped the floors.

The doctor continued forward and opened another door on the far side of the room. Tammy followed. She thought she had the strength for this, but the room began to spin when she saw her baby lying face-up on a long, metal table. She wasn't able to focus on her boy before the vertigo was accompanied by light-headedness. Her jaws clenched. A terrible wail worked its way up her esophagus, as her legs gave up their constant struggle with gravity. She felt herself falling.

Very

slowly.

The doctor rushed forward in time to catch her. From behind, he slipped his forearms under her armpits and softened her descent.

• • • • • •

Dino crept around the side of the house, savoring the refuge only darkness can provide. He knocked on the back door and waited. Inside he knew someone was watching him on one or both of the security cameras facing that entrance.

After a few seconds, he heard the deadbolts sliding back. He still didn't know if that was a good or bad sign. Allowing him entry didn't necessarily mean he was a welcomed guest. Dino knew of at least three men who'd endured severe beat-downs after being invited inside this Como dope spot.

A tall, brooding thug named Skeeter greeted him at the back door. Skeeter was never the friendly type, but Dino thought he looked less sociable than usual tonight. Skeeter was big and black and surprisingly quick. He stared down at Dino with low, threatening eyes. Dino was almost afraid to pass by and turn his back on the brute.

"What's up, cuz?" Dino offered his hand for the customary handshake of their gang. Skeeter had no choice but to return the greeting.

"T Lowe here?" Dino asked.

Skeeter nodded. "Damn near everybody here." His voice was low and gravelly. "They in the front room, waiting on you."

"Cool." Dino thought it was odd that Skeeter didn't say anything about the colossal wound in his face. But he supposed the shootout with HB was old news by then. "What they talking about, in there?" he asked.

"Nigga, I don't know," Skeeter said coldly. "I'm back here watching the door. Is you coming in or what? You can't be hanging out on the steps."

Dino almost let his temper get the best of him. He gave up fifty pounds or more to Skeeter, but that didn't matter. He didn't tolerate people talking down to him. But he figured he was already in hot water, so he humbled himself.

This time.

"Whatever, cuz," he said and stepped into the kitchen.

The house was small and mostly dark. Dino headed for the living room, where he found eighteen members of his gang. Some were sitting, most were standing, all were huddled around the lone television in the room. T Lowe was there. So was Tricky, Stephon and Detroit. Seldom seen Pistol Pete was there along with Shaun, Demarcus, Scooter, Mack and a host of other Sicc Crips who operated T Lowe's dope houses throughout the city. The notable absence was Peanut. Thinking about his friend's death face made Dino's stomach twist unpleasantly.

Everyone in the room looked up at him when he entered, but no one said anything. One by one their eyes floated back to the television. Dino was obliged to watch with them. There was nowhere to sit, so he made his way to the sofa and eased down on the floor next to Tricky. The Crips were watching the Channel Six News. They were reporting on the murder of a ten year old boy.

Channel Six's star reporter, Chad Collins, was at the scene of the horrendous crime on Forbes Street. Directly behind him was the yellow and white house where the two boys lived. Dino saw that some of the neighbors had brought flowers and stuffed animals for a makeshift memorial on the front porch.

"The shooting occurred at approximately 3:45 this afternoon," Chad was saying. "The brothers got off the school bus around the corner on Campbell Street..."

The cameraman panned to get a shot of T Lowe's shot-up dope house. There was still CRIME SCENE tape strung from one side of the yard to the other. The house was well-lit. Investigators were on the scene collecting evidence.

"Police are offering little information at this time," Chad explained. "But according to neighbors, the Sick Crip gang moved into the neighborhood about seven months ago, and they have been causing the community nothing but grief since they got here."

The cameraman panned back to Chad standing in front of the yellow and white house. He looked extremely somber, though his blue eyes glowed like fire against the dark sky.

"This afternoon everyone's worst fears came to be," he said. "The two brothers, ages ten and thirteen, made it to their home just as a gunfight erupted across the street. Apparently the boys were well aware of the danger of firearms, because they both got down on the ground and remained there until the shooting stopped.

"It's a sad state of affairs when our children know to hit the ground at the first sound of gunfire, but that is the world we live in. That's the *city* we live in, and that is a reality the citizens in this neighborhood have to face on a daily basis. Unfortunately even those precautions were not enough to save little Isaiah.

"The police say Isaiah Spencer was struck in the head by a stray bullet. He died instantly from the wound. According to neighbors, his thirteen year old brother held him in his arms. He–"

Chad Collins brought a hand to his thin lips. His eyes grew watery.

"This, I'm sorry. This is a, a difficult story."

Channel Six cut from Chad and filled the screen with a school portrait of Isaiah. The photo was taken a couple of years earlier. The boy looked smaller and more vulnerable than he did at the time of his death. His glasses were huge, his smile big and dorky. That was the kind of picture a prosecutor could show a jury and almost guarantee a guilty verdict.

*Who could harm such a sweet and innocent* **ten-year-old boy**? *A monster, that's who!*

Dino's face burned. He felt sweat trickling down his cheek. He wiped at it with his shoulder and realized it was blood. He felt like everyone was staring at him, but he didn't look around to see.

"After the murder..."

Isaiah's mug disappeared, and Chad Collins was back, moderately more composed.

"...police reports indicate Isaiah's thirteen-year-old brother ran across the street and attempted to apprehend the man he believed was responsible. The shooter fled on foot. Isaiah's brother, whose name is not being released at this time, chased the suspect through the neighborhood but was unable to capture him."

The reporter paused and sighed. He sensationalized a few stories over the years, but this one required no additives. It was depravity at its finest.

"When the police and paramedics arrived on the scene," Chad continued, "they found Isaiah Spencer lying dead in the front yard of his home right here behind me. Across the street, they found another individual, identified as *Roderick Cooper*, also shot dead. And inside the gang house, the police found a third gunshot victim who was taken to Jackson Memorial Hospital with a gunshot wound to her leg, possibly involving the femoral artery.

"The police aren't releasing the name of the surviving victim at this time, but they did tell us she is in fair condition. She's currently in a medically induced coma, so they have not been able to question her about the shooting.

"As for the suspects, police are asking the public for any information they have regarding a gray and black Chrysler 300 that might have been involved in the shooting. The police are also looking for the young man who fled on foot as a person of interest.

"This suspect shouldn't be too hard to find, because numerous reports have confirmed that he has a fresh gunshot wound to the face; most likely on his right cheek. Investigators are confident he will show up at a hospital sooner or later.

"Until then, they're still interviewing witnesses and processing the information they've collected at the scene. At this time police are not saying what physical evidence they have gathered so far. What we do know is the murder of ten-year-old Isaiah Spencer has ignited a firestorm of anger in this community and in the city as a whole. We heard the mayor speak earlier today. Everyone is confident the gunman or gunmen will soon be brought to justice.

"At times the police have had trouble gathering community support when they investigate murders, especially those involving gangs who might retaliate. But no one is keeping quiet about this one. The senseless murder of ten-year-old Isaiah is a black eye for the city of Overbrook Meadows. Everyone wants his murderer behind bars as soon as possible. Jessica..."

The view switched to a split screen of Chad at the crime scene and anchorwoman Jessica Serrano in the newsroom.

"Chad, this is an awful tragedy. Have you had a chance to speak with Isaiah's parents or any other family members?"

"Not yet," Chad admitted. "No one has returned to this residence since the shooting – except the neighbors who came to pay tribute to young Isaiah with the cards, flowers and stuffed animals you see behind me."

"I hope they make an arrest soon," Jessica said with a slow head shake. "Thank you, Chad. We'll be back in a moment," she told the audience.

The two reporters disappeared from the screen and were replaced with the photo of Isaiah. This time Isaiah's school portrait was followed by another picture taken from a regular camera. Isaiah sat in front of a Christmas tree with a huge, beautifully wrapped box on his lap. He had the same big glasses and dopey smile. He wore Spiderman pajamas. To further the effect, Channel Six played somber music in the background. Dino thought he heard one of the Crips in the room sniffle.

"Turn that shit off," T Lowe said.

After a few seconds, Tricky jumped up and switched off the set. Tricky didn't want to return to his spot next to Dino, so he continued to stand next to the television, his arms folded over his stomach.

Everyone was speechless. They stared at the blank television screen, at Tricky or down at their hands; pretty much anywhere Dino wasn't. Each second that passed became more and more unnerving. Dino wanted to jump to his feet and demand that *somebody* say *something*, but he didn't have to. T Lowe rose slowly from the love seat and took center stage.

He wore new blue jeans that were starched and crisp with a short-sleeved Polo golf shirt. The shirt was fiery orange. Not many gangsters could get away with this preppy look, but T Lowe never had to worry about his image or his masculinity. He was the wealthiest and most handsome member of their gang. If he wore over-sized clown shoes to the club one Saturday night, at least three Crips would have their own pair the following weekend.

"Sit down," T Lowe told Tricky.

Tricky nodded and took the vacated loveseat.

T Lowe looked over his crew with clear disappointment furrowing his brow. He studied each face individually before he spoke. Dino sighed heavily and loudly to get things moving along.

T Lowe stated the obvious. "This shit is fucked up."

"Where my gun at?" Dino asked.

The question caught T Lowe off guard. "Cuz, I don't know. Why you asking me?"

"You didn't get it for me?" Dino's eyes were dark and cold.

T Lowe frowned. "Nigga, what is you talking about?"

"I lost my gun," Dino said. "I dropped it when I was fighting with that dumb motherfucker." He nodded in Stephon's direction.

T Lowe put a hand over his mouth and shook his head.

"So y'all just left it there, huh?" Dino asked.

"I know you ain't coming in here with no attitude," T Lowe said. "As much trouble as you done caused us..."

"Trouble I caused who?" Dino asked. "*You*? 'Cause I know you not talking about nobody else."

T Lowe frowned. "I'm talking about the whole Sicc, cuz. You fucked us all up!"

"It ain't even about the Sicc," Dino spat. "It's never about the Sicc."

"What the fuck you talking about?"

"How come didn't nobody get my gun?" Dino repeated. "We supposed to be down, but y'all run off and leave my pistol in the front yard?"

"I didn't see yo gun," Tricky said.

Dino was hoping to hear just that. His secret wish was that he lost his .380 in the garage across the street from Tish's house, or maybe in one of the alleys he sprinted through.

"You left my dope, too?" Dino asked T Lowe.

T Lowe scratched his head. "Nigga, what?"

"My shit I got from Pooky," Dino said. "I guess you ran off without that, too..."

"Yeah I left it!" T Lowe barked. "Cuz, this ain't about no motherfucking dope! That little boy is *dead*. They called out our set on the *news*! Didn't you hear that shit? I had to shut my house down. I can't even–"

"*That's* what I'm talking about." Dino rose and strolled across the room like Perry Mason.

"What the hell you talking about?" T Lowe demanded.

Dino spun on him. "This ain't about that little boy; it's about *you*, nigga! It's always about you. You just mad 'cause you had to shut down your spot. You don't give a damn about the set. You only using us to move your dope; been using us since *day one*. You the only one in here got some real money."

T Lowe responded like he got slapped in the face. "Don, don't try to flip this shit around. You fucked up, Dino, and you need to–"

"Yeah, I fucked up," Dino acknowledged. "So what that mean? Ain't none of y'all ever fucked up before? Y'all ready to throw me under the bus? Is that what it is?"

Dino scanned the room, daring someone to say that was the case.

"We ain't going down with you," T Lowe said. "If they got your gun, they already know your name and everything else."

"How you figure?" Dino cocked his head, unaware that he was bleeding again. "I ain't never been to jail. My prints won't pull up shit."

T Lowe's frown intensified.

"He haven't," Tricky said, which caused everyone to look around in amazement.

Dino's arrest record – or lack thereof – was actually somewhat of an urban legend in their neighborhood. Given the amount of crimes he committed, usually several each day, it was hard to believe he'd never been shackled in the back of a squad car.

"You ain't never been arrested?" T Lowe still didn't believe it.

"Naw, nigga," Dino said.

"Well, they still gon' get you," T Lowe predicted. "What you gon' do about that hole in your face? We ain't the mafia, nigga. I ain't got no doctors on the payroll."

*Bet you'd find one if you got shot*, Dino thought, but he bit his tongue. He sensed the tide was shifting in his favor. "Don't worry about that," he said and then turned to the populous. "I just want to know if y'all still down with me or what? Y'all don't want me in the Sicc no more, say it now. Raise your hands, motherfucker. We taking a vote."

T Lowe had already planned to take a vote, but it was different now that Dino introduced it. The crew looked from their leader to their enforcer. T Lowe had the money and the power, but who could they trust more? If one of them got killed, they were sure T Lowe would pay for their funeral and provide for their kids for a little while. But Dino was the punisher. Dino would seek out their killers and make them pay.

Make them bleed.

And Dino's accusations about their leader struck a chord with many of them. How come they never had meetings like this unless there was trouble? How come they didn't ride on their enemies more often? How come they spent ninety percent of their time in T Lowe's dope houses? How much money did T Lowe have stashed away so far?

Blood is thicker than water, and Dino was right in guessing blood was thicker than money, too. Not one of the Sicc Crips raised their hand. Stephon started to, but he was a born follower. He kept his hand in his lap when everyone else did the same.

"So that's it then," Dino said. "We gon' ride this shit out and see how it goes."

T Lowe was so furious, his ears turned red. "What about yo face, nigga? You can't be walking around thinking ain't nobody gon' see you."

"I got somewhere to lay low for a while," Dino informed him.

"Where?"

"Don't worry about it," Dino said. "I'll call you when I get to a phone." He watched the crew to make sure none of them had anything else to say, and then Dino singled out one of his closest friends. "Kevin, you got yo car?"

A skinny goon dressed in all black stood quickly. "Yeah. It's, it's at the park."

"Gimme a ride," Dino said as he walked out of the room.

Kevin followed with a lot less pep in his step. Back in '94 Kevin took a .25 caliber bullet to the head. He hadn't been one hundred percent ever since. The left side of his body stopped growing after the surgery. His right side was now nearly twice as big. Kevin moved with an obvious limp, and he wasn't worth spit in a fist fight, but his loyalty to the set was never in question. He caught up with Dino outside and gave him a blue handkerchief to wipe his face.

"You bleeding hard, cuz."

Dino took the rag with a grunt, still fuming from the big meeting.

"You, you really ain't never been arrested?" Kevin asked him as they made their way down the side of the house.

"Never," Dino replied. "I put that on my mama."

"How you pull that off?" Kevin wanted to know.

Dino thought back to earlier that day when Isaiah Spencer's brother chased him from the crime scene. "I can run," Dino said with a stray tear in his eye. "I can run like a motherfucker."

# CHAPTER SEVEN
## *CHARLOTTE'S WEBB*

Tammy was still lightheaded when they left the medical examiner. To her recollection, she'd never passed out before. It was an odd experience. Her sister didn't want her to drive home, but Tammy assured her she was fine. By the time they went to retrieve her car from Jackson Memorial, thirty minutes had passed, which was enough time for Tammy to clear out any of the remaining cobwebs in her head.

Or so she thought.

The truth was Tammy was on the cusp of a mental breakdown. Talking to the police and looking through their big folder of gangbangers, that was all done with a mechanical detachedness. But seeing Isaiah with her own eyes brought it all home. Tammy now understood what Jacob had been trying to tell her.

Isaiah was dead.

His blood had been spilled on the front lawn of his own home. Tammy would never see him laugh or cry again. Every dream she had for him and every report card she saved was wasted. Her baby never even made it to his eleventh birthday. No amount of consoling from any doctor, policeman or family member could put him back together again. Tammy understood that her life was inexorably changed forever.

She drove slowly on the freeway, checking her rearview mirror ever so often to see if her sister was still behind her. Pam followed dutifully, right on her bumper. Things got *fuzzy* a few times on that lonely stretch of I-30, but Tammy didn't pass out behind the wheel or veer out of her lane. By the time they reached their mother's house, Pam was convinced her sister was doing better, and Tammy was okay with letting her think that.

Since Tammy's trip to the morgue, many phone calls were made, and a good deal of family had gathered at her mother's house. They were watching the news when Tammy and Pam walked through the door. Everyone was misty-eyed or flat out crying, and that was the last thing Tammy wanted to be around right then.

She feared that if they got her bawling again, she would never be able to stop. She would cry at the wake and cry at the funeral, and when Jacob graduated from high school four years from now, she'd be on the front row, still crying for Isaiah.

"Hey, baby." Florence greeted them in the foyer with a hug and a kiss on the cheek. "How you holding up? How was it?" She squeezed Tammy's upper arm and stared woefully into her eyes.

"I'm okay," Tammy said. "He was, okay. He looked so little..."

Her mother nodded and pulled her close.

"Where's Jacob?" Tammy asked.

"He in the front room," Florence said. "I tried to get him away from that news, but he won't go nowhere. He been sitting in front of that TV for an hour."

"Did he eat anything?"

"Not really," Florence admitted.

"What's on the news?" Tammy asked.

"Isaiah," Florence said, "on every channel. Your Aunt Bertha gave a couple of pictures of him to Channel Six. Hope you don't mind..."

"No, that's fine."

"They got the whole city upset about it," Florence reported. "The mayor was on there earlier. The police chief, too. Everybody say this is the worst thing that happened in this city for a long time."

"Did they get him? They get the one who shot him?"

"Not yet," Florence said. "But he got shot in the face, so it won't be long. Ain't too many places you can go where people won't notice that."

"I'ma go get Jacob," Tammy said. "I'm ready to go home."

"Home? Why don't you stay the night?" Florence suggested. "All your family is here. The police and news people are still at your house, last I heard."

"We been surrounded by people all day," Tammy said. "We need some time alone. We ain't really had a chance to talk."

"Okay. I'll get him for you," Florence said. She let go of Tammy's arm and disappeared in a crowd of people who all looked somewhat the same.

While Tammy waited, a host of relatives came forward to give their condolences.

"I'm so sorry," Aunt Agnes told her. "Isaiah was such a good boy."

"I didn't believe it when I first got word," Uncle Jimmy said. "I told them, *Naw, you must be talking about the wrong boy*. But then I found out they was right. It's a damned shame."

"Niggas ain't no good," Cousin Jesse offered. "I'm sick of watching the news and hearing about all this ignorance in the country. You know, a nigga will kill a nigga way quicker than any white man would. We ain't got no respect. No love for *self*. One day, it's gon' be only three niggas left, and they gon' look around wondering what the hell went wrong."

By the time Jacob came out, Tammy was feeling unsteady again. She grabbed his hand and held on tightly.

"You ready to go?"

"Yeah. You know Isaiah was on the news?"

"That's what your grandmother was telling me."

"They had a good picture of him," Jacob told her. "He looked good."

"Yeah," Tammy said, though the only image she could conjure at that moment was the way Isaiah looked on the cold coroner's table. "He looks real good."

• • • • • •

Back on Forbes Street, there were still a few reporters milling around, but it wasn't anything like the media circus Florence predicted. They did point their cameras at Tammy's car when she pulled into the driveway, but they didn't hound her.

"Ms. Spencer!" one of them called out to her. "Would you like to give a comment about Isaiah?"

Tammy shook her head, and that was it. The reporter backed away and so did his cameraman. Tammy and Jacob entered their home without incident.

She flipped on the light in the living room and yawned lazily, glad to finally be closed off from the world. The detectives picked her up from the hospital at four o'clock. It was eleven o'clock now; around the time she would've gotten home if she'd completed her shift.

"Have you taken a shower?" Tammy asked her son.

Jacob shook his head.

Tammy saw that he had a new shirt on, but there were still dark stains on his pants and shoes that were undoubtedly Isaiah's blood.

"Why don't you go take a shower?" Tammy suggested. "I'm gonna make some tea. You want some?"

Jacob shrugged and shuffled off towards his bedroom.

Tammy made a pot of green tea and retreated to her own room for a much needed bath. When she got out of the tub, she found Jacob in the living room, peeking through the front curtains. Jacob wore gray jogging pants with a white tee shirt he had ripped the sleeves off of. Tammy hadn't noticed how big and strong his arms grew over the summer. Jacob was becoming a strapping young man. But that realization was bitter-sweet.

"What you doing?" Tammy asked.

Jacob jumped and snatched the curtains closed. "Nothing."

The lights were off in the living room, but Tammy distinctly remembered turning them on. She went to her son and pulled him towards the sofa.

"Come here," she said. "Sit with me."

Jacob followed her obediently. They sat hip to hip. He cradled his hands in his lap. Tammy threw her arm over his shoulder.

"What were you looking at?" she asked him.

"Across the street," Jacob said.

"The police still there?"

He shook his head. "No. But they still have the house taped up. Do you think they'll come back tonight?"

"If they're gone, they're probably gone for the night," Tammy guessed. "They might do more investigating tomorrow."

"Not the police," Jacob said. "I mean the, the Crips."

Tammy frowned. "I don't think so. Why?"

"Don't you think somebody should watch for them?" Jacob asked. "In case they come back?"

Tammy shook her head with a sigh. "I'm pretty sure they won't come back at all, Jacob. The story's all over the news. If they come back, they know they'll get arrested." She thought that would make him feel better, but Jacob looked bothered by this theory. "What's wrong?" she asked him.

"How, how we gonna catch them, if they don't come back?" he said.

Tammy's eyes narrowed. "What do you mean, *we*? The police have a lot of leads, Jacob. They gonna find them. Don't worry about that. You shouldn't think you have to do anything to help them."

"But what if they don't get them?" Jacob pondered. "What if they stop looking, and we the only ones who can do something?"

"That's not gonna happen," Tammy assured him.

"But what about Vernon?" Jacob reminded her.

Vernon McCuen was one of Jacob's distant cousins from Cleburne. Vernon was only twenty-two when he was stabbed to death at one of the town's honky-tonks. Jacob was eleven at the time. The police in Cleburne quickly ran out of leads in Vernon's case, and six months later his murder was still unsolved.

A few of Jacob's uncles and older cousins decided to make a special trip to Cleburne, to see what they could do to help. Two days and two murders later, they all returned home, informing everyone that Vernon's murder investigation was now closed. The guilty parties had been judged and sentenced by a jury of their peers.

Tammy hated that her own family resorted to vigilante tactics. Even worse, she hated that Jacob knew about it.

"What happened in Cleburne could never happen here," she told him. "The police in Cleburne couldn't find a piece of gum stuck to the bottom of their shoe. This is Overbrook Meadows. This is a big city. The detectives here know what they doing. Don't ever think about trying any of that Cleburne stuff – here or anywhere else. Don't even let that cross your mind, Jacob. You hear me?"

He nodded. "Yes, ma'am."

Tammy rubbed his hair and brought his head to rest on her shoulder.

"I know it's hard," she said. "It ain't fair."

"I hate them," Jacob said. "I wish they was dead."

"Don't say that."

"I do, Mama. Isaiah never did nothing to nobody. He didn't deserve that. Out of all the people in the world, Isaiah was the main one who didn't deserve that."

"You're right. But even if all of those gangbangers was dead, it wouldn't bring Isaiah back. You would still feel the same way you feel now."

"No I wouldn't." Jacob shook his head. "I'd be happy, Mama. I'd be happy if they was dead."

The callousness of his words sent a chill down his mother's spine. She knew he was serious, and it was unsettling to think that Jacob had progressed through the stages of grief so quickly. Tammy was still in denial, but her son had somehow jumped all the way to anger. Maybe it was because he was at the scene when Isaiah died. That was the only way to explain it.

"Isaiah broke his glasses today," Jacob said. "He was trying to fix them on the bus."

Tammy smiled a weak, faltering smile. "Did he get them fixed?"

"Yeah," Jacob said. "But they was still crooked when he put them on."

Tears flooded Tammy's eyes, but it was a different cry this time. "He in a better place now," she promised. "God fixed his eyes right up – He sure did. Isaiah never has to wear those glasses again."

Jacob nodded, but he wasn't concerned with God or Jesus or heavenly lasik surgeries at that moment. Jacob was still thinking about the bully who broke his little brother's glasses on Isaiah's last day on earth. His mother warned him to leave the Crips alone, but she didn't say anything about him going to the grade school to beat up Isaiah's tormentor.

Earlier today the thought of an eighth grader fighting a fifth grader was considered taboo. But everything was different now. If Jacob could find the little fucker who broke his brother's glasses, he'd touch him up nice and proper.

No, that wouldn't bring Isaiah back, but it would make Jacob feel a little better. It would be a start at least.

• • • • • •

By the time they made it to the freeway, the pain in Dino's face was thundering. Luckily Kevin had a pocket full of pharmaceuticals. Technically the heroin belonged to T Lowe, but no one could blame Dino for needing a couple of freebies after the day he had. Kevin was a little apprehensive about giving T Lowe's dope away, but Dino was past the point of caring what T Lowe had to say about anything.

"Tell him *I* took it," Dino instructed. "If he got a problem with it, he can come see me."

In addition to crack, the Sicc Crips pushed powdered cocaine, better known as *girl*, and powdered heroin, also known as *boy*. They sold the dust by the capsule; ten dollars a pop. Dino took twelve brown pills from Kevin and twisted one open expertly. He tilted his head back and downed half a pill in one snort. After the tingle in his nostril subsided, he snorted the other half.

Dino wasn't a big heroin fan. A ten dollar pill would usually last him a few hours when he chose to indulge. But tonight was different. Tonight he was shot up, embarrassed, and almost excommunicated from his gang. He had blood on his hands. This wasn't the first time he bodied someone, but it was the first time he felt serious remorse about what he did.

He didn't need Channel Six News to tell him Isaiah Spencer was like baby Jesus. Dino saw it for himself every day. That little boy never did a thing to hurt anyone. If ever there was a truly innocent victim, Isaiah was it. And if ever there was a true face of evil, well, that would be Dino.

The heroin coursed through his bloodstream quickly, making its way to his brain in less than a minute. The pain in his cheek didn't subside immediately, but Dino did feel relaxed right away. The heroin drained down the back of his throat and made him nauseous, but that sensation would pass. Soon he would be nodding so hard, he wouldn't be able to keep is eyes open.

Dino got comfortable in his seat and watched the road lazily. He felt like he was floating on a cloud, rather than cruising in Kevin's 2001 Buick LeSabre.

"Where we going?" the driver asked.

"Waxahachie," Dino replied.

"What's over there?"

"You remember that broad I used to mess with back in the day," Dino said, "when we was in the Evergreens?"

"That light-skinned bitch?" Kevin asked.

Dino nodded. "Mmm hmm."

"The one with the fat ass?"

A smile lifted the corner of Dino's mouth. He nodded. "Mmm hmm."

"I thought she took off to get away from you," Kevin recalled.

"I got her in some shit," Dino acknowledged. "She stayed in that fucked up neighborhood, remember? I used to get into it with them niggas across the street from her every time I went over there. After a while, they started fucking with her, since they was too pussy to bust at me."

"Then you shot that fool," Kevin mused.

Dino nodded. "Yup. When I shot that nigga, all hell broke loose. They started fucking with Charlotte real tough."

"That was her name?" Kevin asked. "Charlotte?"

"Charlotte Webb," Dino said with a chuckle. "That's her *real name*: Charlotte Webb. Her mama never made it past the sixth grade. She was a crack head when she had Charlotte. Her last name was Webb, and she thought that shit would be cute, you know, to name her daughter after that book."

"I didn't never know her last name," Kevin said.

"She didn't like telling people," Dino explained. "Anyway, when I shot that dude on her street, them niggas got straight ignorant. They did a driveby on Charlotte's house. They slashed her tires and busted all the windows on her car. I went back over there to show them fools what was really up, but Charlotte didn't want no more trouble. She said she was leaving. This gang shit was too much for her. *I* was too much for her. She moved all the way to Waxahachie."

"You still been talking to her?" Kevin asked.

Dino shook his head. "Nope."

"So why you think she'll let you stay over there?"

"Bitch still love me," Dino said. "She left 'cause bullets was flying at her house, not 'cause she didn't wanna be with me."

"What if she got a man?" Kevin asked.

"I guess we'll go to plan b."

"What's that?"

"I ain't got no plan b," Dino said. "You know niggas don't never plan that far ahead."

Kevin laughed. "That was, that was some heavy shit went down earlier," he said after a minute. "I thought T Lowe was gon' kick you out the Sicc."

"He was," Dino said. "That's why I had to man-up and take control of the meeting. Ain't no way I'ma sit there and let some nigga decide what happens to me. I'm the only one who can decide that."

"You and T Lowe be bumping heads," Kevin noticed.

Dino sighed. "I think I'm finally starting to see that nigga for what he is. Like with my gun; he say he don't know if I left it or not. What kind of shit is that? This nigga's supposed to be my homey, right? My brother. How come he wasn't looking out for me?

"And them three slabs I got from Pooky... T Lowe say he left 'em at the spot. You think I believe that shit? What kind of nigga gon' leave three slabs, just sitting there? You think he left *his* dope, too? Hell naw. He got his shit *and* my shit. I ain't no fool, cuz. That's why I didn't tell him where I was going. I don't want you to tell him, either."

"What you think might happen?"

"I don't know," Dino said. "All I know is that nigga's lying, and I don't trust him. I been thinking about making a move anyhow."

"What kind of move?"

"This just between you and me," Dino said. "Everything we been talking about is between you and me, you feel me?"

Kevin nodded. "I feel you."

"I think it's about time T Lowe stepped down from being our OG," Dino said. "I don't like how he be handling the Sicc. I think he too soft. He only care about his money."

These were serious words, but Dino didn't have a problem sharing his thoughts with Kevin. The two gangsters had been childhood friends since the third grade. Kevin was the closest thing Dino had to a real brother.

"I was listening to what you said back at the spot," Kevin said. "A lot of niggas be feeling the same way you do, but don't nobody wanna say nothing."

"That's 'cause T Lowe putting money in they pocket," Dino said. "T Lowe think the world revolves around money, and it do in a way. But it's more to it than that. You still got to be a man. You still got to stand up for yourself and your homies. When HB came by earlier, T Lowe damned near took his side. He told me to give the dope back and everything. What kind of shit is that?"

"He didn't care about it, 'cause he got his own money," Kevin surmised.

"That's what I'm saying," Dino said. "But what about the Sicc? What about being down for each other? I'm supposed to trust y'all niggas with my life, but I can't trust T Lowe like that. Not no more. He didn't even shoot back when Pooky was busting on us. Didn't nobody shoot back. Nobody but me..."

"You shoulda put it to a vote tonight," Kevin said. "Everybody was behind you. You could be our OG right now."

"It ain't a good time," Dino said. "I'm fucked up. I gotta hide out for a minute. But I'll bring that shit up again when I get back. Best believe it's gon' come up again. And when I'm OG, the first thing I'ma do is kick Stephon's bitch ass out the set. Then I'ma whoop his ass."

"Cool. I ain't never liked that punk motherfucker," Kevin said.

Dino grinned. "That's why you my nigga. We always on the same page."

● ● ● ● ● ●

They rode in silence for a while as Dino nodded from the effects of the heroin. A heroin high is the complete opposite of explosive drugs like cocaine or speed. Rather than make you jumpy or antsy, heroin calms you in a way only morphine or hardcore sedatives can. Dino's eyes were half-closed. His head fell slowly, bouncing back up ever so often, whenever his chin hit his chest.

When they got to Waxahachie, Kevin asked again where they were headed. Dino instructed him to make a right turn off Main onto West Jefferson. Charlotte had her own home on East

Madison. It was after midnight when Kevin pulled to a stop across the street from her humble abode. Dino sat up in his seat and tried to get his eyes to focus.

"Somebody's there," Kevin said.

Dino nodded. There was a light on in the front room and a car in the driveway. It wasn't the car Dino last saw Charlotte driving, but he hadn't seen or heard from her in two years. A lot can change in that amount of time.

"I hope that ain't her man's car," Dino muttered under his breath.

"She got a man?" Kevin was shocked.

Dino laughed. "I don't know, cuz. She is fine. She could have a man."

Kevin shook his head. "So what you gon' do if she does?"

"I told you. I'll go to plan b."

"You said you don't have no plan b."

"I don't," Dino said with a snicker. "Maybe I'll shoot that nigga. You got a pistol?"

Kevin's eyes grew wide. Dino laughed again.

"Look at you, ol' scary ass nigga. I ain't gon' shoot nobody," Dino promised. "I was just playing. But I do need a gun. I don't want to be way over here by myself with no protection."

Kevin shook his head and gestured towards the glove compartment. "It's one in there."

Dino opened the box and removed an all black Glock 21 .45 caliber pistol. He held it up and admired the finish in the scant light from the street lamps.

"*Aw, hell yeah*! I can tear her boyfriend a new asshole with this motherfucker for sho'."

Kevin rolled his eyes.

"Naw, I'm playing," Dino said, snickering again. "I'm just finna go over there and see if she'll let me crash for a while. If she let me in, it's all gravy. You can take off. If she don't let me in, I'll come back to the car. I'm not gon' start no trouble."

"Alright," Kevin said. "But that's my favorite strap. I want it back."

"You'll get it back," Dino assured him. He checked to make sure there wasn't a round chambered before stuffing the gun in his waistband. "You, uh, you got a cellphone I can keep?"

Kevin frowned but dug into his front pocket. "Damn, nigga. You already got my dope and my strap. Now you want my phone, too? What else you want, Dino? You want me to give you my car?"

That didn't sound like a bad idea, but Dino wasn't that much of an asshole. "Naw, cuz. And I do appreciate you helping me out. Don't worry, man. When this shit settles down and I take T Lowe's spot, I'ma hook you up. You gon' be my number one soldier. I put that on the set."

Kevin couldn't hide his elation. He handed the cellphone over and gave Dino the Sicc handshake before his friend got out of the car. Dino crossed the street under the cover of darkness and knocked lightly on Charlotte's front door.

Kevin waited, thinking either a man would answer or no one at all. But a female opened the door a few seconds later. She wore a blue nightgown with a robe over it. Kevin had never seen much of Charlotte, but she was just as beautiful as he remembered from back in the day. She looked a little bigger, but that was all good. Kevin liked women who were thick and voluptuous, and it was no secret Dino did, too.

From Kevin's vantage point, he saw Charlotte register excitement and then shock and disgust when she saw how badly Dino was wounded. Kevin expected her to send him on his way. But after a brief conversation Charlotte's expression changed again. She looked hurt and remorseful, and finally Kevin saw pity in her big, brown eyes.

"That smooth sonofabitch," Kevin muttered as the couple hugged and Dino disappeared inside the small house. Kevin put his Buick back in gear.

It would be a long drive back to Overbrook Meadows by himself. But Kevin had the nice, warm glow of hope to keep him company. Soon things were going to change in his gang. Kevin would get in on the top floor this time. No longer would the crew make fun of his disability; calling him Slue-Foot or Lazy Leg or Lil' Half Dead. His new nickname would be *Big* Kevin. His new position: Dino's right hand man.

Nobody would talk shit to him after that.

# CHAPTER EIGHT
# *THE RUSSELL PARKS SHOW*

*I love going to school!*
*(Going to school)*
*I love going to school!*
*(Can't wait to get to school)*
*I'm going to learn some math and history!*
*(Math and history)*
*When I wake up early on a school day, I'm so glad!*
*I can't wait to see all my teachers and friends.*
*And I promise that we won't talk in classss!*
Jacob hated that song, but of course Isaiah loved it. He had all of the words memorized. Every morning Isaiah would turn the radio on while he brushed his teeth, so he could sing along with the motivational tune. K105 FM played the song every school day at exactly seven a.m.

Jacob didn't have to go to school this morning, but he turned the radio on anyway because K105's morning show was somewhat of a ritual. Normalcy was the thing his mind craved most right now, and hearing that stupid *I Love Going to School* song helped a lot. In the back of his mind, Jacob could hear Isaiah singing along with the recording. It made his heart ache, but it was also a little comforting.

"*Good morning, Overbrook Meadows!*" The smooth voice of K105's DJ cut in after the song. "It's seven o'clock, so get your butt up if you still in bed! Today is *Friday*, and you made it through another long week. Just one more day, and you can stay home in your pajamas all day tomorrow if you want to!

"If you have to be there by eight, you got *one hour left*. But if you're stuck on I-30 East, you might not make it. Let's check in with Wendy Wallace, our eye in the sky, for more about what the heck's going on on I-30. Wendy…"

"Morning, Russell! I'm flying over the interstate right now, and things are pretty bad over here…" Wendy had to raise her voice over the noise from her helicopter, but she still sounded vibrant and sexy. Jacob had no idea what she looked like, but Wendy had always been his favorite voice on the Russell Parks Show.

Jacob walked to the front window and peered through the curtains for the fifth time that morning. The police were mostly done with their investigation at the Sicc Crips' house, but a two-man CSI team was still there gathering the last bits of evidence. One of them walked slowly across the front yard, waving a metal detector over the grass as he stepped.

The other technician plucked bullets out of the wood on the front of T Lowe's dope house. Jacob wondered if they'd already dug up the bullet that passed through Isaiah's head. He figured they must have, because the police showed no interest in Isaiah's crime scene today. The reporters were a different story, but thankfully they weren't like the paparazzi Jacob saw on television.

Since he'd been up, three reporters pulled to a stop in front of their house, but none of them knocked on the door. They just took a few pictures, mainly of Isaiah's shrine and got back into their vehicles and drove away.

Jacob would be glad when all of this attention died down, because there was no way the Crips would come back with so many people hanging around. His mom said they wouldn't come back at all, but Jacob held out hope. One day he would look out of the window and see the man who killed his little brother. Jacob didn't have a solid plan for when that moment arrived, but the killer wouldn't get away from him a second time – that much he knew for sure.

Jacob heard his brother's name on the radio. He closed the curtains and went back to the entertainment center.

"That's why I moved to Mansfield," Russell's female co-host said. "I got three boys, and I didn't want them to grow up around this mess."

"But moving away does not solve the problem," Russell Parks countered.

"It solved *my* problem," his co-host said. "I haven't had no trouble with gangs since I been out there."

"Well, that's just short-sighted," Russell said. "That's the kind of mentality that keeps our people behind: Everyone's always thinking *me, me, me*, and nobody spends enough time talking about *we, we, we*. Man, I miss the sixties. We had some brothers and sisters back then who was down for the people. What we got now? Al Sharpton?"

"That's 'cause they killed all our leaders," his co-host said. "Every time somebody tried to stand up for us, they ended up getting assassinated. Now, don't nobody wanna try. People are too scared."

"Yeah, and you're one of 'em!" Russell observed. "You ran your scary butt all the way to *Mansfield*!"

They both laughed.

"If you're just joining us," Russell said, "We're talking about the terrible, *terrible* murder that took place in the Poly neighborhood of Overbrook Meadows yesterday. Isaiah Spencer, a ten year old honor student, in the fifth grade, was shot dead in his own front yard. What's sad is Isaiah took cover, lying flat on the ground as soon as he heard gunfire, but he still got hit. If you're not safe at your own house, where are you safe? What has our city come to? Plashette says we should all move to Mansfield, but is that the answer?"

"Naw, I didn't say we should all move to Mansfield," Plashette corrected. "I said I moved *my* family to Mansfield. I don't want the rest of y'all following me. My neighborhood will end up looking just like the one I ran away from!"

"Oh, that's cold," Russell said. "But what do you guys think? We've been taking calls all morning, and we've got Maria on line four. Maria, what's your opinion on Isaiah's murder?"

"Hello?"

"Yeah, Maria, you're on the radio."

"Oh, uh, I think it's really stupid what's going on over here. I saw that little boy on the news yesterday, and I cried for him and his family. I called my son and made him come right home. I hugged him, and he was like, 'Mama, what's wrong with you,' and I told him to shut up and hug me back. I get so scared sometimes.

You never know when it might happen to you or somebody in your family."

"How old is your son?" Russell asked.

"He's thirteen," Maria said.

"What part of town do you live in?"

"I live on the south side, and it's just as bad over here as it is in Poly. We have shootings almost every night."

"What do you think should be done, Maria?" Plashette asked. "Do you think there's a solution to this gang foolishness?"

"I want to move out to Mansfield with you!"

"Naw, you need to stay right where you at!" Plashette said with a chuckle.

"Thanks, Maria," Russell said, then, "We've got another caller, Sammy, on line two. Sammy, what you got to say about this?"

"Russell?"

"Yeah, this is Russell. You're on the radio, man. What you got to say about these senseless murders in our community?"

"Well..." Sammy had a southern twang that made Jacob's skin crawl. "You can take a monkey out the jungle, but he's still—"

"Whoa, whoa!" Russell Parks wasn't normally one to interrupt, but he knew a mean redneck when he heard one. "You're live on the radio, man. What kind of racist nonsense are you about to say?"

"I just think you people—"

"Okay, Sammy, I'm going to have to let you go," Russell said. "This is a serious subject, and we've got people calling—"

"*Niggers!*" Sammy shouted and hung up himself.

"Get off the phone, you old fool!" Russell snapped. "Hey, I'm sorry about that y'all," he told his audience. "This is a free country, and some people think they can say anything they want anytime they want. That guy probably never listens to this station. He just heard we're trying to have a meaningful dialogue about our community, and he wanted to do something to disrupt it. That's the devil, y'all. And we don't have to pay him no mind."

"We sho' don't," Plashette agreed. "That fool's probably mad because his trailer fell over in that tornado last month."

"Stop it, girl," Russell said. "Your stereotyping is no better than his. Let's get back to these calls. Who we got next?"

The telephone rang.

Jacob jumped, thinking the radio station had gotten his number somehow. He went to the couch to fetch the cordless phone. He peeked through the front curtains again as he answered it.

"Hello?"

"Hey, who is this?" It was a vaguely familiar male voice.

"Jacob."

"Oh, what's going on, boy? This yo uncle, Myron." Uncle Myron had a gruff, cigarette damaged voice. Jacob hadn't spoken to him in more than a year.

"Hello, sir."

"Sir? What's this *sir* shit about? Call me Unc or Uncle Myron. Don't be calling me no *sir*."

"I'm sorry, Uncle Myron."

"What's going on over there?" Myron asked. "Yo mama still sleep? I ain't seen nothing on the news but yo brother all morning."

"Yes sir, I mean Uncle Myron. She's still asleep. She didn't go to bed until four or five this morning."

"That's some fucked up shit that happened," Myron said. "Them niggas killed my nephew like that."

Myron was one of the few members of their family who wasn't a Jesus freak. His candor used to frighten Jacob when he was younger, but Myron's words seemed very appropriate now. Why say something was *messed up* when it was really *fucked up*? Jacob didn't think that was gratuitous at all.

"They say you went after one of them punks," Myron said. "You did that, boy?"

Jacob nodded. "Yeah, but I didn't catch him, though."

"Why not?" Myron asked.

Jacob's face burned. "I don't know. I ran as fast as I could, but, but he was bigger than me. He was too fast."

"You give up?" It was more of an accusation than a question.

Jacob's eyes filled with moisture, and he blew hot fumes from his nostrils. "No. I was, just 'cause—"

"Calm down, man," his uncle told him. "I'm not trying to give you a hard time, Jacob. I just want to see where your head is at. Tell me something; what was you gon' do, if you woulda caught that nigga?"

103

Jacob frowned and shrugged his shoulders. "I don't know, sir."

"Call me Unc or Uncle Myron."

"I don't know, Unc."

"Was you gon' fight him?"

"I would've killed him."

"What's that, boy?"

"I would have killed him," Jacob said coldly. "If I caught him, I would have killed him."

"What about now?" Myron asked. "What you'll do if you see him now?"

Goosebumps sprouted on Jacob's arms. His first thought was this was a test. His uncle wanted to know if he was a punk or not. But then again, Jacob knew Myron might be hinting at something more serious. When his cousin Vernon got killed in Cleburne, Uncle Myron was one of those who took a trip down there to sort things out.

Jacob never got the specifics about exactly who did what, but he knew two more people wound up dead. Supposedly, these new victims were in some way responsible for Vernon's death. Jacob also knew Uncle Myron was an Iraq war veteran who had personally killed a dozen "sheet heads" before his honorable discharge. *And* rumor had it Uncle Myron amassed a rather nice arsenal since returning to the states.

"I still want him dead," Jacob said, his throat catching on the last word.

His uncle hummed. "You know, it's not all that easy to kill a man."

"Yes, sir."

Myron didn't correct him this time. "Especially in a big city like yours," he said. "That shit that went down in Cleburne, you heard about that, right?"

"Yes, sir." Jacob's heart thundered. Sweat collected between his shoulder blades.

"How you think you'd get away with something like that?" Myron asked.

Jacob knew absolutely nothing about killing folks, but he watched enough murder mysteries to recite the basics. "First I have to find him. Then I have to follow him and learn his schedule. Then I have to catch him alone and kill him. Then I get away and get rid of the gun."

There was a pause, and then Uncle Myron laughed. Jacob squeezed his eyes shut and shook his head in embarrassment.

Myron quieted down and asked, "How you know all that, boy?"

"Huh?"

"I said how you know all that? You sound like you been killing for a while. You killed somebody before?"

Jacob didn't know if that was sarcasm or not, but it didn't sound like it. He opened his eyes, and a cool chill rolled down his chest. "No, sir. I ain't never killed nobody."

"Well, you sound like you know what you doing," Myron said. "Listen, I wouldn't never advocate nothing like this, especially for my nephew, but family is serious business. You always look out for your family. Even if it goes against right or wrong or Jesus, too. That's how you feel?"

"I always looked out for my brother."

"That's good, boy. You got a gun?"

Jacob thought that was a silly question, but his uncle was dead serious. "No, sir. I, I don't have a gun."

"I'ma give you one," Myron said. "I'll be down there for the funeral. How long you want me to stay, to help you out with this?"

Jacob couldn't believe the absurdity of this conversation, but it really was happening. He definitely needed help if he was going to murder someone, but his mom would never let him hang out with his crazy uncle Myron – or anyone else who was involved with the Cleburne project.

"I, I wanna do it by myself," Jacob said. "Isaiah was my brother. My responsibility."

Uncle Myron was quiet for a second, and then he said, "You done grew into a real man, Jacob. I'm proud of you. Make sure you're looking for me at the funeral, so I can hook you up. Tell yo mama I called."

"Okay," Jacob said and hung up the phone. He barely had time to wrap his mind around what just happened when he heard a sound behind him.

"Hey."

Jacob spun and saw his mother standing in the doorway. Tammy yawned lazily with a hand over her mouth. She had dark circles around her eyes. She didn't look like she got any sleep at all.

"Who was that?" she asked.

"That was, uh, Uncle Myron."

Tammy sighed. "What he want?"

"He heard about Isaiah," Jacob said. "He said he's coming down for the funeral. He wants you to call him."

"Maybe later," Tammy said. She sat next to her son and gave him a hug. She backed away, knitting her eyebrows. "What's wrong? You warm, but you're shivering."

"I was, just thinking about Isaiah," Jacob said. "I don't, I don't know what to feel."

Tammy nodded and placed a hand on his cheek. "It's okay," she said. "You can feel whatever you want. Come on. Let me get you some breakfast."

● ● ● ● ● ●

"Hi."

"Hi, Pam," Russell Parks said, his voice deep and somber. "My producer says you were related to the child, who was murdered..."

"Yes," Pam said. "Isaiah was my nephew – he still is. Man. It feels weird to say *was*. It's like, it doesn't even feel real."

"I know what you mean," the morning show host said. "And I'm very sorry for your loss."

"I'm praying for you and your whole family," Plashette added.

Dino turned down the volume and inched closer to the radio. He heard a lot of talk on the news yesterday, but this was the first time he'd hear from someone who knew the dead boy personally. Dino wasn't normally a nail-biter, but he gnawed on his thumbnail like a beaver while waiting for Pam to speak her piece.

"What would you like our audience to know about Isaiah?" Russell prompted.

"Isaiah was a sweet boy," Pam said. "I know this city has a big problem with gangs, and we seem to lose a couple of black men every week – be it to jail or the graveyard. But Isaiah's murder, it's different."

"Mmm hmm," Russell agreed.

"Isaiah was a great student," Pam continued. "He never got into fights. He would get picked on sometimes, because he was small and he wore glasses and because he didn't have a lot of money in his family, but he didn't fight back. Isaiah was peaceful. He was a good, Christian boy. He loved his mama. Everything he did was to please her. My sister didn't deserve to lose her son like that." Pam sniffled. Even over the radio, her grief was poignant.

"How is your sister doing?" Russell asked.

"Better than I thought she'd be," Pam said. "As much as she loves her boys, I don't see how she can walk, talk or even hold her head up, but she's doing it. She's a lot stronger than I ever imagined. And she's not filled with anger like some of us are. She's holding on to God's word. She still believes God has a plan for her and her family."

"What about you," Russell asked. "How do you feel about the man or men who killed your nephew?"

"Oh, well, I believe in God's plan, too," Pam said. "But I've always had a problem when I see innocents and babies suffering. Everybody knows how I feel about that. As far as the punk who killed Isaiah, I think that sorry sonofa– Oh, I'm sorry, Russell. I almost, this stuff makes me so mad."

"I understand," Russell said.

"Okay," Pam said and took a deep breath. "If the lowlife *hoodlum* who killed my nephew is listening right now, I want you to know–"

"Whatchoo doing?"

Dino reached to turn off the radio before looking back. Charlotte stood in the hallway with her baby in her arms. Charlotte was just as sweet and beautiful as Dino remembered her, even more so now, but a lot had changed over the last two years. The most notable difference was the bundle of joy she toted.

When she invited him inside last night, Dino thought he hit the jackpot. His old girlfriend still had the prettiest lips and sexiest eyes in the world. Charlotte's skin was smooth and rich like a cappuccino. And she still had love for Dino. Her compassion was as much an Achilles' heel now as it was when they were dating.

Charlotte gained a few pounds since Dino saw her last, but it all went to the right places. She used to have *nice* hips and thighs, but they were nothing less than *awesome* now. Her booty was rounder, and her breasts jumped up a full cup size. The reason for all of this new voluptuousness was the only downside, and Dino was still trying to come to terms with Charlotte being a mother.

She got knocked up by a college kid named Reggie a little over a year ago. Reggie seemed to have a good head on his shoulders, but Charlotte later learned he was the biggest whore and loser on TSU's campus. Reggie had only seen his daughter twice since she was born four months ago. Last week Charlotte filed the first set of papers to get child support payments started.

"What you talking about?" Dino asked. "I'm just chilling."

"Why you sitting in the dark?" Charlotte asked. Her hair was shoulder length, reddish brown with tan streaks. She wore it pulled back in a ponytail. She hadn't put on any makeup yet, but she was still striking.

"It ain't dark," Dino said. "The sun's already out."

"Was you listening to the radio?"

Dino leaned back on the sofa. "What's up, shorty. Why you asking all these questions?"

"You left a big ass blood stain on my pillow case," Charlotte said.

Dino already knew that because his gauze was caked with blood when he got up. Unlike Tish, Charlotte had plenty of medical supplies in her bathroom, so Dino taped on a proper bandage before going to bed last night.

He changed his dressings in the morning, but it was already clear that his half-ass doctoring wouldn't solve his problem. He saw the first signs of pus seeping from the hole in his cheek, and the inflammation had returned with a vengeance. The swelling moved upwards now, and his right eye was half-closed because of it. The heroin still helped with the pain, but it wouldn't stop the infection that was fermenting in the hole.

"Sorry about that," Dino said.

Charlotte came and sat next to him. She had her robe on, but one of the straps of her nightgown was pulled down. Her baby breastfed complacently, and Dino couldn't help but become a little aroused. He knew breastfeeding was a natural thing, and he didn't consider himself a pervert, but Charlotte's titties were as perfect as he was ever going to see in real life. He looked away from them and met her accusing eyes.

"Was you listening to something about that shooting?" she asked.

"Why you tripping?" Dino said. "Why you keep asking about that?"

"Was you high last night?"

Dino hated the way she was answering all of his questions with more questions. But he wasn't in a position to complain.

"I took something for the pain," he admitted.

"You was out like a light," Charlotte informed him. "Dead to the world. I coulda shot your gun in the same room, and you wouldn't have woke up."

Dino's eyes widened. He had no idea what he did with Kevin's gun before he passed out.

"While you was sleep," Charlotte said, "I went to the living room to see if I could find out anything about your shooting."

Dino's heart rate quickened. He knew his lies were flimsy at best, and Charlotte wasn't ditsy and desperate like Tish.

"It's all over the news," Charlotte said. "They say the one who got shot in the face is the one who killed that little boy. And I know they was talking about it on the radio, because I was standing in the hallway listening."

Dino's anger started to rise, but he subdued it.

"So why you lying?" Charlotte asked. "And why you come over here? Everybody in the city is looking for you, Dino. You know I don't want no trouble. I left Overbrook Meadows because of you. I don't need you coming here with the same shit."

She had him dead to rights, and Dino knew it. But defeat was not an option. He wished he could confide in her, but Charlotte was a mother now. She would never accept him as a child killer.

"It's a lie," Dino said. "They trying to hang me, but it's a lie. I didn't kill that boy."

"So *everybody* got it wrong?" Charlotte said. "The reporters, the police, the *goddamned mayor* – everybody's lying on you?"

"Ain't nobody said it was me who killed that boy," Dino said. "They said I was there, and I'm a person of interest."

"No, they said it was *you*," Charlotte informed him. "You'd better check the news, if you don't believe me. You want me to turn it on now?" She looked around the sofa. "Where's the remote?"

"I don't need you to turn the TV on."

"No, where's the remote?"

"I said I don't wanna watch it."

"Well, you need to read the paper or something, Dino, 'cause you got your facts wrong. Everybody says *the one who got shot in the face is the one who killed that little boy. Everybody says that.*"

"*Everybody don't know what the fuck they talking about!*" Dino shouted. "*I* was the one who was there. I'm the one who got shot. None of them people saying it was me was there when that shit went down."

Charlotte stared into his eyes. For a moment Dino thought she'd call his bluff or tell him HB or Pooky got arrested and they were talking, but that wasn't the case.

"They saying it was me 'cause I took off running," Dino explained. "I was shooting back at them niggas, but after I got shot, that was it. I took off, and I got away, and that's why they trying to pin that shit on me.

"I already told you; I wasn't facing that little boy. He was *behind* me. The same dude who shot me is the one who killed that kid. Once they catch *him* and finish with their ballistic tests – or whatever they're doing – that's when the truth is gon' come out.

"Until then, I don't need you taking sides with them and making me out to be some kind of monster or something. The only thing I did yesterday was defend myself, and I wouldn't even have done that if I saw some kids walking home from school.

"I'm a fuck-up, Charlotte. I know it. Everybody knows it. But I'm not reckless like that. I do have a conscious, and if what they're saying about me was true, I'd kill my motherfucking self – that's how bad I would feel."

Charlotte listened intently. Dino was sure his lies would work again, but she shook her head.

"Dino, look man, I want to believe you. I really do. But I got a baby now. Even if you telling the truth, you still got people looking for you. And I'm not talking about the police; I'm talking about whoever shot you in the face. If they killed that little boy, and they're not locked up yet, then what's to stop them from coming up in here and shooting me and my baby? I left the city to get away from that shit."

Dino felt her pain, but deep down he was elated. It sounded like Charlotte half-believed him.

"Nobody knows I'm here," he assured her. "That's why I came all the way down here. Nobody knows about you, and there's no way they can find me."

"Somebody brought you over here."

"That was Kevin, and I trust that nigga with my life," Dino said. "You ain't got to worry about somebody coming over here starting shit. Kevin is the only person who know where I'm at, and he ain't telling nobody. I put that on my mama."

"But what is staying over here gonna solve, Dino? You need to go to the hospital. And you can't get your story out, if you hiding."

"I just need to stay off the streets until the police figure out what really went down," Dino explained. "Once they say it wasn't me who shot Isaiah, I'll go to the hospital. I know I'm going to jail for the shootout anyway, but I'd rather get locked up for something I did, instead of something I didn't do. It shouldn't take more than two or three days, Charlotte. The truth is gonna come out. That's when I'll turn myself in."

She frowned, but Dino was convincing, and he knew he had her. Who could turn a possibly innocent man over to a lynch mob? Certainly not Charlotte. She had a heart of gold.

She sighed and looked down at her baby. When she met Dino's eyes again, she was on the verge of tears.

"Dino, I don't want no trouble over here. I came to Waxahachie to start over. I'm trying to do right. I messed up and got pregnant, but I'm taking care of my business. I don't have a boyfriend now because I don't need a man. I don't need no stupid promises, and I don't need no help. My baby is all I got. You asking me to put Crystal in danger for you."

"No I'm—"

Charlotte put a hand up to silence him. "You got two days," she said. "I don't know how that's gonna help, but I still care for you, Dino. And if you telling the truth, I owe you at least that much."

He exhaled a pent up breath. "Man, thank you—"

"But if I find out you lying to me... If I find out you really did kill that boy..." Charlotte shook her head. Her nostrils flared. "I'll call the police on you myself, Dino. 'Cause what happened to that boy is *bad*, and whoever did it is going to hell. I hope it wasn't you, but I swear before God I'll turn you in if it was."

"It wasn't," Dino said. "Thank you for trusting me. I won't let you down, baby. I promise."

Charlotte got up. "I told you; I don't need no promises from no man. I need you out of my house in two days, Dino. That's it." She headed for the hallway and disappeared around the corner.

"Alright," Dino said and reclined on the couch. His heart knocked. His last toot of heroin had worn off, and his face throbbed. He felt like a snake for deceiving Charlotte, but war is always ugly. He was currently entrenched in the fiercest battle of his life.

The evil nymph who always sat on his shoulder urged Dino to cut the charades. He still had nine heroin pills left. He could slam them all at once or use a bullet from Kevin's gun if that didn't do the trick.

But Dino shut the evil nymph up. Suicide was a fool's and a coward's way out. His innate drive for self-preservation brought him this far, and this basic instinct would take Dino the rest of the way. Exactly *where* he was headed was still up for debate, but Dino knew Charlotte was right about one thing: There was sure to be fire and brimstones and a shitload of suffering in his afterlife.

Dino could avoid his date with Lucifer as long as his heart was still beating.

# CHAPTER NINE
## *THE FUNERAL*

The first weekend without Isaiah passed dreadfully slowly.

Jacob couldn't sleep much, so he watched a lot of television. On Saturday morning he watched a whole line-up of Isaiah's favorite cartoons. Jacob used to chastise his brother, urging him to hurry and grow out of his animation fixation. But in retrospect, Isaiah's cartoons weren't that bad. They were a lot funnier than the toons Jacob grew up with. And they didn't get too preachy, trying to deliver a moral lesson with every storyline.

After eleven am, most of the networks aired fitness commercials or stupid sports like *bowling*, but Jacob didn't go outside to find a friend to play with like he normally would. Everyone he ran into in his neighborhood would ask a bunch of stupid questions and go overboard, saying sentimental things about Isaiah.

Jacob heard enough sentimental stuff already, because his home looked like a family reunion the whole weekend. Relatives from as far away as Georgia and California came to pay their respect and grieve with Tammy.

A lot of Jacob's cousins came, too. Some were his age or younger, so it became Jacob's responsibility to keep them company while the adults talked about adult things in the living room. Jacob didn't have cable television or a new video game system, so he had virtually nothing to offer his relatives. Mostly they just sat in his room looking sad and bored, waiting for their mother to come and tell them it was time to go.

On Sunday people brought so much food Tammy ran out of room in the refrigerator. Jacob ate turkey and dressing at noon, ham and macaroni at three, and tuna casserole at six. He scarfed down more pie than at Christmas or Thanksgiving, and no one said anything about him being a glutton or not leaving enough for others.

On Monday Jacob stayed home from school again. Tammy said he didn't have to go back until after the funeral on Wednesday. Jacob appreciated the time off, but it was weird having so many days out of school but not being able to enjoy them.

On Tuesday Tammy took Jacob to the Men's Warehouse to buy him a black suit for his brother's funeral. This was the first suit Jacob ever owned. He wondered how his mother could afford it all of a sudden. Tammy explained that she had insurance at the hospital that paid for things she needed for Isaiah's funeral.

Jacob thought it was sad how Isaiah lived poor his whole life, but now that he was dead some insurance company had thousands of dollars set aside for his *needs*. Jacob wondered if he could have his own death money now, and they could throw him in the river for free when he died. But of course he didn't ask his mother that.

On Wednesday morning Jacob got decked out in his brand new suit. It was somewhat of a relief to finally reach the day of Isaiah's funeral. All of the waiting and planning and eating and crying had become a huge source of stress in their household. Everyone was upset for days and days on end. Jacob hoped he would see his mother smile again sometime soon. He doubted Tammy would ever burst into a fit of laughter, like she used to, but just to see her smile would be enough. She was a good mother. She deserved to be happy.

In her bedroom, Tammy looked over her new dress in the mirror mounted on her dresser. Her sister Pam stepped forward to pluck a price tag from the back zipper. Their mother sat on the corner of the bed with her hands clasped in her lap. All three women wore black. They all looked tired and a little older than their years.

"But you said he's eating, right?" Pam asked.

"Yeah, he's eating," Tammy confirmed. "But that's about all he's doing. It's hard to get a read on him now. Sometimes I can tell he's been crying, but usually it don't look like nothing's wrong with him at all. But I know he's thinking about a lot of stuff. You can see it in his eyes. His brain is always working."

"Jacob's been cooped up in the house a lot," Pam noticed.

"That's not because of me," Tammy said. "I asked him all weekend if he wanted to go outside and play basketball with some of his friends. But he kept telling me no. He didn't say why. Normally I would have made him go. But I know he's depressed. Maybe he only wants to be around his family."

"I wouldn't want to play either," Florence said.

"The weird thing is," Tammy said, "I catch him looking out the front window all the time. That's what got me thinking he wanted to go outside."

"Maybe he's scared," Pam offered.

"That's what I'm worried about," Tammy confided. "I think he's looking at the house across the street because he's afraid of those Crips. He don't want to go outside, because he thinks they'll come back and hurt him."

"Have you asked him?" Florence asked.

Tammy shook her head. "Not really. We talked about the Crips a little bit, and I told him they wouldn't come back to that house. I didn't ask if he was scared of them. Every time I say something about him peeping through the curtains, he gets real defensive. If I catch him doing it, he'll yank the curtains closed and look back at me, like I caught him stealing or something."

"Sounds like he scared," Florence decided. "But you can't blame him. Jacob was the only one who was with Isaiah when that mess happened. If that was me, I wouldn't be no more good after that."

Tammy thought about that and wondered if it was possible to have a nervous breakdown at Jacob's age. Her sister was thinking the same thing.

"You might want to take him to a counselor," Pam suggested.

"I thought about it," Tammy said. "The police gave me a card. I was gonna wait 'til after the funeral before I called them, you know, to see how it goes. I'd hate to put Jacob through that, if he don't need it."

"What will it hurt?" Pam asked.

"I don't know," Tammy said with a shrug. "I guess I'm not too keen on the idea of spilling your guts to a perfect stranger and expecting them to solve your problems for you. Even before the shooting, Jacob didn't like to share his feelings. I don't think he'll do good with a counselor. But that could just be my thinking. Maybe it's the way I was raised."

Both women looked to their mother. Florence offered no apologies for their upbringing.

"I don't like counselors 'cause ain't nothing you gon' hear from them you can't find out for yourself," Florence said. "Them people take your money so you can sit there and cry your eyes out. They ain't gon' tell you nothing your mama didn't already tell you twenty times or more. On top of that, some people leave worse off than before they went."

"I'm not disagreeing with you, Mama," Pam said. "But Tammy, this should be your decision. You know if Jacob needs to see a counselor or not."

"I'm gonna wait to see how he is after today," Tammy said. "Then I'll know for sure."

• • • • • •

At nine o'clock the family loaded into two vehicles and headed for Ebenezer Baptist Church, where Isaiah was already waiting on them. Jacob sat in a champagne-colored Escalade with his uncle Jimmy driving and his mother in the backseat with him. Tammy held his hand throughout the trip. Uncle Jimmy had the radio tuned in to a gospel station. Jacob felt stiff and uncomfortable in his new suit, but he didn't complain or fidget at all.

At the church there were more vehicles squeezed in the parking lot than Jacob had ever seen there. There were a few news vans and a shiny, black limousine parked right out front. There was a long string of cars on both sides of the street. Uncle Jimmy dropped Tammy and Jacob and his family off near the main entrance and drove off in search of what was sure to be a faraway parking spot.

Inside, the church was stuffed to the gills with mourners and well-wishers, most of whom Jacob had never seen before. An usher approached Tammy as soon as they entered. He led her and Jacob to their seats on the very first pew. Isaiah's coffin was less than six feet from their reserved seats, and Jacob was hesitant to follow the usher down the aisle.

The casket was closed now, but his mother told him they would open it at the end of the service. Jacob hadn't seen his brother since Isaiah lay bloodied on the front lawn. He was definitely not interested in seeing the corpse again today. He didn't understand why anyone would want such a thing.

This was supposed to be a funeral, not a museum exhibit. Most of the people in the church never met Isaiah when he was alive, but they wanted to see what he looked like now that he was dead. Jacob thought this was a macabre custom. He made a mental note to request that his coffin be nailed shut at his funeral.

The service started much like regular church, except there were no praise and worship songs at the beginning and no announcements from some blue-haired biddy who couldn't read her own notes half the time. Their pastor was a middle-aged man named Jeremiah Taylor. Not surprisingly, he was in rare form for all of the new guests visiting his house of worship today. Pastor Taylor wore a brand new suit Jacob had never seen before, and he spoke with a fevered excitement that didn't match his usual monotone.

His sermon was titled "When I Get Home." Pastor Taylor explained that the evil and suffering people endured on earth would burden them no longer when they got home. He compared going home after a long day's work to going to your eternal home with Jesus.

He said your feet will hurt when you "get home" after work. Your back will be stiff, and you might not be able to sleep, knowing you have to do the same work again tomorrow.

But when you really "get home," all of your suffering is gone for good. He said the Lord called Isaiah to come home, and the trumpets played for him when the pearly gates flew open. The pastor said it may be sad to lose such a young child, but everyone should actually be happy for Isaiah, because going home is never a bad thing. Isaiah was in a much better place now. And when God called everyone else to come home, they could see him again and have a grand, old time.

For the first time in his life, Jacob understood every word of the pastor's sermon. He still didn't think it was cool for God to make a ten year old boy "come home," but it was nice to think of

BLOOD FOR ISAIAH

Isaiah walking through the gates of heaven, with angels playing their trumpets on either side of him. Jacob didn't know if any of that really happened, but it was a vision he didn't mind holding on to.

Towards the end of the service, the pastor invited several people to come forward and eulogize Isaiah. Among touching words from Aunt Pam and Uncle Jimmy, Jacob was surprised to see the mayor, the chief of police and some guy named Al Sharpton take the podium. These men didn't know Isaiah personally, so they spoke mainly about the many black-on-black murders in the city and how the community should come together to build a brighter tomorrow.

The service concluded with the viewing of the body. Jacob thought this would be the hardest part, but it wasn't so bad. The people at the funeral home did an excellent job preparing Isaiah's body for the gawkers. They taped over the hole in his head and applied a layer of make-up that matched Isaiah's skin tone. Jacob guessed their work was similar to the taping and bedding process homeowners use to repair a hole in the wall.

Unless you'd seen the wound beforehand, you wouldn't be able to tell where the bullet entered Isaiah's skull. Jacob and Tammy knew what to look for, but everyone else said Isaiah looked really good. A few people, Mr. Al Sharpton included, stopped to hold Tammy's hand and tell her Isaiah was, "Such a handsome young man."

Jacob expected his mother to scream or maybe even pass out when she saw Isaiah lying on the plush coffin fabric, but Tammy maintained her composure throughout the day. Jacob had no idea she was such a strong woman. He thought his mom had as much poise as Coretta Scott King or Betty Shabazz or even Jacqueline Kennedy.

After their business at the church house, everyone piled into their vehicles and lined up for a procession to the cemetery. The hearse carrying Isaiah's coffin was first in line. The limousine with Jacob and his mom and a few privileged others followed close behind.

Jacob had all but forgotten about his uncle until they got to the gravesite, and he saw the older man watching him throughout the pastor's final prayer. The sight of Uncle Myron made Jacob's heart stop beating altogether for a few seconds. He understood

118

that the time had come to back up his bravado, but he looked away from his uncle and watched the pastor instead. Tammy held Jacob's hand tightly as guests approached Isaiah's casket and dropped flowers on top.

Uncle Myron tried to make his move when they lowered the coffin into the earth and the crowd began to disperse, but Tammy continued to cling to her son, and Jacob made no attempts to break away from her.

After the funeral, most of the guests returned to the church for a home cooked meal provided for the bereaved family. Jacob separated from his mother briefly to use the bathroom, and it was then that Myron initiated an encounter. Jacob exited the restroom and found his uncle standing in the doorway, effectively blocking the hallway.

"Hey," the older man said. "You doing alright, boy?"

Uncle Myron was a short, charcoal-colored brother with long, jet black hair and a wide nose that seemed to stretch from cheekbone to cheekbone. He had quick eyes that saw everything around him without looking around at all. He was one of those rare breeds of men who looked like a tough guy without impressive height or excessive brawn.

Jacob's palms were sweaty, and his mouth was bone dry, but he nodded.

"Yes. Yes, sir."

"Give your uncle a hug," Myron said.

Jacob was confused, but he stepped forward for an uncomfortable embrace. He stretched his arms around his uncle, but Myron did not return the hug. Instead he used their closeness to conceal a move that went too smoothly to be a first time thing. Uncle Myron transferred something hard and heavy to Jacob's inner coat pocket. The weight of the object pulled down on Jacob's sports coat, making it feel all of a sudden cumbersome and ill-fitting.

Jacob knew he would be exposed the next time his mom smothered him with affection, but it was too late to change his mind. The deal was done. Uncle Myron backed away with a blank expression, and just like that thirteen-year-old Jacob was in possession of his very own firearm. His chest knocked against the heavy piece. Beads of sweat sprouted on his forehead.

"I'll give you a call later," Myron said and gave Jacob a hearty slap on the shoulder. Jacob's knees buckled under the force of his uncle's big hand. Myron regarded him queerly. "You alright? If you changed your mind, tell me now."

Jacob shook his head. "I haven't." His voice missed a note, and he sounded like a 3rd grader. He cleared his throat. "I haven't changed my mind."

"Good," Uncle Myron said, staring deeply into his eyes. "Don't forget why you're doing this."

Jacob nodded, knowing he would never forget his little brother's death. He would not forget the deep hole they placed Isaiah in, and he wouldn't forget the backhoe that waited thirty feet away to fill the grave with dirt again. Jacob didn't have any Bible verses memorized, but he would always remember Pastor Taylor's words as they bid their final adieus to an innocent little boy who had to go home much too soon.

*So now we commit his body to its eternal resting place. Earth to earth, ashes to ashes and dust to dust... Amen.*

● ● ● ● ● ●

At three o'clock that afternoon, Dino only had two cans left from the twelve pack of Colt 45 Charlotte brought him the previous evening. Generally Dino hated malt liquor. But when you needed something to *take you there* in a short amount of time, and you were also short on cash, malt liquor was the perfect vice.

The only downside to chugging so much of the poison was the nausea that ensued. But Dino threw up so much in the past few days, he'd grown accustomed to the smell of porcelain and Tidy Bowl. He didn't mind the toilet water splashing back into his face, and he didn't care about the look Charlotte fixed on him whenever he staggered out of the bathroom.

She knew he was sick. And it wasn't just his face – although the wound on his cheek had become quite disgusting over the past five days.

By now Dino was past the point of lying to himself about what may or may not be going on inside the hole in his head. His wound didn't bleed much nowadays, but he couldn't go without a bandage because there was thick pus leaking from it constantly. The swelling had deteriorated enough for Dino to fully open his right eye, but the hole wasn't closing up like it was supposed to. It remained wide open and stinky, like an old witch's vagina.

And it looked different every time Dino took the gauze off. Usually the wound ranged in color, from maroon to black to dead tissue gray. The pus that leaked out was generally solid white, but sometimes it was bright green or reddish green. The swelling around the gash came in almost every color of the rainbow. The pain was constant. Whenever Dino rolled to that side of his face while sleeping, he would awaken with a ferocious howl, his face and chest glistening with sweat.

Charlotte warned him that by the time he manned up and went to the hospital, it would be too late. The doctor would tell him he had gangrene, and all of that dead skin and tissue would have to come off. They would hack up his face and leave him looking like a burn victim; one half of his head normal and the other half sucked in, all the way to the bone.

Dino was physically sick from the infection in his head, but he was also mentally sick because of his dwindling options, his solitude, and a heavy burden of guilt that sat like a boulder on his shoulders and threatened to smother him in quicksand. Every day Dino remained at Charlotte's house, he sank deeper into his pit of despair. Today Channel Six upped the ante by showing footage of Isaiah Spencer's funeral on the afternoon news.

Dino leaned back on the sofa with his eyes transfixed on the television, almost in a stupor. He brought a beer can to his lips and tilted it up. Only a half inch of backwash fell into his mouth, but it was cooler than his tongue. He swallowed it down gratefully. He dropped the can to the floor, where it joined the other eight cans Dino had emptied since he woke up at ten.

Someone inserted a key into the front door. Dino didn't rise from his seat or even look back to see who it was. He'd come to understand that he wasn't in control of his destiny anymore. If it was time for him to die or go to jail, then so be it. But it was Charlotte who walked through the door, rather than someone who meant him harm.

"Hey," he said when she came into the living room. "You get off early?"

Instead of answering, Charlotte dropped her purse on the couch and laid her sleeping baby next to it. She took a deep breath and blew it out very slowly. She looked around her disheveled

121

living room. She looked at Dino, looked at what he was watching on television, checked out his pile of beer cans, and then met Dino's eyes again.

It was clear she already had a hard day at work. Dino knew coming home to him made it that much worse. But he didn't give a damn about her problems. It wasn't like everyone on TV was calling *her* the scum of the earth.

"This has been the longest two days I've *ever* seen," Charlotte commented.

Dino looked at her and then intentionally rolled his eyes back to the television. Charlotte went and stood in front of it. When Dino still wouldn't make eye contact, she reached back and turned the TV off. Dino snatched up the remote, but it fell between the sofa cushions. Charlotte put her hands on her hips, daring him to dig for it.

"I don't wanna argue," he told her.

"I don't either," she said. "I just want to know why you're still in my house."

Charlotte wore tight blue jeans with her red and blue Camp Cuties tee-shirt. Charlotte's ultimate dream was to become a registered nurse, but she had to put her ambitions on hold when she got pregnant with Crystal. She took a job at a daycare center, mainly because they allowed her to bring her baby to work.

"Why you giving me a hard time?" Dino asked. The heroin and malt liquor were playing kickball in his belly. He feared he would throw up again at any minute.

"I said you could stay here *two days*," Charlotte reminded him. "It's been *five days*, Dino. You not doing nothing but getting high and drunk, eating up all my food."

"I hardly eat shit," Dino said. "I probably ate two plates since I been here." That wasn't the exact truth, but it was closer than Charlotte's statement.

"Dino, you're going to *die*," she said frankly. "Your face is..." She shook her head and scrunched up her face. "...*Nasty*. One day I'm going to come home from work and find you dead in here."

"So what if you do?" Dino asked. "What's it to you?"

"I don't want no *dead fugitive* in my house."

"You said you didn't want no trouble over here," Dino reminded her. "And I haven't brought none. You said they were going to come over here looking for me, but nobody came. Now you talking about you don't want me to *die* over here? What's the real problem, girl? I ain't hurting you, and you know I ain't hardly ate shit."

Charlotte lowered her gaze and the tone of her voice. "You know what the problem is, Dino."

"No, I don't. Why don't you tell me?"

"You already know."

"No, you tell me," Dino said. "You been yelling at me for a week. Don't get tight-lipped now."

"You killed that boy."

Dino shook his head and sighed loudly. "You really believe that shit, don't you?"

Charlotte met his eyes and nodded. "Dino, you *know* you killed that boy. Why don't you tell the truth?"

He watched her closely. A fat tear rolled down Charlotte's cheek.

"I told you I didn't do it."

"Yes, you did," Charlotte said. "You said they was gonna change the story, but they haven't. Whatever tests they had to do are done now. That boy is in the ground, and they still say the one who got shot in the face is the one who killed him."

"If you really believed that shit, you would've called the police."

"I did," Charlotte said.

Dino's heart sank all the way down to his gut. He hadn't been fearful of the police since he left Tish's house, but all of that apprehension came back in a flash. Was Charlotte setting him up? The police could be waiting outside right now, hoping she could get a confession out of him. Was she wearing a wire?

"You lying."

Charlotte shook her head and sniffled. "I did call. But, I, I couldn't talk to them. I hung up without saying nothing."

Dino exhaled his pent up breath. "Listen, girl–"

A telephone rang.

It wasn't the house phone, and it didn't sound like the ringtone Charlotte had on her cellphone, either. They both looked around curiously.

"That's your phone?" Dino asked on the third ring.

"No," Charlotte said. "My phone don't even ring like that. Ain't that your phone?"

"I don't have no phone."

"Yes, you do. You had one when you first came over here."

Dino racked his memory, but his brain was mostly mush. He vaguely remembered something about a cellphone. And then it hit him. *Kevin.* He shot to his feet and ignored the havoc this caused his equilibrium. He ran into the bedroom and found Kevin's cellphone under a pile of clothes next to the bed. It wasn't ringing anymore. Dino hit the MISSED CALLS button and called the last number. Kevin answered after just one ring.

"Hello?"

"Who dis?"

"This Kevin."

Dino looked back and saw that Charlotte had followed him into the bedroom. He wanted to tell her to go somewhere and mind her fucking business, but she'd really call the police on him then.

"What's up?" Dino asked his homey.

"Got some news," Kevin said. "HB got arrested today. He got caught at the hospital."

Dino chuckled. He knew the hospitals were on high alert. He prided himself for having more endurance than HB. "What he go to the hospital for?"

"He got shot in that *incident*," Kevin reported. "Him and his brother. Pooky got shot in the arm. HB took one in the stomach."

"Why they just now going to the doctor?" Dino asked.

"Pooky didn't go," Kevin said. "Just HB. Word is they hired they own doctor after that shit happened. It was some retired cat from Oklahoma. You remember that police chase, about four years ago? They finally caught that dude in a red Porsche, and it turned out it was a doctor – high on crack?"

Dino did remember. "They hired that fool?"

"Yeah. He did good with Pooky," Kevin stated. "But HB got hit in the stomach, and it was too much work. The doctor had to cut HB open and take out some of his guts. He ended up fucking that shit up. You can't do that kind of shit in somebody's garage. HB tried to lay up for a while, to see if he would get better.

124

But he was fixing to die, so he had to bite the bullet and go to the hospital."

Dino grinned, remembering the fateful shootout. He thought he hit both brothers but wasn't sure until now. The thought of HB losing a few feet of intestines almost made up for the Isaiah mishap.

"They got his car, too?" Dino asked.

"Naw. He walked in."

"He talking?"

"I don't know," Kevin said. "I haven't heard nothing, if he is. Oh, but that bitch finally woke up, and she *is* talking."

Again Dino had to search his memory bank to remember the girl. "The one who got shot in the leg?"

"Yeah," Kevin said. "She told the police everything she knew about our spot and everybody who was there."

"She was in the house when that shit went down," Dino said. "She don't know shit."

"She don't know nothing about the *shooting*," Kevin confirmed. "But she do know about T Lowe's dope."

"That's his problem," Dino said coldly.

"We having another set meeting next week," Kevin said. "They want me to come get you."

"You told them where I'm at?"

"Naw, cuz. I'm the only one who know."

"Then come by yourself," Dino said. "What day?"

"I don't know yet. I'll call you tomorrow and let you know. I'm out big homey. Holler."

"Holler."

Kevin disconnected, and Dino did the same. He looked up at Charlotte with a big, crocodile grin. In a split second Dino's brain twisted the truth to fit his needs.

"See. I told you they was gon' figure out what happened. They just arrested one of them dudes I was in the shootout with. *He* the one who killed Isaiah. They'll charge him for it pretty soon. You'll see."

Charlotte's eyes grew big. "For real?"

"For real," Dino said. "Go turn on the news. They probably talking about him right now. I told you I didn't kill that boy." He stood and wrapped his arms around her waist. "You almost turned me in for *nothing*."

"I'm sorry," Charlotte said. Her relief was so strong, Dino could taste it. Her smile was wide and infectious.

"You ought to make it up to me," Dino said. He palmed her ass with both hands and pressed his hips against hers, grinning devilishly.

"What you want me to do?" Charlotte asked, but then her expression changed. She wrinkled her nose and pushed him away. "Ooh, boy. Your face *stinks*! Your breath do, too!"

"That ain't no way to get me in the mood," Dino said.

"I'm sorry," Charlotte said. "I want to. I mean, it's been a long time, but..." She shook her head, staring at his blood-stained bandage. "That thing is just too nasty, Dino. It stinks like, like something *dead*..."

"That's cool," he said and headed to the bathroom to change his dressings again.

"I'm sorry," Charlotte said. She tried to follow him, but Dino closed the door on her.

"It's alright," he called. And it really was. Dino had been on a strict diet of heroin and beer for the last 72 hours. He didn't have the energy to satisfy a woman, and he knew it.

Besides, HB was probably snitching on him at that very moment. Who could screw around at a time like that?

*Hoodlums find time for folly*
*Constant friction*
*And addiction*
*Boy/Girl spots get hit up, cuz, listen*
*To these demons*
*Street-level crime caucuses meeting*
*A little death, a few beat-downs*
*Blast the fleeing. Fuck retreating*
*Bustas bleeding. Ooh wee mayne!*
*Life is leaving, maggots feeding*
*Now we even*
*But ain't no peace in this game, dog*
*We scheming*

# CHAPTER TEN
## *THE BOYS IN BLUE*

Jacob was already awake and dressed when Russell Parks played his "*I Love Going to School*" song on Monday morning. He never paid much attention before, but as he listened, he realized there was a whole choir of kids singing, rather than just two or three. Some of the voices were male and others were female. Jacob strained his ear towards the radio, and he could've sworn he heard Isaiah's voice among them.

He knew that was not possible, but, then again, maybe it was. If Isaiah was important enough to get trumpets played for him as he walked into heaven, why couldn't he get his voice on some stupid song no one would notice? No one but Jacob, that is. Maybe that was Isaiah's way of saying he was doing fine in the spirit world. God worked in mysterious ways, or so they said.

Fifteen minutes later Jacob sat at the kitchen table with a bowl of Malt-O-Meal. His mother sat across from him cradling a cup of coffee. Tammy still had her nightgown on, but she didn't look sickly or sleep-deprived this morning. She wasn't back to her old self, but Jacob sensed she was getting there, slowly but surely.

"You don't want me to drive you?" she asked.

Jacob shook his head and downed a spoonful of hot cereal.

"How come?"

"I'm okay on the bus."

"And you're sure you don't want to take another day off school?" Tammy asked.

"There's nothing to do here," Jacob said. "Plus I don't want to get too far behind."

Tammy sensed what her son really wanted was to get back to a normal routine, so she didn't push it. "I'm not going back to work until tomorrow," she said with a yawn. "I always hated Mondays anyway."

"Are you still going to work two jobs now?" Jacob asked.

"What do you mean?"

"If, since it's just you and me, I was wondering if you still had to work all day."

Tammy hadn't thought about that. Her part-time job at the taquería only brought in a hundred and fifty bucks a week. Their monthly expenses wouldn't drop that much with Isaiah gone, but maybe that wasn't why Jacob asked.

"I would like to work only one job," Tammy mused. "I could switch to dayshift at the hospital, and then I'd be here when you get home from school."

"That would be cool," Jacob said. He stood and took his half-eaten bowl to the sink. "I'm finna go."

Tammy stood too. She gave him a hug when he turned back around. "Have a good day, baby. Are you sure you're okay?"

"I'm fine," Jacob said. He gave her a kiss on the cheek and bent to scoop his backpack from the floor.

"Are you taking that to school?" Tammy asked, knowing the big, red book bag belonged to Isaiah a week and a half ago.

"I'm going to have a lot of homework," Jacob predicted. "I'll need something to carry it in."

That was somewhat of a red flag, but Tammy considered this one minor. She'd been taking mental notes of all the odd things Jacob did that might indicate he needed to go to counseling. She knew he hated backpacks and often teased his little brother for carrying one. So was his change of heart a sign of his mental strain, or did he simply want to carry a piece of Isaiah to school with him?

Tammy chose the latter, and she didn't see anything wrong with it. When Jacob left for school, she planned to scour his and Isaiah's room for a few trinkets she could store away in a keepsake box. In particular, Tammy wanted Isaiah's hairbrush, his pocket dictionary and any of his old eye glasses she could find. She wasn't crazy for wanting these things, so Jacob wasn't crazy for wanting his dead brother's backpack.

"I'll see you later," she said as Jacob left the kitchen. "I love you."

"I love you, too," he called over his shoulder. Jacob checked his front pocket to make sure the string with the key was in there, and then he disappeared through the front door.

● ● ● ● ● ●

Outside, the first thing he saw was T Lowe's old dope spot. Jacob's eyes became transfixed on the house, and it was hard to look away. He wanted to cross the street and explore the property. He wanted to see if there was any blood or bullets left in the front yard or on the porch. He wanted to go inside the house to see if anyone was stupid enough to spray-paint their name on one of the walls.

Jacob couldn't go over there now because his mother was home, and she was probably standing in the doorway, watching until he was out of sight. He didn't turn back to check, because that would make him look suspicious. Jacob knew his mother was watching him closely as of late. He didn't want to do anything to draw more attention to himself.

He made a right turn on Campbell Street and walked the same route he and Isaiah walked together for years. On the right, he passed by the alleyway Isaiah begged him to take the day he was killed. The alley was nasty and overgrown with grass and shrubbery, but it wasn't all *that* bad. Jacob thought that if he managed to avoid the paint cans, he could make it through the alley without any permanent stains on his school clothes. He'd be scratched up a little, but those scratches would've healed by now.

Hindsight is 20/20 though, and Jacob wasn't overwhelmed with sorrow over what could've been. His mom thought he was overcome with guilt, but that was no longer the case. In truth, Jacob had already accepted the fact that life is an ugly and evil bitch. Life didn't slow down to cry over spilled milk, so neither did Jacob. All that mattered was what you learned from your experiences and what you did to make things better in the future.

Jacob learned a lot about suffering in the past twelve days, and he was almost ready to make things right. Deep down, Jacob feared he'd probably end up screwing things up worse, but that was out of his control at this point. When faced with the choice to do something for Isaiah or do nothing, Jacob chose to do something. The rest of the chips would fall where they may.

● ● ● ● ● ●

He expected a fair amount of sympathy once he got to school, and Jacob was not disappointed. He was, however, surprised by where some of this sympathy came from. The pity party started as soon as the bus slowed to pick him up from the corner of Crenshaw and Campbell. As he hopped up the stairs as usual, the hard-nosed driver grabbed hold of his arm before he could head for the back seats.

"Hey," Mr. Barnett said, "ain't you the one whose brother got killed?"

Jacob gave him a puzzled look and said, "Yeah."

"I didn't know his name," the bus driver said, "until I heard it on the news. I was watching the news, and I sat up in my bed and said, '*I know that boy.*'"

"Thanks," Jacob said. He tried to walk away, but the driver didn't let go of him.

"Your brother," he said, "he wasn't like nobody else ever been on my bus. I could tell he was smart, and I know he ain't never messed with nobody. He was the only one who would always speak to me. Every time he got off the bus, he'd yell, '*Bye, Mr. Barnett!*' I'm sho' gon' miss that."

Jacob sighed. The other kids were watching now. He felt embarrassed.

"I never said nothing back to him," Mr. Barnett said. "And I'm sorry for that. I want you to know I'm sorry."

Jacob was shocked to see tears in the bus driver's eyes.

*You had three whole years to respond to him, you old fart! Now he's dead, and you want to apologize to* **me**? *What the hell am I going to do with that?*

But Mr. Barnett was not the enemy, so Jacob kept cool. "Alright," he said. "Thank you."

The man let go of his arm, and Jacob quickly made his way to the back of the bus. All of the kids watched him, like he was important all of a sudden.

At school it was much of the same.

His first three teachers stopped him either before or after class to tell him how sorry they were for his loss. None of them had met his little brother, but from what they saw on the news, Isaiah sounded like a perfect angel.

"Don't worry about the assignments you missed," Jacob's math teacher told him. "I'll let you know which chapters we went through, and I'll give you the worksheets so you can practice at home. But you don't have to turn them in. If you need some help after school or at lunchtime, just let me know. I'll stay late for you. Whatever you need..."

During passing period Jacob got another surprise when Camille Parker walked up to his locker. Jacob had a crush on Camille since they were in grade school. He never tried to talk to her, because her family had a lot more money than his. What could he offer a girl who got an actual allowance every week? The last time Jacob asked his mother for an allowance, Tammy told him, *"I'm* **allowing** *you to eat and sleep here for free, boy. Quit begging."*

"Hi," Camille said.

When Jacob met her eyes, his heart froze, and his brain froze too. "Huh, hey. How are... Hi."

"I'm sorry about your brother," Camille said. "I saw him on the news this weekend. I saw you, too. You were at his funeral, in a suit."

"My mom bought me that," Jacob said, and immediately hated himself for it. *My mommy bought it?* Jeez, why the hell did he say that?

"I was so sad," Camille went on. "I wrote you a letter last night. But then I read it and..." She blushed. "I can't give it to you."

Jacob's jaw dropped. "Wuh, why not?"

"It's silly," she said. "I started off talking about one thing, but then I ended up talking about something else."

Without warning, Jacob started to get an erection – right in the middle of the hall. He held a book over his lap. "Can, can I still have it?"

Camille reached into her folder and pulled it out right away. It was clear she meant to give it to him all along.

Jacob took the letter and saw that it was folded four or more times, in a tight square. On one side there was a drawing of a heart with what looked like an arrow poking through it.

"I gotta go," Camille said and took off in embarrassment.

Jacob slammed his locker closed and headed straight for the bathroom. He stood in one of the stalls wondering where his erection came from and what he could do to make it go away. He read Camille's note while he waited. That didn't help his boner problem at all.

● ● ● ● ● ●

By lunchtime Jacob decided that he was having a great day. He would never admit this, and he'd fight anyone who accused him of such, but it was hard not to enjoy the perks of sympathy at school. All of Jacob's teachers and peers were nicer to him than they had ever been. The love letter from Camille was a super-duper bonus.

Jacob might have gone home that day with a big smile on his face if his friend Harold didn't stop by his table and put things back into perspective.

Jacob and Harold had been buddies since the second grade. Back then people called him *Fat Harold* because of his size and propensity to eat a whole box of Little Debbie's in one sitting. Harold used to slather butter on his honey buns before popping them in the microwave.

But two summers ago Harold's parents got a divorce, and he went to live with his tougher-than-leather father. Harold Senior was appalled by his son's eating habits, and he put an end to the gluttony right away.

The next fall Harold returned to school with a flat stomach and no chubby cheeks. Jacob teased him, saying his father must've beaten the weight off of him. Harold laughed, but later he confided that wasn't far from the truth.

Harold took a seat across from Jacob and peered into the paper sack lunch his dad made for him.

"What you got?" Jacob asked.

"Corn on the cob," Harold said. "Some raisins. A turkey sandwich with no cheese, wheat bread. Some apple juice."

Jacob looked down at his school-provided sloppy Joe lunch and snickered. "I thought you wasn't on a diet no more."

"It's not a diet," Harold corrected. "It's a way of life. Most diets fail because people think they only have to eat right for a little while."

"You sound like an infomercial," Jacob informed him.

"You try living with a nutritionist," Harold said, then, "Hey, I'm sorry about your brother. I feel real bad for you, man."

The smile fell from Jacob's lips.

"I wanted to go to the funeral," Harold said, "but I had to go see my mom in Oklahoma on Saturday."

"It's alright," Jacob said. "You didn't know Isaiah anyway."

"Yeah, but I wanted to be there for you, man. I can't believe they had a shootout on your street. How you taking it? I would still be crying, if that was my little brother."

"Crying don't solve nothing," Jacob said. He looked down at his sloppy Joe, and his stomach churned unpleasantly. He pushed the tray away.

"I heard they caught somebody," Harold said.

"They did," Jacob confirmed. "But it wasn't the one who killed my brother."

"How you know?"

"Because I saw the man they arrested on TV last night. He was bald-headed. He didn't get shot in the face. The one who got shot in the face is the one who killed my brother."

"I hope they get him," Harold said. "Whoever he is, he deserves to pay for that."

"He is gonna pay," Jacob assured him. "If the police don't find him, I'll make him pay."

Harold knitted his eyebrows. "What you mean?"

Jacob pulled his backpack onto the table and patted it. "I got something that will make him pay."

Harold looked even more confused. "Something like what?"

Jacob turned the front of the bag towards his friend and unzipped it.

Harold still couldn't see. He had to lift the flap and lean in closer. When he saw what it was, Harold snatched his hand back as if something bit him. His eyes grew as big as quarters.

"Wh–"

Jacob put a finger to his mouth and nodded.

"Wh, what's that for?" Harold was more spooked than Jacob had ever seen him.

"It's mine," Jacob said. "My uncle gave it to me."

Harold looked around frantically. "What are you doing with it *here*?"

"I need to have it wherever I go," Jacob explained. "I might see the one who killed my brother. I have to be ready."

Harold thought he was in an episode of the Twilight Zone. "Jacob, you can't bring that to school! You should–" He leaned closer and lowered his voice. "You shouldn't even have it, man! What's wrong with you? Do you want to go to *jail*? You're going to get expelled!"

"No I'm not, because nobody knows I have it except for you."

Harold put both hands to his head and rubbed his temples. "Oh my God, man. I can't believe this."

"Chill out." Jacob zipped his bag closed and returned it to the floor.

"Are you going to shoot somebody?" Harold asked.

"No," Jacob said. "I don't think so."

"You don't *think* so?" Harold shook his head. "Man, this is crazy. It's like, not even real."

"Just forget about it." Now Jacob's heart was thundering as well. He felt like he had to tell *someone*, but Harold was clearly not the right choice.

"I can't forget about it," Harold said. "And I'm not a good liar, man. If somebody asks me about it, I'll–"

"No one's going to ask you about it, because you're the only who knows about it. What are you going to do, tell on me?"

"No," Harold said. "I'm not. But you can't bring that thing to school no more, Jacob. I mean, I know some bad stuff is happening, but that's not going to make it better. Guns only make things worse."

"*Shut up*! Be quiet, man."

Harold looked around and swallowed a mouthful of spit. "Please don't bring that to school no more, Jacob. I'm scared to death, just thinking about it. You shouldn't have it at all. Give it back to your uncle."

"Alright," Jacob lied. "I'll give it back to him."

"*Today*," Harold urged. "Give it back *today*."

"Alright," Jacob said. "I promise. Now promise me you won't tell nobody."

"I won't," Harold said. "But you need to leave it in your locker for the rest of the day. It might go off and kill somebody."

Jacob wanted to correct his friend's naïveté. Everyone knew that guns don't kill people; people kill people. Jacob talked to his uncle the day after Isaiah's funeral. Myron explained that you first had to put bullets in the clip, insert the clip, cock the gun and take the safety off. Lastly you point and shoot at what you wanted dead. A gun couldn't do all of that by itself.

"Alright," he said. "I'll leave it in the locker and give it back to my uncle today. Now promise you won't tell nobody."

"I promise," Harold said. He calmed down a little and wiped the sweat from his brow. "Man, I think I lost another pound just then; I'm shaking so hard. Were you really thinking about shooting somebody?"

"No. I just wanted to show it to you."

"But you said you were going to make somebody pay, for killing Isaiah..."

"I was just talking," Jacob said. "You know I'm not going to shoot nobody. I wanted to show it to you, that's all."

"Well, don't take this the wrong way, but I don't want to see that," Harold said. "I wouldn't want to see it at your house, and I definitely don't want to see it here at school."

"I'm sorry I scared you," Jacob said. "I don't know why I took it from my uncle in the first place. I don't know what I was thinking."

● ● ● ● ● ●

Jacob was on pins and needles for the rest of the school day. He knew Harold would betray him. He expected to get called down to the principal's office at any moment. There would be cops waiting there to search his backpack. But thankfully that call never came.

When the final bell rang at three o'clock, Jacob rushed to his locker and let out a huge sigh of relief when he felt his gun inside Isaiah's book bag. Give it back to his uncle? That was ludicrous. Not only would Jacob lose his chance to avenge Isaiah, but his uncle would forever think he was some punk little kid.

Harold was a good guy, but he didn't understand the way the world worked like Jacob did. Harold never saw his brother's blood splattered on his front lawn, so he couldn't say what was right or wrong for someone who had.

But Jacob did learn that he had to be a lot more careful in the future. Today's slip up could've cost him everything. But so far it looked like he would make it home with no repercussions.

When he got outside, Jacob headed straight for his bus, rather than mingle with his classmates who turned the parking lot into somewhat of a party scene each afternoon. Halfway to his destination, Jacob saw a group of kids hanging out on the curb. They were wearing all blue. Initially the sight of them made Jacob's muscles tense up. But as he got closer, Jacob saw that the three boys were classmates of his.

There was a strict dress code at the middle school, which required students to wear either blue or khaki pants with a blue or white golf shirt up top. The boys in question pushed the limits of the dress code by wearing blue pants with a blue shirt *every day*. They were the wannabe gangsters at William Joseph Middle School. Jacob never paid them much attention before, but he was pretty sure they wore blue to signify they were Crips.

In truth, the boys in blue were not affiliated with a real gang. Jacob knew they were old friends from the same street, and the three of them was the full extent of their posse. But it still angered Jacob to see them standing there, flaunting their colors.

With Isaiah's backpack slung over his shoulder, Jacob approached the wannabe Crips. He walked right through the middle of their huddle without so much as an *Excuse me*. He knew they would not let the slight go unnoticed.

"Say, watch out, fool!"

Jacob turned and stared at the one who spoke. It was a skinny kid with big eyes and big lips. He was the tallest of the crew.

"What you say?" Jacob taunted.

"I say watch out, cuz," Big Lips repeated.

The word *cuz* made a sneer grow in the corner of Jacob's mouth. He wasn't an expert on gangs by any means, but he knew "cuz" was exclusive lingo for Crips. Crips also referred to each other as "kinfolk," which furthered the illusion that they were *family*, rather than a band of miscellaneous misfits.

"*Cuz*?" Jacob cocked his head. "What you supposed to be, a Crip or something?"

Big Lips' friends stepped forward and stood on either side of him. One was short and stocky. He was fair-skinned, a mix of black and Hispanic, and he sported a beautiful curly afro. The third kid was fat and dopey-looking, but Jacob would never underestimate anyone who outweighed him by thirty pounds or more. All of the fat kids Jacob knew were effective wrestlers, especially in middle school, where everyone's boxing skills were subpar.

"Yeah, we Crips," Big Lips said. "Hardeman." He did something with his hands that Jacob didn't understand.

By then a small crowd, lured by a 6th sense only school kids possessed, had gathered to see if the wannabes had found their latest victim.

Jacob's face grew warm. He knew everything was up to him. He initiated this encounter. He could either walk away or see it through. The interesting thing was Jacob knew these kids were not gangbangers. They went to school and passed most of their classes. They didn't sell drugs or even smoke marijuana behind the gym at lunchtime.

Jacob lived across the street from *real* Crips for more than six months. The wannabes at his school were not on that level. But then again, they represented something Jacob could not turn a blind eye to. A Crip is a Crip, and they were all **The Enemy**, as far as he was concerned.

"Where yo bandanas at?" he asked.

"What?" Big Lips said.

"If you a Crip, where's your bandana?" Jacob repeated.

"Fool, we can't wear that at school," Curly Head said.

"Where're your tats then?" Jacob asked.

"What?" Big Lips said.

"*Tattoos*," Jacob said. "Y'all stupid; don't even know what tats are."

"We do know what tats are," Fat Boy said. He took a step forward.

Jacob held his ground. "I ain't scared of y'all." That was a lie, but the bullies didn't know that. And Jacob could see that it freaked them out a little. Rather than attack, they were hesitant.

There was a zero tolerance policy for fights at William Joseph. Whoever threw a punch would have to spend four weeks at an alternative school. Jacob would take that punishment in his misguided attempt to avenge Isaiah. But the wannabes weren't so sure.

Luckily someone came along and gave them a way out.

"Leave him alone. His brother just got killed."

Jacob looked around and saw Camille standing beside him. She looked worried and angered that the Crips would pick on someone who was in such a fragile emotional state.

"Oh, you the one." Big Lips took a step back. "My bad, cuz. I didn't know that was you. Sorry about your brother. I saw that shit on the news."

The other two wannabes backed off as well. Jacob started walking again, but he wasn't satisfied. His adrenaline was flowing. Plus his testosterone kicked in, now that a girl he liked was on the scene.

"Y'all some punks," he said as a parting shot.

"What?"

Jacob made it to his bus, but he turned back to face them. "I said y'all some punks."

Fat Boy came after him, but Big Lips grabbed his arm.

"Leave that fool alone, cuz. He just trying to start some mess."

Jacob stared them down individually before climbing onto his bus. He went all the way to the backseat, so he could glare at the Crips some more before the bus took off.

Among the crowd of students gathered in the parking lot, Jacob was surprised to see his best friend. Harold didn't ride the bus home. His dad should've picked him up already, but that wasn't the problem. The problem was Harold saw what Jacob did.

The shock was written all over his face. Harold shook his head dolefully, his eyes locked on Jacob's.

His expression made guilt fall heavily onto Jacob's shoulders, and he lowered his head in shame. What was he doing? His mother taught him better than this. Jacob wondered if he was going crazy. He wasn't the best kid in the world before Isaiah's death, but at least there was some civility. If he fought, it was always in self-defense or in defense of Isaiah. And the idea of bringing a gun to school was ludicrous.

The only thing Jacob knew for sure was that he wanted Isaiah to come back alive. He wanted to give up his window seat, so Isaiah could stare out at the world while Jacob protected him from any danger coming down the aisle.

His chest tightened. Jacob squeezed his eyes closed and tried to shut out all of the confusion and ignorance in the world. He wasn't aware that he was crying until he felt the tears snake down his face.

● ● ● ● ● ●

Dino sat on the love seat this time, because that was the best seat in the house, and there was no denying he was the main attraction. If not for Dino, the Sicc Crips wouldn't have called a set meeting that night. And, according to T Lowe, there would be twenty-three members of their gang in attendance instead of fifteen – again, if not for Dino. Dino didn't think anything he did could effectively cut their gang by a third, but he sat back and listened because T Lowe held center stage, and T Lowe loved to hear himself talk.

"It's fucked up, cuz. You need to take responsibility for this."

The noticeable absences from the meeting were Tricky, Papa, Demarcus, Shaun, Bolo, Peanut, Pacman and Detroit. These members couldn't attend because they were currently locked up in the main jailhouse downtown. Peanut couldn't come because he was dead and in full decomposition mode by then.

Dino understood that he was *somewhat* responsible for his gang's string of bad luck, but he refused to accept the full burden. He already had enough guilt from the dead boy. Plus he plain old didn't like T Lowe.

"*You* say it's my fault," Dino countered. "But they all got arrested in one of *your* dope houses."

T Lowe paced the floor like a grumpy silverback. He wore blue Dickey pants with a blue Dickeys work shirt. A blue handkerchief hung from his back pocket, and the shoestrings in his black Nikes were blue. It was time to stand up as the leader of the Sicc. T Lowe had to make it understood that he wasn't some rich pretty boy. He was a full-fledged gangster, like everyone else. He was a Blood-killing Crip, down for the cause, true blue.

"I'm sick of you pushing this back on me," T Lowe spat. "The popos wasn't fucking with us like this until *you* got into that shit with HB. You got our name on the news, and you got our people arrested. Our whole set's coming down, and you wanna hide somewhere and let us take the fall for it. But that ain't happening, nigga. You ain't hanging us out to dry."

T Lowe finished his spiel with a finger in Dino's face, and that was one thing Dino would never tolerate – not from his mama, not from his teachers and not from his supposed leader.

He shot to his feet and delivered a forceful two-handed shove to T Lowe's chest. But T Lowe was prepared for such aggression. He took one step back and stood his ground. His hands remained at his sides. He rolled his shoulders like a boxer and licked his lips.

"What's up, Dino? You wanna go?"

Every muscle in Dino's body tensed. Adrenaline flooded his system, and the house was bathed in a flash of blood red. No one in the room moved to intervene. Dino knew he could take T Lowe. It would be a hard fight. T Lowe was bound to be healthier at the moment. And if he hit Dino on his bad cheek, there would be an eruption of pain like no other. But still, Dino could take him.

If not for Isaiah Spencer, he would've given it a shot.

Dino portrayed himself as a maniacal killer, the proverbial loose cannon, but in truth he had a lot more cunning than his homeboys recognized. Dino did learn from his mistakes. Isaiah's death taught him to look before he leapt.

If he attacked T Lowe, pummeled him to the floor, the gang would watch, and he'd have the coup he envisioned. But Dino would still have to return to hiding afterwards. And it's impossible to maintain a coup if you're not physically present.

Plus T Lowe was right about everything he said that night: While Dino lay around Charlotte's house drinking and snorting and watching old re-runs of *What's Happening*, the police were conducting a massive manhunt for Isaiah's killer. They had only one lead, which they passed on to the city's gang unit. The task force harassed every Sicc Crip they could find. They arrested any of them who had a stray warrant in the system. They raided three of T Lowe's dope houses and made multiple arrests at each location.

The police confiscated large amounts of cocaine and threatened Dino's brethren with lengthy prison sentences. T Lowe had to shut down most of his other operations because they were suddenly under obvious surveillance. The gang took a devastating loss of income.

The police were under such pressure from the mayor, they were willing to cut deals with the very men they persecuted: *We'll drop the traffic warrants. We'll drop the gun charge. We'll make this a misdemeanor. We'll even leave the crack houses alone. Just give up the shooter; the guy who got shot in the face. We want the one who killed Isaiah.*

Dino took a deep breath and let the anger flow from him. The only logical option was to turn himself in. If not for a little thing called *prison*, he might have done it. But Dino couldn't go to prison. Just the thought of those concrete walls made his skin crawl. There were men in prison who had been behind bars for thirty years and still had forty more to go. They wouldn't respect the work Dino put in on the streets of Overbrook Meadows, and they wouldn't respect some stupid gang they never heard of called the *Sicc Crips*.

The men in prison would only care about the ten-year-old boy who got killed. They would make Dino's life a living hell. They would beat and intimidate him year after year. There would be no refuge behind those cold, metal cages. Everyone would hear Dino's screams in the dead of night, but no one would help him. Even the guards would turn a blind eye, because no one likes a child killer. Dino knew that because he didn't even like himself.

"I think we should lay low," he said calmly. "The only reason they fucking with y'all is 'cause y'all still out in the streets; doing the same thing as usual."

"What we supposed to do?" T Lowe asked. "Run to our mama's house? Hide under the bed? Get out of town like you?"

"It's hot," Dino said. "That's what you supposed to do when it's hot; you gotta lay low."

"Naw." T Lowe shook his head. "We ain't hot. *You* hot, cuz."

"And you only worried about your money, nigga." It was the only card Dino still had left to play, so he threw all of his chips in. "The only reason the homies got popped is because you left all those houses open. Cuz, you knew it was hot, but you left yo niggas in the open like that. That ain't smart, nigga. You need to take some responsibility."

T Lowe shook his head but was not angered by these words. "I'm not finna have this same argument with you, Dino. I'm not the only one getting paid. Everybody's getting paper. I worked hard to put this shit together."

"Yeah, and I did too," Dino said. "But I did my shit in the streets, cuz. In the *gutter*. You did yo shit behind a triple beam."

"You think your work's more important than mine?"

It was clear Dino did, but diplomacy was the only way to resolve this.

"Let's put it to the homies," he said and once again left his fate up to the crew. He half turned to face them.

After a few moments, T Lowe did the same.

"Who want this nigga to turn hisself in?" T Lowe asked.

Most of the gang frowned or looked around at their comrades. A few of them stared coldly into Dino's eyes. Stephon was the first to speak up.

"I think you should turn yourself in."

Dino wanted to rush forward and throttle the hell out of him, but he subdued the urge. Violence would only show his weakness, which was the last thing he wanted to display at a time like this.

"I do too," Scooter said.

"That's how you feel?" Dino asked him. He was surprised by this vote, because he and Scooter had a lot of history. When Scooter got jumped by a couple of Bloods who lived next door to his grandmother, it was Dino he called for backup. Without a weapon, Dino bloodied both of those slobs, and Scooter never had a problem with them again.

Scooter lowered his gaze. "I love you, cuz," he said. "But this shit's getting too deep. You gon' take all us down with you, D."

Dino scanned the rest of the group. "Who else?" he asked. "Who else want me gone?"

"I don't want you *gone*," Cooper said. "But I don't see no way around it. You do need to turn yourself in. Get the heat off the rest of us."

Dino nodded. "Who else?" On the outside he appeared calm, but beneath the skin his heart rate grew steadily. Who did these ungrateful niggas think they were? He would pull out his gun and murder every one of his dissenters before he allowed them to kick him out of the Sicc. He watched as one Crip after another urged Dino to sacrifice himself. But thankfully the bloodletting stopped at a number he could deal with.

"So, just six of y'all?" Dino asked.

"Don't forget me," T Lowe said.

Dino looked him in the eyes. "That's only seven."

"The rest of y'all have to vote," T Lowe said. "Ain't no abstaining on this one."

Dino had no idea what *abstaining* meant. He felt like T Lowe was trying to use his superior smarts as leverage.

"What about you, Mack?" T Lowe asked.

Mack shook his head. "I don't know, cuz."

"You got to vote," T Lowe said.

Mack sighed. "I guess I'm with Dino. I don't want my nigga to turn hisself in."

T Lowe pursed his lips and continued with the poll.

"Stevie?"

"I'm with Dino, too."

"Kevin?"

"I'm down with my nigga Dino."

"Head?"

"I can't tell that man to turn hisself in."

"So what's your vote?"

"I guess I'm sticking with Dino."

"Yellow Boy?"

"I vote for Dino."

"Rufus?"

"You know Dino my nigga."

143

"Bear?"

"We can lay low for a while. Shit won't be that bad."

With the vote at seven to seven, T Lowe's stress was starting to show. Dino tried his best to look bored with this foolishness.

"What about you, Calvin?"

Calvin folded his arms over his chest and looked from Dino to T Lowe and then at the worried faces of what was left of his gang. He brought a hand to his chin and rubbed his goatee.

"I ain't voting, man. This shit, this shit's crazy."

"You got to vote," T Lowe said.

"Go ahead," Dino said. "Make it official."

Calvin sighed. He stared into Dino's eyes, and his face grew dark. "You know, my mama asked me about that boy."

Dino nodded. Calvin was one of few Sicc Crips who had a supportive mother and father at home. Dino met Calvin's family a few times. His mother was one of the most caring women in the hood.

"She asked me if I knew who killed Isaiah," Calvin reported. "I told her I didn't. She knew I was lying, and she told me that if I *did* know who killed him, I should stay away from that person. She said whoever did that was going to hell, and anybody around him was going to reap the Lord's vengeance right along with him."

T Lowe nodded. He couldn't have put it more eloquently.

"But y'all know my big brother's locked up at the Stiles Unit," Calvin went on. "He write me letters all the time and tell me how bad that shit is; to be in the pen and have all those killers around you. He said prison is worse than you treat a dog. It's worse than a zoo. It's worse than anything a man can do to another man – outside of killing him – so I can't tell Dino to turn hisself in."

Calvin cleared his throat and pleaded with the boogeyman directly. "But you need to get it over with, D. You got to face what you did and ask God for forgiveness. You need to stop hiding behind your homies and getting us all fucked up. You need to turn yourself in, but I can't vote for you to go to prison. That's something you gotta decide for yourself."

Dino silently blew out a sigh of relief. T Lowe watched him, hoping Calvin's impassioned speech would cause some conviction.

But what T Lowe didn't understand was Dino no longer cared about his soul. He knew he was damned, and no prayer to God or Buddha or the prophet Muhammad was going to change that. If God was so awesome, He wouldn't have allowed Isaiah to get killed in the first place.

"Alright, so I guess that's it," Dino said to T Lowe. "You lost your vote, so quit trying to kick me out the Sicc."

"The homies in jail get a vote, too," T Lowe said.

"Well, when they get out, let me know," Dino said. "Kevin, gimme a ride, cuz."

Dino headed for the back door as Kevin slowly made it to his feet. Dino didn't wait for him because he had never been more eager to get away from his crew. He didn't think the vote would be that close. But he understood that T Lowe had a lot of time to turn the tide against their best soldier, who had become their biggest liability. Dino was hidden away all week with no chance to defend himself.

"Didn't you hear what this man said?" T Lowe called after him. "You trying to take us all to hell, right along with you."

Dino turned and sneered at his OG. He wanted to give a poignant and witty retort, but all he could manage was a lame joke.

"This ain't no Bible study, nigga. If you wanna preach, yo ass shoulda been a pastor."

# CHAPTER ELEVEN
## *RED FLAGS*

Jacob did not take his pistol to school the next morning.
It wasn't anything Harold said that changed his mind, although Harold's reaction to the gun had to be taken into consideration. Jacob now understood the seriousness of Uncle Myron's gift and the possible repercussions if he was to get caught with it. Getting kicked out of school was a major risk, but that was nothing compared to going to jail and having to look his mother in the eyes when she picked him up.

Tammy would want to know where he got the gun from, and Jacob didn't think he could lie to her if she really got in his face about it. Tammy would confront her brother when she learned the truth, and Uncle Myron would know that Jacob was a stupid little boy who went to school showing the gun off rather than using it for the task at hand.

But that last part was his biggest problem: Jacob had no idea how to go about the business at hand. He had a vague idea of what he wanted to do to avenge Isaiah, but the actual logistics of his plan were a total mystery.

His ultimate goal was to kill the Sicc Crip who got shot in the face. But if the whole city couldn't find that creep, how the hell was Jacob supposed to? An alternative was to kill another Sicc Crip, preferably the one the police described as the leader of the gang. But even this was daunting.

Jacob monitored T Lowe's old dope house for two weeks after Isaiah's murder. He was starting to believe that his mother was right about the Crips not coming back. Jacob was aware of other gangs in his neighborhood, but he didn't think any of them were *Sicc* Crips. But then again, he would have no way of knowing unless he walked right up to them and asked.

In truth, Jacob needed a lot more manpower if he truly wanted to kill a man. He needed someone with a car who could drive him around in search of his target. He needed someone who knew the streets well, so they could make a clean getaway after the attack. What Jacob really needed was for his uncle to come down from Denton and teach him the ways of murder.

But Tammy would blow a gasket if Jacob started to pal around with her dysfunctional sibling. Jacob couldn't even call his uncle without stirring up suspicion, because he'd have to ask his mom for the phone number.

He hopped off the school bus that morning with his plot for revenge still undetermined. Jacob spotted his best friend in the parking lot. Surprisingly Harold waited on him, rather than run the other way.

"Hey, man. What's up?"

"Nothing. What's up with *you*?" Harold asked, staring at the backpack Jacob had draped over one shoulder.

"I'm cool," Jacob said. "And you don't have to worry. I don't have it anymore. I gave it back to my uncle."

Harold nodded. He didn't look like he fully believed him, but he had no reason not to. Before Isaiah's death, Jacob didn't lie to his friend.

The boys entered the school together and headed for the auditorium, where they were required to wait until the first bell.

"I was thinking about what you said yesterday," Harold said, "and I guess I see why you felt that way; like you had to do something for your brother."

"There's nothing I can do," Jacob said. "I'm just a dumb kid."

Harold watched him and then said, "I, I wanted to ask you about what happened after school. When you got into it with those Crip dudes, was that for Isaiah?"

"Those weren't *Crips*," Jacob spat. "Those were some more dumb kids, just like me. They don't even know what it means to be in a real gang. If somebody started shooting at them, they'd piss their pants."

"Is that what you were thinking about doing?" Harold pressed.

147

"I wasn't thinking about nothing," Jacob said. "They was just standing there, and it pissed me off."

"Why? 'Cause they said they was Crips?"

"Man, who are you?" Jacob wanted to know, "my psychiatrist or something? Stop trying to figure me out, Harold. *I* don't know what's going on with me, so how am I supposed to explain it to you?"

"I didn't say–"

"Just forget it," Jacob warned.

"I wanna help you, man."

Jacob stopped in the middle of the hallway. "How can you help me, Harold? How?"

His friend shrugged. "I don't know. But I can't stop thinking about what happened with those guys yesterday. That was–"

"What happened yesterday was me being stupid," Jacob said. "I told you I don't know why I did it, so leave me alone about it, alright?"

Harold stared fretfully into his friend's eyes. "I think you need some help. I talked to my dad, and–"

"*You what?*" Jacob grabbed his friend's shoulders and pushed his back into the nearest locker. "What'd you tell your dad?"

"Let go of me."

Jacob did, but he didn't get out of Harold's face. "What'd you tell him? I told you not to tell *nobody!*"

"I didn't tell him about the, the thing," Harold said. "I just told him about your brother and what happened after school. I told him you never got in trouble before, and, and I was scared for you. That's all I said."

"You don't have to worry about me," Jacob said. "And neither does your pops. I'm doing just fine."

"Alright, man. Chill out."

Jacob snorted and turned quickly, heading back the way they came.

"Ain't you going to the auditorium?" Harold called.

Jacob didn't stop. A few moments later he was lost in a sea of students, most of them happy and laughing, all of them totally oblivious to how precious each day of their life was.

● ● ● ● ● ●

Jacob was sitting at his desk working on a suitable plan for murder when his second period teacher called his name. Jacob looked up at her lackadaisically.

"Hey," Mrs. Milligan said. "Are you with us today?"

"Yeah," Jacob said.

"I asked you about the Continental Congress," Mrs. Milligan informed him. "It's okay if you didn't finish your reading from last night, but it would be a good idea to pay attention in class. We're taking a test on Friday."

Jacob shrugged.

"Are, are you taking notes?" his teacher asked.

Jacob looked down at his notepad. There was an amateurish drawing of a gun, a tombstone and what was supposed to be the Sicc Crip's dope house. Jacob looked up at his teacher and closed his notebook.

"Yep," he said.

Mrs. Milligan was normally the nosey type. Jacob expected her to come to his desk and demand to see his drawings, but she just nodded.

"Okay," she said. "Well, try to pay attention for the rest of the period."

"Alright," Jacob told her.

Towards the end of class, Mrs. Milligan gave the students a few study questions to work on until the bell rang. Jacob didn't get too far into his assignment before the teacher interrupted him. She stopped by his desk, speaking softly.

"Jacob, could you step outside with me for a second?"

Jacob blew out a frustrated sigh and then got up and followed her into the hallway.

Mrs. Milligan was a tall woman with dark brown hair and a long, pointy nose. She had crows' feet in the corners of her eyes, but other than that she didn't look very old. She closed the door behind Jacob, so none of his peers would know what they were talking about.

"How's it going, sport?" she asked. She squeezed Jacob's shoulder encouragingly, but her touch had the opposite effect. She'd never touched Jacob before, and he didn't like that she was doing it now.

"I'm fine," he muttered.

"Have you had any trouble with school, since you got back?"

"No," Jacob said. "It's alright."

"So, you're, um, okay with being back?" she asked. "You don't feel like you should've taken more time off? It's understandable if you do."

"I'm fine," Jacob repeated. "Why you so worried about me? There's people in there who go to sleep every day. Just because I missed one question..."

Mrs. Milligan's eyes narrowed. "Well, uh, I guess it depends on their circumstances. Some of the students who fall asleep in class, I'll call their mother and find out they have to work at the family business when they get out of school.

"Sometimes students get sleepy if they had too much for breakfast. It just depends. But I'm not talking about them, Jacob. I'm worried about you right now. You're distracted – and that's totally understandable. If you weren't ready to come back to school yet–"

"I don't need everybody worrying about me," Jacob said. "I always pass my tests."

"This, this isn't about a test, Jacob."

"Can't you leave me alone?" he asked. "I wanna go back and do my work."

"Well, okay," Mrs. Milligan said. "I'm going to let you get back to your work. I was only..." She trailed off because Jacob walked around her and went back into the classroom.

● ● ● ● ● ●

Jacob knew he hadn't heard the last of Mrs. Milligan. He wasn't surprised when a hall monitor came to retrieve him from his next class. Jacob was, however, taken aback when his teacher instructed him to take his books with him.

Jacob caught up with the office assistant outside of the classroom and tried to squeeze some information out of her as they walked the deserted halls.

"Where am I going?"

"To Mr. Sweeney's office."

"That's the uh..."

"The counselor's office."

"What does he want to see me for?"

"I don't know."

"Why do I have to bring my books?"

"I don't know. You have to ask him yourself."

Mr. Sweeney was a medium-sized gentleman who always wore a suit to school, even though he wasn't required to do so. In his three years at William Joseph, Jacob never had any direct dealings with the man. He knew Mr. Sweeney helped students who were pregnant or crybabies, and that was reason enough to avoid him.

Jacob walked into his office, and Mr. Sweeney stood and shook his hand, like they were both adults.

"Hi, Jacob. Have a seat."

Jacob did as he was told.

"How you doing today?" Mr. Sweeney asked.

"I'm alright," Jacob said, glad he left his gun at home this morning. He already threw away the drawing he made in Mrs. Milligan's class. With neither of those things in his backpack, he didn't think there was anything Mr. Sweeney could do to hurt him.

"Do you know why I called you to my office?" the counselor asked. He wore a black suit today with a green shirt and a black tie. He had jet black hair that looked oily. He wore no moustache or beard.

Jacob shook his head. "No. I don't know what I did."

"I talked with your history teacher, Mrs. Milligan. She's worried that you may not feel good enough to be in school."

"I feel fine," Jacob stated.

"She said she tried to talk to you, and you were rude to her," Mr. Sweeney reported.

"I didn't want to talk to her," Jacob admitted.

Mr. Sweeney nodded. "How are things going, since your brother died? Have you talked to anyone about it?"

"What you mean?"

"Well, like your mother or father, for instance. Or maybe your grandmother or a counselor?"

Jacob realized he hadn't, but, "Yeah" was a better answer.

"You talked with a counselor?" Mr. Sweeney asked.

"No."

"That was a real hard thing to go through," Mr. Sweeney said. "I know you were there when your brother died. No one expects you to get over it easily or quickly. Could you tell me how you feel today, Jacob? Are you mad or angry? Are you feeling sad?"

Jacob didn't like any of those questions. "I wish people would quit asking me that."

"We're only asking because we care about you."

"Y'all don't have to care that much."

Mr. Sweeney leaned back in his chair and watched the boy for a few beats.

"Listen," he said. "You're being really defensive, and Mrs. Milligan says you've never been rude to her before. I think this is all normal, considering what you've been through. But I think it may get worse, if you don't let someone help you."

Jacob rolled his eyes.

"I think you should take a few more days off school," Mr. Sweeney suggested, "until you have time to meet with a counselor, someone more qualified than myself."

The smug expression fell from Jacob's face. "I don't want to talk to a counselor."

"I know you don't, Jacob. But it would be in your best interest. If you have too much *stuff* inside of your heart and your mind, it's not good to keep it bottled up."

"I want to go back to class," Jacob pleaded. "I'll be good. Don't kick me out of school."

Mr. Sweeney frowned. "I'm not kicking you out of school, Jacob."

"The teacher told me to bring my stuff."

"Don't you want to take more time off?"

Jacob shook his head. "No. I wanna stay in school. I'll be good. I promise."

The counselor was surprised to see tears in his eyes. "Okay. You can stay in school. But I'm going to call your mother. You need to see a grief counselor, Jacob. You have to. But that's not a bad thing. Try to keep an open mind..."

● ● ● ● ● ●

Jacob hoped the counselor was bluffing about calling his mother, but he saw Tammy waiting for him when he headed for his bus after school.  Jacob didn't think his behavior was that big of a deal – certainly not important enough for his mother to take off work.  He knew Mr. Sweeney blew everything out of proportion when he called her.

The first thing Jacob did was try to diffuse the situation.

"Hey, Mama.  I don't know why Mr. Sweeney was tripping. I don't need a counselor.  You didn't have to pick me up."

Tammy smiled weakly and took her son's hand.  She squeezed it tightly and drew him close for a hug.

"It's okay," she said and kissed him softly on the forehead. "It's alright, baby."

· · · · · ·

Tammy didn't try to strike up a conversation during the drive home.  Depending on which direction their talk went, she might find herself crying again, and she didn't want to have to fight tears and traffic at the same time.

When they got home, Jacob said he had to get started on his homework.  Tammy told him to go ahead.  She took a shower and then made an early supper while he worked.

She cooked for her small family every day, but usually she stored the food in Tupperware containers, so the boys could heat it up while she was at work.  It felt good to prepare a big meal that would be eaten right away, so Tammy made Jacob's favorite; spaghetti casserole with plenty of juicy ground beef and oozing melted cheese.

Jacob was done with his lessons by five, and Tammy had the table set a few minutes later.  His eyes didn't light up like they usually did when he saw his mom's casserole.  Tammy waited until he finished most of his plate before she initiated their talk.

"How's school?"

He shrugged.  "I thought I was doing fine, but everybody else don't think so."

"Everybody like who?"

"Some of my friends, my teachers, Mr. Sweeney.  He think I need to see a counselor."

"Yeah," Tammy said. "He gave me a few numbers. I made you an appointment with one of them. It'll be this Friday, after school."

"Why, Mama? I don't need a counselor."

"I didn't think so either," Tammy said. "Looks like we're both wrong."

"They can't make me go."

Tammy sighed. "Yes they can, Jacob. If they think you have problems, they can make you stay home until you get help."

The boy frowned.

"Mr. Sweeney says you walked away while a teacher was talking to you," Tammy said.

Her son half nodded.

"Why did you do that?"

"She kept asking what was wrong with me. I didn't want to talk to her."

"Are you going to talk to the counselor I made an appointment with?" Tammy wondered.

Jacob shrugged. "I don't know."

"What about me?" she asked. "Can you talk to me?"

"Ain't nothing wrong," Jacob said. "I just don't like everybody trying to figure out how I feel. I tell them I'm fine, but they won't leave me alone."

"That's because we know you're not fine," Tammy said. "There's no way you can feel fine after what happened to you. We want you to open up and get some of your feelings out. It's okay to be depressed or angry right now. But if you don't let it out, you'll stay that way."

"Ain't nothing to let out."

"How do you feel about what happened to Isaiah?"

Jacob's nostrils flared. He didn't speak for a few seconds. His eyes filled with tears, but he refused to let them fall.

"Mama, you already know how I feel. Why you want to talk about it again?"

"I don't think we ever really talked about it."

"Yes we did, Mama. We talked at the police station."

"I want to talk without all the screaming and crying," Tammy said. "It's different now. We both had time to think about it and get used to it a little bit. I don't know about you, but I was still in denial at the police station."

154

"I wasn't never in denial," Jacob said. "I saw what happened. I already knew he was dead."

"Do you feel like, like it was your fault?" Tammy asked. "Do you feel guilty, because you didn't go through the alley?"

The tears spilled from Jacob's eyes, and he hated himself for it. He was trying to "move on," but nobody would let him.

"I don't feel guilty, Mama. God wanted Isaiah to come home, remember?"

"Well, do you blame God?" Tammy asked.

Jacob wiped his face with the back of his hand. "What good would that do? I can't do nothing to God."

"What about the Crips?" Tammy pressed. "You want to do something to them?"

"The Crips are gone, Mama. How am I supposed to do something to them?"

"I'm just asking," Tammy said. "If they were still there, would you want to do something to them?"

"Would *you*?" Jacob asked.

Tammy considered that and realized her question was unfair. Of course she'd want to harm the Crips.

"I gotta go," Jacob said. "I still got some English homework."

"I thought you said you were done."

"I forgot about my English."

"You don't want to talk to me?"

Jacob stood and shook his head. "I thought you wanted me to talk to a counselor or something."

"I do, Jacob. But I'm your mama. I thought…"

He shook his head again. His tears flowed like a stream. "Can I please go?"

Tammy's vision blurred. She told him, "Yeah, go ahead," before she started to cry too. In all her years of parenting, she never thought she'd see the day when her son couldn't talk to her about something. She wondered if she'd failed him somehow.

The only bright spot was that they did have an appointment with a grief counselor on Friday. Tammy had to find solace in that for now. It was possible Jacob could only open up to a stranger, which would explain why he spurned his friends and teachers and his very own mother today.

So, for those reasons, Tammy didn't say anything when she caught Jacob peering through the living room curtains again later that night. Whether he was afraid of the Crips or hoping they'd come back was a secret he didn't want to share just yet.

As much as it hurt her, Tammy had to find the strength to walk quietly back to her room and allow Jacob time to be alone with his thoughts.

*In shrouds, dark phantoms survey the corpses*
*When the soul is divorced from the body. This remorseless*
*Mass murder is like lightening. It's exciting! It's ferocious!*
*Nail-biting, edge-of-your-seat violence, keen and focused*
*Like locust laying waste to the land, grinning shooters*
*Blast first. They blast worst, leaving bile in the sewers*

# CHAPTER TWELVE
## *CHARLOTTE'S LAST STAND*

The next morning Dino sat in front of the television, as he did with 90 percent of his time nowadays. He stopped flipping channels when he saw HB's ugly mug on the Channel Six news. The station's best reporter, Chad Collins, gave viewers an update on the hunt for Isaiah Spencer's killer.

"Algernon Russell," Chad said, "is known on the streets as *HB*. Russell is currently in custody for outstanding warrants unrelated to the shooting, but police are fairly certain he was a key player in the shootout that took the life of ten-year-old Isaiah Spencer."

HB's mug shot dropped from the screen and was replaced with Chad Collins in the newsroom. Chad was a lot easier on the eyes, compared to HB, and the reporter had a cocky swagger as of late. Before Isaiah's murder, Chad didn't know the meaning behind a blue versus a purple bandana. But now he was a bonafide expert on the underbelly of gang violence in Overbrook Meadows.

"As I reported in a Channel Six exclusive," Chad continued, "Russell admitted himself to Jackson Memorial last Wednesday afternoon. He claimed he was suffering from '*stomach pains,*' but doctors later learned Russell had been shot in the stomach a week prior to his visit. It is believed someone performed surgery on him *outside of a hospital*, in an attempt to remove a bullet from his abdomen.

157

"Police are still trying to determine exactly what role Russell played in Isaiah Spencer's murder. He has not given any statements to the detectives regarding the shooting. Russell has hired an attorney to represent him, and at this time his attorney is not making any comments either.

"What the police do know is this: Algernon Russell is known to drive a gray and black Chrysler 300, and multiple witnesses have indicated a car matching that description was involved in the shootout that took Isaiah's life. Police speculate Russell was injured by the same individual who killed ten-year-old Isaiah, which would bolster earlier statements that the man who got shot in the face is *still* the prime suspect in the death of Isaiah Spencer.

"As for where that individual is..." Chad leaned forward with his elbows on the desk. "That is a mystery the police have yet to solve. No one has been admitted to the hospital with a bullet wound to the cheek, and no one has showed up at the morgue with that injury either. So this suspect is *still at large*, and he is considered to be armed and extremely dangerous. If you see him, *do not* approach him. Call the police. The detectives have a task force set up..."

Charlotte walked into the living room with her baby on her shoulder. Dino quickly used the remote to change the station. He found an *I Love Lucy* rerun. Charlotte approached and stood in front of the television.

"Why you always change the channel when I walk in?"

"Move," he said. "I don't be changing the channel."

"Yes you do." Charlotte wore jeans with her red and blue Camp Cuties tee shirt.

It was 7:30 am, and Dino couldn't wait for her to leave for work. He recorded a soft porn program on Showtime last night, and he was eager to masturbate to it. Charlotte was still being stingy with the ass, but Dino didn't need a woman to satisfy his needs. Even if Charlotte was willing, she couldn't keep up with the recent surge in his sexual drive. Dino could have sex four times a day now, easy.

"Why don't you leave me alone?" he said. "I ain't messing with you."

"Don't tell me to leave you alone," Charlotte said. "You must've forgot this is *my* house. I can say whatever I want."

158

"Alright, well move out from in front of the TV," Dino suggested. "Say it over there."

Charlotte cocked her head and rolled her neck as only a sistah can. "You can change the channel all you want, Dino. I already saw that story. Plus I was standing in the hall just now, while you was watching it. You want me to tell you what they said?" She kept talking before he could respond. "They said that bald-headed man didn't shoot that boy. They still say *you* did it; the one who got shot in the face."

"They said they *think*–"

"You know what, boy, you can keep lying all you want to. I ain't trying to hear it. I'm through listening to you. Your time has *been* up, Dino. You gots to go."

"Go where?"

"Out my house."

"So you just gon' throw me out?" Dino sounded incredulous, but the real surprise was how she put up with him for this long.

"I said you could stay here *two days*," Charlotte reminded him. "You know how long ago that was?"

*About two weeks*, Dino thought and said, "But I don't got nowhere else to go."

"That ain't my problem."

"I don't have no ride."

"Call that boy who brought you over here."

Dino shook his head. "Alright. I'll call him later."

"No, you need to call him *now*," Charlotte said. "I'm going to work, and I'm locking my doors when I leave."

"I'll be gone by the time you get back."

"*Open your ears*," Charlotte urged. "You're going to be gone *before* I leave for work. You understand? That means you need to leave *right now*, Dino."

"Alright," he said. "But my homeboy ain't gon' answer his phone this early. You need to give people time to wake up."

"I'll take you," Charlotte offered. "I'll take you anywhere you want to go."

Dino frowned. "Why you tripping? You believing that shit you heard on the news?"

Charlotte sighed. "Look, Dino, I don't even care about that no more. You want to keep saying you didn't kill that boy, that's your problem. You the one who gotta answer to God, and you the one who's going to hell for lying and for murder. I want you to leave 'cause you been acting different since you came back this last time. You think I'm stupid, but I'm not. You not snorting the same stuff you had at first. Whatever you're on now is making you *crazy*."

*Wow*, Dino thought. *I guess you ain't stupid.*

When Kevin brought him back to Charlotte's house after their last set meeting, Dino asked for more heroin pills because he'd depleted his supply. Kevin didn't have any heroin this time, but he had a few eight balls. Dino said he'd give them a try.

Dino didn't think he'd like cocaine after a weeklong heroin binge, but he was a hundred times wrong about that. Cocaine was everything he wanted it to be, and more. Not only did coke work faster to dull the pain in his cheek, but it got him a lot higher, too. And it wasn't some funky, sleepy high either. Cocaine kept Dino on his toes. He could hear everything around Charlotte's house, from the mailman getting out of his vehicle to the squirrels scurrying across the rooftop.

Since he got the cocaine, Dino could stay up late into the night to make sure the police weren't creeping though the backyard or along the side of the house. He could stay up for more than one night if he wanted to. He currently hadn't slept in 79 hours, but he wasn't tired at all. He was more alert than a stalking panther.

There were a few downsides to getting high on coke, but Dino didn't think they were too severe. He hadn't eaten much in the past few days, and his britches were now two sizes too big. He had to hold his pants up whenever he walked somewhere, but that usually never included anything more than a trip to the bathroom and the return trip back to his perch on the loveseat.

In addition to the weight loss, coke gave Dino a nervousness that hadn't been there before. He'd chewed all of his fingernails down to the quick, and recently he started to pick at the hole in his face while he watched TV.

He knew it was bad to get his dirty hands anywhere near his wound, but he couldn't help it. The sensation of self-inflicted pain was soothing, to a certain extent. Even when he went to the bathroom later and saw that he peeled off a whole later of scar tissue, Dino couldn't stop from doing it again later.

Another side-effect of the coke was it made Dino horny as hell, but he didn't think that was a problem. Charlotte had plenty of lotions and baby oils, and Dino was home alone for nine hours when she went to work. Plus Charlotte usually went to bed at eleven o'clock, which left even more time for some late night chicken-choking.

"I'm still using the same stuff," he told Charlotte. "And the only reason I'm taking it is for the pain."

"It's not the same!" Charlotte snapped. "You're a *liar*, Dino! I don't think you can help it. Every time you open your mouth, another lie rolls out."

"Whatever."

"Whatever? You think this is a game? You're peeking through the windows all the time. Sitting in the dark. I woke up last night to go to the bathroom, and I saw you standing in my door. All the lights were off, and you was just standing there." She shivered. "I couldn't see nothing but eyes and teeth, and it scared the hell out of me. I couldn't even get up. I had to hold my pee for the rest of the night, 'cause I was scared to walk around my own house. You know how fucked up that is?"

It did sound fucked up, hearing it from her viewpoint.

"Girl, you know ain't nobody gon' hurt you. Stop playing."

"I'm not playing, Dino. You need to leave. *Right now.*"

"I'm not going *nowhere* right now. I said I'll be gone when you get back."

"How are you gon' sit there and tell me what you're gonna do in *my* house?"

"Just like I did."

Charlotte couldn't believe his insolence. Dino couldn't believe she still didn't get the picture. He was in control of his own destiny now; not the police, not his gang, and certainly not some dumb broad who never should have invited the big, bad wolf inside in the first place.

Charlotte turned and headed for the bedroom. Dino got up and followed her. Charlotte stopped in the hallway and looked back at him. Her daughter was not asleep, and the infant was frightened by Dino's closeness.

"What you doing?" Charlotte asked.

"Where you going?" Dino asked.

"Leave me alone, Dino."

161

"I ain't did nothing to you."

Charlotte turned and continued towards her room. She tried to close the door when she got there, but Dino stuck his foot in the way.

"Leave me alone, Dino."

"What you come in here for?"

She thought quickly. "I came to get my purse."

"Where's your phone?" Dino asked.

"It's in my purse. Why?"

"Let me see it."

"You got your own phone. You don't need mine."

"I do need yours," Dino said. "Let me see it."

Charlotte looked down at the floor where Dino kept his gun under a pile of dirty clothes. She could get to it before he could, and she was sure she could cock it and fire it before Dino had time to mount an offense.

"It ain't under there," he said, following her gaze. He lifted his shirt. Charlotte saw the butt of the pistol poking out of his front pants pocket. "Now, let me see your phone."

Charlotte walked slowly to the bed and lifted her purse from the pillow. She dug inside and found her cellphone, her eyes on Dino the whole time. She handed it to him and pulled the purse strap over her shoulder. She exited the room without a word and walked slowly back down the hallway. Her heart tried to punch a hole through her chest, but on the outside Charlotte remained calm.

The front door was not that far away. Just a few more feet, and Dino could have the house. She didn't care if he had a shootout with the police when they came to get him, so long as she wasn't there when it went down. She could–

"Where you going?"

Charlotte didn't turn around or stop walking.

"I'm going to work," she said. "You said you'll be gone when I get back..."

"You gon' leave your phone?" he asked.

"Yeah," Charlotte said, still moving. "You can, you can keep it. Just leave it on the, on the bed when I, when you get done..."

Four more steps and she would be outside. Two more steps and she'd have the doorknob in her hand. Now one more. She reached for it.

Dino lunged forward. He grabbed her wrist with fingers so skinny they were like claws.

Charlotte screamed loud enough to wake her neighbors on the other end of the block. Dino didn't flinch. He spun her around and pulled her back into the living room. Before Charlotte could yell again, Dino pushed her down roughly on the couch and reached back for a vicious backhand. Charlotte didn't know if he meant to strike her or her child, but the gesture effectively closed her windpipe.

"*Shut up*," he growled. "Don't you say *nothing*."

Dino had been so doped up in the past couple of weeks, Charlotte had forgotten he had this other side of him. His eyes were focused now, and he didn't look high. His hair was wild. His teeth were bared. The bandage on his cheek hung by only one piece of tape, exposing a wound that reminded Charlotte of the diabetic foot ulcer that took her grandmother's big toe and then her middle toe and finally her whole foot.

Charlotte sank deeper and deeper into the cushions, but she couldn't get far enough away from Dino, or his breath. Crystal was crying now, and that made things substantially worse.

"I, I gotta go to work," Charlotte pleaded.

"Why? So you can call the police on me?" Dino guessed.

"No, Dino. I just want to go to work. I promise. I won't call nobody."

"You ain't going," Dino said. "So get that out your head. Just sit there and be cool." He backed away from her and returned to his favorite position on the loveseat.

Charlotte's chest heaved. She feared she might pass out. There was a landline phone in the kitchen, but she would have to go past Dino to get to it. There was another cordless phone in the bedroom, but that route also went past Dino.

"Lemme, lemme call-in then," Charlotte begged. "They gon' know something's wrong, if I don't show up."

Dino dug in his pocket for the last of his second eight ball. Rather than make a line, he stuck his muzzle in the baggie and snorted with both nostrils. Some of the crystallized powder went straight down his throat and made him cough raggedly. But most of the coke remained stuck to his nasal membranes, where it would be absorbed and released into his blood stream. Dino found the remote control and started to flip channels again.

"I, I have to call my job," Charlotte repeated.

"Shut up," Dino said. "You ain't gotta call nobody, and you ain't going nowhere. You ain't getting out of my sight. If you wanna call the police on me, you have to kill me first."

That didn't sound like a bad idea. Charlotte knew the whole city would thank her.

"Well, let me, let me go to the kitchen at least, so I can make Crystal a bottle."

Dino sighed and slowly pushed himself to a standing position. "Alright," he said. "Come on."

● ● ● ● ● ●

Jacob knew he had to be good at school that day. He started by leaving his gun at home. That was a no-brainer. He was sure to be under scrutiny, and he still didn't know for sure if Harold had told anyone about the weapon.

Before he left the house, Jacob put on a happy face for his most skeptical critic. Tammy made bacon, toast and hash browns for breakfast. Jacob finished his whole plate. His table conversation was pleasant, and he tried to sound chipper.

"Wow. You musta got a good night's sleep," his mom noticed.

"I think I just had a bad day yesterday," Jacob acknowledged.

"I did too," Tammy said with a slight grin. "But it'll get better. I know it don't seem like it now, but one day we'll both feel normal again."

"I know," Jacob said. He took his plate to the sink and washed it rather than leave the chore for his mother. He gave Tammy a kiss on the cheek and flashed a crooked smile before leaving. "See you later, Mama. I love you."

"I love you too, baby."

Tammy followed him to the living room and stood in the doorway until he was out of sight.

When Jacob rounded the corner onto Crenshaw, the dopey grin slipped from his face. But it was back by the time he got to school. He met up with his best friend in the auditorium. Harold was happy to see Jacob looking like his old self.

"I'm glad you're feeling better," he said. "You had me freaked out the last couple of days."

"I had everybody freaked out," Jacob admitted. "Sometimes I wake up thinking about Isaiah, and I get depressed. It messes up my whole day. I take it out on the wrong people."

"It's cool," Harold said. "I saw on the news that they still haven't caught the guy who killed him."

Harold wasn't trying to push any buttons, but his comment made Jacob's stomach tighten. Harold didn't notice any change in his demeanor, but he moved on to another topic anyway.

"Hey, did you ever write Camille back?"

Jacob shook his head. "I didn't know what to say to her."

"Well, you'd better think of something," Harold said. "She's on her way over here."

The auditorium was crowded, but Jacob spotted his crush as soon as he looked in the direction Harold was gazing. The row they were sitting in was packed with students, so Camille stood in the aisle and gestured for Jacob to come to her.

"I guess I'll see you later," Jacob said and stood stiffly.

"Yeah, have fun," Harold replied, glad to see so many people reaching out to help his best bud.

●  ●  ●  ●  ●  ●

Jacob didn't get to spend much time with Camille before the first bell rang, but any amount of time with her was enough to make him feel dreamy. He didn't know why she was interested in him all of a sudden, and he didn't question it. Maybe it was fate. Or it could have been God working in one of His mysterious ways.

Jacob was still in a good mood when he got to second period, so the smile he wore for Mrs. Milligan was mostly genuine. His history teacher stood in the doorway during passing period. Jacob approached her, even though his mother didn't tell him to do so.

"I'm sorry for walking off when you tried to talk to me yesterday."

Mrs. Milligan smiled, too. "Oh, it's okay, Jacob. I understand you weren't in a good mood."

"Yeah, but it was still rude, and it won't happen again."

Mrs. Milligan reached out and gave his shoulder a comforting squeeze. Today Jacob didn't mind the affection.

● ● ● ● ● ●

By three o'clock Jacob was ready to certify his behavior that day a success. But changing his mood did not necessarily change his heart. And the devil is always looking for an opportunity to steal, kill and destroy.

On the way to his bus, Jacob had to walk by his school's three wannabe Crips. The sight of them filled him with as much rage as he felt during their previous encounter.

Jacob tried to reason with himself: He could walk by them without speaking. Or he could go back to the parking lot, make a half circle, and approach his bus from a different angle and avoid them altogether. But that was too much like the scenario that got him in this predicament in the first place. If Jacob didn't take an alternate route to save his little brother's life, why do it now?

And why should he ignore them? He wasn't afraid of those losers. They were pranksters, not gangsters. The rest of the school respected them because they talked loudly and always stuck together. But Jacob wasn't impressed by any of that.

In fact, Jacob became increasingly disgusted, the more he thought about it. If the wannabes were so tough, why did they have to gang up to argue or fight with one person? Who gave them the right to run his school with their intimidation tactics? And why were they wearing so much goddamned *blue*? Jacob had come to despise the color, and he couldn't keep his mouth closed when he got within spitting distance of the group.

"Fuck Crips." The words spilled from his lips without warning. Jacob was surprised, but not regretful. "Punk ass."

Big Lips was leaning against the fence, talking to one of many hot-tailed girls who find hoodlums attractive. Fat Boy stood on his left, playing a game of pencil-break with Curly Head. They looked up at Jacob with astonishment and then animosity when they saw who it was.

Big Lips pushed off the fence and crossed his arms over his chest. Fat Boy dropped his pencil and narrowed his eyes.

166

"Why you keep fucking with us?" Big Lips asked. "Didn't your brother just get killed? You ain't learn nothing from that?"

His words cut like a rusty knife. Jacob's memory bank filled his mind with snap-shots of Isaiah's murder. He felt a tingle in his eyes a half second before they filled with tears. He couldn't believe he was going to cry in front of these punks. But since it was going to happen either way, Jacob had to mask his tears the only way he knew how. A lot of middle-schoolers cried during a fight, so Jacob dropped his backpack and swung for the fences.

His first punch was a right cross that everyone saw coming. Big Lips took a step back and threw his arms up; effectively blocking the blow. Jacob followed the cross with a left hook Ali would have been proud of, and Big Lips took it flush on the chin. He staggered backwards, his eyes floating aimlessly for a second.

Curly Head braced his leader before Big Lips hit the ground, and Fat Boy rushed in like a rhinoceros. Jacob threw an uppercut that caught Fat Boy square on the nose, but the big kid's momentum propelled him forward. He crashed into Jacob, shoulder first, delivering the brunt of the impact to his gut.

The air was forced from his body like a stomped balloon, but that was only half of Jacob's problem. Fat Boy wrapped his arms around him, and Jacob lost his footing. He tumbled backwards with the fat kid on top. By then Big Lips had recovered enough to know that he almost got knocked out in front of his peers.

Fat Boy's grip was strong, but he was still reeling from the uppercut. His nose bled freely, and he kept his head down, content with pinning Jacob to the ground rather than advancing to a more superior position. In the meantime both of Jacob's arms were free, so he peppered Fat Boy's ears with the hardest punches he could throw from his back. He used his legs to kick and push, but Fat Boy's bulk was too great. Jacob could not buck him off.

By the time Curly Head and Big Lips joined the fracas, the school's parking lot was filled with chants of "*FIGHT! FIGHT! FIGHT!*" Students hurried to get a peek before the administrators broke it up.

Jacob didn't notice much of the crowd, but he did see Big Lips rush in on his right. He delivered a kick to Jacob's head that should've hurt more than it actually did. Curly Head came in on the other side, and Jacob made a smooth transition from aggressor to defender. He gripped his hands together behind his neck and brought his elbows together in front of his nose. The sneakers started to fall like rain. After a while Fat Boy felt comfortable enough to sit up and take a few shots himself.

Jacob never begged for help, but he was grateful when he heard adult voices mingling with the incessant screams of blood-lusting adolescents.

*"Get off him!"*
"Break it up!"
"Grab him!"
"Get that one!"
*"Get off him!"*

The bodies began to peel away one by one, until Jacob was the only student on the ground. There was so much noise and confusion, Jacob didn't realize he was screaming, too. But he felt his lips moving, and after a while he could hear himself over his thunderous heartbeats.

*"I hate you! I hate y'all! I hate all y'all!"*

● ● ● ● ● ●

Dino never held anyone hostage before, and he didn't believe that's what he was doing with Charlotte, but as each minute became an hour and morning gave way to late afternoon, the word **KIDNAP** became more and more prevalent in his hideaway.

Charlotte was the one who brought the word to his attention. She would still be nagging about it now if Dino hadn't threatened to fatten her lips if she didn't zip them up. Whether he really would have done it or not was up for debate. But one thing Dino knew for sure was he couldn't go another hour with Charlotte's incessant whining:

*This is kidnapping, Dino!*
*You can't keep me here if I want to go.*
*You're holding me and my baby* **hostage**.
*My mama's going to come and check on me.*
*Somebody's going to come and find out you're holding me*
**hostage**.
*They're going to get you for killing that boy and for*
**kidnapping** *me!*

168

*You not gon' get away with this!*

Listening to that shit would drive any man insane, and Dino needed all the peace and quiet he could get. He needed time to think. He needed time to plot his next move, because all of his current paths led to either death or incarceration, and he could accept neither of those options. Dino needed an epiphany. He needed a brainstorm like no other.

Charlotte sat on the sofa watching television with him. Her baby lay next to her dozing quietly. Charlotte's eyes were low. Her body was weary. She still had on the blue jeans and Camp Cuties tee shirt she put on that morning. She would be getting off work right about now, if Dino had let her go. Instead she spent her day being watched and followed by a man who she was increasingly convinced had gone insane.

For the better part of the morning, Charlotte kept her guard up, waiting for Dino to slip up so she could escape with her baby. But as the day progressed, her tension gave way to stress, which ultimately gave way to mental fatigue. Charlotte didn't like to accept failure, but she knew there was no way she could outsmart Dino in his current state of mind.

No matter how many times she tried to get out of his line of sight, Dino didn't go for it. He followed her to the kitchen when she got something to eat. He followed her to the bedroom when she needed more diapers for Crystal. He even followed her to the bathroom when she had to pee.

Dino snorted more powder every thirty minutes or so, and he was always alert. But Charlotte didn't see too much cunning behind his dilated pupils. What she saw was the deranged stare of a man who had gradually become unhinged.

Dino picked at the hole in his head constantly. When the wound began to emit a sticky discharge, he wiped it on his pants leg or on the loveseat, with hardly a care about what he was doing. His ravaged nasal cavity hemorrhaged twice today, but Dino was barely concerned. He grabbed whatever was closest, a diaper in one instance, and bled into it while he continued to flip channels with the blood-smeared remote. He scrambled to the bathroom to vomit once, but he rushed back to the living room before Charlotte could make a move.

At this point, she was done trying. Dino looked crazy enough to kill her, but Charlotte knew he wouldn't last long in his current condition. Either his brain or his heart would give out. Or maybe he'd run out of cocaine and kill himself. Charlotte didn't care how it ended, so long as she and her baby made it through unscathed. Her fate was in her savior's hands now. She knew God would deliver them from this madness before too long.

It was four o'clock now, and Dino hadn't come up with anything thus far. Charlotte was no closer to having her home back to herself, and the police were no closer to arresting "the one who got shot in the face." Dino had the television tuned in to Channel Six. They were airing a press conference the chief of police gave earlier that day.

"The public has been very helpful," Chris Salazar said. He was a bearded man who looked like he could get the job done. "I've been with the police department for more than thirty years, and I don't believe I've ever seen more outpouring of support from the community.

"We have made our first major arrest in this case. The man we questioned earlier, Mr. Algernon Russell, has been charged for the death of Roderick Cooper, who was another casualty in the shootout that killed ten year old Isaiah Spencer. Russell will also be charged for the attempted murder of Latasha Foster, who was shot in the leg during the incident.

"He will also face charges for the death of Isaiah Spencer. We do not believe Russell is the individual who fired the shot that killed Isaiah, but Isaiah was killed during the commission of a felony, which makes Russell culpable.

"Russell is not cooperating with us, and he has yet to make a statement. But based on evidence and eye-witness testimony, we have identified him as the individual who initiated the shootout.

"At this time we are still looking for other individuals who will also be charged for Isaiah's murder. We believe one of these persons was driving or riding in the Chrysler with Mr. Russell. And of course we are still looking for the individual who was shot in the face during the shootout.

"We were fortunate–"

A telephone rang, pulling Dino's attention away from the television. He sat up and looked around wildly, knowing something was amiss. He had already unplugged both of Charlotte's home phones and turned her cellular off as well. Apparently she had a fourth phone he didn't know about, and there would be consequences for such deceit. He stared at her angrily, and Charlotte rolled her eyes.

"That's *your* phone, fool."

Dino's expression changed as recognition dawned. He made it to his feet and took a few hurried steps towards the bedroom. Halfway there, he ran back to the living room to check on Charlotte. She hadn't moved. Dino rushed to the bedroom and found Kevin's phone in the pants he wore the day before.

He knew there wouldn't be good news on the other end of the line. Either the set saw the press conference, and they wanted to re-evaluate Dino's standing in the gang, or a couple of Sicc Crips got out of jail recently, and they were ready to cast the votes T Lowe promised.

Dino took a seat on the corner of the bed and answered the phone on the fifth ring.

"What's up?"

"What up, D?" Kevin said.

"Nothing, nigga. What's up?"

Kevin sighed. "Say, I got some bad news, man."

No surprise there. "What, nigga?"

"You out the Sicc, cuz."

Dino sucked his teeth. "How they kick me out without me being there?"

"T Lowe said you ain't gotta be there. He had enough votes already."

"How he figure that?"

"I don't know," Kevin said. "But that ain't all, cuz. They say they gon' get you, nigga."

"Get me how? Drop a dime or something?"

"They ain't talking about turning you in," Kevin reported. "T Lowe say you know too much about his houses and stuff." Kevin's voice became low and solemn. "They talking about *getting you*, cuz. You know what I'm saying?"

"They gon' *get me*?" Dino frowned. Anyone who ran up on him would be with Jesus shortly afterwards. They had to know that. And, "How they gon' get me, cuz. They don't even know–"

"I had to tell them," Kevin said softly. "I'm sorry, cuz. I had to. They made me tell where you at."

Dino's head spun. He felt like he was spiraling down a dark abyss, like Alice in Wonderland. He knew T Lowe was a stupid sonofabitch, but what in the world made him think he could take Dino out?

"Man, is you serious?"

"You need to move around," Kevin said. "That's why I called. They told me not to, but–"

Dino heard a sound in the living room. He shot to his feet, wondering how long he'd left Charlotte alone. It couldn't have been more than thirty seconds, but that was enough time for her to grab her baby and make a run for it.

"I gotta go, cuz," Dino said.

"What you gon' do?"

"Nigga, what I'm gon' tell you for? So you can tell them niggas again?"

Dino disconnected and shoved the cell phone in his pocket. He ran to the living room and found Charlotte up and on the move. She had her purse, her baby and her car keys in her hand. She looked back at him like a startled deer when he rounded the corner.

"Gimme your keys," he demanded. "I gotta bounce."

"What you talking about?"

"You said you wanted me gone. Gimme your car keys."

"I'm not giving you my car."

Dino thought he broke her will, but Charlotte still had more fight left in her.

"Bitch, quit acting stupid. Some niggas is on they way over here. You need to go to a neighbor's house or something. I'll call you later and let you know where you can pick your car up at."

He held out his hand. Charlotte backed away.

"Somebody coming over here?"

"*Girl is you listening*?! I got to get out of here. *Now*! You do too. Gimme them keys!"

She shook her head. "I'm not giving you my car, Dino! Just leave! *Get out of my house!*"

"Ho, you acting ignorant."

"That's *my* car! I need my car! *Get out of my house!*"

The baby started crying. Dino's frustration grew.

"Give me a ride then!"

"Get away from me!"

Charlotte headed for the door. Dino had to up the ante. He hated to take this route, but his life was on the line. He wasn't

172

going to die over this foolishness.  He pulled the pistol from his pocket and pointed it at her torso.

"Alright," he said calmly.  "I ain't playing no more.  Gimme them keys, Charlotte."

She stood at the front door with one hand on the knob.  She looked back at him, but she didn't look frightened.  She knew he wouldn't shoot.

"Dino, don't point that thing a—"

*POP!*

The sound was much softer than Dino expected.  He didn't believe the gun went off, except it jumped in his hand, and Charlotte's eyes flashed open like shutters.

Dino's eyes widened, too.  He looked down at his gun and saw a small trail of smoke leaking from the barrel.  He looked up at Charlotte in time to see her sliding down the door.  Her eyes were as big as dinner plates, and now her mouth hung open as well.  Her baby kicked in her arms.  As she fell, Dino noticed a small, red stain on the door behind her.

But even as he saw all of this, Dino didn't believe it.  He didn't cock the gun, and he most certainly didn't pull the trigger.  There was a certain logic to these things, and this followed none of it.

But then again, guns don't kill people.

People kill people.

Charlotte's butt hit the floor, and her baby's cries intensified.  Dino saw a raspberry stain blossoming a little to the left of Charlotte's sternum.

"I'm, I'm sorry."  Dino's bottom lip hung dumbly.  His apology was totally inadequate, but he felt like he had to say something.

Charlotte tried to respond, but her mouth filled with blood, and she could only manage a wet cough.  Her nose likewise hemorrhaged.  The crimson tide spilled from her nostrils in rivulets.

# CHAPTER THIRTEEN
## *HOLY HANDS*

The principal sat behind his beautiful cherry wood desk and eyeballed the troubled adolescent in his office. Jacob sat across from him in a much less extravagant plastic chair and returned the stare. Jacob's hair was kinked with a few blades of dead grass still entangled. His white golf shirt was ripped, soiled and bloodied, but thankfully none of it was his blood. The nasty, red stain on his torso came from a fat wannabe Crip who was currently in the backseat of a police car; on his way to the juvenile detention center on Kimbo Road.

The fat Crip's homeboys, Big Lips and Curly Head, were crammed in the back of another cruiser. The police had a fourth set of handcuffs for Jacob, but the principal didn't let them take this last one. William Joseph had a zero tolerance policy when it came to fights on campus, but even the strictest rules can be bent, depending on the circumstances.

Jacob's principal was a large man with a big nose, a big moustache, and a big waistline that he had to have his pants custom fitted for. Mr. Gilliam was balding, but he refused to give up the hair on the sides and the back of his head. This piggish man could end Jacob's career at the school with one stroke of his pen, but he worried that it might come back and bite him in the ass.

"You admit to starting the fight?" Mr. Gilliam asked.

Jacob met the man's eyes and nodded. His knee bounced, but Jacob wasn't really nervous. Nothing this man could do would hurt him more than what the Sicc Crips did to Isaiah. He was only worried about what his mother would say when she found out about the fight. She wouldn't understand – that much he knew for sure.

Tammy told him time and time again that vengeance belonged to the Lord. But if that was true, why did Texas execute so many people every year? Apparently God expected man to take vengeance into his own hands every now and then.

Jacob's fight with the wannabes didn't avenge Isaiah *per se*, but it was a start. Jacob now knew he could back his thoughts up with actions. And he did shed one Crip's blood for Isaiah.

"You threw the first punch?" his principal asked.

"Yes, sir." Jacob's mouth felt funny when he talked. He ran his tongue across his teeth and felt substantial swelling on his lower lip. He also had a knot on the side of his head. But other than that, Jacob wasn't badly injured. He knew that the damage he dished out was worse than all of the blows he took during the fight.

"Who, who initiated it?" the principal asked. "What was the first thing said, and who said it?"

"It was me," Jacob acknowledged. "I said..." He lowered his gaze, looking worried for the first time. "It was a curse word, sir."

"It's okay," the principal said. "You can repeat it."

"I said, 'Fuck Crips,'" Jacob reported.

Mr. Gilliam sighed and scribbled something in the chart on his desk.

Jacob knew that chart had his name on it, and he also knew that anything scribbled in it could haunt him for years to come. He didn't care.

Mr. Gilliam shook his head. "Jacob, do you know where those three guys are right now – the ones you had a fight with?"

The boy shrugged.

"They're on their way to juvenile detention," the principal said. "And when they get out of jail, they won't be allowed to come back to this school. I have to sign papers to send them to an alternative school. I understand they didn't start the fight, but they were all participants, and we have a zero-tolerance policy at this school. Do you understand?"

Jacob nodded. He understood perfectly. It sounded like he was about to go to jail.

"But you..." Mr. Gilliam pursed his chubby lips. "I don't know what to do with you, son. Everybody in the city knows about your brother, Isaiah, and we all want the individuals responsible to get arrested and punished for that *despicable* crime. We also know you were there when Isaiah was murdered, and we know you've been traumatized to a certain extent because of that. I talked to Mr. Sweeney, and he says you're going to start counseling this Friday. Is that right?"

Jacob nodded.

"But there's still the matter of today..." Mr. Gilliam frowned. "If I stick to our zero-tolerance, you'll go to jail right now. And then you'll get kicked out of school. That's what *should* happen to you, Jacob. But I don't think it would play out too well..." He rubbed his chin.

"I talked to a few higher-ups, and we've agreed to give you another chance. This fight will go in your files, but there will be no expulsion from school. You are suspended for the remainder of the week, and I pray you will take that time to reflect on your behavior. If you need more time to work out these feelings you have, I encourage you – and I give you my permission – to take as much time as you need.

"But if you should return to school on Monday with the same aggressive tendencies, then I'm afraid I'll have no choice but to go through with the expulsion, son. By then we will have sufficient documentation of the help we offered you..."

Jacob thought that was a pretty sweet deal. Mr. Gilliam could save his own tail, and Jacob cleared the Crips out of the school.

Someone knocked on the principal's door.

"Come in," he said.

An office clerk stepped inside and eyed Jacob warily. "Mr. Gilliam, Tammy Spencer is here to see you."

"Great," Mr. Gilliam said. "Could you show Jacob to the assistant principal's office? I need to speak with his mother alone for a second."

"Sure," the secretary said. "It's right this way," she told Jacob, gesturing for him to follow her.

Outside the office, Jacob saw his mother standing anxiously near the front desk. When she and her son locked eyes, Tammy's expression melted in a sea of grief that made Jacob feel sick in the pit of his stomach. She rushed to him and hugged him tightly. Jacob worried that some of his peers might be watching them, and he fought the urge to push away from her.

"You alright?" she asked.

He nodded. "Yeah, Mama. I'm sorry"

"It's okay," Tammy said. "We'll get through this. Lord knows we'll get through it."

• • • • • •

Tammy's meeting with the principal lasted twenty minutes, during which time Jacob sat in an empty vice principal's office and pretended to read his history textbook.

At four-thirty Jacob heard his mother thank the principal, and then she appeared in the vice-principal's doorway. She wore no makeup. Her eyes and nose were red and puffy. She didn't look half this bad when she first got there. Jacob could handle a lot of things, but being the cause of his mother's tears made him feel rotten to the core.

"You ready?" Tammy asked.

"Yeah." Jacob gathered his things and followed her out of the office.

Three minutes later Tammy pulled out of the parking lot driving slowly. This was her second trip to Jacob's school in as many days, which would have been bad enough if she didn't bury her other son one week ago. Tammy maintained a loose grip on her sanity by God's grace alone. She didn't know how much more stress she could handle.

"You almost got kicked out of school," she said a few blocks down the road. "That's what your principal wanted to do. The only reason he didn't is because he's worried about what people would think, if the news got hold of your story. He thinks the mayor and everybody else will come down on him."

Jacob figured as much.

"You want to tell me what happened?" Tammy asked.

Jacob slumped in his seat. "They was talking about Isaiah."

"They don't even know Isaiah," Tammy said. "What'd they say?"

Jacob couldn't remember what had pissed him off. "They said he was dead."

Tammy kept her eyes on the road, her hands tight on the steering wheel. "The principal says you started it. You walked up to them and said *F- Crips*. Why would you do that?"

"I don't like them," Jacob said.

"You don't like who, the ones at your school, or the ones who lived across the street from us?"

"None of them," Jacob admitted.

Tammy sighed. "Jacob, I know you're upset about what happened to Isaiah, but you're not being fair. The boys at your school had nothing to do with that, and you know it."

"But they're the source," Jacob explained.

"What are you talking about?"

"They all start out like that; kids who don't know what's going on. They think they're in a gang, but they're not. But then they get older and they drop out of school, and it starts to be real. They sell drugs and they go to jail, and then they start shooting people; just like the ones across the street."

Tammy couldn't believe her son's thinking had become so skewed. "Jacob, what you're saying makes some sense, but don't you see how wrong it is? Let's say the boys you got in a fight with were going to grow up and be bad people. How did you help it any? If anything, you made it worse, 'cause now they have to go to an alternative school. You can't take your frustrations out on innocent people."

Jacob knew she wouldn't understand. "Those punks at my school aren't innocent, Mama. I don't see why you're sticking up for them. They're dumb. They pick on everybody because they're in a gang, and people are scared of them. The principal couldn't do nothing about them, and their teachers couldn't either. But *I* did. They're gone now because of me.

"We should've did the same thing when those Crips moved across the street from us. But we didn't. We sat there and looked at them, and they took more and more control. They made our whole neighborhood scared and ugly, and then they killed Isaiah. But I'm not doing that no more. If I see a Crip, I'm gonna get rid of him."

Tammy looked over at her child in horror, not believing these words were coming from a thirteen year old. "Get rid of them how, Jacob?"

"Whatever it takes," he said, his face set in a dark sneer.

His words were so cold, they gave Tammy chills. She expected a myriad of reactions to Isaiah's death, but she never thought her baby would become violent. If Jacob truly meant to confront every Crip he came across, Tammy feared she'd attend another funeral in the not too distant future.

It wasn't fair. How could God allow such a thing?

"We're going to church tonight," she said, her voice quavering. "I don't know where you're getting these ideas from, but I'm not going to sit back and let you self-destruct, Jacob. I know you miss your brother. But that don't mean you have to be in a rush to go be with him. We need to pray. I'm going to get you some help."

Jacob's nostrils flared, but he didn't say anything. How could his mom think he was the one with the problem, when her solution was to pray to the same God who killed Isaiah – or *allowed* Isaiah to get killed; it was all the same. It was clear *somebody* in that car was delusional, and Jacob knew it sure as hell wasn't him.

● ● ● ● ● ●

Dino did remember cocking his gun.

He'd done it the night before, when he thought he saw ninjas dropping from the trees in Charlotte's backyard. But they weren't really ninjas. They were members of a police task force, dressed all in black. They climbed the trees so they could hide and monitor Charlotte's home from a better vantage point. At approximately three-thirty a.m. they began to drop from the trees and run quietly towards the house.

The only thing is, none of that was what it seemed. Dino neither saw ninjas nor a SWAT team dropping from the trees in Charlotte's backyard. As he stared out of the kitchen window in the wee hours of the morning, Dino gradually came to understand that his eyes were playing tricks on him. Those were just regular trees, with their thick branches and shadowy leaves blowing in the wind. That was all.

Dino finally calmed down enough to return to his spot on the loveseat, but as he thought about it now, he knew he'd made a terrible mistake: He cocked his gun in preparation for the police assault, but he forgot to un-cock it when he realized there was no one there.

The burden of that slip-up felt like a half-ton weight on his chest. Dino had that cocked gun in his pocket for more than twelve hours. He pulled it out a few more times last night, when he heard sounds that might have been the police but turned out to be the house settling. He could have – and should have – shot himself at least once that morning. But fate did not require his blood just yet.

The gun didn't go off until he put his finger on the trigger and pointed it at Charlotte. He didn't think he squeezed it. He certainly didn't mean to. But the proof was coughing up blood on the living room floor. Dino un-cocked his gun and slipped it carefully into his pocket.

"I'm sorry," he said. He knew his apologies didn't matter at that point, but Charlotte was still alive, barely, and he thought she could still hear him. Dino didn't know what the spirit world had in store for her. But if Charlotte could keep at least one memory when her heart beat for the last time, Dino wanted her to know this was a terrible accident. It was important to convey that message.

*Guns don't kill people*

"Oh my God..." Dino put his hands to his head and rubbed his temples. His body urged him to move, in *any* direction, but he could not look away from the mess he'd made. Two weeks ago he saw Peanut in a similar position, but this was different. Peanut was already dead when Dino looked into his eyes. But Charlotte continued to gasp for air. Peanut was a good-for-nothing gangbanger, who some might say got what he had coming. But Charlotte was wholesome and innocent; a young mother with dreams of a better future.

"Aww, shit, man. *No, no, no...*" Dino went from rubbing his temples to banging them with the heels of his hands. His fingers trembled. His whole body shivered. His heartbeats were erratic, and he grew light-headed. He took a few staggering steps backwards, and then he turned away. He had to. The look on

Charlotte's face was gruesome. The way she sat with one leg pinned unnaturally under her body...

Charlotte's baby didn't appear to be injured. Crystal screamed and kicked but was unable to escape her mother's tight grasp. Dino could watch that no longer.

He stumbled towards the bathroom but didn't make it through the door before vomit spewed from his mouth. All Dino had to eat that day was a bowl of Top Ramen, but his stomach continued to void itself for second after agonizing second. Dino stood in the middle of the hallway with his arms outstretched; each hand bracing an opposite side of the wall. In the living room the baby's screams became more high-pitched. Dino knew he had to get out of there.

The gunshot didn't sound that loud to him, but there was a good chance a neighbor heard it. If not, someone would hear the baby pretty soon. And Dino couldn't forget the Sicc Crips were on their way to "get him." No matter how he sliced the pie, doom and gloom was on its way to Charlotte's house. Dino would surely die if he was still around when it got there.

He spit out the last of his puke and stepped over the mess on his way to the bedroom. He'd only brought one set of clothes to Charlotte's house, but she'd given him a few more outfits Crystal's daddy left behind when he decided to catch ghost. Dino didn't have any valuables in those pants pockets, but they were full of his DNA. He stumbled around the bedroom in an attempt to gather all of his clothing, but then he said, *Fuck it.*

If it was DNA he wanted to avoid, he already lost that battle. Dino had dirty clothes in Charlotte's bedroom, used gauze in the bathroom and dirty dishes in the kitchen. And then there was the living room, where he'd wiped his blood on the sofa and left unseen sperm stains from his masturbation marathon. It would take three days to clear all of his DNA from the house, so taking a few pairs of pants wouldn't help any.

*What about fingerprints?*

Dino considered that for only half a second before settling on another, *Fuck it.* Thanks to the cocaine he'd been snorting, Dino had been in every nook and cranny of Charlotte's home. He peeked through the windows, probably touched every blind, and he even snooped through her closet while she was at work. Wiping all of that down was another impossible task.

So, with nothing to pack or clean up, Dino was ready to leave within two minutes of shooting his ex-girlfriend. He had his pistol in one pocket and Kevin's cellphone in the other. The only thing Dino needed was Charlotte's car keys, which were clutched in her left hand the last time he saw them.

Back in the living room, the baby's face was red from all the wailing, and Charlotte had thankfully passed on. Her eyes were wide open, but they didn't follow Dino when he approached her. Charlotte was mostly lying down, with her upper back propped against the front door.

Her left hand lay limply in her lap. They keys hung from one ring that was looped around her middle finger. The hole in her chest continued to spew lethal amounts of blood. Her whole front half was soaked. The last of Dino's sensibilities implored him not to touch the body, but he overrode them.

"*I'm so sorry,*" he said again. Both of his eyes were wet with tears. His nose ran as well. The baby started to scream louder when Dino reached for her mother's lap. He ignored her. Dino plucked the keys from Charlotte's hand and quickly backed away. He took a deep breath and let it out in shudders. Gastric acid burned the back of his throat, but there was nothing left to throw up.

Dino started to turn away, but he saw Charlotte's purse strap on the floor behind her. He bent and grabbed it, but it wouldn't come free. Half of the purse was stuck under its owner. Dino took a deep breath and pulled Charlotte up by her free arm. The purse slipped out, but with it came a dreadful realization that Dino had done something very unholy. Something vile and inhuman. Murder was bad enough, but robbing the corpse would surely send him to an even worse level of hell.

He threw his head back and moaned woefully. He turned and lurched towards the backdoor. Halfway there the piercing screams of Charlotte's baby stopped him in his tracks. Dino would be labeled a monster when the press got wind of this story. That was unavoidable at this point. But how much worse would it be if he left a crying baby in the grips of her dead mother? It might be hours before Charlotte's body was found. Crystal would be ten times more traumatized by then.

Dino gritted his teeth and returned to his problem in the living room. He figured this would be harder than relieving

Charlotte of her purse, but *there's nothing to it but to do it*, as his cousin was fond of saying. Dino held his breath and grabbed hold of Crystal with both hands.

But Charlotte wasn't dead.

Her eyes snapped into focus and she began to scream. Even worse, she fought with Dino, and they became entangled in a hellish tug-of-war.

"*Stop!*" Charlotte shouted. A fine spray of bloody spittle coated Dino's face from forehead to chin. He squeezed his eyes shut and looked away.

"*Let go of my baby! Gimme my baby!*" Charlotte was in a panic. She was belligerent.

"*Let go!*" Dino shouted back. "I ain't gon' hurt her!"

"*Give my baby!*"

"Dammit, girl! Let go! *You finna die!*"

Not surprisingly, Dino had more strength in his coke-ravished body than Charlotte had in her half dead one. The baby slipped into his arms. Charlotte reached with both hands to reclaim her.

"*GIMME!*"

Dino had never touched the child before, but he cradled Crystal expertly and held her against his chest. He turned away. This time he would never look upon Charlotte again. He could hear the life fading from her voice as she continued to scream like a banshee.

"*Give me, gimme! Gi' my baby!*"

Outside the sun was bright. The weather was cool. Dino hopped into Charlotte's Maxima and deposited Crystal on the passenger seat, rather than take the time to secure her in the child-safety seat in the back. He was trembling furiously. He backed out of the driveway with the baby's and her mother's screams ringing in his ears.

He made it all the way to the freeway before he realized he didn't bring a diaper or a lick of milk with him.

● ● ● ● ● ●

Ebenezer Baptist Church wasn't as packed as it had been for Isaiah's funeral, but there was a nice turnout that Wednesday night. Jacob tried to pay attention to the sermon, but their pastor was on another one of his tithes and offerings rants. He spent the whole service talking about how everyone should give him *at least* ten percent of their earnings every week, or every two weeks; depending on their pay schedule.

Pastor Jeremiah Taylor quoted scriptures from the Bible, explaining how ten percent of your salary already belonged to God and keeping it for yourself was essentially *robbing* God. He assured the congregation that they would be blessed tenfold, depending on how honest they were with their tithing. Lastly he threatened the folks who did not pay their tithes, saying they were setting themselves up for a *curse* – not from him of course, but from God.

Jacob thought his pastor was pretty convincing, but he was past the point of believing everything a so-called "man of God" had to say. Sometimes there was an ulterior motive behind sermons. Jacob knew that his pastor drove a brand new, champagne-colored Escalade, for example. Plus Pastor Taylor didn't live in the hood, like Jacob and Tammy. He had a nice, five-bedroom home on the west side of town.

Some might argue that the pastor deserved these nice things for the work he did for the Lord, but Jacob was becoming more and more cynical. He knew that Isaiah's death and subsequent funeral had opened his eyes to a lot of things, like how his mother had spent her whole life doing everything the pastor and the Bible told her to do. But what did it get her? Isaiah was a holy-roller as well, but look what happened to him.

No, Jacob would be a fool no longer. He believed his life was in his own hands, and his future was determined by the decisions he made. He did not believe there was an invisible man in the sky controlling people like puppets. In the Old Testament, God did a lot of things to show people He was up there. They knew when He was happy, and you'd better believe they knew when God was mad.

But where was all of that stuff now? God hadn't burned a city down in a million years, even though Las Vegas was just as sinful as Sodom and Gomorrah. And what about all of the false prophets, like Jim Jones and David Koresh? How come God didn't smite them? There was only one answer to these questions. By the time Pastor Taylor finished begging for money, Jacob had his explanation:

There was no God.

It was scary to think it, especially inside a church house, but Jacob was a man now. He had the right to believe whatever he wanted. If he was wrong, then someone needed to explain why their *God* took Isaiah. Until then, Jacob had to take life at face value. And that meant there was no Santa Claus, no Tooth Fairy and no holier than thou carpenter who got nailed to a cross and came back to life three days later.

After the sermon, the pastor gave his customary altar call; asking anyone who didn't know Jesus to come to the front of the church, so that he may introduce them to the Lord by way of a sinner's prayer. The altar call was also for anyone who may have slipped away from God's grace or for anyone who needed a special prayer that evening. Jacob knew his mother would make him go, and she didn't disappoint. She grabbed him by the arm and walked him all the way to the pastor's podium.

"Hallelujah!" someone in the congregation shouted.

"How you doing, sister?" Pastor Taylor asked. "Would you like me to pray with you tonight?"

"Yes," Tammy said. "For me and my son. Jacob's been acting different since Isaiah died, and he's getting in trouble at school. He needs help, pastor. He got in a fight today, and I think he's getting worse."

Tammy urged Jacob forward with a hand between his shoulder blades. She rubbed the back of his neck and then pushed his shoulders down, until he knelt at the altar.

"Oh, Jesus," the pastor said, stepping around his podium, "I ask that you make your presence known in this church tonight, Lord God. We pray for healing! We pray that you reach out and touch this boy's heart, and touch his *soul*, Jesus."

Rather than wait for Jesus to reach out, the pastor palmed Jacob's head himself. He held on to it throughout the prayer.

"Lord, you know sister Tammy has been through a lot lately. You took her son Isaiah home, and we know you're taking good care of him, Jesus. We know everything happens according to *your* will, and we don't question you, Lord."

"No we don't!" someone behind them agreed.

"We only ask that you continue to bless her, Father," the pastor went on. "Bless her in this time of need, oh Lord."

Tammy dropped to her knees next to her son. He wasn't surprised to see that she was crying again.

"Y'all come up and lay holy hands on this family!" the pastor instructed his flock.

After a few seconds there were dozens of people crowded around Tammy and Jacob. They all prayed individually, mostly with their eyes closed, saying things like, "Yes, Lord," and "Thank you, Jesus." They reached out and put their holy hands on Jacob's and Tammy's shoulders, arms, backs and heads.

"Lord, we ask that you look over Brother Jacob," the pastor said. "Don't let him fall prey to the ways of the devil, Lord. We know he's filled with anger, God. We know he's mad because those people killed his brother, and we understand his feelings, Lord. We understand that the man in him wants to *rise up*! The man in him feels like he has to do something to make it right, Lord."

"Yes, he does."

"He sho' do."

"But we ask that you help him take that anger, that *fire* that's built up inside him... Let him use that fire to get closer to *you*, Lord! We ask that you take his frustration away from him! Give him peace, Lord! Give him understanding! We ask that he listen to his mama and do things that will please you, Lord God. We ask these things in Jesus' name, because we know we're unworthy. We're so unworthy!"

"Yes, we are!"

"We need you, God!"

"We ask these things in *Jesus'* name! And we give you all the honor and all the glory, Lord. We give you all the praise, God. Amen..."

"Amen, brother."

"Amen."

● ● ● ● ● ●

Tammy and Jacob didn't make it home until after nine. Tammy thought the service went well. She was sure God would work a miracle in Jacob's life. But she saw that Satan still had his claws in her son before she even got her shoes off.

Jacob turned on the TV in the living room, and they caught the tail end of yet another tragedy. According to Channel Six News, a twenty-one year old single mother was murdered in Waxahachie earlier that day. The killer took off with her car and her infant child.

Tammy took a seat on the couch with her eyes glued to the television. "Jesus. That's awful," she said under her breath.

"Must've been God's will," Jacob replied callously and went to his room.

# CHAPTER FOURTEEN
## *REVELATIONS*

While Jacob balked at Pastor Taylor's sermon for the evening, Dino cruised down the freeway in his pilfered Nissan Maxima. The baby quieted down as soon as they got on the interstate, but Dino knew it was only a matter of time before Crystal started up again. Dino had never cared for an infant before, but he was pretty sure they liked to eat every few hours or so. Plus Crystal's diaper was already soiled and bloated, mostly from the blood it absorbed while she wrestled against her mother's death grip.

"She think she know so much," Dino said, shaking his head. "But that don't mean she's always right. If somebody killed *my* mama, I wouldn't want to be with her while she died. I'm a no-good motherfucker, but even I know that," he told the baby.

The infant stared up at him curiously. Dino was covered with a fair amount of blood himself. He'd been on the road for three hours so far, and he still hadn't strapped Crystal in her carrier. The baby lay on her back on the bucket seat next to him – but Dino considered her one hundred percent safe. If he had to come to a sudden stop, he could reach over and catch Crystal before the momentum launched her into (or possibly through) the windshield. A lot of people couldn't think fast like that, but Dino knew he could do it.

"She think I don't know how to take care of no baby," he said. "But I know a lot more than motherfuckers think I know."

Dino wasn't normally one to talk to himself, but desperate times called for desperate measures. He had to keep talking because his brain was trying to power-down on him midway through his getaway. He was more than tired. He felt like he was trying to stay awake after popping six Ambiens.

Dino had been wired on cocaine for five days straight. The excitement at Charlotte's house amped him up even more, but he was almost sober now, and his body wanted to recuperate. Dino still had a little more cocaine he could use to counter his biological yearning for sleep, but he didn't want to get high right now. He dared not. He had a baby to look after, and he wasn't going to blow it this time.

Isaiah's death was an accident. Charlotte's death was a mistake as well, but that was the last innocent blood Dino would spill. His main goal in life, at that point, was to ensure Crystal did not fall victim to his wretched curse.

"I'll kill myself, before I let something happen to you," he said with a sniffle. "I swear before God, I'll put a bullet in my head if something happen to you."

The baby watched Dino's face, and she mouthed a few words that wouldn't have made sense if she could talk. Dino looked down at her and grinned.

"You gon' be alright," he promised. He coughed. "Your mama would be alright too, if she gave me the keys." He frowned. There were dried tear stains on his cheeks. "Why come she couldn't give me the keys? I didn't want to hurt nobody. I was gonna take off on foot, if I didn't get the car. I wasn't gon' shoot her. I didn't mean it, Charlotte. Lord knows I didn't."

Dino was on Interstate 35 heading north. When he first got on the freeway, he'd gone south, thinking Mexico was a good destination for them. He made it all the way to Waco before he changed his mind and reversed course.

Mexico was every fugitive's dream, but even if he could make it past the border, Dino didn't think it would be so sweet for him. A rich white man would have no trouble starting a new life down there. But Dino was black, broke, harboring a kidnapped baby, and he was in serious need of medical care. He'd stick out like a sore thumb, and the Mexicans would be quick to extradite his ass.

The bottom line was Dino was a cold-blooded killer, and he understood that he could not escape his fate. The only thing he could do at this point was make sure he went to the morgue rather than the penitentiary when it was all said and done. But before he took his last breath, Dino had to take care of some unfinished business in his hometown.

Isaiah's death was one hundred percent Dino's fault; he could accept that. But he refused to take sole responsibility for the latest murder. Charlotte would still be alive right now if Kevin hadn't panicked Dino with his ominous phone call. So Dino felt there were some Sicc Crips who should be held accountable. Their so-called OG was a given, but T Lowe wasn't the only one who needed a few bullets in his diet.

T Lowe couldn't have made the decision to *get* Dino all by himself.

● ● ● ● ● ●

Traffic started to get heavy when Dino entered Overbrook Meadows' city limits. He began to worry about someone seeing his face, but there wasn't much he could do to conceal it while driving. His best defense was to make sure he remained as inconspicuous as possible, so he obeyed the speed limit and didn't look around wildly, like he expected the police to pop up behind him at any moment.

When he exited the freeway, Dino held his right hand over his cheek, hoping any motorists watching him would assume he had a toothache. That wasn't too much of a stretch, because his wound was literally pulsating by then. He accumulated a few suspicious looks when he stopped at a red light, but Dino didn't stare back at them, and gradually the gawkers' attention was drawn elsewhere.

When he reached his destination, he let out a sigh of relief. Dino had lost more than twenty pounds since Isaiah's death. The missing weight was most noticeable in his face. His skin was stretched taut over his skull. His eyes and jaws were sunken, and his already monstrous teeth gleamed like polished bones in the fading sunlight. Dino grinned at the baby, totally oblivious to how freakish he looked.

"We made it," he told his little hostage. "I told you I wasn't gon' let nothing bad happen to you. We here now..."

*Here* was Sycamore Park, a large, wooded area located in the heart of Overbrook Meadow's Poly neighborhood. Split almost perfectly in half by Sycamore Creek, the park was once the pride of the neighborhood. It was earthy and picturesque; the perfect place for a Sunday afternoon picnic or kite-flying on a breezy autumn day.

That was thirty years ago.

Today Sycamore Park was one of the most loathsome eyesores in the city. When red and blue flags made their way down south in the late eighties, the park became the locale for countless turf wars. But that was nothing compared to the drug killings that took place in the early nineties.

Sycamore Park became so dangerous, the city's recreational department refused to set foot on the property, which left room for the hooligans and Mother Nature to regain control. The grounds were now overgrown with trees and shrubbery. The miles of winding roads within the park were booby-trapped with broken beer bottles, discarded tires and other debris. Gang graffiti covered every picnic bench and gazebo, warning outsiders to keep away, or at the very least be wary.

Many people lost their lives at Sycamore. Most thugs knew it was a great place to dump a body or a stolen car. Dino piloted the shadowy trails expertly, knowing he'd have all the privacy he needed there.

He found a spot he liked towards the middle of the park; about half a mile away from the abandoned recreation center. It was eight o'clock. The purple sky had just a little bit of light left. This was perfect because Dino needed the night to conceal him when he set off on foot. The city was full of creepazoids who only came out when the moon was high. Dino hoped to blend in with them.

He turned the Maxima's ignition off and killed the headlights. He looked around and listened for a few minutes. The park was eerily quiet, except for the zillions of crickets who were in search of a mate and the occasional croak of a bullfrog who was also in search of a date or a meal that evening. Dino looked down at his hostage. Crystal looked up at him. She hadn't cried much since Dino pried her from her dying mother's arms.

"You a good baby," Dino told her. "If I had me a daughter, I'd want her to be just like you."

Crystal giggled and kicked out with her chubby legs.

Dino smiled. A wistful tear filled his eye. Charlotte was a good mother, and there was no excuse for what he'd done to her. He knew he deserved to die, but not just yet.

Dino reached into the backseat and grabbed Charlotte's purse. He dug through it in his lap and found a pacifier close to the top.

"Oh, check this out," he said and offered it to Crystal. The baby opened her mouth and sucked merrily when Dino inserted the faux nipple.

Towards the bottom of the purse, Dino found Charlotte's wallet. There was ninety dollars inside. Dino stuffed the money in his pocket and dug around for anything else he thought he might need for his mission. There was nothing more.

There was nothing else he could do for the baby, either, so Dino got out of the car and locked all of the doors. He tossed Charlotte's car keys as far as he could in the direction of the creek, lest some dope fiend happen upon the ride and take it for a spin.

Before he closed the driver's door, Dino popped the trunk open, looking for more bandages so he could replace the sticky one he'd had on all day. There wasn't any stray gauze in the trunk, but Dino did find a sweatshirt he thought might be useful. It didn't fit him, but he draped it over his neck, so he could use it to conceal his wound if someone got close to him on the streets.

With nothing else to scavenge, Dino closed the trunk without wiping down any of the fingerprint-laden surfaces. There was no need to humor himself. He was sure the police had already found his fingerprints on the .380 he murdered Isaiah with, and his prints were all over Charlotte's home as well. All the detectives had to do was connect the dots. The boogeyman was back in the city, so it wouldn't be too difficult to find him.

As he walked away, the baby started to cry again. The wails tugged at Dino's heart, but he did not run back to her. Instead Dino quickened his pace until Crystal's screams became muffled cries. After a while, he could hear the child no longer.

● ● ● ● ● ●

Ten minutes later Dino exited Sycamore Park with mud on his sneakers and a gaggle of cockleburs stuck to his pants legs. The right side of his face was swollen and shiny and open to the world, because he'd discarded his last bandage in the tall grasses alongside the creek. Dino knew the dressing wasn't helping his wound at all, and the tape and gauze would only draw more attention to his malady.

It was getting chilly out. Dino needed somewhere to lay his head for the night. But before he took a break, Dino took a moment to do his first good deed in the last few weeks. He stopped at a pay phone and dialed 911.

"*911 Emergency. Do you have a police, fire or medical emergency?*"

"Yeah," Dino said. "There's a baby in a red Maxima in the middle of Sycamore Park; right here on the corner of Beach and Rosedale. The baby's mama is Charlotte Webb. She live in Waxahachie. The baby is doing fine right now, but it's getting cold, and somebody need to come get her. She don't have no milk, and she need a diaper."

"*Excuse me, did–*"

"The Maxima is parked close to the old rec'," Dino said. "It's off the road, in some bushes, but you should be able to find it. I locked all the doors, so can't nobody mess with her."

"*You locked the doors? Um, who am I speaking to?*"

Dino dropped the phone but did not hang it up. He left it dangling by the cord and immediately tried to put distance between the payphone and himself. There weren't many people out, so Dino jogged across the street and ducked into the first alley he saw. The alley was relatively clean. He made it two blocks before he ran into a jagged hill of discarded tree branches. He checked for dogs before jumping the fence into the backyard on his right.

Dino kept his head low as he ran towards a nearby house. There were lights on, but he didn't see anyone peeking through the windows. He sneaked down the side of the house and emerged in the front yard. He scampered across the street and jumped the fence into a different backyard.

He performed his alley-to-backyard trick a few more times, until he emerged on a quiet street seventeen blocks away from Sycamore Park. This was the same maneuver Dino used to elude Isaiah's big brother at the beginning of this saga, and it never failed to get him away from trouble.

Halfway down his ninth alleyway, Dino felt a trembling on his inner thigh. Two seconds later his phone rang. Dino pulled Kevin's cellphone from his pocket and stared at it quizzically. He had half a mind not to answer it, but nothing on the other end could hurt him this late in the game.

"Hello?"

"Damn, nigga. You can't stop killing, can you?"

Dino didn't immediately recognize the voice.

"Who this?"

"What you kill that girl for? That shit was uncalled for, ol' ugly ass nigga."

It was T Lowe.

"I'm coming for you," Dino promised him. "You gon' pay for everything that's gone wrong in my life."

T Lowe laughed. "Why don't you just kill yourself, Dino? Get this shit over with. 'Cause that's how it's gon' end. You know that, don't you? Them laws ain't trying to take you alive no more. It's shoot on sight, cuz. They want you dead, Dino. Everybody do."

"Fuck you, cuz. Why don't you tell me where you at right now? We can handle our business tonight."

T Lowe laughed again. There was something altogether unnerving about his cackle. "Nigga, you really is stupid," he said. "You don't go nowhere I don't want you to go, Dino. And you don't make no moves I don't want you to make. Ain't you figured it out yet? The only reason you in this shit is 'cause *I* put you in it. I been pulling the strings since *day one*."

Dino wanted to hang up, but he had to know what T Lowe was talking about.

"Nigga, you ain't running nothing..."

"You sure?" T Lowe said. "Alright, well how come ain't nobody help you when HB got on your ass about that dope? How come nobody didn't shoot back when Pooky got to dumping on your bitch ass?"

Those were very good questions, but Dino didn't bite.

"How come nobody didn't get your gun when you took off?" T Lowe asked. "It was laying right in the middle of the yard. How come it got left there for the police to find it?"

"You did that?" Dino asked.

"I wanted HB to kill your stupid ass," T Lowe admitted. "When Pooky missed all them shots, I figured I'd let the laws get you. But you didn't have no fingerprints on file. I didn't know that shit."

This was more deception than Dino ever imagined. The Sicc was his whole life. He thought they were all his brothers. He tried not to let the shock show in his voice.

"What, what about Peanut?" he asked. "You let Peanut get killed for nothing?"

"I thought you was smart," T Lowe said. "But you ain't, so I'll break it down for your dumb ass one more time: The Sicc is all about money, nigga. One monkey don't stop the show. I didn't want Peanut to get killed, but he knew what he signed up for. That nigga shouldn't have got in a gang, if he didn't want to get shot at."

Dino's head was spinning. "Alright, so what about me?" he asked. "Why you had beef with me in the first place?"

"You think I don't know what you was planning?" T Lowe asked. "All this shit you was doing, all that *work* you called yourself putting in. You wanted to take over the Sicc, Dino; way before that boy got killed. I saw you trying to make some moves. The homeys was starting to look up to your dumb ass, so I had to get rid of you. Plain and simple. I don't let nobody fuck with my money, especially not some retarded nigga like you."

"I'm smarter than you think," Dino growled. "Keep underestimating me. You'll see when I got this pistol in your face."

T Lowe laughed. "Nigga, you ain't smart. I bet you don't even know the police can track a cellphone, do you? You been talking on this motherfucker for, what, three minutes already?" He laughed again. "Ignorant ass..."

Dino disconnected and chucked the cellphone as far as he could. He clenched his teeth, and his nostrils flared. The whole alley was awash with fire and bloody red. Dino kept marching through the pain and the flames.

● ● ● ● ● ●

Jacob hopped off the school bus and rushed home to drop off his backpack and grab his pistol. He thought he saw something terrifyingly wonderful when the bus rounded the corner onto Campbell Avenue a few minutes ago. Jacob wasn't positive, but if he saw what he thought he saw, things were about to get very interesting in his gang-infested neighborhood.

Inside his house, Jacob lifted the mattress on Isaiah's bed and found his handgun right where he left it. He kept the gun under Isaiah's mattress for two reasons: First, if his mother was snooping around for proof of Jacob's insanity, she'd be less likely to look for incriminating evidence among Isaiah's things. And second, Jacob thought it was fitting to store his gun close to where Isaiah once slept. Isaiah was sleeping eternally now, but the gun would ensure that he did not rest in peace alone.

Jacob took the pistol off safety, but he did not cock it before stuffing it into his waistband. A month ago he wouldn't dream of concealing a gun there; with the barrel less than an inch from his manhood. But Jacob knew about guns now, and he was not worried that it might go off by itself. That's not how things worked in the real world. The gun would only go off when Jacob wanted it to, because he was the decider of life and death. He was the Grim Reaper and Satan and God, all rolled into one.

His pistol ready, he ran back to the front of the house and stepped out into the afternoon sunlight. Jacob did not lock the door behind him because he might have to run back home in a few minutes, and he didn't want his escape to be impeded in any way. If someone dared to burglarize his home in the short time he was gone, they'd better be willing to die for their ill-gotten gains – because Jacob had a gun now, and his uncle told him to shoot first and ask questions later.

Jacob jogged to Campbell and made a right turn, heading north. He jogged all the way to Crenshaw and continued across the intersection. Jacob didn't stop running until he got to South Little John. He slowed to a walk and made another right on that quiet street.

Up ahead on the left, the vision Jacob saw from his school bus window was still there. His mouth went dry, and his pulse quickened. He couldn't believe it. A red and white U-Haul truck was backed into the driveway of a small, brick house. There were five or more men standing in the front yard; most of them toting items from the back of the U-Haul into the home. All of the movers wore blue, but that was not as important as the man who appeared to be in charge of the crew.

196

In the middle of the yard one gentleman stood with a bullhorn in one hand and a clipboard in the other. He barked orders at his minions, and they were obedient to his every wish. The leader was tall and handsome. He had short hair styled in a crew cut, and he wore a thin goatee. His skin was dark bronze. His eyebrows had the best natural arches; perfect for the look of disappointment he fixed on some of his subordinates.

This was the same man Jacob pointed out in the homicide detective's big book of gang members. This was the man Jacob lived across the street from for six months – up until the day Isaiah was murdered. This was also the man who held Jacob back when he tried to attack the one who got shot in the face. Jacob didn't think they had the gall, but the Sicc Crips were back. They were trying to set up another dope house within a mile of their last one.

The Crips had balls, but balls without smarts will only get you so far. Surely they knew someone was waiting on their return. Or did they really think they could go on with business as usual? Jacob waited until he was closer before he pulled his gun.

"Say, put that box in the kitchen," the man with the bullhorn instructed one of his homies. "Take that one to the bathroom," he told another. "Put that one..."

T Lowe trailed off when he saw Jacob approaching. He lowered his megaphone and frowned. "Say, little nigga, what you doing over here?"

Jacob raised his pistol. He cocked it and pointed it at the leader's face. His hand trembled, but Jacob had eight bullets in the clip. He was bound to hit him with at least one of them.

"You killed my brother," he said. His face was hard like stone, flushed with heat.

The man with the megaphone put his hands up and began to walk backwards.

"Say, cuz, quit playing. I didn't kill your brother. You know that. The one who got shot in the face killed your brother."

"You was with him," Jacob said. "I tried to get him, but you stopped me. You held me back."

"I didn't want you to get hurt," T Lowe said. "The one who got shot in the face would've killed you, if you caught him. I saved your life that day."

"Too bad nobody's gonna save yours," Jacob said. But he was wrong about that. Before he could pull the trigger, two Crips sneaked up behind him. They grabbed his arms, and in the ensuing struggle, Jacob dropped his pistol. He fell to the ground, and the Crips started to hit him and kick him. Eight more goons rushed from God-knew-where, and they joined in the brawl.

With ten people on top of him, Jacob could do little more than protect his face. But these gangsters weren't like the wannabes at his school. They pinned his arms down and targeted his head repeatedly. His lips split and bled. They broke his nose and knocked his teeth out. One of them gouged Jacob's eye and yanked it completely out of the socket.

Jacob fought his hardest, but he could no longer defend himself. Just when he thought he would pass out or die, a small hole parted in the crowd, and the leader poked his face into it.

"Why you come over here?" T Lowe asked. "You want the one who got shot in the face, not me."

Jacob nodded. *Yes, that's what I want. Now let me go, so I can find him.*

The leader read his mind. "It's too late for that now, lil bro. You wanted to do it like this, so now we have to finish it. *Just like this.*"

T Lowe squeezed his fist into the crowd. Jacob saw that he had Uncle Myron's handgun.

"No!" Jacob screamed. *"NO!"*

But it was too late. T Lowe squeezed the trigger, and Jacob saw a bright flash of light.

**"NOOOO!"**

● ● ● ● ● ●

He awakened and sat up in bed with a jerk. Jacob's chest heaved. His head pounded. Sweat glistened on his neck and face. He reached for his eye, which was still in the socket. Jacob looked around frantically. It took a moment to realize he was not outside. He was not surrounded by Sicc Crips, and no one shot him in the face. It was all just a dream, or a nightmare, or maybe even a premonition. But it wasn't real, that was the important thing.

Jacob sighed and wiped his face with his sheets. He wondered why his subconscious would taunt him with such a dreadful scenario. If he still believed in God, Jacob might consider his dream a warning from the Most High. But since there was no God, he had to decipher his vision on a worldly level.

*Why did I get killed?*

Jacob thought about it for only half a minute before he had his answer. It was simple: In his dream, he went against his uncle's most important instruction. Uncle Myron told him to shoot first and ask questions later. This was supposed to be a murder he was committing, not some talk show interview.

When the time came to kill a Crip, Jacob could not show pity or compassion. His mission was to kill and flee. He now understood how quickly the tables could turn on him, if he allowed his victim to beg for mercy. The Crips outnumbered him ten – or maybe even twenty to one, so Jacob could not beat them with superior firepower. His best weapon was his superior smarts. He would remember this when it was time to do the deed.

He laughed at himself.

A megaphone? That alone should have made it clear that he was dreaming, but the mind is a peculiar thing. Very strange indeed.

Unable to fall back asleep, Jacob got out of bed and went to the living room. He peeked through the front curtains, more out of habit than necessity at this point, and saw that the old Sicc Crip dope house was still vacant.

He went to the bathroom and then stopped to check on his mother before returning to bed. Tammy never slept with the door closed. Jacob saw that she was curled under the blankets in the center of her bed. Tammy had the biggest bed in the house, a queen size. She looked lonely lying there by herself. Jacob wasn't too keen on the idea of her finding a man, but sometimes he did wish she had a companion. Everybody needed *somebody*. His mother was no exception.

Back in his own room, Jacob went to the closet and shuffled quietly through the hangers on the back row. On the far end he found one of Isaiah's old winter coats. Jacob unzipped the inner pocket and pulled out the gun Uncle Myron gave him. It was a Colt .32, semi-automatic. It was completely black, except for the dark brown wood grain on the handle. It was a beautiful weapon, well oiled, in mint condition.

Jacob loved the gun so much, he wanted to take it to bed with him. But this was serious business, not some kid's toy.

After a few minutes of quiet time with his new friend, Jacob returned the pistol to its hiding spot and climbed back into bed. He closed his eyes with a slight smile on his face. He hoped he could catch up with his previous dream and handle things differently this time. If not, he would be happy with a totally new dream, so long as he got to shoot a Crip in it.

Real or imagined, Jacob was in a hurry to get down to business.

He could hardly wait.

# CHAPTER FIFTEEN
## *MAMA*

"Say, is you gon' get up?"

Dino's eyes flashed open, and he brought the pistol up in one smooth motion, pointing it at the voice that awakened him. His gun was cocked and the safety was disabled, but he did not shoot Mama in the face.

Gradually his eyes adjusted to the sparse lighting, and he lowered the weapon. He stared curiously into the eyes of a dark-skinned woman in her mid-fifties. Mama wore big glasses with thick lenses. Her hair was short, salt and peppery, but she wore a wig today that was long and jet black. She was a full-sized woman, and although Dino did like a gal with shapely hips and thighs, he never once found Mama attractive. In fact, she was the epitome of *unattractiveness*, in his humble opinion.

"What you want?" Dino growled. He tucked his pistol beneath the sheets and kept it warm between his legs.

"You, uh, you said you was gon' give me some more money tomorrow. I, I mean today."

Mama knelt next to the bed with a wild look in her eyes. Her breath stank. She didn't turn on the light in the bedroom, but the hallway light was on, and the door was partially open. Dino saw a shadowy figure walk through the hallway. He sat up quickly.

"Aww, *shit!*"

An immediate burst of pain exploded on the side of his face. It was so intense, he saw bright flashes of pink and red behind his pupils. The source of the pain was as disgusting as it was predictable: Last night Dino slept without gauze covering his wound for the first time in two weeks. His sore excreted its usual pus and blood during the night, and the goo effectively glued his pillow to his face. The same thing happened a few times with the gauze, but this was the worst ever. When Dino sat up, the whole pillow came with him.

"*Goddammit!*" He lowered his head and the pressure subsided a little. "What the hell is going on?" Dino's face was twisted and mean.

"It's, it's yo face," Mama said. "You stuck to the pillow."

"*Fuck!*" Dino's eyes were red and menacing. He sat up slowly this time and stopped when the pillow case began to tug. He reached with his grimy fingers but could not get a mental image of what he was feeling. "Is it coming off?" he asked Mama.

She shook her head. "Uhn uhn. You gon' have to *jerk it* – real hard."

"Fuck that," Dino said. He opted to peel it off slowly instead, but the pain was excruciating. Every tug felt like he was trying to pull his brain out of that hole.

"*Aarrgh!*" He growled. His eyes welled with tears. "*Is it coming?!*"

Mama shook her head. She ducked down for a closer look. "Let me turn the light on," she offered.

"*Close that damned door first!*" Dino ordered.

Mama got up and closed the door. She turned the light on and rushed back to the bedside and told Dino to, "Sit up."

"*Bitch, I ain't finna sit up!* This shit hurt!"

"I'll get the pillow," Mama explained.

She reached under the pillow and braced it for the move. Dino didn't want to trust her, but he couldn't lie like that all day. He slowly made it to a sitting position, and Mama, true to her word, never let the pillow case pull his skin. She leaned in again and studied the dilemma with her beady eyes.

"It's in there good," she declared. "Why you sleep on that side of your face?"

"I wasn't gon' sleep facing a wall," Dino explained. He thought that was common sense.

"Well, you gon' have to just, yank it out," Mama deduced. "It's gon' hurt, but it won't hurt for that long."

"Fuck that," Dino said. He figured he could take the pain, but the ensuing bleeding would be bad. And Mama didn't have anything to wrap it up with afterwards. "Go get some scissors," he decided.

"What for?"

"So I can cut this pillowcase."

"That's, that's *my* pillowcase."

"Bitch, it's already messed up now. Go get some scissors!"

Mama flinched and then got up to do as she was told.

"And keep that goddamned door closed!" Dino called after her.

In a normal setting, it would have been taboo for Dino to refer to an older woman as *bitch*, especially one affectionately known as *Mama*, but this wasn't a normal setting, and Mama was no Mother Teresa.

Mama was a junkie who lived on the east side of town, in a neighborhood called Stop Six. She had been smoking crack for decades. She would have been living on the streets by now if not for the fact that Mama was a professional thief and a seasoned scam artist. She was notorious for her slip-and-fall lawsuits, spread across four states. But ironically, Mama's biggest score came from a legitimate personal injury claim five years ago.

While pacing the aisles of her local Walmart, looking for a good opportunity to conceal the camcorder she had in her cart, Mama happened upon a small puddle of olive oil, and she took one of the greatest falls in civil court history. Her injuries included a broken hip, facial lacerations and two fractured fingers on her left hand.

The Walmart folks had great lawyers, but the accident was captured on video, and Mama's injuries were indisputable. The most damning portion of the video showed a Walmart employee breaking a bottle of olive oil and wiping most of it up with a paper towel less than two minutes before Mama pushed her buggy up that fateful aisle.

With the proceeds from her lawsuit, Mama wisely bought a house and then went on a six month crack binge with the rest of her money. A lot of people in the neighborhood laughed at her for going broke so soon. But Mama knew her house was an investment that would never stop paying interest.

She turned her home into a "smoke house" and opened the doors to any dopefiend who wanted a safe place to get high. Mama also welcomed prostitutes and their johns as well as regular homeless folk who wanted to get out of the environment. Mama's fees depended on the length of stay. She would accept payments in cash or preferably crack cocaine.

Oddly enough, Mama never had any children. Her real name was Gloria Swanson. Everyone called her *Mama* because of her nurturing personality. She would help almost anyone in their time of need and take her cane to any punk who hurt one of her prostitute friends. Mama had enough clout to be a pimp if she so decided, but running a smoke house was a lot less stressful, and she made enough money to stay high all day long, every day. She didn't even have to shoplift anymore.

She returned to Dino's bedroom with a huge pair of sewing scissors that looked sharp enough to cut off an arm, or most certainly a finger.

"My granny gave me that pillow case," she muttered under her breath. "I ain't got too much left from my granny as it is..."

Dino frowned at her. "You might as well kill that noise, 'cause I ain't paying you for it. If you cared so much about it, you wouldn't have it on this bed in the first place. All kinds of nasty shit go on in this room."

Mama sighed and offered him the scissors. "Here."

"You gotta do it," Dino said. "I can't see."

"Well, here, let me get the pillow out first."

Dino held the case steady while Mama slipped the pillow out of it.

"What you want me to do?" she asked, "just cut around it, or what?"

"Cut it as close as you can," Dino instructed. "What time is it anyway?"

"Six o'clock."

"Why you wake me up so early?"

"You been here since ten o'clock last night," Mama reminded. "That's eight hours." She started to cut, and Dino winced when the sharp blades came close to his eyes.

"You got some Tylenol?" he asked.

Mama shook her head.

"Advil?"

"Nope."

"What you got in there? I know you got something."

"I got some hydrocodones," she said. "But them my personals."

"I'ma need them," Dino said. "This shit hurt like hell."

"Them my personals," Mama repeated.

"What you need 'em for?" Dino asked. "You don't even be popping pills."

"I sell them," Mama said. "Everybody likes something different. I got people who buys them."

"How much?"

She shrugged. "Four for ten."

"I'll pay you," Dino said.

Mama nodded and backed away with what was left of her granny's pillow case. When she held it up, Dino saw a rather large patch of fabric missing.

He stood and went to the mirror over the dresser. He still had about two inches of fabric hanging past his wound in all directions.

"Why didn't you cut it closer?"

"You can cut it closer if you want," Mama said and gave him the scissors. "I ain't no nurse, and that's as close as I'm getting to that thing."

Dino shook his head and inched closer to the mirror. He started to trim up his new, permanent bandage, but Mama didn't go anywhere.

"What?" he asked her.

"I need some money," she said.

"I gave you twenty dollars last night."

"I know. And today's a new day."

Dino dropped the scissors on the dresser and dug the bills from his pocket. He only had seventy dollars left.

"I can't give you no more cash," he said. "I'll give you two dimes, but I have to score first."

"When?"

"Bitch, I don't know."

"You gon' get a fifty?"

Dino frowned at her. Mama knew the dope game well. Dino could buy seven crack rocks with his seventy dollars, or he could purchase a bigger block of dope for fifty dollars. A "fifty" could be cut into twelve or thirteen dime rocks that would bring in between $120 to $130. Dino could buy two more fifties after that and make $260 from the initial $50 investment. Math like that was why drug dealing was so attractive to young boys in the hood who never had a pair of Jordan sneakers until they started doing runs for the local dope man.

"Yeah, I'ma get me a fifty," Dino said.

"You want me to get it for you?" Mama offered.

Dino's frown intensified. Sending a dopefiend to score your crack was like asking a pedophile to babysit your kids. But Dino was stuck between a rock and a hard place. It would be daylight soon, and he didn't have a car. He'd have to expose himself to get the drugs, and most of the dealers in the city knew him well.

"Where you gon' get it from?" he asked Mama.

"Amanda, the pink house," she said.

Amanda was a street rather than a person. Dino knew they had good stuff there. He counted the money out and gave it to her. He gave her his last twenty dollar bill as well.

"Bring me two boys," he said; street talk for the heroin capsules Kevin got him hooked on.

"Okay." Mama snatched the money and turned to leave.

"Hold up," Dino said. "You probably already know this, but I'll kill you if you fuck off my money or my dope. That's all the money I have, and I ain't got nothing to lose." He looked her dead in the eyes. "I will kill you, Mama. And if you don't come back, I'll set this house on fire. I know you ain't paying the insurance."

Mama's expression confirmed that she wasn't. "I'm coming right back," she promised. "Don't worry about me."

"Bring me two 40's too," Dino said. "Colt 45."

Mama looked at the money in her hand. "I ain't got enough."

"You can get them boys two for fifteen," Dino said. "That means you'll have five dollars left. You think you was gon' keep that for yourself? I told you; don't try to fuck me."

"Oh, okay then. I, I didn't know I could get 'em two for fifteen. I don't never get none of them..."

"Whatever," Dino said. "And hurry up. Bring me them hydrocodones before you go."

"Alright."

Mama left the room and came back a minute later with a brown pill bottle. She even brought a glass of water and a can of

Vienna sausages, because you weren't supposed to take the pain relievers on an empty stomach. She was a fuck up, but Mama's nickname was well-earned.

Dino turned on the television and watched the daybreak news while she was gone.

● ● ● ● ● ●

Not surprisingly, Charlotte's murder was the top story of the day. Channel Six's finest reporter, Chad Collins, sat in the newsroom looking as somber as ever.

"Charlotte Webb was only twenty-one years old," Chad was saying. "She was a single mother, working hard to make ends meet. Her daughter, Crystal, is four months old. The tragedy unfolded early yesterday morning, when Charlotte didn't show up for her job at Camp Cuties Day Care. Her manager says she was a model employee, and it was unlike Charlotte to miss a day. What made the situation even more perplexing was Charlotte never called-in to say she wasn't coming.

"The manager at Camp Cuties made several calls to Charlotte's residence as well as to her cellphone, but she didn't get an answer. The manager says she had a bad feeling. She tried to contact Charlotte's relatives at that point. One of the calls she made was to Charlotte's mother, who lives in Overbrook Meadows."

The shot cut away to a woeful, middle-aged woman who was standing outside of a brick building, possibly a police station.

"I had a message on my phone when I got off of work," the woman said. Thick tears spilled from her eyes. Her voice was shaky. She wiped her nose with a well-worn paper towel.

"I didn't get off until five, or I would've had a chance to do something sooner," she explained. "The message was from Charlotte's job. They was saying she didn't come to work today, and they couldn't get in touch with her. I called Charlotte myself, and when she didn't answer either phone, I knew something was wrong.

"I got my boyfriend to run me to Waxahachie. I didn't see Charlotte's car in the driveway when we got there. But I saw..." She put a hand to her chest and shuddered. "I saw blood coming out from under the front door. I told my boyfriend to call the police, and I shoulda waited 'til they got there, but I couldn't."

She put a hand over her face and shook her head. The tears squirted like a sliced vein.

"I went in there, through the back door, and I found Charlotte myself. She was dead. *Blood was everywhere.* I couldn't find Crystal nowhere..." The bereaved mother screamed. *"God, they didn't have no reason to kill my baby! No reason!"*

Thankfully, Charlotte's mom disappeared from the screen at that point. They went back to Chad Collins in the newsroom. He shook his head dolefully.

"A manhunt for the suspect quickly ensued," he said. "But police believe the killer had at least a two hour head start. They've processed evidence at the crime scene and learned that Charlotte's killer had possibly been living with her for days, if not weeks before the crime."

The reporter clasped his hands together. "The detectives worked the case throughout the night, and they now have *definitive proof* that Charlotte Webb's murder is tied the murder of ten-year-old Isaiah Spencer. The police informed us that multiple fingerprints collected from Charlotte's home match those found at Isaiah's Spencer's crime scene.

"They are now saying that the most likely suspect in *both* of these crimes is a man they've already warned the public about. At this point he is still unidentified, but the police maintain that he is a member of the Sick Crips gang. He is an African American male of average height and build, and he suffers from a bullet wound to the right side of his face. Police believe this wound has still not been treated by a doctor."

Chad paused for a moment to let all of that sink in. "This story could have been more tragic than it already is," he said at length. "But thankfully the suspect did not harm Charlotte's four month old daughter. He abandoned Charlotte's car with the baby still inside, and according to police, he called 911 himself to notify them where they could retrieve the infant.

"We're going to play *the actual 911 call* for you now. And we ask the public to please pay close attention. The police believe this is the killer speaking, and someone out there may recognize his voice. The detectives need all the help they can get. Okay, go ahead and roll it..."

Channel Six played the entire 911 call. Dino marveled at how dreadful he came across. He thought he was doing a good deed by reporting the whereabouts of the baby, but even with this he sounded cold and calloused. He didn't sound like he cared at all about Charlotte's murder or the emotional trauma he put her baby through.

Someone knocked on the door, and Dino turned the television off.

"Who is it?"

"It's Mama."

"Come on," Dino said.

Mama stepped into the room and made sure to close the door behind her. She had two 40 ounces of booze under one arm and a plate in her other hand. She sat the beer on the dresser and gave Dino the plate. He noticed there was a clean razor blade on top. Mama reached into her bra for the fifty and his two brown pills.

Dino took the dope and eyeballed it carefully. Everything seemed to be in order. He snorted half of one of the brown pills and then took a seat on the bed and cut up his crack. Mama stood over him, but she didn't speak. Dino cut only twelve rocks from the fifty, but they were fat. He knew they would sell quickly. He gave two of them to Mama, and she headed for the door, her fist wrapped tightly around her fix.

"Hold up," Dino said. "Who in there? I heard some noises while you was gone."

"Just Tracy and Monica," Mama replied.

"Who are they?"

"Some girls from down the street. They stay the night with me sometimes."

"You told them I was in here?"

Mama shook her head. "I didn't tell nobody, Dino."

"Who'd you say was in here?"

"I told them to mind they business."

Dino nodded. He had no choice but to believe her. "I need to sell these rocks," he said. "If somebody come by who wanna buy something, get the money from them, and come get it yourself. I don't want nobody coming in here but you."

Mama nodded. "Alright."

Dino knew that was a good deal for her, because Mama would chip a piece off of every rock she sold. Plus the longer Dino stayed there, the more dope he'd have to pay her.

"I know I already told you," he said, "but I'ma say it again, in case you forgot."

"I didn't forget," Mama said.

"Don't tell nobody I'm in here," Dino said anyway. "I know you been watching the news, so you know everybody want to get me. I got niggas on the streets who want to get me, just like the police do. If them niggas find out I'm over here, they just gon' come in here shooting. They don't care who they hit."

Mama didn't say anything.

"I don't wanna hurt nobody, but I'll tear this motherfucker up if you snitch on me," Dino assured her. "I like you, Mama. But I'll kill you. I put that on the..." Dino almost put it on his set, but he remembered that he wasn't a member of a gang anymore. "I put that on my mama," he said.

"I'm not gon' tell nobody," Mama assured him. "I swear."

Dino stared into her eyes. Again he had no choice but to trust her. It was only seven in the morning. He needed somewhere to hideout until nightfall. As long as he fed her crack, Mama's house was as good a place as any.

"Alright, get out of here," Dino said.

Mama left the room and closed the door tightly behind her. Dino popped the top on one of his 40's and took a man-sized swig of malt liquor.

As he drank, he considered the things he needed to exact his vengeance against the Sicc Crips. That brainstorm didn't take long. When he was done, there was only one item on his shopping list: *Bullets*. He needed lots and lots of them. He would send Mama to pick some up from Walmart after he sold his second fifty.

Dino turned the television back on, but he would not watch the news anymore that day. The media was making him out to be some kind of ghastly, blood-thirsty creature. Dino didn't think they were wrong about that, but he didn't want to hear it every five minutes.

*Jeez.* Even monsters have feelings.

# CHAPTER SIXTEEN
## *THE PIE MAN*

Tammy left her boss' office and marched towards the front of the restaurant. She wanted to walk right out of the front doors, but she stopped at the counter and took a few deep breaths.

"Damn, girl, what's your problem?" Sarah asked her. Sarah was Tammy's only real friend at the job. She was a young girl, only nineteen years old. But she wasn't the youngest employee at the restaurant.

Juan's Taquería was a thriving business located on the north side of town. Tammy had been working there part-time for almost four years, and she knew that some of the dishwashers who came in after school were no older than thirteen. On the weekends, the owner brought his ten year old daughter with him so she could take orders and bus tables.

"Nothing," Tammy told her work buddy. She reached into her apron for her pencil and order pad. Looking out at the crowded dining area, Tammy knew she could still make thirty dollars in tips that morning if she put on a happy face and got a little pep in her step.

"You don't look like it's nothing," her co-worker said. Sarah was thin with nice hips and thighs, killer legs that seemed to go on forever. She had long, dark hair and a sweet disposition. Sarah was a great waitress, especially for that neighborhood.

Tammy looked back to make sure no one was eavesdropping before she confided in her.

"I might get fired."

Sarah's jaw dropped. "No. Why?"

Tammy shook her head. "Sam's being an asshole. I went in there to give him my two-week's notice, and he blew up."

That was even bigger news. "You're quitting?"

"I have to," Tammy said. She looked over her shoulder again. "I can't talk about it right now. Sam's in a bad mood. If he comes out here talking noise again, I'm going to say something bad to him."

Sarah grabbed her arm. "No, honey. You're going to tell me about it." She pulled her friend towards the side entrance, but Tammy dug in her heels.

"It's not my break time yet," she protested.

"If you're quitting, what does it matter?" Sarah asked.

That was a good point. Tammy loosened up and followed her colleague outside.

● ● ● ● ● ●

The weather was unseasonably cool that Friday morning. Most of the trees in the neighborhood had relinquished their leaves to the coming winter, and Tammy hated how barren and ugly everything looked. Some people liked the sights of fall; the browns and oranges, the overcast skies. But none of that appealed to Tammy. She was definitely a spring kind of girl.

Her work uniform consisted of tight black slacks with a long-sleeved blouse, but Tammy still began to shiver right away.

"It's cold, girl. I don't want to be out here."

"Tell me why you're quitting," Sarah pressed. She pulled a box of smokes from her apron pocket.

Tammy grinned, knowing that was the real reason for the outing.

"So what's the deal?" Sarah asked.

"It's Jacob," Tammy said. She folded her arms over her chest and turned her back to the wind. "I need to drop down to one job, so I can spend more time with him."

"He's been depressed since Isaiah?" Sarah guessed.

Tammy sighed. "Yeah, but I didn't think it would be like this. He's not sad. I haven't seen him cry since the funeral. He's just so..." She shook her head. "He's mad all the time. I never raised him to be mean. I don't know where it's coming from."

"Who's he mad at?" Sarah asked.

"Pretty much everybody," Tammy said. "He been talking back to his teachers and–"

"You too?"

"No." Tammy shook her head. "He is getting a little mannish, but it's the violence I'm most worried about. He got in a fight the other day at school."

Sarah blew out a thick plume of smoke. "What for?"

Tammy shrugged. "Jacob saw three boys standing at the bus stop, and he decided to start a fight. He says they were wearing blue, and he don't like Crips 'cause of what happened to Isaiah. He says it's his *duty* to confront Crips. It's probably just a phase, but I'm worried about how far he'll take it. If he'll pick a fight with three people, maybe he'll say something to an older kid – or a grown man."

"They jumped him?"

"Yeah," Tammy said. "And the worst part is all of them got kicked out of school, but Jacob didn't. So now he feels like he got rid of them."

"He talked to a counselor?"

"We have an appointment today," Tammy informed her.

"Why don't you quit your *other* job?" Sarah suggested, "so you can stay here with me."

Tammy frowned. "Girl, please. You know I actually get *benefits* at the hospital. I already talked to my supervisor. She said I can move to dayshift whenever I want."

"So how's Sam going to fire you, if you gave him two-week's notice?" Sarah wondered.

Tammy shook her head. "He talking about, '*This is family. If you want to leave the family, why stay two more weeks? I'll hire somebody else tomorrow.*'"

Her friend giggled, because Tammy mimicked his accent perfectly.

"I been here *four years*," Tammy said. "This is how he treats me?"

"He's just mad," Sarah guessed. "He don't want to lose you."

"And how are we a family?" Tammy wondered. "He's Iranian, his wife is white, I'm black and you're Mexican. All of the cooks are Asian, and nobody likes each other. And this place is called *Juan's Taquería*. Who the hell is *Juan*?"

Sarah laughed. "I been wondering that, too."

"I just hope this counseling works out for Jacob," Tammy said, her mood somber again.

"Who are you going to?" Sarah asked.

"I forget his name..."

Sarah nodded, and then her eyes brightened. "Hey, you know my little brother had to go to a counselor when he got arrested for bringing a gun to school. They tried to send him to see this old lady, but he didn't like her, and they was getting into arguments. And then they sent him to this other guy on the east side. He's real low budget. He got along with my little brother right off the bat, and Jesus started to change. He started to do good in school and everything. And he still hasn't went back to jail or nothing."

"What you mean *low budget*?"

"He works off, like, grants and stuff," Sarah explained. "He don't hardly make no money for hisself. He got a program in the MLK center on Truman. He used to be in a gang, and he work with all of those gang kids. They respect him, 'cause he was in prison, and he talks real with them."

Tammy found herself growing more intrigued as she listened. "He sounds great. What's his name?"

"Steve, something..." Sarah knitted her eyebrows. "I don't remember his last name, but I know they used to call him the *Pie Man* back in the day. He don't let the kids call him that now. But everybody knows about it, because he got it tattooed on his arm."

"What's a pie man?" Tammy wondered.

Sarah shrugged. "I don't know."

The restaurant's side door swung open. Their boss stepped out with a big scowl pulling his cheeks down. Sarah tossed her cigarette, but not quickly enough.

"This is not your break," Sam told her. "Are you still working here, or are you quitting too?" His accent was so thick, it was almost cliché.

"I'm still working," Sarah said. She scooted past him on her way back inside the restaurant, but Sam stopped Tammy before she could follow.

"Listen," he said when it was just the two of them out there. "I didn't mean to say the things I said to you. I think you are great person, hard worker. And I would like for you to stay for two more weeks, if that is what you would like to do."

"I would," Tammy said. "I need the money."

"If you would still like to work on the weekends, instead of quitting," Sam said, looking down at his shoes, "that would be fine also..."

"Thanks, Sam." Deep down Tammy knew her boss had a good heart. It was refreshing to see him show it every now and then.

He opened the door for her, and Tammy graciously returned to her post.

"I been wondering," she said when they got inside. "Who's Juan?"

Sam shrugged. "*Juan* is good name for taquería. Would you buy taco from ShahkAm Pournavab?"

Tammy giggled. "I thought your name was Sam."

"I am whoever America wants me to be," the restaurateur replied. "This is great country, yes?"

● ● ● ● ● ●

Steven Stewart, no longer known as the Pie Man, looked up from the pile of papers on his desk. His small office was quiet, but the community center was always noisy. He listened to the echo of basketballs and competitive shouts from the gym around the corner.

Steve had only one window in his office. It didn't offer much of a view. He looked out into the hallway and saw a young girl drinking from a water fountain. An athletic boy close to her age leaned against the wall next to her. He grinned and spat the best game he could muster, but even from his desk twenty feet away, Steve could tell the girl was not interested.

On the wall above the water fountain hung pencil drawings and paintings created by the children in the daycare. Their subject for the week must have been still life, because all of the sketches depicted a bowl of fruit, a flower pot or an old watering can.

To the right of the water fountain was a marble bust of Martin Luther King Jr. The sculpture sat on an exquisite column. It had only been defaced once that Steve was aware of. But that was before he came to work at the community center. No one would dare do anything that disrespectful now – or at least Steve was sure none of *his* kids would.

The big man leaned on his desk with his eyes narrowed. His breathing slowed as he tasted the air, like a cobra. Steve stood six feet, three inches tall and weighed almost two hundred and thirty pounds. According to the medical charts drawn up by the powers that be, Steve was considered overweight.

But even his doctor agreed there were always exceptions to the rules; especially for someone who was as overtly muscular as Steve was. He was in great shape. He could run faster and longer than any of his young students, but physical fitness was the last thing on his mind at that moment.

He rose from his seat and cocked his head, listening intuitively to the sounds coming from the gym. The dribbling basketball was constant, but there was something else... So far it was just talk, but one of the voices was laced with anxiety. It was a subtle tone ninety percent of the world's population wouldn't notice, but Steve was always aware of these delicate shifts. Not only did it help with the work he did today, but his keen ear helped him avoid many bloody situations at the Fort Leavenworth penitentiary eleven years ago.

Steve exited his office, but he was stopped by an attractive female before he made it to the gym.

"Excuse me..."

He half turned, eager to tend to his business on the court, but also not wanting to be rude. "Yeah. Can I help you?"

"Hi," the woman said. She wore black slacks with a white blouse that reminded Steve of a hostess. She had smooth, mocha skin, large brown eyes and full pink lips. Her hair was frizzy, borderline curly. She had it pulled back into a ponytail. "I'm Tammy Spencer," she said. "I spoke to you earlier..."

"Oh, hi," Steve replied. "It's nice to meet you." He shook her hand briefly. "I'm sorry, I, uh..." He looked away. The dicey conversation he heard a moment ago was now a full-fledged argument.

*"Get out my face, ho!"*

*"We don't know you, nigga!"*

*"What you doing here in the first place?"*

The voices came from around the corner. Steve felt bad for exposing his visitor to such language.

216

"I'm, I'm sorry," he said. "I have to check on that. You could, you can have a seat in my office. I'll be back in a second..."

He gestured for Tammy to enter his office, and she did so, with a little reluctance, Steve thought. But his guest wasn't about to get jumped, so Steve had to redirect his focus. He turned his back on Tammy and jogged to the gym's main entrance. None of the basketballs were bouncing by the time he got there. There were almost fourteen boys in the gym. They were all watching a confrontation between a new kid and two of Steve's regulars.

"*Mike!*" Steve's voice boomed, and he effectively ended the altercation from thirty feet away. "*Mike!* What the hell's going on, man?"

Mike backed away from the new kid and folded his arms over his chest. Mike was a tall, caramel-colored brother. He was once the fierce leader of the Truman Street Bloods; inciting fear and chaos in his neighborhood. His peers called him Psycho Mike because of his explosive temper, but Steve taught him to use his leadership skills for the betterment of the community – or so he thought.

"This fool started it," Mike complained, "talking about I shot his brother."

The fool in question was a student Steve had never seen before. He was short and stocky, and his mean glare was only a front. Much like a canine, Steve could smell fear. For him, the scent was as pungent as fresh bacon.

"And what you doing, Tyrone?" Steve asked the third troublemaker.

"He was talking about Mike shot his brother," Tyrone explained. "I was trying to tell him to leave that stuff in the streets. We don't got no beefs up in here."

Steve shook his head. "I coulda sworn I heard you say, '*We don't know you, nigga.*'"

Tyrone looked down at the shell toes on his sneakers.

"And what are you getting in his face for?" Steve asked Mike.

"I told him to kill that noise," Mike said. "But he kept talking."

"That nigga shot my brother," the instigator said.

"See," Mike said.

"What's your name?" Steve asked the newcomer.

"Lil Ced."

"What set you claim?" Steve asked.

"I'm Crippin'," Lil Ced said. "Bideker Boys."

"Alright," Steve said, "first of all, we don't use those street names in here. What's your real name? Cedric?"

The boy scowled but nodded.

"Second of all," Steve continued, "There ain't no gangs in this building. There's no Bideker, there's no Truman, there's no Crip and there's no Blood."

"That's what I tried to tell that fool," Mike said.

Steve spun on him. "How the hell you gon' tell him anything like that? I told you not to get in nobody's face. And you damned sure don't need Tyrone co-signing on your shit. If both of y'all ran up on me talking like that, I'd wanna bust some heads, too."

Mike frowned. He was by far the most infamous ex-banger in the building. A lot of people still looked up to him. Whenever he slipped back into his old persona, Steve was there to rebuke him. Fortunately Mike always took his scolding like a man.

"My bad," he said.

"You gon' have to gimme fifty," Steve said.

Mike opened his mouth to say something, but he thought better of it. Tyrone tried to walk away, but Steve couldn't let him get off so easily.

"You owe me fifty too, Tyrone."

"For wha–"

"For *co-signing*," Steve said. "You don't gang up on *nobody* in here, physically or verbally."

Tyrone's shoulders dropped. He walked off to a quiet corner to start his push-ups.

"The rest of y'all get back to your game," Steve ordered. A moment later the balls started bouncing again. "Hold up, Mike," Steve called.

Mike came back and glared at the newcomer.

"Fix your face," Steve instructed, and the boy did. "You shot his brother?" Steve asked.

Mike frowned. "Man, I don't even *know* his brother."

"What's your brother's name?" Steve asked Cedric.

"Monte. Monte Payne."

"What he go by on the streets?" Steve asked.

"That's it," Cedric said. "Everybody call him Monte."

"You shoot somebody named Monte?" Steve asked his veteran.

Mike shook his head. "I don't know that dude."

"When did he get shot?" Steve asked.

"Last October," Cedric said.

Mike huffed. "Homey, I was locked up last October. Wasn't I, Steve?"

Steve nodded. "This man was locked up when your brother got shot," he told Cedric. "I know this for a fact, because I went to visit him. He was locked up from July last year 'til January this year."

Cedric's eyes registered confusion. It was a look Steve knew very well. A lot of the boys at the center hated people they didn't even know. Oftentimes their beefs had trivial origins. On the streets, Mike and Cedric might have had a shootout, without ever knowing the truth behind their feud. Even worse, neither of them was more than sixteen years old.

"I think you owe this man an apology," Steve prompted.

Cedric's frown intensified. In the hood apologies were so rare, they were almost forbidden. Making Cedric admit to his wrongs was one of many barriers Steve had to break down before he could truly reach the boy.

"My, my bad then," Cedric said without looking Mike in the eyes.

"It's all good," Mike said.

"Alright, now you gotta drop and gimme fifty," Steve told the new kid.

He looked up in confusion. "What that mean?"

"You owe him fifty push-ups," Mike informed him, showing the leadership skills Steve admired so much. "Come on. We can do 'em over here."

Mike headed off towards the side of the court. Cedric followed grudgingly.

"It ain't that bad," Mike told him. "They hurt at first, but after a while they won't hurt no more. It'll make you stronger."

"Come holler at me when you get done," Steve told Cedric. "We need to go over the rules, so this won't happen no more."

Cedric shrugged and nodded.

Steve sighed and looked over his whole group before returning to the visitor in his office. But when he neared the gym's exit, he saw his guest waiting in the doorway.

"I'm sorry," he said when he was close enough to speak without yelling. "I thought you was waiting in my office."

"I wanted to see what was going on in here," Tammy said. "If I'm going to bring my boy, I need to know what you do."

"Oh, well, stuff like that don't happen all the time," Steve said. "That was a new kid I've never seen before. Sometimes they come in fresh off the streets, and just..." He trailed off because Tammy was smiling.

"It's okay," she said. "I think you did real good."

● ● ● ● ● ●

Back in his office, Steve was surprised to learn that Tammy was the mother of Isaiah Spencer; the slain ten-year-old he'd heard so much about on the news. Steve immediately felt empathy as Tammy told her story. A lot of mothers came to his office to complain about things their boys were doing, but none of them were as sweet and kind or as passionate as Tammy was that day.

Usually after listening to a mother's side of the story, Steve could point out many things she was doing to contribute to her child's delinquency. But with Tammy there was nothing. She was a smart woman, she was a praying woman, and she was hard-working. She clearly loved her son and gave him all of the attention and discipline she could. Jacob sounded like both a product of his environment and a product of his circumstances.

But there was one thing Tammy did have in common with the other mothers who dragged their children to the community center. This particular characteristic went much further than mere statistics. It reached into the heart of almost every black family Steve knew and ripped it apart at the seams: Through no fault of her own, Tammy had to raise her surviving child without a male role model in the home. Jacob's father abandoned them many years ago.

When she was done talking, Tammy looked up at Steve with large eyes that were wet but hopeful. "Now," she cleared her throat, "tell me about you."

"Okay." He smiled. "My name is Steven Stewart. My position here is counselor and mentor. But I've never gone to college, so I don't have any official certifications. I grew up in Stop Six, not too far from here. And, like your son, I grew up without a father to teach me how to be a man. I had to learn from the thugs on the streets, and they taught me a lot of things I had no business knowing – at any age.

"I started selling drugs when I was thirteen," Steve said. "I started getting arrested around the same time. But I didn't do any real time until I was twenty-one. By then I was a bonafide menace to society. I was a certified gang-banger. I was involved in fights and shootouts all the time.

"I went to jail so much, the guards yelled, '*Welcome home*,' whenever they saw my face. I was selling mostly cocaine back then. I wasn't just selling it; I was cooking it. My so-called friends nicknamed me *The Pie Man* because I was such a good cook. And, like the fool I was, I embraced that name. I was proud to be The Pie Man.

"But, I ended up getting busted again," Steve said. "That last time was the worst. The judge said he was sick of seeing me in his courtroom, and he gave me fifteen years. I did ten flat. Those ten years in the joint changed me. But I won't lie and say I changed right away. For the first five or six, I was just as bad as I was on the streets. Actually, I was worse. I fought regularly. I stabbed people. I'm not proud of those things, but that's the kind of person I was. That's who I thought I had to be to survive."

Tammy nodded.

"But then I found out I didn't have to live like that," Steve said. "I started going to church, and I found God." He chuckled. "It was just like in the movies: I was reading my bible in my bunk one night, and the whole cell suddenly filled with light. I knew it was the Holy Spirit, and I started to shake. I cried so hard. I couldn't help it.

"The next morning I threw all of my drugs and weapons away, and from that point on, I only wanted to become a better man and help others see the light. I knew I hurt a lot of people in this city. So when I got out the pen, this is where I started; on the same streets I used to do so much dirt on."

"That's beautiful," Tammy said.

"Well, it's not all I want it to be," Steve said. "But I do my best. Every year I see boys in here that I can't reach. Sometimes I hear about boys I thought I *did* reach, but they ended up getting killed or sent to the penitentiary."

"You can't save 'em all," Tammy said.

"I know," Steve replied. "But from what you've told me about Jacob, I'm pretty sure I can help him. When are you going to bring him by?"

"I'm not sure," Tammy said. "We already have an appointment with a grief counselor this afternoon, but I think he'd do better with you, since you know so much about gangs."

"Well, whatever works best for him," Steve said. "I'm here every day, from noon until ten p.m. You never need an appointment."

He smiled, and Tammy smiled too.

"Okay, well, I'd better get going," she said. "It was really nice meeting you."

She stood and offered her hand. Steve stood before he shook it. He walked her out of the office.

"It was nice meeting you too, Ms. Spencer."

In the hallway, Steve saw Cedric sitting on the floor across from the MLK bust.

"I didn't see you come by," he said.

"You told me to come talk to you after I did my push-ups," Cedric stated. "I saw you already had somebody in there, so I waited over here."

"Oh," Steve said, glad to see the boy had some manners. He had an excellent success rate with teens who came in with their basic social skills already intact. "Alright, come on," Steve told him. "But we gotta hurry up. I'm taking everybody out for pizza in a minute. You hungry?"

Cedric nodded. "Yes, sir."

● ● ● ● ● ●

Tammy got home at two o'clock, and she and Jacob left at three-thirty to meet his grief counselor. Despite the encounter with Steve, Tammy held out hopes that her son would bond with the therapist. But when Jacob exited the counselor's office an

222

hour later with his head hanging low, Tammy knew they didn't get off to a good start.

"How'd it go?" she asked when they got to the car.

Jacob shrugged. "Alright."

"Did you like the counselor?" Tammy asked.

Jacob shrugged again. "He alright, I guess. But he don't know what I feel like. All he knows is what his books say I'm supposed to feel like."

Tammy nodded. "That's okay. I talked to another counselor today who will probably understand you better."

Jacob buckled his seatbelt with a frown. "Mama, I don't wanna start going to all these different people."

"Hopefully it'll just be one more person," Tammy said. "His name is Steve, and he didn't learn counseling from a book. He's been in a gang, and he's been to prison. He doesn't even have a degree."

Jacob furrowed his brow. "For real?"

"For real," Tammy said. "He's a good dude. You'll see."

# CHAPTER SEVENTEEN
## *DEVIL REDS*

On Monday Jacob's suspension was officially over, and he was happy to get dressed that morning while listening to the *I Love Going to School* song on the radio. Isaiah had been dead for three weeks now, and Jacob had only been to school three days since then. He never thought he'd say it, but school was a welcomed respite from all of those tedious days spent at home.

It would be different if he was off for summer vacation and he had something to be happy about. But smiles were few and far between in the Spencer household. Isaiah was usually the one who cracked everyone up with his intentional and unintentional goofiness. His absence left a huge void in their lives that had yet to be filled.

Tammy made oatmeal and toast that day, and Jacob gobbled up every bite.

"I gave my two-weeks notice at the restaurant last week," Tammy told him as he downed a glass of orange juice.

"You quit?" Jacob clarified.

"Yeah. My last day is next Friday."

"You're just going to work at night at the hospital?"

Tammy shook her head. "No, Jacob. I'm moving to day shift. I'm going to work seven 'til three, so I'll be here when you get home from school."

He nodded. "That's cool."

"I'm going to start taking classes in a couple of months," Tammy said, "so I can be a medical assistant. They make more money, and I'll probably be able to get us a house somewhere else, after a while."

"Somewhere like where?"

"I don't know. Where do you want to live?"

Jacob didn't really care. Isaiah was already dead, so it sounded like a case of too little too late. But he knew his mother wanted to interact with him, so he said, "I heard it's nice over by Hulen Mall."

"It is," Tammy agreed. "But we probably can't afford a house over there, even if I get promoted. I was thinking more like Forest Hill, or maybe Everman."

"Everman's cool," Jacob said. "Then when I get to high school, I'd be a bulldog instead of a *parrot*."

Tammy chuckled. "I always thought it was funny that Poly's mascot is a parrot. I wonder who thought of that..."

"I know it wasn't nobody black," Jacob said.

"How you figure?"

"They didn't let black kids go to Poly until 1971," Jacob informed her.

Tammy cocked an eyebrow. "Where'd you learn that?"

"Our teacher told us last February," Jacob said. "We only get one month to learn about black people, so I always pay attention."

● ● ● ● ● ●

When he got to school, Jacob felt like something was different as soon as he stepped off the bus. There was a new electricity in the air. It didn't take Jacob long to realize he was the cause of it. His fight with the wannabe Crips was still on everyone's mind. The students were divided on how they should respond to him.

Some of them stared in awe: Jacob had done something none of them were brave enough to do. They wondered why he didn't get kicked out of school like the Crips. Others gave Jacob a wide berth; thinking he was a predator now, and any of them could be his next victim.

It didn't matter that Jacob had technically lost his fight, because in middle school victory and defeat are not always clear cut. The important facts were Jacob took the first swing, he bloodied one Crip's nose, and he almost knocked another one out cold. The wannabes ganged up on him, but Jacob emerged from the assault virtually unscathed. And most significantly, he was still attending classes at William Joseph, but the Crips were nowhere to be seen.

So now, whether he wanted the title or not, Jacob was the Big Man on Campus. After fighting through a curious crowd that felt like paparazzi, he found an empty spot next to his best friend in the auditorium. Harold regarded him oddly as Jacob took a seat.

"Man, do you see how everybody's looking at me all crazy?"

"Uh, yeah," Harold said sarcastically. "If, if you haven't noticed, I'm looking at you the same way."

Jacob met his eyes and laughed.

"It's not funny," Harold said. "Sometimes I feel like, like I don't know you no more."

"Why you say that?"

"I asked if you were okay," Harold reminded. "I asked about those boys, and you said everything was fine. But then you started another fight with them anyway."

"Man, so what? They gone, and I'm here. What difference do it make?"

"I guess it don't matter now," Harold said. "Except you lied to me, man. If you didn't want to talk about it, you should've said so. You didn't have to lie."

"I didn't lie about nothing."

"Then tell me why you kept messing with them."

Jacob rolled his eyes. "Can't you let it go?"

"You could've got kicked out, too," Harold informed him. "If you tell me what's going on, maybe I can help you."

"I already got too many people trying to help me, Harold. I don't need no more help."

"My dad says you're going through–"

"Fool, didn't I tell you to stop telling your dad shit about me?"

Harold was so surprised he flinched. "I only told him–"

"You weren't supposed to tell him *nothing!*" Jacob spat. "But you can't help it, can you? You can't keep your fucking mouth shut."

Harold's eyes were wide and fretful. "I, I didn't tell him about your gu–"

Jacob punched him hard in the chest before Harold could get the word out. The blow forced the air from Harold's lungs and sounded off with a muffled *THUNK!*

"*Nigga, what's wrong with you?*" Jacob growled.

"*What's wrong with **you**, man?*"

Jacob looked around to see if anyone saw what happened. A handful of kids did.

"Why you keep bringing that up?" he hissed. "I told you: Don't never talk about it again!"

"I didn't tell nobody about it!" Harold squealed.

"But you keep bringing it up! I don't want you to say *nothing* about that to *nobody*. Not even me!"

Harold grabbed his backpack and rose to his feet.

"Where you going?" Jacob grabbed his arm.

"*Leave me alone!*" Harold shouted, loud enough for everyone in a ten feet radius to hear. He jerked his arm away roughly. Jacob saw tears in his eyes.

"Wait, man..."

Harold turned his back and slowly made his way down the other side of the aisle. Jacob would've gone after him, but he knew Harold was crying, and that's one thing a man should always be allowed to do in private.

● ● ● ● ● ●

Before he went to homeroom, Jacob stopped in the bathroom and locked himself inside one of the stalls. He sat on the toilet and cradled his backpack in his lap. When he heard the noise trickle down to one, and then no students in the restroom with him, Jacob unzipped his backpack and removed a white handkerchief folded around a hard, metal object.

He unwrapped his pistol and examined it under the flickering florescent lights. The gun was beautiful to him. He loved the cold steel, the wood grain handle, the way it fit so perfectly in his hand.

The tardy bell rang. Jacob rewrapped his uncle's gift with shaky fingers. He knew he had no business bringing the firearm to school today, just as he had no reason to go to the bathroom and check on it. He had plenty of excuses for his behavior, but none of them added up to much.

The truth was Jacob liked to have his pistol with him. He liked to tote it, he liked to touch it, and he liked to look at it. It gave him a rush, and it comforted him at the same time. It made him feel powerful. Jacob had never felt so in control.

But all of that changed the moment he walked into his homeroom class. Before he could take a seat, Jacob's teacher summoned him to her desk. He expected a reprimand for his tardiness, but she had something else to tell him; something so shocking, Jacob almost shit his pants right there in front of everyone.

"The principal would like to see you," Mrs. Hymel informed. She gestured towards a hall monitor who was waiting to escort him to the office.

Jacob's jaw dropped. His whole body went numb. His first thought was Harold stabbed him in the back and told about the gun. His second thought was *What the hell am I gonna do with this backpack?* The obvious answer was to not take it with him, but his alternatives were limited.

If he stopped by his locker on the way to the office, that would look suspicious. But he didn't want to leave his bag unattended in the classroom, either. Mrs. Hymel's homeroom was as wild as it gets. No one had assigned seats. Half of the students were walking around at that very moment.

"Whuh, what do I have to go to the office for?" Jacob asked his teacher.

"I don't know," Mrs. Hymel said, barely looking up from her grade book.

Jacob debated a moment longer before making his decision. If the principal knew about the gun, he would've sent policemen to escort him, rather than some snotty-nosed sixth grader.

"Alright," he said. Jacob threw the backpack over his shoulder and followed the hall monitor out of the room.

• • • • • •

Mr. Gilliam wore a purple button-down with a black tie that morning. He lounged behind his desk with a cup of coffee and a half-eaten box of Krispy Kremes. There were eight other staffers who worked in the main office. It didn't appear that Mr.

Gilliam shared his doughnuts with them before taking the box to his desk.

Jacob sat across from him and placed his backpack on the floor between his feet. He looked up anxiously. The principal leaned back in his chair and licked his chops.

"How you doing today, Jacob?"

"I'm, I'm fine, sir."

The fat man nodded. "I called you in here, just to check in with you, see how things have been going since we talked last Wednesday..."

"Oh, I'm, uh, fine, sir."

The principal looked him up and down. His eyes seemed to settle on Isaiah's bag, but that might not have been the case. Either way, Jacob's underarms became moist. He prayed the perspiration wouldn't bead on his forehead as well.

"Did you meet with the grief counselor on Friday?" Mr. Gilliam asked.

"Yes, sir."

"How'd it go?"

"It went great," Jacob lied. "I liked him a lot."

"How often are you going to see him?" the principal wanted to know.

"Once a week," Jacob said. He noticed Mr. Gilliam's cheeks drooping into a frown, so he added, "But my mom found another counselor I can see every day after school."

"That's good," Mr. Gilliam said. He grabbed a doughnut from his box and ate half of it with one bite. He licked his fingers clean. "When are you going to meet with this other counselor?"

"Today, sir."

"What about the other thing?" the principal asked. "How are you feeling about gangs and people who wear *blue*? You know, on the way in here this morning, I saw quite a few students wearing blue shirts with blue pants. The first thing on my mind was, *I wonder if Jacob is going to attack this boy next, or this girl...*"

That was a coincidence, because Jacob wondered the same thing. Everyone in the hallway who wore all blue caught his eye. But none of the students he scrutinized were Crips or even wannabes. The color alone didn't push Jacob into a rage. It took the color *and* the gangster mentality to piss him off. He sensed the principal knew that. "I don't have a problem with people wearing blue."

"That's not what you said last week."

"I was mad at those guys because they said they were Crips, *and* they said bad stuff about my brother. But even if that happens again, I know I don't have to fight them. Words can't hurt me, and it's not worth the trouble."

The principal grinned broadly. Jacob knew he'd like that answer, because he got that exact sentence from his counselor. And his counselor learned a lot of smart things from all of those books on his shelves.

"That's great," Mr. Gilliam said. "That's the attitude I'm looking for. I hope the incident last week was a one-time thing, and you're ready to move on with your schooling. If you have anything you would like to talk to me about, don't hesitate to stop by my office. Mr. Sweeney is also available whenever you need."

"I'm fine," Jacob said. He waited a couple of beats and then asked, "Is, is that it? Can I go back to class?"

"Sure," Mr. Gilliam said. "Enjoy your day, son."

Jacob grabbed his backpack and hurried out of the office. When he got to the hallway, he wiped his forehead and realized it was indeed slick with sweat. If the principal noticed, he didn't say anything. But how could he not see it? Wasn't he trained to be aware of subtle things like that?

The only thing Jacob knew for sure was that he was being watched, and he definitely shouldn't have brought his gun to school. The stress was starting to make him feel queasy, but he would have to tolerate his bubbly stomach for quite a while longer. It was only eight-thirty am. He had a long way to go before he could take his gun back home.

● ● ● ● ● ●

There was no more excitement by lunchtime, and Jacob decided he was probably in the clear as far as the gun was concerned. But he kept a death grip on his backpack for the rest of the day; just in case. He saw his friend Harold when he went to the cafeteria, but Harold quickly cut his eyes and buried his nose in his dad's paper bag lunch. Jacob went through the line to get a hot plate. Harold still wouldn't make eye contact when Jacob walked towards his table.

*Fuck you then*, Jacob thought. He found an empty table on the other side of the cafeteria, but he didn't stay unaccompanied for very long. Four students he didn't have any classes with approached and asked if they could eat with him.

"I don't care," Jacob said.

The students crowded around him; one on either side, and the other two sat across from him. The school lunch for the day was pizza. This was probably the most adored and coveted meal served in the cafeteria. Jacob was immediately apprehensive when the boy sitting across from him wanted to give his slice away.

"You, you want my pizza?"

Jacob looked up at him, expecting a trick. The boy was tall and skinny. He was Hispanic, with long hair that was past due a haircut. He had bushy eyebrows with clusters of nasty pimples on his cheeks. He looked away nervously.

"Who are you?" Jacob asked.

"I'm, I'm Ricky," the boy said.

"Why you don't want your pizza?" Jacob asked. "What's wrong with it?"

"I had some chips earlier," Ricky explained. "I'm not that hungry."

Jacob reached over and grabbed his pizza, his eyes still narrowed. He stacked the slice on top of his and made a double-decker.

"I'm Willie," the student on Jacob's left said. He was short and thin with skin the color of whiskey. He had large eyes that could have been described as curious or *scary*. Jacob chose the latter.

"That's Mark," Willie said about the boy on Jacob's right. "And that's Jonathan," he said in regards to the fourth student.

Jacob didn't know this was going to be a meet-and-greet, but he didn't want to be rude. Plus if Harold wasn't talking to him anymore, Jacob might need some new losers to pal around with.

"I'm Jacob."

"Oh, we know who you are," the one introduced as Jonathan said. He was a skinny, cocoa-colored brother. Jacob didn't know him directly, but he'd heard Jonathan had the sickle-

BLOOD FOR ISAIAH

cell disease. That may have been a schoolyard rumor, but Jacob thought the whites of his eyes looked a little yellowish.

"We know your brother got killed," Willie said.

Jacob started to get upset, but Ricky added, "Yeah. We're sorry about that."

"And we know you don't like those crabs," Mark said. Mark was chubby like Harold used to be before he went to live with his dad.

Jacob had no idea what he meant by *crabs*, but he didn't want to admit it and risk looking foolish in front of this new crowd. Based on how the word was used in the sentence (English was Jacob's favorite subject), he knew *crabs* had to have something to do with the Crips who got expelled.

"No, I don't like them," he said.

"We don't like them, either," Ricky said. "I'm glad they gone."

"Dumb ass erickets," Mark said.

Jacob's mind raced. That was another term he wasn't familiar with, but he was a fast learner. Apparently people who don't like Crips don't refer to them as Crips. They call them crabs and erickets. Jacob understood *crab* right away, but *ericket* took some brainwork. Jacob assumed they were insulting Crips by comparing them to *crickets* – but he might have been wrong about that.

"Are you a Blood?" Willie asked.

Jacob said, "Yeah," before he considered the consequences.

"I told you," Willie said to Mark.

"Is that why them crabs killed your brother?" Jonathan asked.

That explanation sounded a lot better than, *I didn't want to get my pants dirty that day*, so Jacob said, "Yeah," again.

Jonathan nodded.

"That's why I don't like them fools," Willie said. "They always starting shit."

"They should all die," Ricky said.

"CK *all day*," Jonathan agreed.

Jacob was totally lost by then, but he did understand that all of his new friends felt the same way he did about Crips – *crabs* that is. And now that he thought about it, all four of the boys at his table had some sort of defect that would have made them easy targets for bullies at the school: Ricky had pimples from hell, Willie was undersized, Mark was fat and Jonathan had sickle-shaped rather than regular red blood cells.

It was highly likely the crabs picked on all four of these boys before Jacob came along and *vanquished* them from the school. Jacob didn't know what more they wanted from him, but Mark's next words cleared things up.

"Can, can we be in your gang?"

That was so funny, Jacob forgot to laugh. "Alright," he said. *Why the hell not?* If this band of misfits wanted to help him avenge Isaiah, they were certainly welcome. The more the merrier. Plus his new friends already knew more about hating crabs than Jacob did.

"What's the name?" Jonathan asked.

"The name of what?" Jacob said.

"Your gang," Jonathan said. He grinned mischievously. His jaundiced eyes glowed like a cat's.

Jacob thought fast. He felt that he had gone too far already, and retreat was the best option. If he backtracked and said he was just kidding, there would be no repercussions. He would lose face, but the boys at his table were losers, so their opinion didn't matter.

But in a way, they did matter. Jacob was intrigued by their lingo, and avenging Isaiah was still a necessity. So far Jacob had done virtually nothing for his dead brother, but there's power in numbers.

Plus Jacob couldn't deny how good it felt to have people look up to him. If they joined his imaginary gang, Jacob would be their leader. He could have a double-decker pizza anytime he wanted. And Jacob would teach them to be a *respectable* mob; to only go after their true enemies, rather than pick on random kids just because they were different.

Jacob came up with a gang name that expressed his disdain for erickets as well as his rejection of God.

"We called the *Devil Reds*."

The boys were quiet for a few moments. Jacob thought they would laugh at his stupid gang name, but Jonathan said, "That's tight, man. We wanna be down with the Devil Reds."

"Alright," Jacob said. "We'll talk about it some more later. But I have to lay low for a while. The principal's watching me, 'cause of that shit last week."

"That's cool," Willie said. "We'll stay under the radar; like a submarine."

That was so corny, Jacob wanted to throw his juice at him. But Willie was his homey now, so he had to accept him as he was.

"Yeah, nigga," Jacob said. "Like a submarine."

# CHAPTER EIGHTEEN
## *MLK*

After school Jacob was finally able to breathe a sigh of relief. He made it through the whole day without anyone finding out about his gun. Jacob expected the worst from his friend, but Harold wasn't a snake, rat or tattletale. Even with the friction between them, he'd kept his mouth closed about the things that mattered most, and Jacob knew he owed his buddy an apology.

But before he could get to that, Jacob had new friends to entertain, and his rift with Harold got moved to the back burner.

Jonathan met Jacob at his locker after school. It was clear he wanted to be his new sidekick.

"Say, you ride the bus home, don't you?"

"Yeah," Jacob said. He pulled books from his locker and placed them carefully into his backpack; not wanting to scratch or damage his pistol in any way.

"I live right around the corner," Jonathan said. "I walk home."

"Yeah?" Jacob said.

"You, you should come to my house after school one day," Jonathan offered. "Ricky and Mark be coming almost every day."

"What y'all do?" Jacob asked.

"Umm, nothing..." Jonathan looked down in embarrassment. "We play video games and basketball sometimes. But we really don't have nothing to do. That's, that's why you should come."

Jacob had never met anyone so eager to be a follower. It was intriguing. "It's some crabs by your house?" he asked.

Jonathan's yellow eyes lit up. "Yeah. It's some down the street from me. We be wanting to say something to them, but we, I mean, if you came with us..."

Jacob almost laughed at him. This was borderline ridiculous and majorly ironic: This whole mess started because Jacob wanted to avenge his little brother; to shed blood for Isaiah. Now he was about to *become* a Blood for Isaiah. This was classic. It was better than the movies.

"How I'ma get home, if I go to your house?" Jacob wondered.

"My mama will take you," Jonathan assured him. "She's on disability, and she's there all the time. Plus she kinda, you know..." He tapped his temple. "She nice, but, she..."

"She slow?" Jacob offered.

"Yeah," Jonathan said. "She'll do whatever I tell her to. You can spend the night, if you want."

"Hey, what y'all doing?"

Jacob looked back and saw Ricky and Willie approaching. He removed his last book and slammed his locker closed.

"I'm finna bounce," Jacob said.

"I was asking him about coming to my house after school," Jonathan told his cohorts.

"Yeah, that would be cool," Ricky said.

"I can't come today," Jacob said quickly.

"Jacob!"

Jacob looked up and saw his crush at the end of the crowded hallway. Camille wore the same Dickeys pants and golf shirt as everyone else, but she still managed to look cuter than all of the other girls. She always had her shirt tucked in to accentuate her waistline. And her budding breasts were like magnets to the eyes of pubescent boys.

"That, that's your girlfriend?" Jonathan asked.

In middle school you're considered to be in a relationship with anyone you received a few love letters from, so Jacob said, "Yeah."

"She pretty," Willie said.

Jacob grinned, his chest swelling like a bag of Jiffy Pop.

• • • • • •

Jacob exited the school with his girl on his right and his Devil Reds following behind. He didn't think he could get any cooler.

Jacob felt like he could snap his fingers and have someone carry his books or bring him a soda from the vending machine. This feeling of superiority faded when he saw his mother's red Chevy waiting for him in the faculty parking lot. Jacob broke away from his crew as quickly and as politely as possible.

"Aw, man. I forgot my mama was picking me up today. I gotta go, y'all. I'll see you later."

"What about—"

"I'll holler at you tomorrow," Jacob told Jonathan. He speed-walked away from the group without looking back, but not quickly enough to allay his mother's curiosity.

"Who are they?" Tammy asked when he climbed into the passenger seat.

"Just some friends."

"Some new friends?" She studied the group closely before putting the car in gear.

"I knew them before," Jacob lied. "I just never hung out with them."

"You got a girlfriend?" his mom asked.

Jacob blushed. "No. That's just Camille."

"I remember her," Tammy said. "Y'all was in the fifth grade together."

*Third through eighth*, Jacob thought, but said, "Yeah, I think we were."

"Where's Harold?" Tammy wanted to know.

"I think his dad already picked him up."

"That Camille is real pretty," Tammy noticed.

"She alright," Jacob said. "Are we still going to see that counselor?" he asked, eager to change the subject.

"Yep," Tammy said. "But after today you're going to have to ride the city bus over there. I can't take off work anymore for a while."

That was fine with Jacob. The more his mom worked, the less time she'd have to stick her nose in his business. "Cool."

● ● ● ● ● ●

## BLOOD FOR ISAIAH

The eastside MLK center was a beautiful structure, both inside and out. It was built in 1971, the same year Overbrook Meadows followed the Supreme Court's orders to integrate all of the public schools. The community center was located in the heart of Stop Six, which was a predominately black neighborhood. The goal was to instill a sense of hope and accomplishment in the hearts of the downtrodden citizens in the area.

But like so many other poverty-stricken communities, the residents of Stop Six seemed to have more self-hate than self-pride and work ethics. The crack epidemic of the mid-eighties made things considerably worse. As the body count in Stop Six rose to grotesque numbers, few residents took a moment to un-cock their pistols and ask themselves, *What would Martin Luther King Jr. think?*

Even the community center was not spared from Stop Six's era of black-on-black violence and Negro degradation. In 1989 a Stop the Violence rally was held on the bright green hills and basketball courts adjacent to the MLK center. It was a lively event, with local artists performing anti-violence raps and R&B tunes for an excited crowd. Free hotdogs and soft drinks were provided, paid for by the city council. Unfortunately free bullets were provided as well.

The crowd dispersed at the first sound of gunfire, and chaos quickly ensued. When the dust cleared, eight year old Samica Jeffries lay dead with a bullet wound to the side of her head. Nineteen year old Jamarcus Sands lay motionless in the sandbox with a bullet lodged in his spine and another one in his liver. He survived for five days after the shooting, but only because of a machine that breathed for him. When his mother gave permission to pull the plug, Jamarcus couldn't take one breath on his own. He went to be with Jesus within seconds.

In 1993 another shooting brought more negative publicity to the eastside MLK center. This one occurred in the parking lot. Because of a $400 drug debt, Rodney Freeman and his girlfriend Patricia Crowley, affectionately known as Fat Pat, were executed in broad daylight, while terrified students from the daycare looked on. A total of 34 shots were fired into Rodney's Cutlass Supreme. People likened it to the slaying of another infamous Texas couple named Bonnie and Clyde.

Tammy pulled to a stop in the community center's parking lot – not far from where Fat Pat's blood leaked from her boyfriend's car two decades ago.

"You gonna be alright?" she asked Jacob.

"Yeah. Why? You leaving me here?"

"This meeting is just for boys," Tammy confirmed. "Steve's gonna call me when it's time to pick you up."

Jacob was not eager to get out of the car. Everything he heard about this place was bad. But being fearful was not part of the new persona he was trying to construct for himself. Plus he still had his gun with him. What's the worst that could happen?

"Where do I go?" he asked, staring out of the window.

"Go through those main doors, and you'll see his office; the first one on the left. If he's not in there, he's probably in the gym around the corner."

Jacob watched two teenagers enter the door his mother was referring to. He wondered if they were crabs or Bloods. They didn't have any colored rags in their pockets or colored shoestrings. But if they were going to the same meeting Jacob was going to, he figured they were one or the other.

"Alright," he said. "I guess I'll see you later." He pushed the passenger door open, but his mother stopped him.

"Gimme a kiss."

Jacob rolled his eyes and planted a kiss on her cheek.

He got out and threw his backpack over his shoulder. Jacob approached the main entrance with confidence, but most of his courage left him when he looked back and saw his mother driving away. He couldn't believe she was really leaving him. She didn't even wait to make sure this *Steve* guy was even there.

Jacob sighed and entered the building cautiously. The first thing he saw was a bunch of ugly pictures on the wall to his right. They were obviously drawn by young children, but even kids should have a better understanding of perspective and shading, Jacob thought. Next he came across a beautiful bust of Martin Luther King Jr. planted atop a Roman-style column. As Jacob drew nearer, he found that he could not take his eyes off the sculpture.

Martin Luther King Jr. knew more about pain and suffering than most of the white American leaders in the history books. He bravely marched down the street while people spat and threw rocks and called him a nigger and other vile names. According to his last speech, MLK knew he was going to die, but he kept marching anyway because his cause was just. As crazy as it was, Martin Luther King Jr. cared more about others than he cared about his personal well-being. Jacob knew he'd never meet a man like that.

"Can I help you?"

Jacob turned and found himself in the presence of one of the biggest men he'd ever seen in real life. The guy wasn't big-*fat*, he was big-*strong*. He wore a gray golf shirt with black wind pants and sneakers. His chest was swollen like two oil drums. His biceps bulged like a recently fed python. He was brown-skinned with a thin moustache and goatee. His hair was shaved low, the same length all around.

Confronted with such manliness, Jacob unconsciously reverted to the most un-cool kid imaginable.

"My, my, my mama said to come in here..."

The muscle-bound man smiled. "Are you Jacob?"

The boy nodded.

"I'm Steve," the counselor said. "Why don't you step into my office, and tell me why you hate Crips so much."

Jacob's jaw dropped.

Steve grinned. "It's okay. Everybody here came in hating either Crips or Bloods – or Latin Kings or Sur Trece. You'll fit right in."

●●●●●●

Around the same time Jacob stared at a bust of Martin Luther King Jr., wondering if he would ever meet a man with such character and resolve, Dino rolled over on a stained mattress that smelled like piss and vomit. He opened his eyes for the first time that day, but he had to wipe the sweat from his face before he could see anything.

He didn't cover up with a sheet or blanket when he passed out earlier that morning, even though it was cool outside as well as inside the dilapidated bedroom. Dino understood that the steady heat he felt came from within, and his fever would not subside until he got some antibiotics. Or he could simply die. That would cure his infection as well.

He squinted at the afternoon sunlight bursting through the tattered window blinds as he looked around the squalid environment he was forced to call home. His mind was so jumbled, it took him a moment to understand where he was. By degrees it came to him: He was in another smoke house. This one was similar to Mama's, but it was on the south, rather than the east side of town.

This new house was owned by a crackhead named James. But James wasn't a lifelong junkie like Mama. He bought his home fair and square with paychecks from a steady job he worked five days a week for twenty years. James didn't try crack for the first time until he was forty-three, but from that point on, his and Mama's lifestyles were virtually identical.

James was a full-fledged addict now, and he was desperate enough to harbor the city's most wanted fugitive in exchange for a few measly rocks. Dino didn't trust James nearly as much as he trusted Mama, but so far his new landlord hadn't called the police on him, and that was all Dino had going for him nowadays: So far he didn't get caught. So far he didn't get shot. So far the hole in his head was mostly black, with shades of gray, but the infection hadn't killed him yet, so Dino had time for a little more mischief.

It was Monday now. According to an alarm clock next to the bed, it was four o'clock in the afternoon. Dino had been back in Overbrook Meadows since he left Charlotte's baby at Sycamore Park last Wednesday.

In the past five days Dino did a lot of plotting and scheming, a little shucking and jiving and even some wheeling and dealing. But he had yet to accomplish any of his goals for revenge. The only thing he'd done since returning to the city was push his mind closer to insanity and his body closer to the grave. Dino would consider himself a total failure at this point. But he'd been having a ball as of late, and failing never felt so good. He reminisced with a wretched smile stretching his skeletal features.

The first night at Mama's house was the most profitable. Mama bought his first fifty on Thursday morning, and by noon it was all gone. Dino sent her back for two more, and he sold all of those rocks before nightfall. Dino planned to go after the Sicc Crips under the cover of darkness, but news from the streets made him reconsider.

According to Mama, all of the crackheads in the neighborhood were skittish because of the overwhelming police presence. There were roadblocks set up on virtually every corner. The cops were even stopping pedestrians randomly to check their IDs. Dino knew he couldn't operate under such scrutiny, so he made the wise decision to stay inside. Mama was selling his dope as fast as he could cut it up, and she kept him supplied with heroin and booze to dull the pain from his cheek wound.

On Friday Dino woke up with his mind fully set on killing at least one Sicc Crip. But Friday was payday, and Mama's house was busier than the day before. Dino sold so much crack, he decided to reward himself with an eight ball. By the time he remembered what the cocaine did to him the last time, it was too late. His eyes were wide and his teeth were numb, and he couldn't stop peeking through the window shades.

Mama noticed his condition, and quickly found a way to capitalize on it. She asked Dino if he wanted a whore for the evening. She could send in one of her trustworthy friends (a girl who would never *ever* snitch on him) for only four extra dime rocks. Dino accepted the deal, and this is how he came to live with Peaches for the next two days.

Peaches was an insatiable crack addict, and she wasn't an attractive ho by any means, but Dino was filthy and ugly himself. Half of his face was rotten, and he stank like three-day-old road kill. Peaches didn't complain about his grossness, and Dino didn't complain about her unsightliness, and they were both so high, the hours rolled by with hardly any recollection of what was going on.

Dino spent all of Friday night with Peaches. She sucked him whenever he wanted, and she swallowed every time. She even went to wash her ass when Dino tried to hit it from the back but was unable to maintain an erection because of her stench. All Dino had to do in return was put a rock in her pipe every now and then. He continued to pay Mama rent for the room as well as rent for Peaches' company, and Dino still made enough money to break even.

Saturday was a virtual mirror image of Friday – except Dino started to show signs of stress as the cocaine ate away at his sensibilities. Business at Mama's smoke house was great, but Dino became less and less trusting of his environment. He had come to understand that Mama was chipping off of his fifties before she brought them to him, and Peaches was also stealing crack whenever Dino closed his eyes for more than thirty seconds. Both of the women denied this, of course, but Dino was no fool.

On Sunday Dino's paranoia reached a boiling point, and he no longer wanted Peaches in the room with him. He couldn't allow her to leave, however, because she knew too much about him. She was sure to drop a dime the moment she left the house.

With no more crack coming to her, Peaches was no longer in the mood to be in the presence of a dying lunatic. But Dino threatened to shoot her if she so much as touched the doorknob. Mama was 100% against these new arrangements, but Dino swore he'd burn her whole operation down to the ground if she went against him in any way.

Time slowed down after that, and Sunday proved to be Dino's longest day *ever*. He continued to snort cocaine whenever his high came down, and Peaches continued to beg for her freedom – or at least a hit of crack, so she could stay high like her abductor. Dino tossed her a few crumbs every now and then. Things didn't hit the fan until early Monday morning.

When it was time to buy four more fifties, Dino was shocked to see that he could only afford to purchase one. After three days of constant drug dealing, he only had fifty-two dollars to his name. He called Mama to his room for a conference, and she tried to explain that he was spending his money just as fast as he was making it. Dino was up to two eight balls a day, he was paying rent on the room, and he was still paying Mama rent for Peaches. Dino wanted his money back. All hell broke loose when Mama looked him in the eyes and swore it was all smoked up.

Dino couldn't recall much about the actual fight, but he remembered punching Mama in the mouth and kicking her in the head when she went down. He remembered Peaches jumping on his back, clawing like a rabid bobcat. The crack whore was as thin as a water hose, but Dino had trouble defending himself. Just when he thought he had Peaches under control, Mama made it to her feet and rejoined the brawl.

After a whirlwind of kicking and scratching, punching and cussing, Dino somehow made it to his gun. He didn't have to use it because crackheads value their lives just as much as teachers and firemen do. Mama and Peaches threw their hands up and backed away, their eyes as big as lemons.

The next thing Dino remembered was running outside. It was dark and it was cold. All of the alleys looked the same, and it took Dino a while to compose himself and get his bearings. He headed west, making sure to avoid all major streets and intersections. He noticed a few patrol cars out, but the police presence wasn't as bad as it had been on Thursday and Friday night.

In one of the backyards Dino leapt into, he found a long-sleeved sweater hanging on the clothes line. At the same residence, he spotted a mountain bike leaning against the back steps. It was four in the morning. Dino was confident everyone inside the house was fast asleep. He took his time tearing the sweater into a makeshift scarf he could wrap around his face. It wasn't freezing that night, but it was fairly cold, so he didn't think a scarf was *totally* out of order.

His disguise in place, Dino opened the gate and rode his new bike casually out of the backyard. He rolled down the driveway and made a left, heading south.

● ● ● ● ● ●

Dino knew James from back when times were simpler; from four years ago when Dino bought his first pair of hundred-dollar sneakers after flipping his first fifty. James Spratt was Dino's first steady customer. He was the first person to teach Dino the true value of the crack rock and the power a dealer could yield over his customers.

Dino was only thirteen when they first met. He laughed at James' tears on more than one occasion. A sadistic bastard way back then, Dino made James get on his knees and beg for his rock sometimes. Occasionally, Dino made him do a song and dance, if James staggered down the block begging for a freebie.

These memories fresh on his mind, Dino pedaled his mountain bike into Mr. Spratt's driveway at five a.m. on Monday morning. He knew his old customer would not turn him away. Dino was not surprised by the look of concern James fixed on him when he opened the door.

"Damn, boy. You, you fucked up."

"I know," Dino growled. He pulled the makeshift scarf from his face so he could talk.

James recoiled in fear.

"You, you the one everybody's looking for," he said, his eyes wide. "You killed that boy, and, and that lady."

"Let me in," Dino told him. "I did kill them people. I ain't gon' lie about it. But I ain't gon' hurt you. I need somewhere to spend the night. I'll give you three dimes."

Dino dug the rocks from his pocket. They were dirty and covered with lint, but they were fat. The sight of them made James' mouth water. Dino could hear the dopefiend's stomach bubble.

"For, for how long?"

"'Til tonight," Dino told him. "When I wake up, I'll score a fifty and give you three more."

James thought about it for only half a second. He snatched the crack from Dino's hand and held the screen door open for him.

"You can have that room across from the bathroom," he said, pointing down a dark hallway.

Dino stumbled in that direction, pausing only long enough to give his usual threat.

"If you tell somebody I'm here, I'll kill you, cuz. I'll burn yo shit down to the ground..."

Dino's voice was slurred, but James was accustomed to dealing with unintelligible demons.

"I ain't gon' tell nobody, D. We straight."

Dino shook his head and followed the walls to his room. His eyes were mostly closed. He could barely put one foot in front of the other. The bedroom was filthy, and it smelled of rotten chicken. There were no sheets on the bed, and Dino thought he saw a hypodermic needle glistening on the floor.

None of that mattered. Dino fell onto the mattress and was asleep before he could remove his gun from his pocket.

● ● ● ● ● ●

When he woke up, it was four in the afternoon. Dino's fever was worse than it had ever been. His head thumped like a subwoofer. Someone knocked on the bedroom door, and Dino knew his landlord had been spying on him for quite a while.

"What?" he groaned.

James opened the door. He poked his head inside and grimaced at the waste of human life sprawled across his guest bed. James was only forty-nine, but he looked sixty. His hair and five-o'clock-shadow was mostly gray. His eyes were almost completely bloodshot. "You woke?" he whispered.

"Nigga, you see my eyes open, don't you?"

"I was, I was just..." James stepped cautiously into the room. "I was wondering if you was still gon' do that... You said you was gon' get a fifty?..."

Dino sighed and dug the cash from his pocket. "You gotta get it for me." He held the bills out to him. "I can't go outside right now."

James' eyes grew large. No dealer ever trusted him with such a task. He snatched the money and asked, "Is you okay, man? You don't look good."

"Just go get the shit, nigga," Dino ordered. "Don't worry about what the fuck I look like."

James nodded fretfully and backed out of the room. When he was gone, Dino pushed himself off the stinky mattress and sat up on the bed. Two minutes later he gripped the headboard and was able to make it to his feet. He staggered to the bathroom and relieved his bowels. Before leaving, Dino leaned on the sink and stared at his ugly mug in the mirror.

"Huh..." He chuckled. What he saw was not at all funny, but sometimes shit gets so bad, all you can do is laugh.

Dino's hair was wrecked. After more than three weeks without a cut, his edge-up was nonexistent. The hair on the left side of his head was mashed down tight. The hair on his right side was dirty and tangled, with random tufts, like a sheep's hide.

His bullet wound was now a deep crater. Dino had never seen anything so disgusting. It looked almost two inches deep. He thought he could stick a finger in the hole and touch his cheekbone, or maybe scratch his top molars.

The patch of pillowcase he'd inherited at Mama's house was a part of him now. Dino could barely see the fabric through a fresh coat of blackish slime that covered his sore from top to bottom. His face was swollen again, but it was the atrophy that held Dino's attention the longest.

Charlotte once told him that the skin around his wound would *die*, but it's hard to visualize what that might look like until

246

you see it with your own eyes.  What Dino saw was blackness intermittently broken up by gray pockets of pus.  The blackness was darkest at the center of his wound, but the discoloration spread all the way to his nose and down past chin.  The exposed muscle and tissue looked dry and burnt.  Dino's right eye was swollen closed.  When he pried his eyelids open, he saw that his sclera was completely red.

In addition to this, Dino's face was covered with new scratches and contusions from the scuffle with Mama and Peaches.  He looked like the living dead, but Dino didn't feel like death was upon him just yet.  He'd squandered his chance to kill T Lowe, just as he'd squandered every other opportunity given to him throughout his life.  But Dino thought he had a little more time.  All he had to do was stay focused.  He got away from Mama's house, and that was a start.  He was no longer high on cocaine, and that was even better.

Dino turned off the bathroom light and returned to his bedroom.  He still had his gun, and he had a pocket full of bullets Mama brought him from Walmart.  Dino would get a little more rest today, and at nightfall, he would hunt.  He would not get high, and he would not drink any beer.  He would not end tonight's mission until somebody (or preferably somebodies) was good and dead.

*You strapped, you down, down for gunplay*
*You deep, and bound to get a piece*
*No peace 'til y'all control the streets*
*This thang, it's strange, this ghetto gang*
*This set we claim, this dope we slang*
*This place were hoodlums know your name*
*Like Cheers, except this kind of fame*
*Is sick. It's hard to coexist*
*Your foes fill clips, and when you slip*
*That's it, you blasted, face in the mud*

# CHAPTER NINETEEN
## *THE HUNT*

At seven p.m. Jacob climbed into Steve's fiery red F-150 and placed Isaiah's backpack between his feet. His gun was still safely hidden inside the book bag. After getting away with it for the second time, Jacob had grown more confident about toting his pistol. No one ever asked to search his backpack before his brother got killed, and this was the same case now. To allay suspicion, all Jacob had to do was stay under the radar, like a submarine. He buckled his seatbelt and cupped his hands in his lap like a good boy.

Steve's truck was immaculate, even though it was more than five years old. All of the surfaces were smooth and shiny. Jacob could smell the lemon-scented Armor All Steve used to make his dashboard glow. The radio was tuned in to a rhythm and blues station, but Steve had the volume down low, presumably so he and Jacob could talk some more.

"So, what do you think of the center?" he asked. "Did you learn anything today?"

Jacob looked out of the passenger window and shrugged. It wasn't that late, but because of daylight savings time, the sun was already starting to set in the western skies. The purple clouds looked dark and forlorn. The few people out on the streets wore thick winter coats and stocking caps to ward off chills from an unseasonable cold front that blew in Sunday evening.

"You finish your homework?" Steve asked.

Jacob nodded.

"What about that math?"

"I did that too," Jacob said.

"How about the other guys?" Steve asked. "It looked like you got along with everybody pretty good."

Jacob nodded again. His counselor was both right and wrong with that assertion. Some of the teens who came to the community center after school were real gangsters, and some of them were wannabes. Some were court-ordered to spend time with Steve, or they'd have to go back to jail for serious offenses. Others, like Jacob, simply got into gang-related fights, and their visits to the community center were a preemptive measure.

Jacob was frightened by some of the boys he met today, but he also found a couple of guys he got along with right away. There was supposed to be a rule against discussing your gang affiliation or glorifying your tales from the hood while at the center, but it was impossible to enforce that one hundred percent of the time.

Jacob befriended two students after he heard them discussing a crab they wanted to beat up at their school. Jacob listened closely to everything they said, and he found the Bloods to be a virtual treasure trove of information. Jacob learned more gang lingo he could take to school tomorrow to impress his Devil Reds.

"Mike says you was hanging out with Kenneth and Darren," Steve said.

Jacob looked over at him. One of his new friends was named Darren. He didn't remember what the other one said his name was. "Who's Mike?" he asked.

"Mike's one of my veterans," Steve said. "He's the tallest kid in there. He had on a long-sleeved button-down today."

Jacob did remember that guy. Mike had led Jacob away from his new Blood friends twice this afternoon.

"It ain't good to hang around those fools," Mike had said. "Some people in here is really trying to do better for theyself. Some people just here 'cause they got to be."

249

"Kenneth and Darren are still new to the program," Steve said. "It's probably not a good idea to hang around them too much."

Jacob frowned. Apparently Mike was an extension of Steve, and Mike was also a snitch. Jacob knew he had to watch himself around Mike from that moment on.

"Don't feel like everybody's coming down on you," Steve said, reading Jacob's disposition. "It's all about choices, little homey; in my program and in the real world. Like with Mike, you can choose to get mad at him for trying to help you. You can call him a snitch or whatever. That's your choice, Jacob."

Steve's insight was remarkable. Jacob never met a mind-reader before. It was impossible not to pay attention to the brawny counselor.

"You're not supposed to bring your street life to the center," Steve went on. "But there's thirty boys in there sometimes, and this ain't no school. I'm not their mama, and I'm not their babysitter. If a couple of them choose to huddle up and talk about some crab they wanna kill, I'm not always there to stop that conversation from taking place. But what I can do is warn you about getting caught up in shit like that."

Jacob was speechless. It was like listening to a teacher who could say whatever he wanted without fear of getting fired or sued.

"Darren and Kenneth don't want to change," Steve said. "They like to play basketball, and they like the free food. But they leave everyday with just as much hate in their hearts as they had coming in."

"How, why you let them come then?" Jacob wondered.

"My doors are open to everybody," Steve informed him. "It's just like the church house. You don't see the preacher standing at the front door, telling this one he can come in but this other one can't: *Naw, Sister Thompson. You can't come to church today. People done told me what you was doing in the bathroom at the Waffle House last Saturday!*"

Jacob chuckled. Steve did too.

"Naw, brother," the counselor said. "I let everybody come, and I do what I can while they're with me. I hope I can reach all of them some day, Darren and Kenneth included."

Jacob nodded. That was a noble cause indeed.

"If you want to make friends with somebody, you should make friends with Mike," Steve suggested. "Do you know anything about him?"

Jacob shook his head.

"Mike used to be a straight *goon*," Steve stated. "When I first met him, I thought he was a lost cause. All he was talking about was *Eff this* and *Eff that*, *nigga this, nigga that*. He was getting into fights at school. He got kicked out of Dunbar. He was selling dope. He was real deep in his gang. He did a lot of dirt, and he moved up in the ranks. He eventually became the leader. He was the youngest OG in the city."

Jacob paid attention to the story, and he also picked up new terminology to boost his reputation with the Devil Reds. *Doing dirt* was something you did (usually illegal) to show your loyalty to the gang. An *OG* (original gangster) was the leader of a gang. He already learned that gang ranks also included *YGs* (young gangsters) and *BGs* (baby gangsters).

"When his mama got killed, that's when Mike really lost it," Steve said.

"His mama?" Jacob didn't think he heard right.

"See, Mike was out there bad," Steve explained. "He was doing drivebys all the time. I don't know if you remember this, but there was a shooting at Dunbar's homecoming dance two years ago. A boy and a girl got shot."

Jacob did remember that. Everyone on TV talked about what a shame it was and how this new generation was headed for self-destruction.

"Mike played a part in that," Steve said. "Half the city wanted him in jail, and the other half wanted him dead. So not too many people got upset when somebody shot up his house. Mike's mama was the only one home, and she got hit in the arm and in the chest. But she was a crackhead, so nobody cared about her. Her murder didn't even make the front page in the Metro section. It was buried so far in the back, you wouldn't find it unless you was looking for it."

This was incredible. Jacob felt guilty about Isaiah, even though he wasn't directly responsible for his little brother's demise. He couldn't imagine how bad Mike must've felt, knowing his evil deeds brought death right to his mother's doorstep.

"He came to stay with me after that," Steve recalled. "Mike was so high and depressed, I didn't think I would ever reach him. But I did. He wanted to go out and make somebody pay for what happened to his mama. I had to teach him that beef would never end like that. In order for his cycle of violence to end, he had to take a loss. Do you know what that means?"

Jacob shook his head.

"It's like this," Steve said. "If I steal from you, then you'll probably feel justified to steal from me, right?"

That sounded about right. Jacob nodded.

"So you steal from me," Steve said. "But then I get mad and steal from you again."

"That's not right," Jacob said. "I only stole from you because you stole from me first."

Steve smiled. "But let's say you and me been stealing from each other for ten years. Let's say me and you sit down to talk about it one day, but we can't remember who stole from who first. You say it was me, and I say it was you. The only way to stop it at that point, is to take a loss. Somebody got to do it. If I stole from you last, you probably won't feel good about giving up. You'll probably think, *Well, it's my turn to steal from you, and after I do that, **then** we can end it.*

"But the problem is, your enemy's thinking the same way. He wants to get you last, so he can say he won. So how do we end this beef, Jacob?"

"Somebody gotta take a loss," he said.

Steve shook his head. "Not just somebody, Jacob. *You* have to take the loss. You can't expect your enemy to do it. You have to tell yourself, *Screw it. I don't care what else they do to me, I'm done. It's over. I'll take the loss*. That's what I taught Mike, and that's the only reason he's still alive today. They killed his mama, but he still put his gun down and said to hell with it.

"That's all it takes to make a change, little homey. No matter how many of your partners got killed, and no matter how bad you feel inside, sometimes you have to suck it up like a man and take it. You think you're man enough to do something like that, Jacob?"

Jacob knew he was talking about Isaiah now, and this conversation wasn't cool anymore. If a jilted lover threw a cup of juice on him, he could take that like a man. If someone stepped on his new sneaker and left a scuff, Jacob could let that slide as well. But how was he supposed to forget about what the Sicc Crips did to his little brother? That was not possible. Steve was wrong for even suggesting such a thing.

Luckily the counselor made the last turn onto Forbes Street, and Jacob saw his yellow and white house. Jacob knew his mother wanted him to call her at work when he got home. Tammy would have a lot of hard questions for him as well, but at least she wouldn't ask him to do anything silly, like forget what the erickets did to Isaiah.

"I guess I'll take that as a no," Steve said. He pulled to a stop in Jacob's driveway and turned to stare at his latest conundrum. "This is your house, right?"

"Yeah," Jacob said. He unfastened his safety belt and bent to retrieve his backpack.

"Your mama thinks you're headed for self-destruction," Steve said. "She thinks you're so upset about Isaiah, you don't care what happens to yourself anymore. That true?"

Jacob didn't say anything.

"The thing is," Steve went on, "if you don't learn how to let your anger go, you could end up hurting more than just yourself, Jacob. Like with Mike, he didn't think his actions would get back to his mama like they did. He eventually learned to take a loss, but do you know how hard it was by then – after going to his mama's funeral? I know how bad it hurts, Jacob. But you have to make a decision to either move on with your life or escalate things. *Niggas* love to escalate shit, but *black men* are smarter than that."

"Alright," Jacob said. He pushed the door open and hopped out of the truck. "I'll see you later. Thanks for the ride."

"Anytime," Steve said. "Just think about what I said. You're at a crossroads right now. You can go whatever way you want to. One path leads to peace. The other one leads to more pain and bloodshed. I know you're smart, Jacob. Think real hard before you decide which way you wanna go..."

"Alright," Jacob said again. He closed the door and stepped quickly towards his home. His counselor made a lot of sense, but Steve's logic was also intrinsically flawed, because it's not human nature to turn the other cheek. All of the great leaders in history fought fire with fire. The punks who didn't fight back got rolled over, like France and Poland.

Jacob wasn't a great leader, but he wasn't a punk either. Isaiah deserved retribution. Jacob couldn't let it go until *after* he evened things up. Anything less would be downright un-American.

• • • • • •

Dino sat on the corner of his stinky mattress and munched on a huge turkey leg. His humongous plate still had a serving of macaroni and cheese, a cup of green beans and two golden brown biscuits. Dino ate slowly because his jaw hurt when he chewed, and he couldn't eat on the right side of his mouth at all. Plus his stomach hadn't processed any real food in weeks. Dino's belly twisted and tightened with each swallow.

His gut tried to force the food back up his esophagus a few times, but Dino would not allow himself to vomit. He knew tonight would be demanding, and he needed every bit of strength he could muster. Each morsel and every vitamin was vital.

Dino only took one nap during the day, because too much sleep made him lazy and lethargic. At seven o'clock he started a push-up regimen but could only get three done before collapsing onto his chest. He tried jumping jacks instead. These came easier, thanks to the long trip to James' house the night before. Dino road his stolen mountain bike almost five miles when he left Mama's house, and his legs were still strong and limber. At nine-thirty Dino ate two bowls of Cornflakes with milk, and he was able to get through six pushups after that meal.

It was eleven o'clock now. Dino planned to leave in a couple of hours. His scrumptious dinner came from a neighbor down the street. Dino didn't know the neighbor's name, but he thought she was an excellent cook. Her turkey leg was tender and juicy, and her macaroni was the cheesiest Dino had ever had.

The neighbor actually made the meal for James, whom she had a crush on. But she was unaware of James' addiction. She had no idea he traded the whole plate for a five dollar crack rock. James kept his habit hidden as much as possible, which is why his home wasn't filled with dopefiends like Mama's was.

It took nearly forty minutes, but Dino finally finished his plate. He burped hoarsely and reached for the pill bottle on his pillow. He emptied half a dozen Tylenols into his hand and downed them with a glass of cold milk. The Tylenols wouldn't dull his pain completely – no over-the-counter drug could at this point – but they did help a little. Without them Dino couldn't function at all. With them he felt good enough to try a few more push-ups.

He dropped to the floor and assumed the position. Back in the eighth grade he could do three sets of fifty, but tonight Dino couldn't do one set of ten. His arms started to buckle on his ninth push up. Sweat drenched his hair and dripped from his forehead like blood. The pull of gravity made his face throb dreadfully. Disgusted, Dino rolled to a sitting position and rested his forearms on his knees. His breaths came hard and heavy.

*Can't do ten goddamned push-ups...*

It was depressing, but Dino didn't let it get him down. He didn't expect any hand to hand combat tonight anyway. If all went well, his trigger finger would be the only muscle he had to flex, and he didn't need any exercise for that. He could flex that motherfucker all night long if need be. When the police came to stuff his body in a black bag, his trigger finger would still be twitching.

*No.*

Dino caught himself. That wasn't going to happen, because he wasn't going to die tonight. He was going to kill T Lowe, and then he would flee, and then he would get high and have a suicidal shootout with the police when they finally tracked him down. That was the order of things. This was Dino's destiny. The Sicc Crips wouldn't kill him because he was better than all of them. He had always been better. Even his three-week drug binge didn't change that.

A shadow in the doorway caught his attention.

Dino looked up angrily, still breathing hard from his aborted workout. The shadow hesitated in the hallway and then came back. James' eyes were wide and dilated. He was sweating profusely, but not from any pushups or jumping jacks. James was high as hell, and he was skitzing hard. His look of desperation and weakness filled Dino with rage, although he wasn't sure why.

James looked down at the floor and then up at Dino. The dopefiend eyed the floor again and then knelt to pick up a little piece of sheetrock. Or maybe it was a stale bread crumb. Either way, it wasn't what he hoped it was. James figured this out when he brought the debris to his mouth and tasted it. He looked up at Dino again and shrugged.

Dino knew full well what James wanted, but he wouldn't give him anything until the crackhead asked for it. He still might not help him out, because Dino's debts were paid in full. It wasn't his fault James accepted drugs rather than cash for his services. James had to know he wouldn't have anything to show for it in a couple of hours. But then again, that's the problem with junkies: They don't plan ahead for shit.

"Dino, you, um... Do you think, uh..."

"Nope," Dino said coldly. "I already paid you, nigga."

"I know," James said. He looked away, his watery mouth twisting uncontrollably. "But, I uh..."

Dino shook his head. "Why you always begging, cuz? You get on my nerves with that ho shit."

"I'm, I'm sorry," James said. But he didn't go anywhere. "I'll, I'll let you stay here another night, if you want..."

"Man, this house smells like straight *shit*," Dino informed him. "I ain't coming back – *never*."

"I'll..." James thought for a second. "I'll give you my TV."

There was only one television left in the house, and it was old and dusty. It didn't get good reception on any of the major channels, and it took a few minutes to warm up. If the pawn shop would take it, James would've gotten rid of it long ago.

"What the hell I'ma do with a TV?" Dino asked. "Next time you hear about me, I'll be dead, cuz. I don't need that shit."

"What, what if..." James thought hard, but he had nothing left to barter with.

"Sing me a song," Dino offered. This was an old game for them. James didn't look upset at all.

"What song?"

"From the Wiz," Dino said. "Sing that, '*Ease on Down the Road*,' shit. And I want you to dance, too; like the scarecrow."

"I, I don't know that song good," James said.

"Then get the fuck out my face."

"Hold, hold on. Oh, okay," James said. "Wait. I remember now."

He pulled up his britches and commenced to sing and dance for Dino's amusement. Making James dance a jig would normally put Dino in a good mood, no matter how bad he felt, but it didn't work tonight. Dino stared at him and grew more and more introspective.

Because of crack cocaine, this grown man chose to humiliate himself for the amusement of a half-dead fugitive. Because of crack, Pooky chose to open a dope house around the corner from the Sicc Crips on Forbes Street. And because of the value of cocaine, Dino robbed Pooky and refused to return the drugs to his big brother HB.

Crack ruined Dino's life, just like it ruined Mama's life. Crack ruined Isaiah's and Peaches' and James' lives as well as the lives of countless men and women in the penal system. Dino was on the verge of a profound understanding, but James got to his favorite part of the song, and Dino forgot what he was thinking about.

*"You just keep on keepin' on the road that you choose,"* James crooned. *"Don't you give up walkin', 'cause you gave up shoes, no!"*

Dino laughed. He dug a dime from his bag of rocks and broke it in half with his fingernail. He tossed a piece on the floor. James had no trouble keeping up with it. He scrambled on all fours and picked it up with a smile.

"If you want the other half," Dino said, "you gotta sing another song."

"Okay," James readily agreed. "You want me to finish that one?"

"Naw," Dino said. "I wanna hear *Amazing Grace.* I'm feeling spiritual tonight."

● ● ● ● ● ●

Dino left James' house a few minutes after one a.m. He took everything he owned with him, but that only included the clothes on his back, his pistol, his bag of crack and a long, flat-head screwdriver he found in James' guest bedroom.

It was 39 degrees outside. Dino took full advantage of the wintry weather. He wore a black stocking cap along with a navy blue scarf that concealed his wound completely – a real scarf this time. Dino found it in James' closet, and he acquired it without asking. He also found a pair of cotton gloves in there, but he didn't take those because they were snowflake white. He planned to move under the cover of darkness tonight, and stealth was much more important than personal comfort.

Dino left on his stolen mountain bike, but he didn't ride it for long. He casually cruised the south side streets looking for a car he could steal with nothing more than a screwdriver. In a better neighborhood, he'd probably be out of luck. But this part of Overbrook Meadows was filled with old clunkers. Dino found the ride he wanted after only a ten minute search.

He pedaled past his prize and made a left on the next corner. Dino hopped off his bicycle and stashed it in an alley. On foot, he leisurely returned to the house he'd selected a moment ago. Parked in the driveway was a 1985 Oldsmobile Cutlass. It was a two door bucket with dark, tinted windows and no hubcaps on any of the wheels.

The hood was cold, but the car was clean. Dino was sure it had been driven recently. If he couldn't start it, he would run back to his bike and make a speedy getaway. If someone came outside and tried to apprehend him, he would shoot them and still make his getaway. His escape route planned, Dino took a deep breath and got down to business.

The passenger window was rolled all the way up, but Dino was still able to wedge his screwdriver between the glass and top of the door frame. He wrenched his tool upwards, and the window bowed outwards. He applied a little more pressure, and there was a **POP** as the glass shattered.

The noise sounded deafening, but no one turned on a porch light or peered through the windows of any of the nearby houses. Still, Dino waited and watched for two minutes before he made his next move. He listened to dogs barking, and he listened to his own rough breaths, but there was nothing more.

Dino reached inside the jagged hole he created and unlocked the passenger door. He opened it and leaned in to open the driver's side. He felt a few shards of glass scratching his butt when he took a seat behind the wheel, but given everything he'd been through in the past few weeks, this was a very minor discomfort.

Using the Cutlass' dome lights, Dino broke the plastic shell covering the steering column with his screwdriver. Beneath that was a plastic cover that was also easily removed. With the ignition switch fully exposed, Dino had only to pull back on the slide lever to start the car. The whole process took only sixty seconds.

The Cutlass' engine roared to life, and Dino threw it into REVERSE. He rolled out of the driveway and made a right turn. He took another right at the next corner and then made a left; heading towards Berry Street. Before he hit the busy thoroughfare, Dino turned on his headlights and leaned over to pull the passenger door closed. He was sweating again, but the broken passenger window provided an endless breeze of cold air. Dino knew he'd cool down by the time he got on the freeway.

● ● ● ● ● ●

T Lowe's dope house in Como was dark and desolate. The average visitor would drive on by, assuming the place was shut down for the night. But Dino knew how things operated, and he knew the house was full of drug dealers. Hopefully T Lowe was among them.

Dino would normally leave his car at the park up the street and make his way back on foot, but he wanted to be extra careful tonight. He drove two blocks past the park and left his Cutlass in an apartment complex.

The steering column was fully exposed, so when he returned to the vehicle, it would take less than ten seconds to start it again. Dino was sure that would be enough time. If not, he would keep running until he found another means of escape. The Sicc Crips were amateurs when it came to life and death struggles like this. Dino couldn't think of a single one who could catch him.

On foot again, Dino found an alley and followed it back to T Lowe's spot. He thought he'd have an easy go at it, but the alleys in Como were a lot more congested than other neighborhoods. At one point Dino had to climb over a pile of severed branches that seemed nearly five feet tall. He wondered if he could make it out the same way if he was being chased.

In addition to the physical obstacles, the residents of Como had a lot of dogs; nearly one per household. The canines set off a racket as Dino crept past their territory, but he would not let them deter him. This was a bad neighborhood. Surely the homeowners were used to their mutts barking at all hours of the night.

After traversing a wild wilderness that felt like a jungle, Dino finally made it to the back of T Lowe's place. Despite the cold, he was sweating so hard his shirt was matted to his chest. From his vantage point, Dino saw that there were a few lights on inside the drug house. The back porch light was also on, which was an indication that the dope game was fully underway. Dino saw a shadow move in the kitchen. He knew that was the doorman; a humongous Negro named Skeeter.

Dino didn't see T Lowe's car in the driveway or in the backyard, but that wasn't necessarily a bad sign. It was late, but crack peddlers don't move with the clocks of regular men. Like doctors, they were always on call.

Dino found a tree to lean against while he waited.

After a while the dogs stopped barking.

An hour passed.

Dino watched a steady stream of dealers come to the back door in search of a large amount of crack for their customers. Dino's heart knocked like an old washing machine each time Skeeter opened the door to serve them. But when T Lowe finally showed up, Dino was peculiarly calm.

T Lowe drove a brand new Infiniti G37. He pulled into the driveway and continued around the back of the house, until his sedan was no longer visible from the street. The Infiniti had bright headlights and Dino was bathed in their glow, with only a four foot shrub concealing him at one point. Dino held his breath, but he wasn't afraid he'd be discovered, because niggas only expect the obvious.

If he'd ran alongside the house and tried to ambush them, or if he did a driveby, T Lowe would be fully prepared to defend himself. But T Lowe didn't search the alley because he didn't have the mind of a killer like Dino did.

Sure enough, the Infiniti's headlights went off a second before T Lowe killed the engine. Dino exhaled his pent up breath as his eyes readjusted to the darkness. He pulled the pistol from his pocket and cocked it slowly. The metallic click sounded monstrous in the alley, and one of the neighbor's dogs started to bark again. But T Lowe hadn't opened his door yet, and Dino knew he didn't hear him.

With the target in his sights, Dino's body grew warm again. The fence separating him from his prey was only four feet away. T

Lowe's Infiniti was parked twelve feet beyond the fence. Dino was pretty sure he could land a chest shot from that distance, but he wanted to be closer.

T Lowe opened his door. Dino took half a step out of the darkness. He would've continued further, but the backdoor of the dope house swung open also. Skeeter stepped out with a pump shotgun in his hands.

Dino grinned. They couldn't outsmart him, so they opted to outgun him. It was a nice try, but Dino didn't fear Skeeter in the least. The shotgun had virtually no range at that distance. The most Skeeter could do was spray a few random buck shots.

Dino inched closer, as the passenger and back doors of the Infiniti popped open. It didn't surprise him that T Lowe wasn't riding alone, but he did feel a tug at his heart when he saw Kevin exit the Sedan.

Kevin was the only friend Dino had left in the gang. He'd stood by him when they tried to vote Dino out of the Sicc, and Kevin warned Dino to make a move when T Lowe decided to take him out. If at all avoidable, Dino wanted to spare Kevin's life. But war is war, and everyone in the Sicc was his enemy at this point.

T Lowe slammed his door closed as Tricky emerged from the Infiniti's backseat. Dino's breath caught, and his heart fluttered again. Tricky was another thug who voted to keep him in the Sicc. The only thing Dino could do for him at this point was keep his gunfire directed at their OG. But if his old friends returned fire, they would have to die as well. It was four against one. But Dino had covertness on his side. He was only moderately apprehensive about the battle that was about to ensue.

Dino took another step forward and a twig snapped under his sneaker.

Everything stopped.

Everyone heard it.

T Lowe was the first to understand what the sound meant. The Sicc Crip OG turned towards the alley and stared with all the intensity of a lion on the prowl. Dino stood very still, but he was mostly exposed by then. It didn't take long for T Lowe to put the shadows together in a way that made sense to him. T Lowe looked from Dino's chest, up towards his face. The two men locked eyes.

At first Dino thought he was still concealed, but T Lowe's expression changed by degrees. His eyes grew large, and his jaw became unhinged. He looked like he saw a ghost, which was highly appropriate, because he was about to be one very soon.

*"Oh, shit! It's Dino!"*

T Lowe's shout was like the opening bell of a boxing match. His scream set everything into motion. And, like the shootout with HB, Dino saw everything with freeze-frame clarity.

Rather than reach for a weapon, T Lowe turned tail and ran towards the house; ducking his head like a turtle. Dino ran to the fence and opened fire. The Glock bucked in his hand. That was a welcomed feeling. It was warm and familiar, like a mother's embrace. The flash from Dino's gun barrel lit up the backyard like fireworks. The sound was as deafening as dynamite.

*POP!*

*POP!*

*POP!POP!*

T Lowe went down. Dino didn't know if he was shot or dodging, so he continued to aim at his back and hindquarters.

*POP! POP!*

*BOOOM!*

The blast from the shotty was much louder than Dino's pistol. He looked up and saw Skeeter advancing from the back door.

*Cha-CHICK – BOOOM!*

Dino saw something like a dragon sneeze, and he felt the heat all the way in the alley. He didn't think the shotgun pellets could hurt him at that distance, but he was wrong about that. Dino felt an instant barrage of fiery wasp stings on his arms and chest, and he couldn't stop a scream from bursting from his lips.

*"Aaah!"*

Bolstered by the sound of injury, Skeeter continued forward. T Lowe was still scrambling towards the backdoor. But he was a noncombatant. Dino had to reassess his priorities. He swung his gun in Skeeter's direction and let off two shots before Skeeter could chamber another round.

*Cha–*

*POP!POP!*

It was dark, but Dino saw Skeeter's body jerk violently; unnaturally. The shotgun fell from his hands, and Skeeter clawed at a new hole on the left side of his chest. He fell backwards and landed hard on his butt.

With his legs outstretched, Skeeter pawed at his wound and looked up at the ghoul standing on the other side of the fence. He didn't look upset at all. As a matter of fact, Skeeter looked peaceful. He could have been sitting on the living room floor with a bowl of popcorn in his lap, watching the Cowboys beat the Eagles on Sunday afternoon.

But Dino saw the blood squirting through his fingers. He knew Skeeter would never watch football again – not unless they had bowl games in hell.

His biggest threat down, Dino returned his attention to the true source of his fury. He was surprised to see that T Lowe had made it all the way to the back steps. The Sicc leader was on his hands and knees. Dino was sure he was injured, but it wasn't over until–

**BAP!**
**BAP!BAP!BAP!BAP!**

The barrage of gunfire came from Dino's left. He was so stunned, his legs got twisted beneath him; both trying to go a different direction. Dino fell to the ground. He looked up and was horrified to see Kevin pointing a gun at him. Dino didn't think he was hit, but the sheer shock felt like a gunshot to the chest.

*"You ungrateful mother..."*

Dino rolled to his side and returned fire. He hit his old friend in the thigh, and Kevin cried out in pain. He fell onto his side, and the two men were face to face, no more than six feet apart, separated by a mere chain link fence.

Kevin's eyes bugged and begged for mercy. Dino's eyes were cold and filled with bloodlust. Dino aimed his pistol for a headshot, but at that moment an army of Sicc Crips rushed out of the dope house like ants from a stomped mound. None of them knew where Dino was exactly, but they knew he was in the alley somewhere. They began to fire in that direction randomly.

The night air was filled with screams and gunshots. Some of the bullets zipped through the fence and sliced leaves and shrubbery very close to their target. Dino knew it was time to make a move.

Low-crawling on his elbows like a Green Beret, he made it to the adjacent backyard before he got to his feet and started running. The pile of dead branches he had trouble navigating on his way in was no obstacle for him this time. Hot blood laced with adrenaline raced through his limbs.  He scaled the debris like an Olympic hurdler.

Dino burst out of the other side of the alley and was running full speed before the first Sicc Crip jumped T Lowe's fence and decided to give chase.  By then it was no contest.

Dino made it to his stolen Cutlass and got it started with plenty of time to spare.

*Why should we love when we can hate?*
*Why build her up when we can rape?*
*Why should we ask when we can take?*
*Clear 'em out and clean the slate*
*This is the life we choose to live*
*Can't stop it now, this train is rolling*
*This train is going, faster now*
*Spitting sparks. This bitch is stolen!*

# CHAPTER TWENTY
## *SMALL WORLD*

On Thursday afternoon Tammy's boss threw her a going away party at the taquería. He decorated the restaurant with balloons and brought her a huge cake from Walmart. And, knowing Tammy preferred Italian over Mexican food, Sam surprised everyone by bringing in a meal from another eatery. Tammy had lasagna and fettuccine for lunch. She was stuffed like a tick when quitting time came at twelve-thirty.

She only had two hours before her next shift started at the hospital, but Tammy had something to check on first. She called her supervisor and told her she might be a little late. Tammy knew her attendance had been sporadic at work since Isaiah's death, but things were getting better.

When she moved to first-shift on Monday, she didn't plan on missing any more days at the hospital – unless Jacob did something horrible at school again. Tammy didn't think that would happen, but she'd have a better idea about her son's state of mind after she made a trip to the east side of town to speak with his counselor.

● ● ● ● ● ●

The Martin Luther King center on Truman Street looked desolate during the lunch hour. There were only a few cars parked out front, and Tammy didn't hear any basketballs dribbling when she entered through the double doors.

Down the hallway on her right, she did hear excited shouts from one of the daycare classrooms. It did her heart good to hear children's laughter. It reminded her of how happy and fun-loving Isaiah was throughout his short life. Thankfully, this thought didn't break Tammy's heart like it normally would.

In the first office on the left, Steve sat behind his desk flipping through a pile of papers. He stood with a smile when Tammy knocked on the door.

"You busy?"

"Oh, hey, Ms Spencer. Come on in." Steve wore a short-sleeved Polo shirt with faded blue jeans. He was freshly shaved, and Tammy thought he smelled good. He offered a huge hand to shake.

"Hi," Tammy said. Her dainty mitt was almost swallowed up by his bear claw, but Steve's handshake was gentle, despite his eye-catching physique.

"I'm glad you stopped by," he told her. "Have a seat."

Tammy did so. She crossed her legs with her hands in her lap. She wore the usual uniform required for her waitress job at Juan's Taquería, but she had her hair down today. It was mostly black with reddish highlights that complimented her skin tone. She wore red lipstick to work that day, but after eating lunch, there was just enough left to tint her mouth a perfect pink.

Steve took a seat and leaned forward with his forearms on his desk.

"You worked today?"

"I just left one job," Tammy confirmed. "I'm on my way to my other one at the hospital."

"You said you were quitting one of your jobs...?"

"Tomorrow's my last day at the restaurant."

"What do you do at the hospital?" Steve asked.

"I'm a housekeeper," Tammy said, somewhat embarrassed about the menial profession. "But I'm going back to school to be a nurse's aide," she added.

"My mama was a housekeeper," Steve said. "She was the hardest working woman I've ever known. I always admired her and felt grateful for the sacrifices she made for our family."

Tammy didn't know if he said that to make her feel better, but his words did just that. "That's sweet. Do you have a big family?"

"Two brothers and a sister," Steve said. "We had three different daddies between us. But you didn't come here to talk about me. You want to know how Jacob's doing..."

Tammy nodded. "Is he any better?"

Steve pursed his lips. "Honestly, it's hard to say after only three days. Monday I didn't think he liked me at all. But he's been better the last couple of times. I think he's coming along. How has the stuff on the news affected him? What has he told you?"

Steve was referring to the well-publicized shooting in Como on Monday night. One gang member was killed and two others went to the hospital with serious injuries. Tammy thought it was just another tragic hood story when the first reports came in. But in the days that followed, the police linked the shooting to the still unsolved murders of Isaiah and Charlotte Webb.

Furthermore, the surviving gangsters were no longer keeping quiet about "*the one who got shot in the face.*" Everyone now knew the suspect's name was Derrick Douglas; known on the streets as Dino. The police were confident Dino was the man who shot Algernon "HB" Russell in the stomach. In that same shootout, it was his stray bullet that killed Tammy's little boy. The police said Dino went to Waxahachie to hide for more than a week before, for some unknown reason, he took Charlotte Webb's life and fled with her infant child.

According to the news reports, the Sicc Crips protected him for as long as they could, but Dino had become increasingly erratic and irrational. When they turned their backs on him, Dino went after his own gang; shooting three, one fatally. At this point, the police had all of the evidence they needed to make an arrest, with two glaring exceptions: They didn't have a mug shot of Derrick Douglas to show the public, and they still did not know where he was.

"It's good to have some of the pieces put together," Tammy acknowledged. "But they haven't made an arrest yet, so I don't think Jacob feels any better. He watches the news a lot, but I can't say he's *happy* about any of it."

"There's, there's something I need to tell you," Steve said. He frowned. He lowered his gaze, and Tammy was surprised by the sudden mood change.

"What's the matter?"

"It's about that guy," Steve said. He put a hand to his mouth and rubbed his lips. He stared into her eyes. Tammy returned the gaze.

"What's wrong?" she asked again.

Steve sighed. "I know him," he said at length. "Derrick Douglas; the one who killed your boy, I know him. I'm related to him. He's my nephew."

Tammy's eyes widened.

"When I heard his name on TV," Steve went on, "I can't tell you how bad I felt. I mean, the situation's already depressing enough, but to find out someone I know is responsible for your son's death, it made me sick to my stomach."

"He's your *nephew*?" Tammy didn't know how to feel.

"I haven't seen him in nearly four years," Steve said. His brow furrowed. "I think Dino's life was screwed up from the very beginning. The first time I spent any real time around him was after his mama's funeral. My sister was a prostitute, and she got beat to death by her pimp; a skinny punk named Chucky P. Back then I was – not a good person, Tammy. I told you about my old life. I told you I was a thug, and I did ten years for robbery and manslaughter..."

Tammy nodded vacantly.

"Part of the reason I did that time was because of Dino," Steve said. "I was furious after my sister got killed. I knew my vengeance wouldn't bring her back, but I felt like she deserved retribution, you know? Plus if I didn't do nothing, I would lose face on the streets. I couldn't go on with my life while my sister's killer was still roaming the same neighborhood I was in, you know?"

Tammy shuddered. She didn't want to know this, but Steve's story was connected to Isaiah's like a spider's web. She had no choice but to listen.

"So I killed Chucky P," Steve said. "Most people said he was Dino's daddy. Others say Dino's real daddy was a john, and there was no way of finding him. Either way, Dino didn't have a mama or a daddy after I did what I did. And then I went to the penitentiary, so he didn't have me either."

Tammy slowly shook her head.

"When I got out, Dino was twelve," Steve said. "I tried to get in touch with him, but he was gone already." He tapped his temple. "Not physically, but mentally. My mama raised him, but she was sick herself, so there wasn't no discipline.

"Dino was gang-banging and selling drugs when he was twelve. He dropped out of school when he was fourteen. I had my counseling thing going by then, and I can't tell you how much it hurt to know that I couldn't reach my own flesh and blood. I dragged Dino to the center a bunch of times, but then he started avoiding me, like I was out to get him.

"It hurt me bad —not just because I couldn't reach him," Steve said. "It hurt because I felt like I *created* Dino when I killed his father. Deep inside I knew that wasn't true. I mean, I think he would've been just as messed up if a pimp raised him instead of his grandma. But I never gave Chucky P a chance to change. Dino's earliest childhood memories were drenched in blood, and his life is the same today."

"Do, do you know where he is?"

Steve shook his head. "I don't, Tammy. I called every relative I know, and no one's heard from him. But Dino turned his back on us long ago. The gang was the only family he needed. And now that he don't have them no more, he could be anywhere. My gut tells me he's dead. But nobody's found a body, so I don't know what to think."

Tammy didn't either. She knew Steve wasn't responsible for his nephew's behavior, but familial ties are strong, and the counselor was now a part of Isaiah's death, no matter how indirect.

And that was painful.

Steve noticed her distress. He shook his head and looked down at his desk.

Tammy wiped her eyes and caught the tears before they spilled.

Steve stood and came around to her side of the desk. He took her hand and held it tightly. She looked up at him and sniffled. Steve knelt to one knee beside her chair.

"I'm sorry," he said.

Tammy shook her head. "It's not your fault."

"I know," he said. "But your loss hurts me, every time I think about it. When I found out my family was involved–"

"You can't let–"

"I always felt like Dino was my fault," Steve said. "Before the murders. When I was in prison and I heard about how he was turning out, I hated myself every night. And when I got out, and I couldn't help him... And then he ended up killing your boy. It's all a cycle. His parents started it, but I played a part in it too. I did." Steve winced. When he opened his eyes, Tammy saw that they were glossy.

It was strange to watch any man cry. But this was even more unexpected, because Steve was such a virile man. Tammy reached for him before she thought better of it. Steve returned the embrace.

His touch was frightening. A shiver bolted down Tammy's spine. But at the same time, his strong arms around her body felt comforting and natural. Tammy liked the feel of his face close to hers, his breaths on her neck. His body was warm. His back was hard and rigid beneath her fingers. Tammy's heart rate increased. Her underarms became moist. She was confused. She abruptly let go of him, and Steve did the same.

"Don't, don't tell Jacob," she said. At that moment she was talking about the hug as much as Steve's ties with Dino. The counselor seemed to know this.

"I won't," he said.

They were still close enough to kiss, and a part of Tammy wanted to do so. But at the same time, she was relieved when he backed away and returned to his seat on the other side of the desk. He wiped his eyes and was back to his old self within seconds.

"I, I won't tell Jacob," he promised.

● ● ● ● ● ●

Three hours later the final bell rang at William Joseph Middle School. Jacob left his 8th period class and went to his locker to gather the few books he needed for his homework that night. He tossed the texts nonchalantly into his backpack because he did not bring his gun to school that day, so there was no need to be cautious.

So far Jacob had toted his pistol with him three times that week, and he no longer worried about being found out. The only reason he left it at home today was because his mother came to his room to talk while Jacob got ready for school that morning. He tried to go back for it after he ate breakfast, but Tammy was walking around by then, and it was too risky.

Jacob loved his firearm so much, he now kept it under his mattress when he slept. If a serial killer was unlucky enough to target his home in the wee hours of the morning, Jacob would have no qualms about shooting him dead. His mother would be upset at first, but after she looked at everything in perspective, Tammy would be glad Jacob had a gun handy. And then he wouldn't have to hide it or keep secrets from her anymore.

Without his pistol, Jacob felt like he left the house with no shoes on. But this was just for one day. Tomorrow he'd put the gun in his backpack *before* he got dressed, because his mom never came to talk to him until he had some clothes on.

Jonathan approached Jacob's locker with his chubby friend Mark following close behind. Jonathan looked as emaciated as ever, but his eyes weren't yellow like they were the first time Jacob met him. His sickle cell illness was a big mystery. So far Jacob hadn't worked up enough nerve to ask him about it.

"What's up, J Dog," Jonathan said.

"What it be like?" Jacob said. *J Dog* was actually not Jacob's preference for a gang name. He considered it common and cliché. But it was hard to make up a whole identity on the spur of the moment. On Tuesday Willie asked him what his street name was, and "J Dog," was the first thing that came to Jacob's mind. Now he was stuck with the moniker.

"What's up, Blood?" Mark said. He munched on a cinnamon roll he'd had in his backpack since lunch that day. It was mashed pretty good, and Jacob saw that most of the icing was stuck to the plastic wrap. But Mark was a fat kid, and he never let something like basic standards spoil his snacks.

"It's all good," Jacob told him. He threw his backpack over his shoulder and headed for the exit.

Jonathan and Mark followed.

"You, you still coming to my house?" the skinny one asked.

271

Jonathan had been trying to lure Jacob to his place for four days straight. Jacob really didn't want to go, because Jonathan was a buster, and any activity he had planned for them was sure to be lame. Plus Jacob would have to ride the city bus home afterwards or get a ride from Jonathan's mom; who was said to be lacking in the mental department.

But on the other hand, Jacob was interested in the crabs who supposedly hung out up the street from Jonathan. Isaiah had been dead for more than three weeks, and Jacob had yet to shoot anyone.

"Yeah, I'll go," he said. Jacob thought about Steve at the community center and decided it would be okay to miss one day. He was only going on a volunteer basis anyway. And Steve had so many guys in there, there was no way he could keep track of every single one of them.

"Cool," Jonathan said. "I mean, *bool.*"

A deep sneer suddenly marred Jacob's features. Some wannabe gangsters take shit too far. The idea was Bloods hate Crips so much, they won't use the letter "c" – at all, even in everyday conversation. It was the epitome of niggerish behavior, in Jacob's opinion. He wouldn't allow it in his gang.

"Stop saying that dumb ass shit," he told Jonathan. "Act like you got some sense, Blood."

Jonathan's smile fell immediately. "But Lil Wayne said–"

"I don't give a damn what Lil Wayne said," Jacob barked. "Y'all niggas always trying to act like somebody else. You not even in a gang."

"But, but you said you was gon' let us in the Devil Reds," Jonathan whined.

"I'm not letting you in nothing," Jacob said. "If you want in, you have to get *jumped* in, like everybody else."

He thought the threat would make him back down, but Jonathan grew more excited.

"Yeah. That's what I want to do to today. Mark do too." He looked back at his friend and Mark nodded.

"I wanna get jumped in today, too."

Jacob felt a flutter in his chest. Once again his mouth was writing checks his ass couldn't cash. And this one would actually hurt people. But sometimes if you want to beat your enemy, you have to become like your enemy.  Jacob couldn't remember where he heard that, but it made sense.

"Alright," he said.  "Is Ricky and Willie coming, too?"

"Everybody's coming," Jonathan confirmed.

"Come on then," Jacob said.  "Let's go find them."

Outside the school busses were mostly gone.  Jacob didn't see Harold or Camille anywhere, but he did see his bus waiting on him in its usual spot alongside the curb.  Jacob's last two Devil Reds were loitering along the fence line.  Jacob felt like he was at one of those crossroads Steve told him about.  He hesitated for only a moment before joining up with his gang.

"What's up, niggas?"  He shook their hands briefly.

"Aw, shit, what up, J Dog?" Ricky said.

"What it do?" Willie added.

"Y'all still down or what?" Jacob asked.  "Y'all wanna get put down with the Devil Reds today?"

"Yeah, we down," Jonathan said.  "Everybody down.  We ready."

Jacob looked them all in the eyes, and no on dissented.  "Alright, let's do it," he said.  "Where you stay?"

"Aww, hell yeah!" Jonathan said and started laughing.  He walked ahead of them and led the way.

Jacob wondered if he'd think it was so funny when the first lip got busted.

• • • • • •

Jonathan lived in a house less than twenty blocks away from the school.  Jacob knew his new friend was poor, but he never expected the level of degradation Jonathan went home to every day.  His front yard was a literal junkyard, complete with a whole car (a '76 Nova that was missing most of the parts that made it run), a few rusty bicycle frames, several boxes of ravaged roofing shingles, and a cheap children's splash pool that was filled with dead leaves, green water and soggy pecans.

A thick extension cord snaked out of one of the side windows to a neighbor's house that supplied Jonathan's family with electricity.  Jacob saw a water hose rolled out of another window.  The house itself had serious foundation problems.  Jacob wasn't an expert on these things, but he was pretty sure the whole place would fall down in a matter of years. Jacob had absolutely no intentions of going inside to see how many rats and roaches called this place home. Surely there were plenty of them.

Throughout his whole life, Jacob thought he and Isaiah had it bad. But he now knew Tammy provided for them pretty well. It was a sobering realization, but it did not divert Jacob's attention from the business at hand.

"We going to the backyard?" he asked.

"Yeah," Jonathan said, sounding nervous for the first time. "We can go back there."

The backyard was a mirror image of the front, except there was more grass and weeds and more room for clutter that made it impossible to push a lawnmower through. The only clear spot was under a leaning basketball goal with a broken rim. Fast feet that yearned to be like LeBron James wore down the grass over the years, leaving dirt so hard it was like asphalt. For the business at hand, this area was perfect.

All of Jacob's new friends knew what it meant to get "put down" in a gang, but Jacob explained it thoroughly and gave them another opportunity to back out while they still had a chance: The initiation basically involved one individual getting "beat down" by the rest of the gang for an unspecified period of time. Since Jacob was already a member of the gang, he would not have to go through the procedure. Also, because Jacob was the leader of their set, he would throw the first punch.

If the new recruit were to fall down during the initiation, Jacob banned his soldiers from kicking or throwing any punches until the recruit made it to his feet again. If anyone chose not to fight back during the initiation, the beat down would be considered a failure, and that individual would not be a member of the gang until he went through the process again and took a few swings the second time around.

Because this was Jonathan's house (and his idea), Jacob volunteered him to go first. All of the boys laid their bags against the back door and made a tight circle around their leader and their first target. It took a lot of will power to take a swing at a boy who had done nothing to him, but Jacob did not hesitate. He took a deep breath and raised his fists. His first punch was a right hook that landed flush on Jonathan's cheek. It wasn't a hard blow, but it sounded off like it was, and everyone was scared stiff.

Everyone but Jonathan. He swung back with a speed that belied his disability. Jacob threw up an arm to block the shot, but he still got caught on the left ear. The blow hurt a lot. Before he could react, Jonathan threw a left jab that caught Jacob square on the nose. The pain was immediate and almost blinding this time, which made Jacob ball his fists in earnest.

He and Jonathan went at it for nearly thirty seconds while the rest watched in horror. At first Jacob's punches were wild and angry. But he had to slow down and really box, because Jonathan knew how to fight. For a while the match was dead even. Jacob thought about how embarrassed he would be if he got beat up by the sickle cell kid, and he finally delivered a damaging combination that toppled his new friend.

Jonathan struggled to get to his feet, breathing roughly, and Jacob was the clear victor.

"Y'all supposed to be jumping in," Jacob reminded the others. "This ain't one-on-one."

Ricky, Willie and Mark reluctantly attacked their homeboy. Jacob let them squabble for twenty more seconds. Jacob didn't throw any more punches, and Jonathan held his own against the other three. When Jacob hollered, "That's it!" Jonathan was still standing. Jacob walked to the middle of the circle and gave him a handshake and a manly hug.

"Y'all come and give this nigga some love," he instructed, and his minions followed suit. "You down now," Jacob said, breathing heavily himself. "You a Devil Red now."

Jonathan's lip was busted, and one eye was starting to close, but he grinned at his abusers.

Jacob had never seen anything so obscene.

● ● ● ● ● ●

With the format in place, the other three beat downs went a lot smoother. Jacob threw the first punch each time, but he didn't get into anymore one-one-one situations like he did with Jonathan.

Spurred on by an increasingly persistent bloodlust, the five boys beat each other like enemies for nearly ten minutes. When the dust finally cleared, everyone had new cuts and bruises. Most of them had soiled and ripped clothing. All of them felt like they had accomplished something great and noble.

But Jacob had mixed feelings about the role he'd played in this foolishness. He knew he created something vile and gross that day. But he also felt like he stepped into a situation that was already in full swing. The wannabes were going to get involved with *somebody's* gang whether he came around or not, so the Devil Reds weren't solely Jacob's fault. He was merely at the right place at the right time.

"So, so what we gon' do now?" Jonathan pondered.

During the initiations, Jonathan showed the most resilience and boxing skills. Without anyone saying it, he was Jacob's number two in command.

Jacob stood and paced before his soldiers. Mark was fat and lazy, but if he used his bulk to his advantage, he could be a formidable opponent. Willie was the smallest, and he took the most punishment during the initiation. He barely fought back. If Jacob stuck to his rules, Willie owed them a re-do. But no one wanted to beat up on the pipsqueak anymore. Ricky was another one who surprised Jacob with his fighting prowess. But all in all, his crew was clearly lame.

Luckily, Jacob had something to help even up the playing field.

"I got a gun," he announced.

Everyone quieted down and stared at him. Jacob knew he was risking a lot, but if you can't trust your own gang, who can you trust?

"For real?" Jonathan asked.

Jacob nodded. "For real. My uncle gave it to me. I was gon' kill that crab who shot my brother, but I can't find him. I'm still gon' bust on *somebody*, though..."

Willie looked like this was more than he signed up for. But the other three were very interested, especially Jonathan.

"It's some crabs up the street," he said and pointed.

"I know," Jacob said. "You told me already."

"You wanna go bust on them?" Jonathan asked.

Jacob hesitated. A shiver tapped down his spine, like someone walked over his grave. He knew this was another one of those crossroads his counselor warned him about. The only problem was Steve never said Jacob would be rolling downhill when he reached this fork in the road. Jacob was stuck in the middle of a snowball. It was impossible to reverse course.

"I didn't bring my gun today," he said. "But I'll bring it tomorrow, if y'all down."

He looked each of his brothers in the eyes, and they all swore their allegiance to him.

"I'm down," Willie said.

"Me too," Ricky said.

"I'm down with you," Mark said.

"You *know* I'm down," Jonathan said, grinning maniacally. "From the cradle to the grave; Devil Reds for *life*. It's whatever you wanna do, J Dog. I can't stand them punks."

# CHAPTER TWENTY-ONE
## *DINO'S LAST STAND*

"Get up, Daddy."

"I ain't sleep."

"Come on, man. Get up."

"I ain't sleep."

"Open your eyes, Daddy."

Dino did open his eyes, and he regretted it immediately. His date for the evening was very close to his face. And she was hideous. She called herself *Alizé*, but there was nothing smooth or classy about this whore. She was a yellow-bone, which made her highly popular when she first hit the ho stroll. But that was thirty years ago. Today Alizé was but a shell of her former self. She was missing both of her bunny rabbit teeth and a few on the bottom of her jaw as well. She was overweight and bald-headed, and she had old, dark sores all over her arms that looked like leopard spots.

Dino didn't know exactly what affliction caused the spots, but he did know Alizé was HIV positive, and she had gonorrhea too. He knew this for a fact. For these reasons, no john from the neighborhood would fool around with Alizé, even if she slashed her prices and they put on four condoms. No matter how horny you were, you were better off sticking your dick in a coffin. But Dino was nearly dead, so he could care less about the cooties. He not only lived each day like it was his last, but Dino lived each hour and each minute that way, too.

Alizé wore baggie work pants with a tank top and a heavy coat. Her titties were big, but her belly was big too. Her ass was surprisingly and depressingly flat. Her real hair was short and sparse, like a pile of roach antennae. Her wig helped her appearance considerably, but it was dirty and knotted, like she found it on the street somewhere. Her nose was wide, and her nostrils were constantly flared. Her lips were chapped and bruised from smoking crack with a metal tire gauge.

It was hard to find something good to say about Alizé, but Dino was a nice guy, so he thought long and hard until he came up with something: He decided he liked her left eye. He would've liked them both, but Alizé's right eye was lazy, and the way it rolled around in the socket creeped him out a little. But Alizé's left eye was beautiful; the color of a sundrenched wheat field, and that one was as quick as a whip. Dino stared at it, wondering if an angel or a demon lurked behind that pupil. If it was a demon, he wondered if he could kill it by shooting Alizé in the eye.

Awful thoughts like this bombarded his mind all the time. It was a wonder Dino hadn't killed a lot more people. The devil was the only homeboy he had left, and he was completely subservient to his new buddy. Dino would rape a child if his dark lord wanted him to. He would kill a nun and ejaculate on her corpse. If given the chance, he would slap the pope and piss on him and then slap him again if His Holiness complained. Dino's date had no idea how completely deranged he was at that moment, so she continued to talk rather than run for her life.

"Gimme a hit, daddy." She reached for his pockets when he didn't respond.

Dino slapped her hand away and sat up angrily. "Don't never touch my fucking pockets."

"I'm sorry, papi. Why you tripping? Don't be like that, daddy..."

Alizé was a seasoned whore from New York City. She migrated to Texas twenty-six years ago, when her pimp (Tik Tik) killed a man and had to lay low for a while. After a couple of months in Dallas, he killed a second person, and the police scooped him up before he could flee again. Tik Tik was currently serving a 40 year sentence at the Stiles Unit in Beaumont. Alizé had been on her own ever since.

She was almost fifty years old now, which made her a dinosaur in prostitute years. But Dino wasn't in a position to be picky, so he'd let her kick it with him for the past couple of days. Alizé couldn't be choosy either, so she shared a bed with the half dead gangster and tried her best to make Dino think she loved him.

He stared at her for a long time, his eyes shifting in and out of focus.

"What you want?"

"Gimme a hit," Alizé said. She had her pipe ready; this one was glass with a clean clump of Chore Boy stuffed in one end. Dino was both disgusted and intrigued by the contraption. He reached for it.

"Let me see that."

Alizé's smile faltered, but it didn't go away completely.

"This my pipe, baby," she cooed. "You gotta get your own."

"No, I wanna use yours," Dino told her.

There was a part of him that still thought smoking crack was wrong. Dino thought he could pacify the voices in his head by not owning his own pipe. As long as he borrowed someone else's tool, he was not a crack smoker himself. He was merely experimenting. Alizé frowned and handed him the glass.

Dino took the pipe and placed it gently on his lap. He dug the bag of rocks from his pocket and stared at it woefully. He only had five dimes left. Truth be told, they weren't even full dimes. When he first cut them, they were fat and beautiful. But that was before he started smoking crack. Dino went back into his bag eight times yesterday and chipped off of every rock, until they all looked pathetic. He could probably still sell them, but Dino hadn't sold any dope since Wednesday morning.

He plucked the smallest rock from the baggie and broke it in half. He gave one piece to Alizé and kept the other for himself. The prostitute reached instinctively for her glass, but Dino blocked her hand. He admired the pipe for a second and then placed his rock on top of the spongy filter.

"Let me see your lighter."

Alizé sneered. "Let me hit mine first."

Dino sneered right back at her, and he was a lot better at it. "Bitch, gimme yo lighter."

Alizé handed it over, and Dino brought the pipe to his mouth. He put fire to the other end and watched a thick plume of smoke roll towards his lips. The crack sizzled rather than *cracked* as it melted into the scouring pad, which made Dino think they should rename the drug *sizzle*. But then he took a deep inhalation, and he could think of nothing at all for the next twenty to thirty seconds.

A crack high is the absolute opposite of a heroin high. It's similar to the rush from raw cocaine, but really it's incomparable. Dino's salivary glands quivered and his bowels did as well. He stared at Alizé until his vision blurred. His pupils dilated to the size of pencil erasers. Dino's heart rate increased as beads of sweat sprouted on his forehead. His body urged him to do twenty different things at once, but Dino couldn't do any of them. All he wanted to do was sit there and not move and not talk, while his brain took a rocket ride beyond the moon and quasars; to black holes and distant galaxies.

One month ago, if someone told Dino he'd end up smoking crack, he would've laughed in their face and maybe kicked their ass, depending on who it was. Not only did Dino despise crack, but he hated crackheads. He'd felt that way ever since he learned that his mother was a dopefiend on the streets of Overbrook Meadows. She was a whore who sucked strange dicks in dark alleys, just so she could have something to put in her pipe. Dino hated his birth-giver, and he hated all women like her.

As he grew older, Dino's disdain grew steadily worse. Crack was the only way to make a little money in the hood, so Dino became a peddler of the very product he detested. And gradually he began to see what the drug did to families. He saw mothers and fathers who would rather get high than feed and clothe their children. He profited from their misery for a long time. So in a way, it was almost fitting that Dino should experience their pain first hand before he went to be with his father, Satan.

"Gimme my pipe." This was Alizé's fifth request, but it was the first time Dino heard her. He tried to hand her the glass, but he couldn't get his arm to move correctly. Alizé took a seat on the bed next to him. She leaned over and plucked the device from his fingers. Dino watched her vacantly, still unable to speak.

His eyes were wide and sunk deep in the sockets, like a prisoner of Auschwitz. Dino's hair was messed all over. The few pounds he gained at James' house were all gone now, as well as a few additional inches from his waistline that Dino could hardly afford to lose.

He weighed only one hundred and thirty-six pounds at this point, which looked terrible on his six foot frame. The whole right side of his face was black and crusty. Dino didn't care what he looked like because he thought he'd be dead by now. For the life of him, he couldn't understand how he avoided the Grim Reaper day after day.

The shootout on Monday should've been his undoing, but Dino single-handedly shot three people without taking any serious damage on his end. Skeeter was the only one to die that night, but T Lowe got hit three times, and Kevin took a bullet to the right thigh. Dino made it to his stolen Cutlass with no one hot on his tail. He didn't even have to speed away from the crime scene.

When he got back to the south side, Dino didn't take any extreme measures to remain anonymous. He bought a room for thirty dollars a night and waited for the police to kick the door in. He cocked his gun and kept it in his lap and was too afraid to even go to the bathroom. But soon the sun came up. Tuesday was upon him, and he was still among the living.

Baffled, Dino decided to get a little puntang before he died. He peered out of his motel window until he saw the perfect hooker walking by. He lured Alizé inside with an offer she couldn't refuse: "I just want somebody to kick it with. I got some crack..."

That was two days ago. Dino used Alizé to help sell his dope for a while, but eventually he asked himself, *What's the point?* What was his goal now? He already got his revenge against the Sicc Crips. He didn't kill T Lowe, but he did shoot the OG in the ass, which was enough to make him feel better.

The only thing left on Dino's *To-do* list was wait for the police to come and kill him, so why make more money? He couldn't come up with an answer, so he stopped. As for his remaining rocks, well, Dino couldn't take them to the grave with him. It seemed senseless to throw them away or give all of them to Alizé, so Dino tried his drug for the first time on Wednesday morning. It was now Thursday evening, and he was officially in love with crack cocaine.

Dino lay back on the bed and looked up at the ceiling. After only two minutes, his high started to come down. But that was okay. Dino still had four rocks in his baggie and twelve dollars in his pocket. Alizé was the one with the problem. The dopefiend scratched her wig and looked around the bed anxiously. She bent over and picked the floor for any crumbs she might have dropped today or the night before. Her good eye finally rolled back to her provider.

"Gimme another piece," she said.

Dino shook his head. "Nope."

"Come on." She patted his thigh. "Come on, papi. Hook me up."

"I just gave you a hit."

"It was too little. You kept the biggest piece for yourself."

"It's *my* shit," Dino explained. "I ain't giving you the most. You ain't do shit for it."

"I'll hook you up," Alizé said. She put her pipe down and went for Dino's zipper with both hands. He wasn't in the mood, and he had the worst case of funky balls *ever*, but he didn't stop her. If she was stupid enough to put her mouth on his mucky member, that was her problem.

Alizé frowned when she got his pants open. Dino knew the fumes were bad enough to melt paint off the walls. But the hooker held her breath and gave it her all. She gobbled him up like candy. Dino sat up on his elbows, so he could watch her.

Alizé was the most skilled he had ever seen when it came to fellatio, but most of Dino's bodily functions had shut down already, in preparation for death, he assumed. After five minutes, Alizé still couldn't coax an erection.

But in the game of prostitution, the service rendered is all that mattered. Alizé stuffed his penis back inside his pants and zipped him up with a smile on her face.

"Alright, now hook me up."

"I didn't even cum," Dino said.

"That ain't my fault."

"I didn't tell you to do that."

"You shoulda stopped me, if you didn't want it. Now quit playing. Gimme a dime."

Dino chuckled. "Bitch, you gots to be out yo rabid-ass mind. I ain't giving you shit."

Alizé's mouth fell open. She folder her arms over her chest. "That, that ain't right, daddy."

Dino shook his head, still grinning. He couldn't believe the slut was serious. After everything she experienced in her long, ugly existence, she still expected life to be fair. Dino laughed hoarsely. "Alright, let me see your pipe."

Alizé's eyes narrowed. "Let me hit mine first this time, daddy."

"Nope." Dino shook his head. "I always go first."

Alizé handed the pipe over and watched while Dino smoked another five dollar piece. She was used to him spacing out for a while, but after three minutes he continued to avoid eye contact.

"Alright, gimme mine now," she said.

Dino shook his head. "Ain't."

Alizé's eyes widened. "But you said—"

"This all I got left," Dino said, gripping his diminishing dope sack. "I'm keeping it for myself."

Alizé looked sad enough to cry. But Dino had just begun to ruin her day.

"Well, gimme my pipe back then," she pouted.

Dino shook his head and gripped it tighter. "Nope."

"Quit playing, papi. Give it back."

"I need it," Dino said. "What I'ma smoke the rest of this shit with?"

"I don't give a damn what you smoke it with," Alizé spat, and Dino knew he'd pushed her too far. "That's my pipe! You can't keep my pipe!"

"*That's my pipe*," Dino mocked her. He stuffed his remaining rocks in his pocket and produced his handgun. He didn't cock it or point it at her, but just having it exposed was enough of a threat. "I'm keeping this pipe," he said, "unless you bad enough to take it from me."

Alizé stared in total horror. She couldn't believe this was happening. In her many years on the streets, people stole a lot of things. They took her drugs and took her money. The bastards even stole her health, youth and her beauty, but never had a *dealer* stole her straight-shooter, at gunpoint no less.

The prostitute almost lunged for her pipe anyway. Dino was armed, but he weighed less than she did. Plus he was so close to death, Alizé thought she could break his arm with a rough jerk. Dino's face was rotten like a zombie from *The Walking Dead*, and he had buck shots in his arms and chest that looked like tiny moles burrowing under his skin.

Alizé was pretty sure she could take him, but it would be just her luck if the coward got off a lucky shot. The last thing she needed was a trip to the emergency room over a glass pipe that only cost a dollar. Besides, she knew of at least four people who were in the streets looking for Dino at that very moment. One of them would give her some crack, if she gave up his whereabouts. They'd give her more than Dino had in his funky dope sack.

She stood with her hands on her hips. "Gimme my pipe, or I'm telling where you at."

"Telling who?" Dino asked with a smirk.

"I'ma tell them niggas out there looking for you," Alizé said. Right away she regretted her words. She thought Dino might shoot her for making the threat, but he kept grinning. There was something surreal and altogether frightening about his skeletal features. That toothy grin. His teeth were much too big for his mouth. Alizé felt like she was in the presence of Satan himself.

"Go ahead and tell 'em," Dino said. "I'll be right here waiting for 'em."

Alizé grabbed her purse and headed for the door. "I'ma tell 'em for real, Dino."

"Hurry up and go!" Dino shouted. "Tell them I'm right here waiting on they monkey ass!"

Alizé stared into his eyes, and her resolve faded visibly. "Just gimme my pipe, papi. I don't want no trouble."

Dino jumped from the bed and rushed towards her. "Get yo–"

Alizé was gone before he finished the sentence.

Dino's heart raced, but a cool serenity fell upon him at the same time. This was it. Ever since he killed Charlotte, he knew it would come to this. The end was upon him. Dino had no doubt the whore was telling the truth about people looking for him. The only question was who these men were.

The Sicc Crips were the obvious guess but not the only option. The police wanted him too, and they were bound to have undercover officers on the streets. Or maybe it was a gang of vigilantes.

But knowing *who* was coming was not as important as preparing himself for what was going to happen when they got there. Dino slammed the motel door closed, but he did not lock it. There was no point in that. He didn't want to avoid THE END; he wanted to greet it with open arms. His face was mangled, his "family" had abandoned him, and he was the murderer of women and children. Homicide was the only fitting conclusion to this bucket of shit he called a life.

With that in mind, Dino took a seat on the floor directly in front of the door. He sat far enough away for the door to swing open freely, but close enough for the men who entered to see him right away. Dino ejected the magazine from his pistol and checked to make sure he had a full clip. He punched it back in and cocked his weapon. He sat with his back against the wall and his hands in his lap. Tears streamed down his face, but he was hardly aware of them.

After a few minutes of waiting, Dino remembered he still had crack in his pocket. He fished it out and got up to retrieve the whore's pipe from the bed. Dino returned to his spot in front of the door and smoked a whole dime in one long inhalation. His high was immediate and frightening. Dino's heart kicked like a donkey. And he heard a freight train so clearly, it felt like he was sitting on railroad tracks. He grabbed his pistol and pointed it at the door with shaky hands.

By the time his high came down, Dino was drenched with sweat. His eyes bulged and his teeth chattered. No one had come to the door yet, and his pipe was caked with residue. And he had two and a half rocks left. Dino put his gun down and put fire to the pipe again.

Life was strange. Ten minutes ago he cared about nothing at all. But now he hoped he'd have time to smoke the rest of his crack before the gunmen burst through the door. Dino finally understood what his mama, his daddy, Rick James and Chris Farley all knew years before him: Crack cocaine is the best drug in the world. And if you gotta die, there's no better high.

Dino snatched up his gun again and burped. He turned his head and threw up on the carpet next to him. He was so high, he didn't move when the puddle of puke started to expand towards his butt and soak his pants.

# CHAPTER TWENTY-TWO
## *THE COMFORTER*

Jacob didn't get home until after seven p.m. That wasn't necessarily a bad time, considering he was usually in counseling past sunset. But his mother confronted him in the living room as soon as he walked inside.

"Where were you?"

Jacob hesitated. Tammy wore the purple uniform for her housekeeping job at Jackson Memorial, but her shift didn't end until ten-thirty. Jacob knew something was wrong, if she took another day off work.

"*Answer me!*" Tammy nearly screamed. She closed the distance between them, and Jacob backed against the front door.

"Wha, what's wrong?"

"Tell me where you were!"

She was so close, Jacob could feel her breath on his face.

"I was, I went to counseling."

"You gonna stand right there and lie to my face?" Tammy had her hand on her hip, but she didn't look very strong right then. As a matter of fact, Jacob saw tears in her eyes.

"I went to my friend's house," he admitted.

"*To do what?* What friend?"

"Mama, what's wrong with you?"

Her tears spilled like blood. "Where'd you get this?" she breathed.

Jacob looked down and was shocked to see his most prized possession in her hand. Tammy didn't hold the gun by the handle, rather she cradled it in her palm uncomfortably, taking care to keep her fingers outside the trigger guard.

Jacob was so stunned, he couldn't respond. He looked from the gun to his mother's dreary eyes. His face burned. Her look of disappointment reminded him of when Tammy chastised him for picking on Isaiah when they were younger: *That's your little brother, Jacob! If everybody in the world makes fun of him, you're supposed to be the* **one** *person he can turn to for help. But you want to hurt his feelings like the rest of them. I, I don't know what to say about you.*

Only this was monumentally worse because his mother was crying. Jacob would walk through hell and high water to make his mama happy.

"Where did you get this?"

"I don't know," Jacob said. He lowered his gaze in submission, but Tammy pressed the attack.

"You're going to tell me where you got it!" She shoved him in the chest with her free hand. *"Where did you get it?"*

Jacob shook his head. "I can't tell you."

Tammy's eyes widened. "Jacob, I'm not playing with you."

His chest swelled, and he gritted his teeth. He looked up at her, his expression hard and cold. "I'm not playing either, Mama."

Tammy's jaw dropped. She put a hand to her chest as her head slowly cocked to the side.

"It's my gun," Jacob said. His nostrils flared. "It don't matter where I got it from. It's mine!"

Deep down Tammy always knew there would come a time when her son would stand up to her and declare his position as a man. But she never dreamed it would happen in the eighth grade. She felt like she'd wandered into a parallel universe.

"Give it here," Jacob said. He had the nerve to reach for the gun. That snapped Tammy back to reality. She threw her arm behind her back.

"No, I'm not giving it to you! What the hell is wrong with you?"

Jacob tried to reach around her. Tammy shoved him back against the door.

*"You gon' take it from me?!"*

Jacob paused and seemed to consider this. Tammy's heart ached. She knew she couldn't outmuscle him. But Jacob's shoulders dropped, and his eyes filled with tears.

"I need it," he whimpered. "You don't know. You don't understand."

Tammy cried too. "Tell me what I don't understand, Jacob. Talk to me. What's going on?"

"I'm in a gang!" Jacob blurted. "I can't do nothing by myself. But, but I got help now."

"What gang? *What are you talking about?*"

"*For Isaiah!*" Jacob cried. "Nobody wants to do nothing for Isaiah, so I have to do it myself. *Everybody wants to forget about it!*"

"Nobody's forgetting about it," Tammy reasoned. "Everybody's trying–"

"No they not, Mama!" Jacob's lips quivered. "They haven't did nothing! Everybody's telling me to forget about it and forgive them people. But I can't! Them crabs killed my brother, and I gotta kill them." The tears streamed down his face and dripped from his chin. His breaths came in shudders.

Tammy shook her head. She knew her son was troubled, but this went past even her worst speculations. "You don't have to do anything, Jacob. The police are already–"

"Yes I do, Mama." His nose started to run as well. He snorted roughly. "I do have to do something."

"You're gonna get yourself killed!"

"No, I'm not."

"Yes, you are. And you don't even care! You don't care what happens to yourself, and you damned sure don't care about me! You–" Tammy's throat caught on the last word. She turned away from him with a fist to her mouth. "Jesus, I don't believe this." The floor shifted beneath her feet. She took a wobbly step and had to reach for the entertainment center to steady herself. "Help me, Lord..."

"Mama..." Jacob rushed forward, but Tammy jerked away from him violently.

"Get away from me!"

Jacob withdrew. He had never seen that look in his mother's eyes. He never saw her teeth bared, like she would tear his arm off.

"Mama, I–"

"You gotta give this up," she said. Tammy's voice was deep and hoarse. Her eyes were low and soulful.

"Give, what?"

"This dumb gang *shit!*" Tammy yelled. "This gun, this anger, this, this *hate* you have, Jacob. Are you done? Tell me you're gonna give it up," she pleaded.

Now her eyes were soft and hopeful. Jacob was on the verge of lying, just so they could put this mess behind them. But he was tired of keeping secrets. He longed for honesty and openness between him and his mom, like it used to be. And now they had it. And even though the truth was a vile and ugly thing, it was still better than living a lie. The child in him could placate her, but the man in him would hide in the darkness no longer.

He shook his head. He wiped his nose with the back of his hand.

Tammy's face twisted in agony. She emitted a long and miserable wail and then turned and rushed from the room. Jacob tried to follow, but Tammy made it to her bedroom and slammed the door hard behind her.

"I'm sorry," Jacob yelled through the wood.

Tammy didn't believe him, and a few seconds later Jacob proved her right. What he said next chilled every ounce of blood in her body.

"I need my gun back," Jacob said calmly. "I, I'm sorry, Mama. But that's my gun. And I want it back."

Tammy turned towards the door and slowly backed away from it. She took quick breaths through her nose and stared at the doorknob. If it turned, she would have a heart attack. But Jacob still had a little respect left for his mother. After a moment, his shadow under the door disappeared, and she heard him retreat to his room.

Tammy stood guard for a few minutes, and then she placed the gun on her bed with trembling fingers. She took a seat and then lay down next to it. Curled in a fetal position, she cried and waited. She didn't think Jacob would come back late in the night to retrieve his pistol, but the mere possibility was dreadful enough.

Tammy closed her eyes, fully aware that she was on the verge of insanity. If she lost both of her boys, that would surely be the end of her. She barely held it together when she saw Isaiah on the coroner's table. The only reason she didn't give up then was because she knew Jacob needed her to be strong.

Tammy's cellphone rang, and it startled her. She dug it from her pocket and cleared her throat before she answered.

"Huh, hell, hello?"

"Tammy?" It was a deep, strong voice. She knew it was Steve without checking the caller ID.

She sniffled. "Yeah."

"Is he home yet?" Steve asked. "Did you ask him about the gun?"

She exhaled slowly. "Yeah, I did. He didn't deny it."

"What's going on? Where is he now?"

"He's in his room," Tammy said. "But he wants his gun back. I don't want, I need to get it out of this house."

"How you holding up?" Steve asked. "You don't sound too good."

Tammy shook her head. She wiped her eyes roughly. "I don't know what to do," she said. That was one of the hardest things she'd ever had to admit. "I tried to be there for him," she cried. "I always listened to him. We went to church. We go all the time. I've been on my knees so much, I just, I can't, I don't understand it. He said he's in a gang. He, he, he wants to shoot somebody. He told me that. He looked me right in the eyes and told me that."

"Do you want me to come over there?"

Tammy thought about it and decided against it. Jacob was volatile right now. She didn't know how he would react if Steve showed up at their house. If nothing else, it would probably ruin their counseling sessions.

"No, but I, I do need somebody to, I want this gun out of my house. Are you still at the center? Can I come see you?"

"I'm closing up right now," Steve said. "But I live right down the street. I'll be home in five minutes. I know it seems hopeless right now, but it's not too late to change things. I'm here for you, if you need me."

Tammy sat up on the bed. "Wha, what's your address?"

Steve gave it to her, and Tammy said she was on her way. She disconnected and did not say goodbye to her son on the way out of the house.

● ● ● ● ● ●

Steve Stewart lived in a two bedroom house on the corner of Truman Street and Stalcup Avenue. His home was by no means lavish, but it was cozy and comfortable. He didn't live in a great neighborhood, but his neighbors were friendly, and everyone tried to look out for one another.

He walked into his house at eight p.m., and, as was customary, he did a quick walk-through before he lowered his guard and felt completely safe there. This was somewhat of a gloomy custom, but it's always better to be safe than sorry. It only took him thirty seconds to make sure no intruder was in the living room or the kitchen, the bathroom or the bedrooms.

When he first got out of prison, this habit was much worse. Steve would drop to his knees to look under the beds, and he'd check behind all of the curtains in the front room as well as in the shower. Before she passed away, Steve's mother complained about his routine.

"Boy, what you done did this time?" she would ask. "Who's after you? If a man can't find peace in his own house, he ain't gon' find it nowhere."

Steve agreed with that, and he never tried to explain things to his mother, because his mom had never been to prison. She didn't understand what it was like to spend a full decade behind bars. She didn't know how hard it was to let go of some of the things you learned there.

Back in the living room, Steve left his briefcase next to the computer desk and turned on the television. He cursed himself and turned it back off immediately. He tossed the remote on the sofa and vowed not to touch it again for at least two hours. Television was another one of his bad habits, but gradually he was getting this one under control. He wouldn't watch more than an hour and a half of TV a day – unless he got caught up in an educational program about the prison system or black history.

Steve turned on the stereo instead. An old school Public Enemy CD began to play. He liked the record, but the visitor he expected might not, so he switched to R&B tunes on a slow jam station. After a moment he thought better of it and turned the stereo off as well. Although soft music might be a nice backdrop for the somber conversation he thought he'd have with Jacob's mother, Steve didn't want Tammy to think he was hitting on her in any way.

Their hug at the community center was still fresh on his mind.  But Steve was a man of tact and discipline.  He understood that the emotions he and Tammy shared should not be confused with the passion lovers felt for one another.  He and Jacob's mom were united by a common evil; a skinny punk named Dino.  That was as far as their connection went.  Steve couldn't deny he was attracted to Tammy, but he was now working as a counselor for her, just as much as he was for her son.

He checked his watch and decided he did not have time to cook dinner before his guest arrived.  Instead he took a seat behind his computer and went through an ever-increasing heap of emails.  Most of them involved community functions he was required to attend.  But every now and then there was a message from a student he'd worked with in the past.  Tonight he received an email from Raheem Mitchell; a junior living on campus at Texas Southern University.

Four years ago Raheem thought THE WHITE MAN wanted him dead, and he had no real control over his life, because it was already decided that he should sell drugs and go to the penitentiary.  Today Raheem understood that he was the true keeper of his destiny, and the best way to prove THE WHITE MAN wrong was to become successful, despite how many odds were stacked against him.

Raheem wrote to tell Steve that he continued to excel in school, and he recently became engaged to marry a beautiful ebony queen named Phyllis.  Raheem wanted to know if Steve would come to his wedding next year.  Steve wrote him back and said he would be delighted.

When someone knocked on the door, Steve became apprehensive.  He rose from his desk, wondering why Jacob's mother made him feel that way.  Tammy was beautiful, but not exceptionally so.  And so far all of Steve's memories of her were laced with agony, rather than the poise and confidence that usually attracted him to a woman.

He opened the door, and there it was again:  Tammy's eyes were wet and miserable.  Her face was pink and puffy.  Her cheeks were pulled down in an interminable expression of sorrow that struck Steve like a punch to the gut.  He reached for her instinctively, drawing her inside with a hand on her arm.

"Hi, Tammy.  Come in, please."

She entered without a word, and he closed the door behind her. Tammy stood demurely before him. Steve noticed that she had on the purple scrub uniform for her housekeeping job at the hospital. He knew she'd missed another day of work because of her wayward son, but ultimately all of her problems were caused by his murderous nephew. Steve saw that she had a pistol in her hand. He carefully plucked it from her fingers. He placed it on the computer desk and looked deeply into her eyes.

Tammy wiped her nose and stood with her hands down by her sides. She looked innocent and totally overwhelmed by the pressures of a world she was no longer familiar with. Steve gave advice for a living, but he could think of no words that would make this woman feel better. He stepped to her hesitantly and put his arms around her. Tammy quickly returned the gesture. She laid her head on his chest and began to cry again. Steve ran a hand up her spine and caressed the back of her neck.

In the back of his mind sirens went off; reminding him of his role as a counselor. But there are no definite rules when it comes to healing. Sometimes a hug will help more than a long talk. Sometimes a kiss worked better than a Band-Aid, so Steve pecked the top of her head and then her forehead. When she looked up at him, Steve felt a sharp pang of guilt and uncertainty, but Tammy closed her eyes and kissed him back.

It would be wrong to categorize the next hour's activities as lovemaking, because Steve and Tammy were not in love, and they had not gone through any of the courting rituals that normally led up to intimacy. But Steve thought it would also be wrong to describe their time together as mere sex. The bond they shared that night was on a totally unexplored level that transcended pain and suffering, loss and heartache.

They became one on the couch. There were no words exchanged as they undressed and took time to marvel and explore each other's bodies. Steve had admired Tammy's physique before, but tonight her nudity did not excite him on a strictly physical level. Steve was more excited by the inner peace that came over her. He was captivated by her heart and her soul. He was charmed by her strength and resolve, the tradition and power flowing beneath her smooth, black skin and the treasure that was her womb.

When he entered her, Tammy made the first and only sound she would make that night. She emitted a soft whimper that incorporated all of her hurt and loathing and longing in one quick breath. Steve took that sound and he stored it away, deep inside his heart. Suddenly there was so much he wanted to say. But he knew that he was a fool, and none of the words in his brain or the dictionary could compare to the magnificence their bodies communicated on their own.

So he kept his thoughts to himself, and Tammy did the same. Multiple eruptions could not stop their coupling, but sheer exhaustion did, nearly an hour later. Steve lay back with Tammy in his arms, and they held each other for another hour. Neither wanted to speak on what happened, and neither wanted their time together to come to an end.

Tammy finally rose at a quarter 'til midnight and got dressed in the darkness. Steve walked her to the door, and they embraced again under the soft porch light. They kissed softly and passionately before she left. Deep down, Steve sensed that would be the last time they touched.

Tammy felt this too, but she left the counselor's house with no regrets.

● ● ● ● ● ●

Dino was not at his post when the gunmen showed up at his motel room. He was on the floor next to the bed; on his hands and knees picking the carpet for tiny bits of crack he or Alizé might have dropped last night or earlier that day.

Dino used to think this was one of the most pitiful customs of a crackhead, but it made perfect sense now. Crack is hard, and he was sure crumbs fell off each time he broke a dime in half. When he chopped it up with his razor blade, he knew little chunks flew here and there. He didn't care about them back then.

Now he cared about them a whole lot.

Dino smoked his last rock forty-five minutes ago, and he was in full skitz-mode now. He didn't understand how he ran through all of his crack so quickly. He didn't understand why he gave Alizé so many free rocks. He didn't understand why he wanted more crack so badly all of a sudden, but he did.

And it wasn't just a flippant craving. Dino felt like he *needed* more crack. He felt like he would die if he didn't get more crack. He knew that he would readily take a penis into his mouth for more crack. He was sweating profusely, and his nerves were shot, and his motel room was wrecked because of his exhaustive search to find more rocks.

The problem was crack came in so many shapes, sizes and textures, virtually everything on the floor resembled a rock. Dino had picked up nearly eighty items so far and tasted them, hoping his tongue would get numb. Even when it didn't, Dino smoked a few faux-rocks anyway – just in case. At one point he smoked candle wax, and another time it was a piece of bar soap he put in his pipe. The smoke from this debris was wretched and foul. But after he finished choking, Dino was not dissuaded from looking for more white pebbles on the floor.

When someone knocked on the door, Dino knew it wasn't the police, because the visitor knocked politely rather than pound with their fist. He planned to say something cool when THE END came, like *"Come on in, bitch nigga!"* or *"Say hello to my little friend!"* But Dino discovered something else about drugs that night: No matter how tough you are while sober, crack turns you into a little bitch. Dino's heart raced, and he no longer wanted anything to do with the people on the other side of the door.

He stopped moving and became very quiet. He held his breath, but the gunmen knew he was in there. They knocked again, and then they tried the doorknob. The door didn't swing open because Dino locked it when he started to pick the floor. But the motel was old and raggedy. It would only take one good kick to get past his defenses.

The stranger on the other side used his shoulder instead, and the **BOOMP!** sound was loud and horrifying. Dino shrieked like a girl as he watched the door push inwards; bending easily, like an archer's bow. Dino dove to the bed and snatched up his gun just as a second **BOOMP!** pushed the door in completely. Dino tried to point his weapon as he rolled over the mattress and hit the floor in a twisted heap.

It was odd to want death yet fear death at the same time. Even stranger was how Dino still thought about crack as the first gunshot exploded in the room, sounding-off like a cherry bomb in a washing machine.

*I'll never get high again*, Dino realized.

And out of all of the horrible things that happened in the past few weeks, this was now the tragedy that he regretted the most.

*My eyes deserve to well with tears*
*Memories of my sins appear*
*Like flashbulbs burning deep within*
*My soul. Accusing. No pretense*
*Abusing. Now the acid rain*
*Stains blissful memories. The pain's*
*Like solemn melodies. My heart*
*Clings fast to fleeting dreams. Depart*
*From me – this bitter sting. Be gone!*
*Regrets, this stress, this somber song*
*Relief is mine. In Him I claim*
*Peace, shelter from this acid rain*

# CHAPTER TWENTY-THREE
## *BODY COUNT*

The shootout did not go as Dino expected.

His original plan was to take a seat in front of the door and start shooting at whoever was standing there when it flew open. He knew they would be shooting, too. And if Dino was completely stationary, the chances of him getting hit at least once were pretty good. Either way, Dino planned to save his last bullet for Plan B. If he was still alive when the dust settled, he would deep-throat his pistol and separate his spinal cord from his brain stem with a fiery explosion that would send him to hell within seconds.

That was how things should have gone, but crack cocaine changed all of that. Dino was not in position when the door swung open, and he was no longer eager to die when the first shot went off. The drugs rewired his brain. Next to finding more crack, self-preservation was the most important thing on Dino's mind.

The first shot was a deafening **BOOOM!** from a shotgun. Dino recognized the sound immediately. It was the same shotty he heard when he attacked T Lowe in the alley three days ago. Skeeter toted the double-barrel then, but Skeeter was dead. Dino

298

knew that another Sicc Crip brought the shotgun, because it was supposed to be a good omen to avenge a fallen soldier with the dead man's weapon.

The motel room was small. The first rain of buckshots would've disemboweled Dino if he got hit, but the shooter aimed for his position on the bed, rather than make adjustments for his forward progress.

Dino hit the floor with a heavy grunt and found himself stuck between the bed and the wall. Next to him was an old air-conditioning unit. Dino rolled onto his belly and poked his head around the air-conditioner just in time to see the shooter cock his weapon and take aim again.

*Cha-CHICK!*

**BOOOM!**

The gunman was a ghoulish Negro named Pacman. Pacman was in jail when the Sicc Crips cast their votes to evict Dino from the gang. Dino was pretty sure Pacman would've had his back if he was there. But that didn't matter, because Pacman certainly didn't have his back now.

Dino ducked behind the air-conditioner and managed to shield his face and torso from most of the scorching blast from the shotty. But his legs were fully exposed. Dino felt a sudden pain in his lower extremities that was comparable to nothing he'd experienced in life thus far. The pain was followed by a wetness, like he was wading in molten lava. Dino screamed and Pacman grinned, but the smile fell from his face when Dino showed his hand.

Without really aiming, Dino raised his arm over the air-conditioner and let off five shots in less than two seconds.

**POP!POP!**

**POP!POP!POP!**

One of the slugs caught Pacman in the upper arm. Dino saw the impact clearly: One second Pacman was standing boldly, with two hands on the shotgun. In the next instant his left shoulder jerked back roughly, like he was doing the Harlem Shake. A clumpy spray of blood splattered on the wall behind him.

**"Fuck, nigga!** *Shit!"*

Pacman let go of the shotty and clutched the wound with his free hand. Before the double-barrel hit the ground, Dino's killer instincts took over. He made it to his feet in a blur, ignoring the pain in his thighs and knees. He secured his gun with two hands, like a policeman. By the time Pacman realized he was in deep shit, Dino was less than five feet away. He pointed his pistol directly at Pacman's nose, and though his hands were shaking like he had Parkinson's, there was no way he could miss.

Pacman's eyes grew big like clamshells. He took a step backwards, but there was only one exit, and he was heading away from it. He raised his hand and said, "Hold on," but Dino pulled the trigger anyway, because this was no game, and war only has a pause button if you're experiencing it on an Xbox.

***POP!***

Pacman was brown-skinned with a neatly-shaved moustache and goatee. He was twenty-two years old. He had a nice build; not particularly muscular, but he wasn't fat at all. Pacman had been with the same girl since high school. They had four children together. Pacman had promised to marry her one day, but *next year* always seemed like a better time to jump the broom. Next year had already come and gone four times since he first proposed to his high school sweetheart. But whenever she confronted him, Pacman said he meant *next* next year.

Pacman did not get his nickname from his eating habits, but rather from his exploits on the football field. Before he tore an ACL and got cut from his college team, he'd played defensive end. He got more sacks his freshman year than any other player in his conference. People used to say he gobbled up quarterbacks like his famed videogame counterpart gobbled up dark blue ghosts.

Dino thought of all of this as he watched a new hole appear on Pacman's head, above his left eyebrow. Pacman's eyes went blank instantly. His mouth fell open. He didn't have time to reach for his wound before his knees buckled, and he fell slowly to the floor.

He hit the carpet softly and casually rolled to his side, like he was taking a nap. Dino saw that the bullet exited the back of his skull. It was a gross, yet intriguing injury. Dino's body wanted to flee the scene, but his brain was stuck. He watched Pacman's leg twitch two times, and then it stopped.

Dino lowered his gun and leaned forward to get a better look at the damage he inflicted, but then he saw movement out of the corner of his eye. He jerked his gun in that direction. He was not surprised to see his old friend Tricky trembling in the doorway. Tricky's eyes flashed from the corpse to Dino. His jaw became unhinged. He mouthed words of horror that never made it past his vocal cords.

Tricky had a gun, but he dropped it and threw his hands up, like he was being robbed. He fell to his knees and started crying. He tried to speak, but it took a few seconds before he was intelligible.

"*Please don't shoot me, Dino! Please!*"

Tricky was a good friend when Dino was in the Sicc, but at this point he didn't have a good reason *not* to shoot the coward. Pacman had come there to do him in, and Tricky was obviously there for the same purpose.

"Why I shouldn't shoot you?" Dino asked him. "You came to kill me, nigga."

Dino took a step towards him, and his knee buckled under his own weight.

"Aww, shit, cuz–"

He stumbled forward and had to use the wall to support himself.

"Say, man..." Dino looked down at his legs quizzically and saw that his new injuries from the shotgun were a lot worse than he first assumed. With his pants on, it was impossible to assess the exact damage. But Dino saw that both of his legs were soaked with blood. His pants were torn and burnt, and a few flaps of skin hung from his left thigh like a tattered flag.

The evil nymph on his left shoulder urged him to do the right thing: *This is it, homey! It's time to suck on that pistol. Do it, cuz. Do it now!*

"Yeah," Dino said aloud. He lowered his head in despair. He knew the voice in his head was right, but when he tried to raise the gun to his face something stopped him. Dino grunted and tried again. He got the gun all the way in his mouth this time, but for the life of him, he could not pull the trigger.

Dino was stupefied. It didn't make sense that he should have any desires to live on at that point. But his brain wouldn't allow him to commit suicide.

Frustrated, Dino screamed and cracked himself upside the head with the pistol. The pain was immediate, but the stars that swam before his eyes were not blinding. Dino saw Tricky still standing in the doorway. He pointed the gun at him instead.

301

"*No!*" Tricky threw his hand in front of his face, much like his dead friend had done. The move didn't save Pacman, and Dino thought Tricky was a fool for expecting a different outcome.

"*You came to kill me!*" Dino bellowed.

"*No, I didn't,*" Tricky cried – literally. Tears streamed down his face like rain on a window pane.

"*Yeah, you did!*" Dino shouted. "Pick up that gun, nigga! *You came to kill me, then kill me!*"

"*Naw, man...*" Tricky shook his head furiously, and Dino knew he wasn't going to do it.

Dino had half a mind to shoot him anyway, but as with any good gangster tale, he had to let someone live, so they could tell the story.

Ultimately Dino would die a failure, but on the streets he would be immortal. Hate him or love him, Dino was by far the most dangerous and most deadly goon Overbrook Meadows had ever seen. He murdered with total disregard for morality and decency. And even on his last leg, he was still more powerful than his enemies. The community would never forget him. He would be revered and feared like the Boogeyman.

*Bloody Dino.*

*Bloody Dino.*

If they called him a third time, he would appear in the night and kill them and take their baby.

"Who out there?" he asked Tricky.

"Huh, whuh, what?"

"I said who else out there?"

Tricky was stuck on stupid, but he finally understood what Dino was asking.

"*Nobody, D. It, it was just me and Pac, Pacman.*"

"You got a car out there?"

"*It's, it's right by the door, cuz. Please don't shoot me, man. Please, Dino.*"

"Nigga, stop crying like a little, ol' bitch. I ain't gon' shoot you. Put yo hands down, ho."

Tricky lowered his arms cautiously, but they shot up again when Dino stepped towards him.

"*Please, Dino! Don't shoot me, man! Please!*"

"Nigga, I said I wasn't gon' shoot you. *Move!*" Dino pushed him aside and peered outside. It was close to midnight.

The sky was exceptionally dark. There was no moon, and a thick cloud cover blocked most of the stars' radiance. Dino saw a Ford Taurus idling in front of his motel room with the keys still in the ignition. He grabbed Tricky by the collar and pulled him into the room.

"Get yo ass in here!"

Tricky yelped like a puppy and fell to the floor next to his dead comrade. He rolled onto his back and threw up his arms and legs in defense.

"*No, Dino! No!*"

Dino looked down on him with a sneer. "Cuz, I should shoot yo coward ass on *principle*! When'd you get to be such a ho ass nigga?"

"*Always*," Tricky assured him. "I always been like this, D…"

Dino shook his head in disgust, but he kept his word and did not murder his old friend. He exited the room with gun in hand and tried his best to ignore the racket of pain from his mutilated legs.

By the time Dino got inside the Taurus, his sneakers were soggy with blood. He heard sirens getting closer. He threw the car into DRIVE, but he didn't have a destination. That was just as well, because he wasn't sure he'd make it five miles down the road.

● ● ● ● ● ●

Jacob was still awake when his mother returned home. He went to the living room when he heard her car pull into the driveway, and he opened the front door for her. Tammy got out of the car looking a lot more peaceful than she did the last time Jacob saw her. But her expression changed when she saw her son standing in the doorway.

"What are you doing still up?" she asked. She looked like she was afraid of him. That was something Jacob hated to see in her eyes. She stepped past him, and he closed and locked the door behind her.

The living room lights were off, but the kitchen light was on, and they could see each other fairly well.

"Where'd you go," Jacob asked.

Tammy gave him a look. "Why?"

He shrugged. "Just asking."

Tammy kept her eyes narrowed. "I got rid of that gun."

"Did you, did you throw it down the street somewhere?" Jacob asked.

"You're not getting it back," Tammy assured him.

Jacob shook his head. "No, I just... You were gone a long time..."

"I don't think I owe you an explanation," Tammy responded. "If anything, you need to explain yourself to me."

Jacob nodded and then shook his head. His eyes filled with tears, and he cried unabashedly. Tammy's heart melted. She took his hand and led him to the couch.

"Sit down," she instructed, and Jacob did so. Tammy sat next to him and held his hand in her lap.

"You want to talk to me now?" she asked.

Jacob nodded and shivered a little.

"Where did you get that gun?" Tammy asked. If he still couldn't tell her, their conversation wouldn't go anywhere. But Jacob surprised her by speaking up right away.

"Uncle Myron."

That wasn't a huge surprise, but it still struck Tammy like a slap in the face. She knew her brother was a knucklehead, but she never thought he would try to corrupt one of her children.

"But don't tell him I told you," Jacob tacked on.

"I don't know if I can do that," Tammy said.

"*Please*," Jacob pleaded. "He gon' think I'm a punk."

Tammy thought about it for a second and said, "Alright." She didn't know if she could keep the promise, but she knew she had to remain open-minded, if they were going to have an open discussion. In addition to grieving for his brother, Jacob also had to contend with puberty and growing into manhood. As a woman, Tammy knew she couldn't tell him it was okay to be a *punk*.

"Tell me why you think you need to hurt somebody for Isaiah," she said.

Jacob shook his head and sniffled. "Because, because it *hurts*, Mama. They, they keep doing this, to everybody, because won't nobody stop them."

"Who, Jacob? Who are *they*?"

"The cra, the Crips, Mama. They think they can do whatever they want. They killed Isaiah, and nobody did *nothing*."

Tammy was actually glad he made that point. "But you told me you joined a gang, too..."

Jacob shook his head, still crying. "It's not a real gang, Mama; just some stupid kids from my school. All of them used to get picked on by the Crips, so they wanted to be Bloods. I hate Crips too, so I said I was a Blood."

His logic made sense, but at the same time it was terribly flawed.

"Jacob, don't you see what you're doing? The real Bloods in L.A., how do you think they got their start?"

Jacob had no idea. He was pretty sure his mother didn't know anything about it, either.

"They were just regular people," Tammy informed him. "They got tired of getting picked on, so they got together and started a gang. But the thing is, a gang might start for one reason, but after a while other stuff happens. They started selling dope and robbing people, and pretty soon they were no better than the Crips or anybody else. They became part of the problem."

Jacob knew how easily that could happen. His wannabe gang was already eager to do evil.

"Why can't you forgive the people who hurt Isaiah?" Tammy asked.

"I can't," Jacob said.

"But why not?"

"Because then won't nothing happen to them."

"Vengeance belongs to the Lord," Tammy reminded him.

"But what if He don't do nothing, either?" Jacob wondered.

"You have to trust God's word."

"But what if, what if I don't believe in..." Goosebumps sprouted on his arms, and Jacob couldn't say it. It was bad enough to think it for so long. He thought his mother would be upset, but she put an arm around him and pulled him closer.

"You think you're the first person to feel like that?" Tammy asked. "When they came to my job and told me what happened to Isaiah..." The memory brought a lot of the pain back, and Tammy found herself crying, too. "I told myself that no God who loved me would allow something like that. Isaiah was the sweetest, most beautiful boy in the world. How could God let him die like that?"

Jacob's eyes widened. "You thought that?"

"Yeah," Tammy said. "Sometimes I lose faith, just like everybody else. That doesn't mean I don't love God no more, and it definitely doesn't mean He doesn't still love me."

"But what if I said there was no God," Jacob pondered.

"He still loves you," Tammy said. "So long as you ask for forgiveness."

"But what if I said it while I was at church?"

Tammy rubbed his shoulder. "It's okay, Jacob. God knows your heart. He's not going to strike you down, just because you're mad at Him one day. You do believe God loves you, don't you?"

Jacob nodded.

"You still believe in Jesus; that He died for your sins?"

Jacob nodded, and he wasn't trying to appease his mother. He really did believe that.

"Then ask for forgiveness," Tammy suggested. "If you haven't said your prayers in a while, do it tonight. I'll pray with you, if you want."

"Okay."

"Do you remember what happened to Jacob in the Bible?" Tammy asked.

Jacob heard the story before, but he didn't remember. He shook his head.

"According to the word, Jacob wrestled with God," Tammy recounted. "He wrestled with an angel all night long, because he wanted a blessing. God thought Jacob was already blessed, and He wondered what more Jacob could want. The angel broke Jacob's hip, but he kept fighting until he got his blessing."

Jacob's chest grew warm.

"But what about all the bad stuff I did?" he asked his mother.

"Did you shoot somebody?" Tammy asked anxiously.

Jacob shook his head.

"Did you point the gun at somebody, or anything like that?"

Again he shook his head.

"Then it's nothing that can't be forgiven," Tammy said. She smiled and squeezed him harder.

Jacob returned the embrace. He never felt so close to her.

"So you're back," Tammy asked. "You ready to be my good, little boy again?"

Jacob smiled but said, "I'm not little no more."

"I know," Tammy said. She rubbed his head. "You can be my good, *big* boy."

Jacob chuckled and wiped his eyes. But then he remembered the Devil Reds.

"What about my gang?"

"I thought you said they were just some stupid kids."

"They are," Jacob said. "But we're a real gang now. We did initiations and everything."

Tammy didn't want to know what those initiations entailed. "Can't you just tell them you don't want to be in the gang no more?"

Jacob was sure he could do just that. He started the gang, and he could disband it anytime he wanted. His new friends might not like it, but he didn't need to be friends with them. His real friend was Harold; had been all along.

"Mama, you know it's blood in – blood out," Jacob teased. "Once you get in a gang, you supposed to be in it for *life*."

"Do I need to go find that gun?" Tammy asked. "I'll come up to your school tomorrow and shoot all of them, if I have to. Would that get you out?"

Jacob chuckled. "Yeah, how about you *don't* do that. I can, I'll take care of it."

"Good," Tammy said. She slid off the couch and got on her knees with her elbows on the cushions. "You ready to pray?"

"Yeah," Jacob said, and he assumed an identical position next to her.

Jesus said He would be in the midst, whenever two or more people came together in His name. Jacob knew that was true, because he felt the Holy Spirit settle upon him as soon as he clasped his hands together.

"Lord," Tammy started off, "please forgive us for our many, many sins. Wash us and cleanse us with your precious blood..."

# CHAPTER TWENTY FOUR
# THE FINAL CHAPTER
## *A PLACE FOR DINO*

Dino's world swam in a blur of brake lights and street lights. His head rocked slowly, like he was on the nod, though he hadn't used heroin in over a week. On one level Dino understood he was dying. But that didn't make sense because he also knew he was still driving. And it's impossible to operate a motor vehicle while you're dead. Dino never did well in school, but he knew his math and biology.

But if that was the case, then what the hell was going on? Dino didn't see a road anywhere, just a multitude of lights; reds and yellows, greens and whites. He wondered if it was possible that he was already dead – he just didn't know it yet. Maybe he was floating up to heaven, and those were *celestial* lights he was seeing.

"Yeah right."

He chuckled. If he was going to heaven, then the preacher man had been lying to him his whole life. Hell, the preacher man had been lying to everybody if a nogoodnick like Dino could make it up there.

But if he wasn't going to heaven, then those lights must've been coming from the streets, which meant something was going terribly wrong.

*You should probably hit the brakes.*

That was his conscience talking. Dino was surprised to hear some good advice from that motherfucker.

*Where were you when I killed that little boy?* he wondered. *How come you didn't have shit to say when I shot Charlotte?*

His conscience didn't respond, because it knew it was dead wrong. It didn't have an explanation for keeping quiet when Dino needed it the most.

*Fuck you*, Dino told the voice in his head. *If you ain't have shit to say to me then, you shouldn't have shit to say to me now.*

But even as he argued with himself, Dino knew his conscience was right about one thing: He was definitely moving. And if he wasn't floating up to heaven, he should probably hit the brakes.

Dino told his brain to tell his leg to pass the message along to his foot, but the process was slower than cold molasses. By the time Dino's big toe twitched, it was too late. The Ford Taurus slammed headfirst into a telephone pole and brought all forward progress to an instant and metal-crunching halt.

***CRHEUNK!***

"*OOOHF!*"

Dino wasn't wearing his safety belt, but thankfully he was only traveling ten miles per hour at the moment of impact. Still, he fell out of his seat and hit his chin hard on the steering wheel.

"*The fuck, man...*"

An additional array of stars blended with the bright lights and swirling darkness he already saw, and Dino knew he had finally reached THE END. He would pass out and bleed out, and someone would find him slumped over the steering wheel the next morning.

The city would cheer and throw parties and have a ticker-tape-parade. Instead of a float, they would load the Taurus onto a trailer with Dino still inside. They would cut the roof and the doors off the car and roll it around Overbrook Meadows, so everyone could get a good look at the big, bad wolf. They would...

● ● ● ● ● ●

Dino came to four minutes later. He was still in the Ford Taurus, and the front end was still crammed against a telephone pole. It was cold, and it was dark. Dino blinked slowly, and the world took its sweet time settling itself.

Dino pushed off the steering wheel and looked around the interior of the vehicle. There was blood everywhere. From the waist down, Dino looked like scraps from a butcher table. He knew he wouldn't be able to walk, but when he tried to tap his right foot, his ankle worked just fine.

He bent his knee. The pain that radiated from the joint was enough to make the average man scream for mama. But Dino had been in so much pain for so many days, this was just another sore spot for him. He tried the other leg. It was stiff, but he could move that one too, if he gave it his all. All he had to do was...

• • • • • •

Dino woke up again. He sat up with a start this time. He looked around frantically and realized he was still in the goddamned car. Same spot, same telephone pole, same bloody legs like the meat market.

*Naw. You ain't getting in that parade*, he told himself, but by then he had no idea what he was thinking about.

The temperature was near freezing now. Dino's shallow breaths left thin billows of smoke with each exhalation. His ears were numb, and so were his fingers. He wished he could say the same for his legs, but they were blazing hot.

Dino knew he didn't get hit in a major artery, because he would've bled to death by now. But his new injuries were very serious. He didn't think he could limp around on those legs for very long. Luckily he crashed right around the corner from his destination. And if he gave it his all, he was pretty sure he could make it to his kinfolk's house.

He sensed getting out of the car would be the hardest part, and he was right about that. Dino barely had enough strength in his arms to open the car door. And then he had to pull himself out of the vehicle like a paraplegic, because his legs were weaker still. By the time he made it onto the sidewalk, he felt the blood running anew. It wouldn't be hard for the police to track him from the wreckage.

He staggered up the block, looking more like a zombie than ever before, and he made a left onto Stalcup Avenue. It was after midnight. Thankfully he didn't run into any cops or drug dealers on his short journey. He saw a couple of crackheads on their nightly stroll, but they were in bad shape themselves. They didn't notice the squishing sounds Dino's shoes made with each bloody step.

Dino's plan was laced with delirium, and he didn't know if his relative would help him. But either way, this was Dino's last stop. If he got turned away, he wouldn't leave his kinfolk's property. He would go around to the side of the house and lie down on the dewy grass. The next morning when they found him dead, they would feel bad about denying him entry. It was probably wrong to use his death as a tool to hurt one last person, but Dino felt he had the right to die in any fashion he pleased.

He made it to the house six minutes after crawling from the wrecked Taurus. Dino hadn't seen his uncle in more than four years, but he knew this man would let him in. Not only did his uncle bend over backwards to help disadvantaged youths every day, but he owed him personally because he'd killed his father back when Dino was two years old. He already served ten years for the murder, but he never paid any restitution to Dino directly. It was time for Dino to cash in his chips.

After three knocks, Steve answered his door. He was a big man, a lot bigger than Dino remembered. He wore only boxer shorts and a tee shirt, but he didn't look like he'd been asleep. His eyes widened when he saw the creature on his porch, but he didn't look too surprised.

"You killed my daddy," Dino said. It was the first thing that came to mind. It was also the golden key to gain him entry into his uncle's house. The counselor might be willing to turn his back on a relative, but he had to show compassion for the child of a man he murdered.

Before Dino could find out for sure, the world went black again, and he felt himself tumbling down a deep well. Steve stepped forward and caught him before he hit the concrete.

● ● ● ● ● ●

Seeing his nephew on his doorstep filled Steve with revulsion and relief and confusion, all at the same time. He felt like he was given the solution to a humongous puzzle, but he also knew this was a terrible burden. In a split second he decided that he did not want Dino at his home. He was disgusted by him; the boy reeked of death and decay. But at that moment Dino's eyes rolled to the back of his head, and he fell forward.

Steve had no choice but to catch him. And once he had Dino in his arms, he felt obligated to bring him inside.

*You killed my daddy.*

Yeah. That'll obligate you alright.

● ● ● ● ● ●

The next sixty minutes were like sleepwalking through a nightmare.

Steve toted Dino to his guest room and deposited him on the bed; fully aware that the sheets were instantly ruined and the mattress may be as well. Dino was in such bad shape, Steve thought he would die at any moment. He paced in the living room while Dino moaned and sweated on the soft mattress.

The obvious course of action was to call the police. But Steve had lived most of his life on the other side of the law. It was hard to let go of his lifelong abhorrence for the po-po. When he was committing crimes on the streets, Steve's harassment was well-warranted. But the way the corrections officers treated him in prison was vastly unjustified.

And when he got paroled, Steve faced even more discrimination at the hands of the Overbrook Meadows Police Department. They pulled him over regularly and illegally detained him for thirty minutes or more once they looked up his record and found out what a bad apple he was.

When he started working as a counselor, Steve thought his relationship with the police would improve, but things remained strained. His main goal was always to help the children he mentored, but the cops only wanted to lock them up. He had knowingly harbored a handful of fugitives in the past few years while he helped them obtain a lawyer.

The fact that Dino was family made it that much more difficult to turn him in. But, then again, Dino was vile and corrupt. If anyone ever *deserved* to be in jail, he certainly did. He murdered men on the streets. He murdered a young mother and took her baby. And he murdered Tammy's little boy. They wouldn't just send Dino to prison; they would put him on death row for all of that. All Steve had to do was make one phone call to get the wheels of justice rolling.

But he couldn't do it – at least not until he talked to him. When Dino said, "*You killed my daddy,*" his words struck a chord in ways Dino would never understand. Dino didn't know about all of the nights in prison when Steve couldn't sleep because of a heavy burden of guilt that squeezed his heart like a vice.

Killing Dino's no-good daddy probably saved the community tons of heartache, but Steve was not God. It was not his job to decide another man's fate. The moment he committed that ultimate sin, Dino became his responsibility. Everything his nephew did up to this point was ultimately his fault, because he wasn't there to clean up the mess he made. He wasn't there to show Dino love in a world that was increasingly filled with hate.

Now that his chickens had come home to roost, Steve had to man up to his mistakes. He had to pay what he owed. Dino had no mother or father or anyone else who loved him, but he had Steve now, and Steve had to be all of those things. This encounter was foretold by God, and it was not too late to make things right.

After thirty minutes of pacing and thinking, Steve went back to the bedroom. He was surprised to see Dino was still alive. The entire right side of his face was black like charcoal. And his legs looked like he barely escaped a lion's den. Steve couldn't do anything for his face, but he cut Dino's pants off and assessed his wounds. The shotgun blast messed him up pretty good, but no major arteries were severed. Dino would survive, if he went to the hospital.

Steve gritted his teeth and went to the bathroom in search of medical supplies. It was hard to care for someone who had been accused of so many atrocious things. But Steve kept his mind on the bloody work at hand and didn't concern himself with the how's or why's.

• • • • • •

Dino didn't wake up until three a.m. Steve was sitting at his bedside, watching over him like a doting nurse. Dino lifted his head from the pillow, and it took a few moments for him to understand where he was. He knew he wasn't at Mama's or

James' house, because it was much too clean and sanitized. When he saw Steve, Dino inhaled sharply, and his eyes filled with tears.

Steve was upset too, but he carried his emotions on the inside, mostly. He leaned forward with his elbows on his knees and stared his nephew in the eyes, unconsciously shaking his head from side to side.

Dino felt pain in more places than he could count, but he also felt clean. He felt loved and ready to die, and once again he didn't understand why his heart continued to beat. It was a sick joke. Death was mocking him.

"Huh, hey, Uncle Steve." He spoke softly, barely above a whisper.

Steve nodded. "Derrick."

"I, I fucked up..." Dino said.

"Yeah," Steve said.

"Why I ain't dead?" Dino wondered.

"You almost there," Steve assured him. "If you don't go to the doctor, you won't make it another day. You hurting?"

Dino nodded. He had the sheets pulled up to his shoulders. The tears spilled from his eyes and got lost in his hair. "It, it hurts everywhere."

"You wanna go to the doctor?" Steve asked.

Dino shook his head right away. "I don't want to go..." He coughed. "I don't want, don't wanna go to the pen..."

Steve nodded and pursed his lips.

"So, what's your plan then?"

Dino shrugged. He looked around the room again. "I'm not gon' get better?"

Steve wished he had a big enough mirror to show the boy his dire straits.

"Naw, man. You ain't gon' get better without a doctor."

Dino nodded and swallowed roughly. "Where my gun?"

"You didn't have one," Steve said.

Dino coughed again. His tears became heavier. He reached up to wipe his face. "I can't do it anyway," he said. "I tried, but I can't."

"Can't do what?" The hairs stood on Steve's arms. The world stood still while he waited for Dino to answer.

"I wanna kill myself."

Steve maintained a stern disposition. "So, did you do it? You killed that little boy?"

Dino's face contorted in a frown so extreme, it looked like a cartoon. He nodded.

"Yeah."

"You killed that girl too, and took her baby?"

Dino continued to nod. His grimace was the ugliest thing Steve had ever seen. His tears were like rivers. Steve's eyes blurred, and he started to cry as well. He slowly rose to his feet and left the bedroom. Dino began to moan and wail wretchedly. He quieted down when Steve returned with a gun in hand. It was the .32 Tammy gave him earlier that night.

Steve felt it was wrong to facilitate a suicide, but the alternatives were just as grim. Dino might linger and suffer for days if he let him die on his own. And the penitentiary was the closest Steve had ever come to hell. Dino would be harassed daily if he went to prison. He would go insane on death row; counting down the days before his execution.

No. This was family business, and Dino was under the care of a loved-one now. If he was a rabid dog that needed to be put down, then it was up to his family to do it – not some cold-hearted judge working for the state of Texas.

Steve looked around until he found a handkerchief to wipe the gun down with. Dino watched his every move but said nothing. Using the handkerchief as a glove, Steve popped the magazine out, checked for bullets and then pushed it back in. He chambered a round and casually handed the piece to his nephew. Dino stared in shock. Steve didn't think he would, but after a few moments, Dino accepted the weapon.

"I'm sorry," he said. "I, I didn't mean it." He shook his head. "I didn't mean to kill that boy."

"It's okay now," Steve said. "It's almost over."

But Dino continued to purge. "I, I didn't mean to shoot that girl, either. I, I took her baby, 'cause, 'cause I didn't want to leave her with her mama, when she was dead. I, I tried to do the right thing. I didn't hurt that baby. I tried to do right..."

"You did do right," Steve said. He wiped his eyes and folded his arms over his massive chest. "Now go on; handle your business."

"Uh, huh, oh, okay..." Dino's fever raged, but he shivered like a wet puppy. He opened his mouth and slowly inserted the barrel. "Uh, huh..."

"Deeper," Steve instructed. He saw that Dino had the pistol at a bad angle. Not only would it hurt like hell if he missed the crucial spot, but the redo would be absolute torture.

"Uh, ug..."

Dino got the gun where it needed to be, and he put his finger on the trigger.

But thirty seconds later he was still moaning and trembling.

Steve approached the bed and looked down on him one last time. "If you can't do it, I gotta call you an ambulance." Tears poured down his face.

Dino's eyes widened. Steve turned his back on him and left the room. He went to the living room and took a seat on the sofa. Steve's heart hammered. Sweat accumulated on his face and chest. He waited another minute, straining his ears for the sound of gunfire and death.

When that sound didn't come, Steve put a fist to his mouth and closed his eyes tightly. He didn't want to get any more involved than he already was. But if he had to assist Dino further, he would do it. But when he rose from the sofa, a solitary gunshot cut through the stillness like cymbals crashing in a quiet theatre.

**BLAK!!**

Steve's breath caught in his throat. His heart slowed to almost imperceptible beats, and he sank heavily back into the couch cushions. He cried, not because his nephew was dead, but because Derrick never had a chance to become anything *but* Dino. He was doomed from birth. But it was over now. His weary bones were finally at rest. Steve had to find solace in that.

After a few minutes, he got up to check on the body, and then he called the police. Steve placed another call to Tammy while he waited for the authorities to arrive. By then it was three in the morning. He planned to only let the phone ring twice, so he wouldn't wake her, but Tammy answered on the second ring.

"Hello?"

"Hey," he said. "It's me, Steve."

"What's, what's going on?"

"My nephew's here," Steve said. His voice was low and somber. "He showed up on my porch an hour ago."

Tammy gasped. "*Dino?*"

"Yeah."

"He's there? What, what do you mean? *You need to call the police*! He's dangerous. Where, where is he?"

"It's okay," Steve said. "He ain't gon' hurt nobody else. That, that's why I called. I wanted to tell you that."

"What, what do you mean?"

"He committed suicide. He killed hisself."

"Oh," Tammy said. "I'm, I'm sorry."

"Don't be," Steve said. "It's, uh, it's what he wanted."

"Oh."

"It, uh, it probably don't help any, but he said he was sorry, about Isaiah. He..." Steve sighed. "He was pretty upset. I'm sure he meant it."

Tammy's eyes became glossy. She didn't know how to respond. Steve kept talking.

"He, uh... He didn't mean to hurt that girl either. Like I said, I'm sure it doesn't mean anything at this point–"

"No, it does," Tammy said.

"It, you uh..."

"It's good to know," Tammy said. She sniffled. "I'm glad he told you that."

"Yeah," Steve said. "Me too."

"Thank you," Tammy told him. "For everything."

"But, I haven't done anything. I don't feel like–"

"You did a lot. Trust me."

"Okay," Steve said. "I, uh, I have to go now. The police are on their way. I'll talk to you later."

"Thanks for calling," Tammy said. "And God bless you."

"You too, Ms. Spencer. God bless you, too."

# EPILOGUE

Tammy didn't think she'd be able to get through the holidays. But she had a huge family, and they were supportive. Jacob was slow in returning to his old self, too. But he was there for her when Tammy wanted to stay in her room, curled in a ball in the middle of the bed.

"How come you didn't make those Rice Krispie things?" he asked her one afternoon.

Tammy met his eyes and then buried her face in the pillow. "I only made those for Isaiah," she said. "That's, that's not even Thanksgiving food. We're supposed to eat pies and stuff."

"Yeah, but I like them," Jacob said. "And my cousins like them, too."

Tammy looked up at him with a frown. "You don't like Rice Krispie treats."

"Yes, I do," Jacob said with a hearty nod. "I always liked them. You probably didn't notice, 'cause Isaiah was the one begging for them all the time. But I think I always ended up eating most of them."

"For real?" Tammy asked.

"For real," Jacob said.

So Tammy stuck with tradition and made Isaiah's favorite treat that year. She thought the nostalgia would upset her even more, but the memories of Thanksgivings past made her smile. And she was happy to see Jacob waiting anxiously for the first serving, like Isaiah used to do.

● ● ● ● ● ●

Depression tried to rear its ugly head again in December, and it was Tammy who had to be there for Jacob this time. She noticed he wasn't talking as much as usual. And whenever she wanted to do some shopping, Jacob never wanted to go with her.

"What's wrong?" Tammy asked him one frosty morning. School had been out for a week already, but Jacob still didn't have any Christmas spirit.

"Nothing," he said. He sat on the couch flipping through sales papers that came in the mail.

"You looking for a gift?" Tammy asked him.

"I already got you something," he said without looking up.

Tammy took a seat next to him and noticed he had a Toys R Us circular.

"You think Isaiah would've liked this," he asked, pointing at a beginner's chemistry set.

Tammy smiled. "Yeah. I think he would've liked it a lot."

"Me too," Jacob said.

"Is that something you would've bought for him?" Tammy asked. The item in question cost nineteen dollars. Tammy had a new job at the hospital by then, and she'd started giving Jacob an allowance a few weeks ago. He also had a little money saved from a leaf-raking venture he started with a friend from down the street.

"Yeah, I would've," Jacob said. "Or this thing..." He pointed to another toy.

"I'm going to the mall after lunch," Tammy said. "Why don't you come with me? You can buy it and give it to somebody else for Christmas..."

Jacob knitted his eyebrows. "Somebody like who?"

"Maybe a poor kid who might not get nothing else," Tammy suggested. "Or a homeless child..."

Jacob thought about it and said, "Okay."

His mood didn't brighten any when they got to the toy store, and he was still gloomy when they wrapped his gift later on that night. Tammy began to wonder if she'd made a mistake. Thankfully things got better when they took a trip to the homeless shelter the next day. They didn't have to go inside, because it was early in the afternoon, and most of the families were camped out on the sidewalk.

Tammy saw quite a few kids who looked worthy of Jacob's gift, but her son was very picky. He wanted his chemistry set to go to a child who looked like he might actually use it; preferably one whose parents wouldn't sell it for crack as soon as Tammy drove away.

He finally spotted a Hispanic family with only one child; a little boy. The youngster was around Isaiah's age, and he wore a thick pair of glasses, too.

"Him," Jacob said. "I wanna give it to him."

Tammy grinned. "Well, go ahead."

Jacob got out of the car, and Tammy watched through the windshield. She couldn't hear the conversation, but she saw that Jacob approached the family and spoke with the father first. He then handed the gift to their very appreciative son and headed back to the car. Before he made it, the boy's mother stopped Jacob and called him back. She gave him a hug.

Jacob was blushing when he got back in the car. Tammy's heart was nearly bursting with pride and just a little bit of sorrow. Her eyes were filled with tears.

"That was nice," she said. "You did a real good job."

"It felt good," Jacob said. He was absolutely glowing.

• • • • • •

After Christmas, life sped up a little when Jacob returned to school. Tammy was still getting acclimated to her new responsibilities as a medical assistant at the hospital. She really enjoyed her new job. A few nurses on her floor said she was a fast learner. They encouraged her to go back to school *again* and train to become a registered nurse.

Tammy was skeptical, but by February she thought she might be able to squeeze in a few classes a week. Jacob was doing well in school. And he went to the MLK center every day, so Tammy didn't have to be home by three o'clock if she didn't want to.

• • • • • •

By April Tammy had saved up enough money to move to a better neighborhood. But when she told Jacob the good news, he surprised her with a difference of opinion.

"We shouldn't move out, Mama. Houses are pretty cheap over here. You won't have any extra money, if the new house costs more."

"I'll have enough to pay the bills," Tammy assured him.

"But what if you want a new car? And who's gonna buy me a car when I'm sixteen? And then I'ma need money for the prom..."

Tammy cocked her head. "Boy, I hope you're gonna get a job to help out with some of that stuff."

Jacob laughed. "I will help out. But I still don't think we should move. It's better to have money in the bank than to have a big, fancy house."

Tammy frowned. "Who said that?"

"My teacher."

"I'll bet your teacher already has a big, fancy house," Tammy guessed.

"I don't think so," Jacob said. "She said she lives close enough to walk to school."

Tammy rubbed her forehead. "So you *want* to stay in the hood?"

"No, I don't *want to*," Jacob responded. "But this neighborhood is not that bad. And my teacher says the economy's messed up now because everybody wants a big house they can't afford. She says people should live in between their means."

"*Within their means*," Tammy said with a chuckle. She shook her head. "Alright, Jacob. But when I get a nursing job, we're definitely moving."

"Cool," he said, then, "You're getting a nursing job?"

"I'm thinking about going back to school. It would be a three-year program."

Her son's eyes lit up. "That's *tight*! My teacher says the more you know, the more you grow."

"Who is this teacher that's telling you all of this stuff?" Tammy wondered.

"Mrs. Helms."

"I don't think you've ever quoted a teacher so much," Tammy noticed. "She must be cute."

Jacob grinned. "Puppies are *cute*, Mama. Mrs. Helms is *gorgeous*."

• • • • • •

When school let out for the summer, Tammy was glad to hear that Steve's program at the community center ran all year long. The center was different during the summertime. Steve had a lot more extracurricular activities lined up for the students. One of them was a basketball league.

Tammy thought her son was only moderately interested in hoops, but after a couple of practices with the team, Steve told her Jacob had tons of God-given talent. He went as far as saying the boy was a *natural*.

Tammy didn't get a chance to see for herself until the league's first game in early June. She was off that Saturday, so she volunteered to drive Jacob to the gym. Tammy also had time to pick Harold up, so he could watch the game with her from the stands. Jacob usually misplaced a few million brain cells when he hung around his best bud, but he was mature and focused that afternoon; trying to *get in the zone*, as he put it.

"Fool, you know you can't play basketball!" Harold taunted from the backseat.

"Be quiet," Jacob told him, his eyes forward, his jaw stern. "I'm getting in the zone, man."

"He can't play basketball, can he, Ms. Spencer?" Harold asked.

Tammy grinned and shrugged. "I don't know, Harold. I guess we're going to find out pretty soon."

"The only zone I've ever seen Jacob in is the *B.O.* zone!" Harold joked.

"Man, shut up," Jacob said. "You the one who stink."

"Neither one of you stinks," Tammy said. She couldn't stop giggling.

"Oh, we wanna make fun of Jacob today?" Jacob asked. "That's okay. You're just mad 'cause you can't play basketball *at all*," he told Harold. "And the only reason *you're* coming," he said to his mother, "is because you got a crush on Coach."

Tammy's eyes widened. "I do not have a crush on your coach."

"Who's the coach?" Harold asked.

"My counselor, Steve," Jacob said. "My mama liked him since last year."

322

"I like him as a *friend*," Tammy clarified.

"Mmm, hmm." Jacob didn't buy that for a second. "They go out on a date almost every week," he told Harold. "Watch how she starts smiling when she sees him. You can see for yourself."

"*Anyway...*" Tammy changed the subject: "I do think you're gonna do good today. Me and Harold will be rooting for you."

"Yeah, I'm glad you're doing something positive," Harold said, and he meant it.

"Whatever happened to those *Devil Bloods* anyway?" Tammy asked.

Harold thought that was funny.

"What?" Tammy said.

"They joined the baseball team," Harold told her.

"Really?" Tammy hadn't heard that.

"It was the Devil *Reds*," Jacob said. "And it's not funny."

"Naw, you right," Harold said and managed to get his chuckles under control.

Tammy was still surprised. "They joined the *baseball team?*"

"I told them it was better than a gang," Jacob said, "'cause you'll always have a bunch of people with you, but you'll never get shot at. They didn't really wanna be in a gang anyway. They just wanted something they could say they was part of."

"And you steered them in the right direction," Tammy noted. "I'm proud of you."

"I'm proud of you, too," Harold said. "But I'm still gon' laugh if you miss all your shots today."

"I won't miss any if you be quiet and let me get in my zone!" Jacob whined. "Dang. It's like y'all don't want a brother to make it."

"Okay, let him get in his *zone*," Tammy told Harold. She stifled her last snicker. "'Cause we *do* want this brother to make it."

"Thank you," Jacob said.

They drove in silence for a while, and Tammy began to think of Isaiah, as she often did. Isaiah looked up to his big brother so much. Tammy knew he would've loved to see Jacob compete on a basketball team. Thoughts like this normally dampened her spirits, but Tammy remained upbeat today. Her memories didn't have to be bitter sweet; it was all about attitude and perception.

Sometimes she would hear that *I Love Going to School* song on the radio and immediately become overwhelmed with sorrow. Other times she would think about how happy Isaiah became when the song came on, and she would find herself smiling; with a warm feeling in her heart that stayed with her throughout the day.

"I wish Isaiah could come," Jacob said.

Startled, Tammy said, "I was just thinking the same thing."

"Steve said as long as I keep him in my heart, then he *is* still here," Jacob recounted.

Tammy grinned. "I believe that."

Jacob smiled back at her. "Isaiah is always here then, 'cause I *always* keep him in my heart."

Tammy's eyes did fill with tears then, but it was a good cry. "Me too, baby," she said. "Me too."

# THE END

# BY KEITH THOMAS WALKER

# ABOUT THE AUTHOR

Keith Thomas Walker, known as the Master of Romantic Suspense and Urban Fiction, is the author of more than a dozen novels, including *Fixin' Tyrone*, *Dripping Chocolate* and *The Realest Ever*. Keith enjoys reading, poetry and music of all genres. Originally from Fort Worth, he is a graduate of Texas Wesleyan University. Keith was nominated for an Emma Award in 2010 for Debut Author of the Year. In 2012 Keith was the recipient of a BRAB Book Club Award for Male Author of the Year (for Harlot) as well as a SORMAG Award for Fiction Author of the Year. In 2013 Keith was the recipient of a BRAB Book Club Award for Male Author of the Year (for Dripping Chocolate). Visit him at www.keithwalkerbooks.com.